ROCINANTE
An Aerial Adventure

by

Wes Boyd

This is a work of fiction. Names, characters, places and incident are either the product of the author's imagination or are used fictitiously, and any resemblance to actual persons, living or dead, business establishments, events or locales is entirely coincidental.

ROCINANTE
An Aerial Adventure

Published by Spearfish Lake Tales
http://www.spearfishlaketales.com

ISBN 978-0-6152-1498-6

To Kathy

Who's put up with my writing all this time.

Part One

It Runs In The Family

1.

It wasn't until Hjalmer Lindahlsen turned down County Road 919 that Jackie Archer realized that the only place he could be heading was Turtle Hill.

Jackie wasn't sure she wanted to go to Turtle Hill with Hjalmer. Turtle Hill was probably the best-known spot around Spearfish Lake for kids to go out and park in the late hours of a date. It had a beautiful view of the Turtle Lakes, and Spearfish Lake beyond, a view that was considered sufficiently romantic to lead to some serious necking -- and more. Sometimes much more; Jackie could remember the hints she'd gotten back in high school from her girl friend Kirsten Langenderfer, about what had gone on out there in the back seat of Henry Tovio's old Ford.

Even the thought of Henry made Jackie sad; he'd been missing in action in Vietnam for nine months now, since last summer, and poor Kirsten was half our of her mind with loneliness and despair.

The thought of Henry and Kirsten added to Jackie's unease a little. Not that she was above a little innocent kissy-face with Hjalmer, even though it was their first date; she'd had little enough of it in her nineteen years, and the prospect seemed a little exciting and daring. She'd always been a tall girl, lanky and gangly as long as she could remember; at an even six feet, she was a head taller than all the other girls in her class, taller than almost all the boys, and unusual enough that she'd not been popular.

And, always, there were the whispered stories of her mother -- not Sarah, but her real mother -- stories that were well-known in a town as small as Spearfish Lake.

As a result, the number of dates -- real dates -- she'd had in her lifetime was small enough to count on one hand, so a little casual necking could be enjoyed, if it went no farther. It was a hell of a long walk to anywhere on this chilly, clear, spring Friday night, but she'd walk home if she had to if things got out of hand. She was used to walking, after all.

Not that Hjalmer wasn't a nice guy. She'd known him for years, but a first date was a first date, and she wasn't the sort of girl to let things get out of hand on the first date, or even the thirty-first. Whether that was what Hjalmer had in mind, she didn't know, and there was a part of her that didn't want to find out, at least tonight. Perhaps if they'd gone out a couple of times, first . . .

But that was neither here nor there, now. If she didn't go along, at least a little bit, there might not be another date, anyway. She'd just have to keep it from going too far.

Hjalmer slowed his Pontiac for the turn up the two-rut lane that ran to the top of Turtle Hill. Though Jackie didn't know it, he knew there was no danger of getting stuck in the narrow, sandy trail through the woods, now in the middle of the spring thaw. Just on the off chance that Jackie might be amenable to a little necking, he'd driven out to make sure the track was open, before he picked her up to take her to the movie down in Albany River.

He figured there was a good chance of a little necking, and perhaps eventually more. A girl like Jackie didn't get a lot of chances at romance. In addition to her height, which he knew put off a lot of guys, she let herself be rather plain. She could be pretty, he thought, if she'd let her cropped brown hair grow, and maybe get rid of those ugly, black-framed glasses -- and, if she'd let herself be pretty.

Dropping to second gear, he eased his car up the path. So far, so good, he thought: she'd put up no protest. His chances of getting on the scoreboard tonight were approximately zero, he figured, but he could lay a foundation on which to build. Not that he thought that he'd ever want to marry this girl, but if a few dates did ultimately lead to some back-seat action, it would be worth the trouble. And, tonight would be fun, anyway, even if nothing else ever happened.

"The view from up here after dark is terrific," he said, as much to put her at ease as anything. "The stars seem so close, it's like you could reach out and touch them."

She didn't reply, but slid over next to him; a good sign, he thought. He reached up and put his right arm around her, while he continued to steer the car up the twisting trail with his left. Already, he was anticipating what would come next; he'd stop the car looking out over the lakes, shut off the engine, pull her close, kiss her gently on the lips, and then maybe a little more. At some point along in there, he'd "accidentally on purpose" brush his hand over one of her breasts, although he doubted if she'd notice. He suspected those none too prominent bumps on her chest consisted largely of cotton armor padding. Depending on how she reacted, he'd be able to assess if they could go further.

It seemed like a lot of work in these days when girls reportedly would drop their pants before they asked your name, but this was Spearfish Lake, after all, not California.

Only a few more seconds, now. The car burst out of the clearing at the top of the hill; he'd turn right and . . .

"Oh, shit." In his headlights, he could see half a dozen cars, most with trunks open. There were several people standing with their backs turned; there were tables and equipment scattered about.

"What is it?" Jackie asked.

"Damned astronomy club's out here," he replied, his mind racing. Well, that blew this location, he thought. Where else could they go? How about the driveway to the West Turtle Lake Club? The gate would be locked, but there probably wouldn't be anyone there, this time of night, this time of year. It was a poor second best; it didn't have the romantic view, and a lot of people around Spearfish Lake got bad vibes from the West Turtle Lake Club. He didn't know if Jackie was one of those people that nudists made nervous. It would be close, though . . .

"Oh, neat," Jackie said, actually interested, although relieved to have an excuse to break up Hjalmer's plans without actually saying anything. "Let's go out and have a look."

"Might as well," Hjalmer grunted. It might make her a little less defensive later, or next time, or whenever, he thought. This probably wouldn't take long, after all. He shut off the lights had to hurry to keep up with her as she hurried toward the cluster of telescopes.

"Hi," she said to no one in particular. "Can we have a look?"

"Sure," a dark form near her said in a deep voice. A red light flicked on in his hand, lighting up the eyepiece on the side of a short, white tube.

Jackie had to squat down and bend over quite a ways to get to the eyepiece; the telescope was on a short stand. She saw a dim glow looking back at her. "What's that?" she asked.

"M-51," the man with the deep voice said. "The Whirlpool Galaxy. Your eyes are probably not real dark adapted yet, but if you study that for a while, you can begin to make out some of the spiral structure."

"I can start to see it," she said. "Parts are glowing more than others."

"That glow is millions upon millions of stars," the man said. "Now, you look off in the corner, there, you can see a fainter glow. That's another galaxy, that crashed through the Whirlpool recently, only a billion years or so ago. You can't see it in here, but in photos you can see how the collision scattered stars from hell to breakfast."

Jackie realized that it would be more comfortable if she got down on her knees, but the ground was wet and cold. She studied the galaxy in the eyepiece as long as she could stand to be bent over.

"You guys going to be out here long?" Hjalmer asked, as innocuously as he could.

"All night," the man said. "We want to wait for some summer and early fall stuff to come up."

Jackie stood up, to let Hjalmer take a look. "Why not just wait for fall?" she asked.

"That's kind of a long story," the man said. "Two hundred years ago, there was a Frenchman by the name of Charles Messier. Now, old Chuck was a comet hunter, and he spent hours and hours hunting around the skies with a telescope not a lot larger than Dave's Unitron over there, although Dave's is better. He was hunting for comets that might blaze real bright across the sky. You remember Ikeya-Seki, about six years ago?"

"I got up before dawn several mornings to see it," Jackie said. "It was so beautiful I couldn't believe it."

"I did, too," the man admitted. "Anyway, old Chas was looking for the faint, fuzzy objects in his telescope that might turn into something like that, and he found a few. But, as he kept hunting around the sky, he kept finding these faint, fuzzy objects, that didn't move against the surrounding starfield from night to night. They couldn't be comets, and he started to get mad. I mean, here he's scanning the skies, and he finds some faint, fuzzy object, and he gets all excited, thinking he's found a comet, and he goes back to look at it a night or two later, and it's obvious it's not a comet, and he started to get disappointed. I mean, take a look at M-51 there, and you can imagine how, in a poor telescope, it might look like a comet."

Jackie nodded her head, although in the pitch darkness the man couldn't see. "I can imagine," she said, when she realized how silly nodding her head was.

"Well, anyway," the man went on, "After a while, old Chuck got wise, and he started keeping a list of these faint, fuzzy things, so when he found one of them while he was searching, he'd know he hadn't found a comet. Over the years, the list reached 110 objects. Now, nobody would remember Charles Messier today, if it weren't for the fact that this list of 110 objects is pretty much the list of the best deep-sky objects to look at in a small telescope. Along about this time of year, if you start right at dark and work right into the dawn, you can see all 110 on a dark night. It's the only time of year you can do it. I've seen them all, but not all of them in one night. That's what we're trying to do out here tonight, and it'll take us all night."

"Well, we shouldn't keep you from it," Hjalmer said, trying to get back to what he had come here for.

"Oh, no big deal, right now," the dark figure said. "We're kind of in a flat spot. I'm just kind of waiting for the Virgo Cluster to get a bit higher before I get started on it. I've pretty well wrapped up everything to the west of it."

"What's the Virgo Cluster?" Jackie wanted to know.

"It's a cluster of galaxies, about ten degrees across, in the constellation Virgo. There's hundreds of them there, and about twenty of them are on the Messier list. They're pretty faint, which makes it one of the toughest parts of the list."

"Can you show us what it looks like?"

"I can, but frankly, it won't look like much," the man said. "You've got to be used to looking at really faint stuff to make much sense out of Virgo. I'll show you a couple of other neat galaxies, though."

While she and Hjalmer waited, the man took the telescope and pointed it to the right, and down a bit. He bent over the tube, and twisted it this way and that. "I always have a little trouble finding this," he said. "There aren't a lot of easy markers nearby. Ah, there it is . . ." he said, standing up, and flicking on the red light to show where the eyepiece now was.

Jackie bent over to have a look. In the eyepiece was another spiral galaxy, seen at a little more of an angle. "You can really see the dark part of the spiral well," she said.

"Look down," the man said softly.

Jackie looked lower in the field of the eyepiece. "Oh, it's pretty," she said. Under the spiral galaxy, there was another one, almost edge-on, a bright streak with a brighter core. She stood there, bent over, studying the two galaxies for a long time before she asked, "What are they called?"

"M-81 and M-82," the man said. "I don't know if they have given names."

Jackie stepped back from the telescope, to let Hjalmer have a courtesy look. "Can we see something else?" she asked.

"Sure," the man said. "Let me change eyepieces to drop the power down a little, and I'll show you one of the real showpieces of the sky." Jackie stepped back, to let him fiddle with the telescope for a minute; then, he aimed the telescope off to the west. "There you go."

Again Jackie bent over the telescope, and let out a gasp. "Wow, that's pretty," she said. "What is it?"

"Beehive Cluster. Another Messier object. It's one of the few you can make out with the naked eye under a dark sky."

She stood up to see, and he showed her were to look. Out of the corner of her eye, she could just make out a dim glow. "I can see it," she said, "But it's better in the telescope." She turned back to it for another look.

The two of them stayed there for a while longer, looking at several star clusters and a couple of double stars. Jackie had been perhaps a little more familiar with the sky than most girls; some of the things that her father had taught her on their camping trips had stuck with her. It was a real joy to look through the telescope. She was glad she'd come out here with Hjalmer, after all.

After a while she began to get cold, in spite of being dressed for cold weather like any sensible northern girl at this time of year. The astronomers were dressed a lot warmer, with snowmobile suits and long underwear and heavy boots; they knew how cold they would get before morning, and there was no way Jackie and Hjalmer could stay with them. "I guess we'd better get going," she conceded finally.

With a degree of relief, Hjalmer got back in his car and got the heater going, while Jackie sat down next to him; not snuggled up to him like earlier, but close.

He thought of suggesting a brief stop in the driveway to the West Turtle Lake Club, but she said, "I guess I'd better be getting on home. I've got to work in the morning."

There wasn't a lot Hjalmer could do but take her home. They sat in her driveway talking for several minutes, and they did kiss a little. In their squirming around, Hjalmer did manage an "accidentally on purpose" touch of her breast, but couldn't conclude whether there was cotton or girl there. "Can we do this again, sometime? Like maybe, next Friday?" he asked.

Dates came infrequently enough to her, and this one had gone all right. "Don't see any reason why not," she told him. She smiled to herself and thought that maybe the next time she let Hjalmer take her out to Turtle Hill, she'd let him sneak a better feel of her breast.

Sarah was sitting in the living room, reading a murder mystery, when Jackie went inside; not necessarily waiting up for her, but up, none the less. Her father would not be home this evening; it was a night on the road. Ever since he had been bumped off of his regular Spearfish Lake run a couple of years ago, her father, Walt, had to drive to Camden every third day, spend a day running a train to the division point at Syracuse, spend the night there, and run a train back to Camden the next day. Sometimes he had to be gone two nights in a row. Perhaps one day he would be able to bid back onto the Spearfish Lake Subdivision of the Decatur and Overland Railroad, but for now, it made life inconvenient.

"How did your date go, Jackie?" Sarah asked conversationally. Sarah may have been Jackie's stepmother, but Jackie never resented it. She had come into the Archer family about the time that Jackie was starting to get old enough to need more than her father's guidance, and Jackie had been glad of it.

Sarah was as much a friend, as anything, and Jackie didn't mind talking to her. "Pretty well," Jackie said. "I didn't particularly care for the movie, but we had fun afterward." She decided not to mention running into the astronomy club on Turtle Hill; Sarah may have been a friend, but Jackie thought it was better to not raise the question of why they had been on Turtle Hill in the first place.

"Are you going to go out with him again?" Sarah asked gently.

"Probably," Jackie said. "Next Friday night, I guess. He's O.K." She looked at her watch and yawned. "I'd better get to bed. I've got to be in at six tomorrow morning."

"I suppose I'd better go to bed, too," Sarah yawned, trying to not let on that she'd been waiting up for her stepdaughter's return.

Jackie went up to her room. Growing up an only child, and with her mother gone so long ago, she had spent many a lonely night there. She felt lonelier now, with the memory of Hjalmer's arms around her, and the warmth of his kiss, the touch of his hand. For a while tonight she hadn't felt lonely at all.

Hjalmer would do to have a date or two with, maybe a little necking, but she couldn't see marrying the guy. She peeled off her clothes and put on her warm, fuzzy flannel pajamas, the better to be snug and cozy on a cold night like this. As she threw back the covers and crawled into bed, she wondered how the guys in the astronomy club were doing. She suspected they'd be a lot colder before morning.

As she waited to fall asleep her mind replayed parts of the evening. She suddenly realized that the part of the evening she had enjoyed the best had not been the movie or the little bit of necking they'd done, but their visit to Turtle Hill. Hjalmer might have been disappointed to know that she fell asleep dreaming of star clusters and galaxies.

The alarm went off far too early the next morning. She and Hjalmer hadn't been out real late the night before, but it was more than late enough on a day that she had to work mornings. Jackie was tempted to hit the snooze alarm and get ten minutes more shuteye, but she knew that she'd already set her schedule as tight as she dared. Begrudgingly, she threw the covers back, and prepared to meet the new day.

As full of sleep as she was, it was hard to pull on her white uniform. This morning she resented it more than most. Being a waitress at Rick's Cafe was a lousy job. She was on her feet more than she wanted to be, tipping had never taken hold in Spearfish Lake, and the pay was nothing to be happy with. Still, she wasn't spending a lot of money, and was able to save a bit. It was more of a job than anything else she'd been able to find since she'd graduated the spring before, even though she knew it wouldn't last forever. It was still better than babysitting for her four year old step brother.

Dressed and ready to go, she pulled on a pair of jeans under her dress; she would take them off once she got to work, but she knew it would be too cold outside for bare legs. It was still pitch dark when she went out to the garage, and again she wondered if the astronomy club was still out on Turtle Hill. The sky looked different, now; she knew enough about the constellations to realize that she was looking at the skies as they would look in the evenings next summer.

Once she had the garage door open, Jackie fired up Sarah's car. It took some juggling, but she managed to get along without a car of her own; it would be easier tomorrow morning, when she could drive her dad's car to work. It was worth it to save money; she had plans to try junior college the next year, but didn't want to get buried under a student loan until she was sure she could handle the work.

It was still dark when she parked the car in back of Rick's, but she could see a dim glow in the east that forewarned of the coming dawn. Inside, she began getting the tables set up for the early breakfast customers; in the back, Lori already had the grill going. As soon as she had a Silex filled with coffee, Jackie poured herself a cup, and another one for Lori.

A couple of pulpcutters were the first customers to arrive; Jackie could tell at a glance they'd been out too late at the Pike Bar the evening before, and hadn't recovered from it yet. She managed to get coffee on the table and the menus down before getting the first suggestive remark from one of them. Once she got the order, she took it back to the kitchen and mumbled to Lori, "God help me if I ever get desperate enough to marry a logger."

"I know what you mean," Lori agreed. "I married one. I don't ever want to do that again, either."

Over the next half hour, a half-dozen more customers filtered in, one by one and two by two. All of them took booths or seats at the counter. Then, all of a sudden, it was as if the bears had arrived: six big men in snowmobile suits all arrived at once, and began to peel off their outer clothing.

As Spearfish Lake was a northern town, nobody was too surprised to see people wearing snowmobile suits, even this late into the spring; but as Jackie watched, she realized that these guys were all wearing Carhartts UNDER their snowmobile suits! These guys were really dressed for cold weather.

As Jackie watched she saw the brown work suits that had been under the snowmobile suits come off, and realized that these guys really weren't bears, but were dressed very warm. "Let me tell you," one of them said to another, "My hat's off to the guy that can roust M-30 out of the morning sky without setting circles." That voice was familiar -- it was the one from the dark mass the night before, the one that had showed her some celestial sights, and she realized that this must be the arrival of the astronomy club.

As she served them coffee, she asked, "Well, did you all see all 110 of your Messier objects?"

"Naaah," one of them, a guy who looked to be about fifty, said. "I don't think anybody got M-30. I missed on M-76 and M-33 last evening, so I was up the creek from the start, then I missed on M-72 and M-73 as the sun was coming up. Young-eyes Gravengood, over there, got everything but M-30, I think."

"I just barely got M-73," the man with the familiar voice said. "You know, if old Chuck had stayed in bed the night he logged M-30, think of how much easier it would have been for the rest of us."

Jackie turned to look at him. He was a tall young man, perhaps a little older than she was, with a somewhat gaunt look, thick horn-rimmed glasses, and short hair -- in this day of Beatle cuts, and even longer hair on men, beardless in a day when it seemed every other guy had a beard. He seemed vaguely familiar. "Your dad is Phil Gravengood, isn't he?" she asked.

"Yeah, I'm Mark," he said. "You're Walt Archer's girl, aren't you? I'm sorry, but I've lost your name."

"Jackie," she said, her mind starting to fill in blanks. There wasn't any real reason to remember much about him; he'd graduated about the time she'd been in seventh or eighth grade. "I thought you were in the Army," she added.

"Got out last fall," he told her.

"Hey, look," she said. "I want to thank you for showing me those galaxies and clusters last night. That was really neat."

Mark frowned a little, then said, "That was you and your boyfriend?"

"He's not my boyfriend, not really," she said defensively. "It was just a date."

"Well, I'm glad you enjoyed it," he said. "I kind of like showing off stuff in the sky. I just wish you'd been there earlier. There's a couple of things that are maybe the neatest things in the sky that you missed. They'd set by the time you got out there."

"Would you show them to me some time?" she asked, surprised at how forward she was.

"It's going to have to be in the next few days," he said. "They're pretty low in the west. Another couple of days, we're going to have moon in the west, and when it's gone, they will be, too."

"Could we do it tonight?" she asked. "I'm not doing anything."

"Might as well," Mark said. "I'm planning on sleeping all day today, anyway. Do you want to meet me someplace?"

"I'm not sure I can have a car tonight," she told him. "Can you pick me up?"

"Sure," he said. "About six all right?" She nodded, and he went on, "You still live with your dad at the same place?"

"Same place," she said. "Now, would you guys like to order?"

In the next two minutes, Jackie took a pile of orders for waffles, French toast, bacon, hash browns, and all of the other breakfast goodies. These guys were hungry.

As she turned to go to the kitchen, she heard one of the older men say, "I don't know how you do it, Gravengood."

"Do what?" the young man asked.

"Get a date with the waitress even before we get to order."

Jackie thought about it as she handed Lori the stack of orders. Well, yes, it could be counted as a date, she thought, although it wasn't going to be the normal kind -- but it was still something to wonder at: dates two nights in a row, a different guy each night. It was something that had never happened to her before.

Mark was yawning and groggy as he drove his old '56 Vicky Ford home. The car was a clunker; he'd paid fifty bucks for it, but figured he could get 35 from the junk yard when he wanted to get rid of it. It started in the winter, and it got him around town, even though it needed a muffler and used only slightly less oil than it did gas. He wouldn't need it much longer, anyway.

Despite -- or perhaps, because of -- being so tired he couldn't see straight, Mark was just the least little bit needled at McComber's teasing him about putting off breakfast in order to get a date with Jackie. He didn't really think of it as a date; she just wanted to see some more of the sky. Besides, the last thing he needed in his life right now was a girl friend, no matter how much he'd like to have one.

Whenever the thought of a girl friend crossed his mind -- and it did often -- thoughts of Mei-Ling were never far away. She'd been a paid girl friend, true, but in the less than a week they spent together, she'd brought out a part of him he never thought had existed.

He'd met -- perhaps "hired" is a better word -- Mei-Ling on his second R&R, the one he took to Bangkok, after he'd extended for six months in Vietnam. The first one, he'd taken in Australia, because he had wanted to see the Magellenic Clouds, Omega Centuri, the Southern Cross, Eta Carina and NGC 5128, along with some of the other sights of the southern Milky Way. He had been able to find an amateur astronomer in Sydney that had taken him out to dark skies for a couple of nights.

The second R&R, in Bangkok, came on a whim. He hadn't wanted to spend the money it would cost, but the slots were open, and some friends were planning on having a good time. Realizing that he'd probably never have another chance to see an oriental city other than Saigon, he decided to go along, too. He hadn't realized that the first stop his friends would make would be to hire girls for the week, and there was no graceful way for him to avoid it, too.

Mark had not been much of a social lion while in high school, or the year he spent in college. He wasn't the handsomest guy to come down the pike; he'd been kind of introverted, too, and really more interested in other things, anyway. Not that a girl friend wouldn't have been nice, but why wish in vain?

So it happened that the few days he spent with Mei-Ling were about the only time he'd spent with a woman in a social/sexual situation. For a week, she had been his, and it had been a memorable week. He had not been surprised when she'd lifted his virginity within half an hour of picking her out of a lineup at random. It had been an exciting experience that had opened a world of doors to him. She had, at least apparently, been surprised when he ask her to take him to sample some real Thai food; she'd said she'd been surprised when he said he liked it. She said she'd even been a little relieved when they went right back to the hotel room instead of going out drinking; in good English, she said she'd gotten a little tired of guys that tried to screw her while they were puking drunk.

Over the next few days, Mei-Ling showed Mark a good deal of the city, including some magnificent temples and pagodas, and he'd had a taste of how the people lived. Moreover, she'd showed him a lot in the hotel room, too; things that he'd never dreamed of in his life.

But, most importantly, this little Chinese/Thai girl showed him just how pleasant it could be to be with a woman -- and that was the greatest door of all that she opened for him. When they finally kissed goodbye, he knew that he would never see her again, but he knew, too, that he'd never forget her until his dying day.

It wasn't a long distance to go home. He hadn't bothered to put the Carhartts or the snowmobile suit back on, and he was a little bit chilly as the old Ford's heater struggled to keep the windows clear, but Mei-Ling was on his mind, now. That had been just about two years ago, and he still thought of her often. The memories still haunted him; for a few days, the door to another kind of existence had been open, and he'd had a peek through it.

Yes, a girl friend would have been nice, but there were other things that wanted to get done, too.

Once at home, he grabbed his heavy clothes and headed inside. The telescope could stay in the car; he'd want it again tonight. He hung the clothes in the back hall, then stumbled up the stairs to his old room, where he peeled off his clothes down to the inner layer of his long underwear. Before he crashed onto the bed, he did something he'd been trying to avoid doing: he dug down into a drawer and stared for a moment at one of his pictures of Mei-Ling, as if her image weren't burned into his mind.

She was still smiling in his mind's eye when sleep came over him.

2.

The sun was still up when Mark drug himself out of bed. It was going to be hell to get back onto something resembling a daytime schedule, not that it mattered a lot right now. At least it was warmer in the old hanger in the daytime, but not enough to make any difference, He'd spent a lot of cold evenings out there over the past winter.

A shower and a shave made him feel almost human again. He glanced out the window; it was still clear, although he could see that it was blowing a little, so he knew it probably wouldn't stay clear much longer. It probably meant more snow, as if they hadn't had enough this winter. He got dressed in clean clothes and went downstairs.

"I suppose you're going to be either out at the hanger or out with the telescope again tonight," his mother said accusingly.

"Both, I think," he replied. "I've got someone that wants to see M-31 and M-45, and when I get done with that, I guess I'll work on the ribstitching some more."

"Are you going to be late?" his mother asked.

"Hard to say," Mark told her. "I'll probably spend an hour or two with the telescope, and then see how I feel about working on the wing."

"And you'll be half the night," his mother replied, understanding him perfectly. She knew that Mark was feeling time pressure on him as the days marched by. "I'll leave some leftovers for you in the refrigerator, if you want some."

Mark had a sandwich and a cup of coffee. Noting the time, he pulled on his Carhartts and headed out the door. Outside, the wind was even sharper than he had thought it would be. It would be cold after the sun set; probably he wouldn't have the telescope out much.

His old Ford started on the first try. It wasn't far to the Archer house, only a mile or so, so Mark left it running outside when he went to the door. The thought crossed his mind that he was sorry he had set this up; it would not be a good night for observing, and he really had other stuff he needed to do.

Jackie was waiting for him when he got there, dressed casually now, in jeans and a flannel shirt. "Are you ready to go?" he asked.

"I guess so," she said.

"Better bring something warm, like a snowmobile suit," he warned her. "It's going to be cold out there tonight."

"I can wear dad's," she said, and went to get it.

While he was waiting, he talked with her stepmother a little. Soon, Jackie was back, carrying the bright red snowmobile suit over her shoulder. "I'm ready," she said.

The car's heater had been going long enough now to warm it up a bit. Mark went over and opened the right-side door for her, not necessarily because it was the courteous thing to do, but because the latch was tricky and the door had to be lifted up to close properly. "Hope you don't mind this piece of junk," he said, "But I needed a cheap car that only had to last me for a few months."

"It's all right," she replied. "Are we going out to Turtle Hill again?"

"I don't think so," he said. "With this wind, it's going to be awful cold out there. Besides, you and your boyfriend weren't the only couple whose plans we screwed up last night, so tonight, I think we'd better let the romantic life of Spearfish Lake march on like normal."

"He's not my boyfriend," Jackie again protested. "Don't get the wrong impression. We only had the one date. I was glad when I saw you out there last night, since it meant I wouldn't have to walk home if he couldn't keep his hands to himself."

"We don't go out there often," Mark smiled in the gathering darkness. "But when we do, it always seems like we get a car or two an hour. They pull up, and someone rolls the window down and asks, 'Are you guys going to be here long?' We always answer, 'Not long, maybe three or four AM', even if we're packing up. It's kind of fun."

"That's not nice," she laughed. "Didn't you ever go out there with your girlfriend when you were in high school?"

"Never did," he replied truthfully. The fact that he had never had a girl friend in high school had nothing to do with it.

"Where are we going, anyway?" she asked.

"Out to the airport, I guess," he said, realizing that he hadn't thought about it, but it would allow him time to get the heater on and the office warmed up. "We can set up downwind of one of the hangers, and be out of the worst of the breeze."

"That's right," she said. "You're a Gravengood, aren't you? Do you fly, like your dad?"

"Soloed on my sixteenth birthday, but I'd been flying for years before," he said.

"Did you fly in the Army?"

"No," he told her, the disappointment still biting. "My glasses are too thick.

They won't take you into flight school if you wear glasses. Besides, it's all helicopters, any more."

Spearfish Lake's airport hardly deserved the name; it was a grassy, open area, where the soil had been too thin to grow trees after it had been logged over a century before. At some time back in the thirties, the WPA had cleared off what remained of the stumps, leveled the ground, reseeded it to grass, and built a small hanger. In the forty or so years since, a couple of T-hangers had been added, but it was still a grass strip, still unlighted. Normally, only four planes were kept at Spearfish Lake year-round, but on summer weekends there might be a dozen or more that people flew in from their homes down south. There were a number of junky old cars parked behind the main hanger, owned by those summer visitors, and only used to run out to summer cottages around the lake.

Mark drove in the driveway, noted the wind direction from the windsock on the main hanger's roof, then pulled to a stop on the concrete pad in front of the main hanger. It was about as out of the wind as they would be likely to get. "I've got to run inside for a minute," he said. "You can stay here, out of the wind, while I get set up, if you like. I'll have to help you with that stupid door, either way."

"Can I go inside to put my snowmobile suit on?" she asked. "It'll be easier than trying to do it in the car."

"No reason why not," he agreed, then opened the car door and got out. He helped her with the Ford's right door, and went over to the airport office. Inside, it was cool and still as soon as he got the lights on. It was a cluttered room, with trash and papers strewn about, stuff stacked high in the corners. On the wall hung a calendar opened to October, 1970 -- six months out of date, now.

While she busied herself pulling on the snowmobile suit over her clothes, he lit a fire in the big, old oil space heater. In a while, it would take a chill off of the room, although it probably wouldn't get real warm. He put a teapot full of water on top of the heater; after a while, he would be able to mix a cup of coffee.

As he did this, she looked at him with an unspoken question in her eye. "I'll be coming back out here after we're done," he explained. "It gets cold out in the hanger after dark, and it helps to have a place to warm up. After last night, I might be out here most of the night."

"What would keep you out here most of the night?" she asked. "Stargazing?"

"No," he said. "Rebuilding an airplane."

"Can I see?" she asked.

"Can if you want," he said. "It's not much to look at, right now."

He led her through a side door in the office and out into the little hanger, where he threw on the lights. Crowded into the little hanger were a couple of small planes; a yellow one that she had seen flying over once, and the red, white and black one that Mr. Gravengood had taken her flying in once, years ago.

In the back of the hanger were what she recognized as pieces of a plane, a small, silver-colored one, sitting wingless against the back wall. One of the wings, bare of fabric, sat leaning against the wall; the other was leading-edge down on a kind of stand improvised out of scrap lumber, with fabric spread over it. "Like I said, it's not much to look at," he said. She stood there looking for a moment before he went on, "Look, I'd like to get the telescope set up before it gets fully dark. I'll get it set up, and then we can come in out of the wind until the stars are out."

She didn't have to go outside in the chill breeze to help him, but it was interesting to watch. She had not had a good look at the telescope in the darkness the night before, but now she could see that it was smaller than she had imagined -- only about two and a half feet long. It was mounted in kind of a box, which fitted to the top of a homemade tripod. It did not take him long to get it set up -- only a few minutes -- and then he fitted an eyepiece into the focuser, and another one into the finder.

The sun had setting in the west in a colorful red ball just as Mark had picked her up; now, the sky was aglow in colorful reds and oranges. "That's quite a sunset," she said.

"Yeah," he agreed. "Look at those mare's tails. There's going to be some weather coming our way." He took the telescope, looked in the finder, and scanned the sky off to the west. "It's probably too early to see Mercury, yet, and we might not with all those clouds." He kept looking for a few minutes, then said, "Well, I guess not yet. Let's get out of this wind."

Inside the cluttered, grimy airport office, the space heater was making ticking noises and almost gave the impression of giving off some heat. At least it was out of the wind. Jackie sat down on the couch, while Mark sat in a battered kitchen chair. "It's cold out there, tonight," she said.

"Yeah, I don't like it much, myself," he said. "Although, I will admit, there were many days in Vietnam that I prayed to see another Spearfish Lake winter day."

"That's right, I heard you were in Vietnam, weren't you," she responded. "Wasn't it horrible?"

"Jackie, you have no idea," he said, seriously. "I have never been so consistently, completely . . ." he was silent for a moment, and for an instant she thought perhaps he was reliving the agony of battle " . . . bored shitless in my life."

She giggled a little with relief. "I can't believe I spent eighteen months there," he went on. "I think I probably worked half an hour a week, and tried to look busy the rest of the time. I was in the 82nd Airborne, and you'd think I was out in the boonies all the time. Mostly, I installed and fixed phones in the division headquarters."

"I thought you only had to stay there a year," she said.

"Yeah," he said. "But the NCO in charge of the phone section left about a month before I did, and they didn't have a replacement for him, so they offered me an extra stripe to stay on for another six months, so I said, what the hell, you know? Two weeks after they gave me the stripe, an old sergeant showed up to take over the section, and after he got there, I did absolutely nothing for the rest of my time there. Except during Tet, back in '68, I never heard a shot fired in anger, except artillery in the distance."

"You were there that long ago?"

"I spent a year and a half in Germany after that," he explained. "I was just about as bored there, too. I don't mind working, but I'm not too good at just sitting around, doing nothing."

"What have you been doing with yourself since you got out last fall?" she asked.

"Mostly, I've been right out there in the hanger, rebuilding that plane," he said. "Every couple of weeks I go down to the unemployment office and pick up my check. How about you?" he added, trying to change the subject a little. "Have you been doing anything but waiting on tables?"

"No," she said. "I got real tired of sitting around after I graduated, until that job came along. It's not going to be too much longer, just until Marjorie gets over having her baby. If I can get another job to hold me through the summer, I guess I'm going to go to the Community College down in Camden, next fall. But, I don't know how that's going to work out."

"Didn't work out too well for me," he said. "I guess I'd just sat in classrooms too long, and I was tired of it. Then, Mr. Corman, over at the phone company, suggested that I join the army and go to advanced phone systems school. I had to give up an extra year to get that, but it was worth it. Let's go out and see if we can find Mercury, again."

The sunset outside had lost a lot of its sheen. It was considerably darker now, and stars were beginning to come out overhead. It was considerably colder, too; the wind seemed to have picked up a bit. Interested as Jackie was in looking through the telescope, it was clear that she wouldn't want to make a night of it, at least this night.

After a few minutes searching, Mark spoke up, "Well, for what it's worth, there's Mercury." He stepped away from the telescope, and she stepped up for a peek. All she could see was a bright, tiny dot in the eyepiece. She told him so.

"That's about all you ever can see, in a small telescope," he told her. "It's not real large, and it's usually pretty close to the sun, so not a lot of people have seen it. He looked around the sky. "Saturn's out," he said. "That's a lot more interesting."

In but a few seconds, she was marveling at the sight of the ringed planet, tiny but sharp in the eyepiece. "Isn't that pretty," she said. "I mean, I've seen pictures of it, and all, but it's nothing like seeing the real thing. It's so . . . real."

Mark stepped back from the telescope and let her study it as long as she wanted to. "Can you see the different colors in the rings?" he asked.

"Yes, they're very sharp."

"If you look carefully," he went on, "You can see the shadow of the rings on the surface."

"Why yes," she said. "Of course. You know, somehow, I never thought that they'd leave a shadow."

"There's a couple of little flecks of light in the field of view, too," he said. "The bright one is Titan, Saturn's largest moon. I don't know if the other one is a moon or a star."

"That is so neat . . ." she said, her voice trailing off as she continued to stare into the eyepiece. For an instant, she was standing in the porthole of an interplanetary spaceship, drawing close to Saturn after a long voyage from earth, the cold of space pressing in on them -- but then she realized that she was still standing on the hanger apron of the Spearfish Lake Airport, looking through Mark's telescope. It wasn't the cold of interplanetary space that was making her teeth chatter in spite of her space/snowmobile suit; it was just the chill wind off of the lake.

"It really is cold out here tonight," he commented. "It isn't quite dark enough for M-31 yet, and we've still got an hour or two for M-42. Why don't we see if that stove is putting out yet?"

It turned out to be a little warmer in the office; the heater was taking hold, a little, and it was out of that miserable wind. "Thanks for showing me that," she said, sitting down.

"I can spend hours looking at Saturn," he agreed. "I don't know how many hours I've spent looking at Saturn since I built that telescope."

"You built that?" she asked.

"Back when I was in junior high. Ground the mirror, the whole shot."

"How do you grind a mirror like that?"

"Very patiently," he told her. "It's very tedious, especially to grind a mirror with that short a focal length. You start with two pieces of glass and some grinding compound, and spend hours, and hours just grinding the curve out of it. Then you have to polish it and figure it, and that takes hours and hours, too. I spent most of a winter at it, down in my basement, but it's the most amazing thing how accurately you can work. The curve of that mirror is accurate to within millionths of an inch."

"And you were . . . what? Thirteen, fourteen? Did you build the rest of the telescope, too?" she asked.

"Well, yes and no," he replied. "The tube is just a piece of irrigation pipe. Some of the other stuff, I built in the beginning, but over the years, I've replaced it with stuff that I've bought. I've fiddled with that telescope for ten years, now. The mount is new, for example; I built it down in the basement, this winter, when it was too cold to work on the Cessna." He looked out the grimy window and added, "We need to get back out there if we want to see M-31 tonight, and that's a sight you don't want to miss."

Jackie wasn't warmed all the way back up yet, but her curiosity was enough to propel her out the door. In a minute, Mark had the telescope pointed low in the west, and Jackie was again looking in the eyepiece. There was a bright spot at the center, and long, filmy extensions to either side. "What is it?" she asked "I can see it's a galaxy, but it's so much brighter than the Whirlpool, last night."

"Galaxies don't get any better than that," he told her. "That's the Andromeda Galaxy. It's more than two billion light-years away, and just a little bigger than our own galaxy. It's practically a next-door neighbor. The only galaxies closer than that are diddly-squat little things."

"I can see some lighter and darker areas. What are they, spiral arms?"

"You picked them right out. Study the field. Do you see anything else?"

Jackie looked through the telescope again, then said, "Oh, there's another galaxy, right below it. It's smaller. And, there's another one, right close in."

"Congratulations," he smiled. "You have just discovered M-32 and M-110."

"I can't make out much detail," she said. "They're just faint, fuzzy spots."

"You can't make much out, even in a large telescope," he told her. She stood studying the view oblivious to the chill, biting wind. Mark had shown M-31 and other sights in the sky to people over the years, but no one he had ever introduced to the telescopic sky had ever shown the intense interest this girl had.

"Let me show you everybody's favorite," he said when she stood back upright. He moved the telescope to the left and up a little. "Now, where we're going to look is Orion. You know Orion?"

"That's the rectangle of stars over there?" she pointed off in the west.

"Sure enough," he said. "You see the three bright stars crosswise, right in the middle? There's another row of three fainter stars perpendicular to them."

"The belt and the sword," she said. "Dad taught me."

"You got it. We're going to look at the middle star of the sword." He bent over the telescope's finder and centered it, then offered the main eyepiece to her.

"Oh, wow," she said. "What is it?"

"M-42. It's a star-forming region. You see right in the middle there, that little group of four stars? They're very young, still getting going, almost. Those are called the Trapezium."

"But what is the whole cloud?," she said, looking at the glowing tendrils and clouds that filled the whole field of the eyepiece.

He smiled. The area was his favorite, too. "The whole region is called the Orion Nebula. It's a tremendous cloud of gas and dust, light years across. It's lighted by the starlight of the stars you see. At that, the view in the telescope doesn't do it justice. Now, in color photographs, it's really spectacular."

Mark wasn't as heavily dressed as he had been the night before -- after all, he had intended to spend most of the evening in the hanger, with frequent warmup breaks because his hands got cold. "I suppose we'd better get out of the wind for a few minutes," he said after a while.

The old space heater had taken a lot of the chill out of the office, and warming up in there didn't seem quite a futile a gesture. It was quite relaxing to be in out of the wind, and they fell to talking. "You know more about the sky than most people," he told her. "Most people know the Big Dipper, if they know anything about the sky at all."

"Dad taught me," she said. "We spent a lot of time together before he married Sarah. We used to go camping and fishing every chance we got. We still go some. It was a lot of fun to sit around the campfire, out along the Spearfish River, and he'd show me the sky, and talk about the constellations. We had a little book, and we both learned a lot of the constellations. One summer we took a pair of binoculars out camping, and we looked at the Milky Way down in Sagittarius a lot. That's really nice."

"In a good pair of binoculars, it can be downright awesome," he agreed. "That may be the best way to see it."

"I wish now that we'd done it more. Maybe we'd have gotten a telescope, and I wouldn't have had to have waited all this time to see some of the things you've shown me tonight. But then, it was just something to do, and Dad was always trying to find something new for us to do."

Mark nodded his head. "Why was that?" he asked, and then instantly wished he'd not asked the question. After all, he remembered why.

"That was right after my mother had to go away," Jackie said. "I was still pretty young, but dad knew we had a lot to put behind us."

"Did he teach you how to fly-fish?" Mark asked, trying to change the flow of the subject, without having to look like he was doing it. Although he didn't know the details, he did know that Jackie's mother had been in the state mental sanatorium down in Camden for more than a decade, and he suspected that there was more pain in Jackie's statement than he wanted to know about.

"He showed me how, but I guess I was still a little young," Jackie said. "I never really learned to enjoy it, but we fished with bait and spinning gear a lot, and I still like to fish. Dad and I still try to get out a few nights a summer though, to go camping and go fishing, and I still enjoy my time out in the woods with him."

"What do you these days besides work?" he asked.

"Not a heck of a lot," she said. "I don't particularly care for television, so I spend a good part of my time at the library. I've tried to look for work that's more permanent than Rick's, something where I'm not on my feet all the time. But, that's hard this time of year."

"I know," he said. "At least, that's something I don't have to worry about."

"Why's that?" she wanted to know.

"Well, back when I was thinking about going into the Army, Mr. Corman told me that if I learned everything the army could teach me about phone repair, then to come and see him after I got out. Well, I did, and I kept in touch with him every time I came home on leave. He sent me special study materials, so I could learn something about civilian systems. I had a long talk with him when I got out, and he's promised me Bruce Frybarger's job when he retires."

"How long is that going to be?"

"He's looking to retire in time for deer season, next year. Mr. Corman said that would be the first opening he had unless someone dropped dead on him." Mark shrugged. "It's a little longer off than I had hoped, but I'll make it work out. The thing is, I know that if I wait just a little while, I'll have a good job that I can work at as long as I want to. That's worth the wait."

Jackie smiled. That was an enviable position to be in; she wished she had something as good going for her. "So what do you do? Spend all your time out here, working on your plane?"

"Not all of it," he said. "But a lot of it. It's taking me longer to get it done than I'd hoped. When I originally got it, I'd hoped to be pretty well done with it by now, but I ought to know that things never go that smoothly. By busting my butt, I'm only a couple of weeks behind schedule, but I think it's going to get worse before I get done with the ribstitching."

"Ribstitching?"

"Yeah, you have to sew the fabric to the wings. Each stitch has to be knotted shut with a special knot, and the knot has to be right, or the inspector won't buy off on it. I've had to do most of it by myself. Dad has helped a little, but his fingers are getting all full of arthritis, so there's a limit to how much he can help. It's just damn slow working by myself."

"How come?"

"I keep having to run back and forth around the wing, about four times for each stitch, sometimes more. It's taking me five minutes to a stitch, and there's several hundred stitches. And, working out in the hanger, I can only work so long before my hands get too cold to tie that stupid knot."

She shook her head and stretched; some of the cold was coming out, now. "I guess I feel a little guilty," she said. "I've been keeping you from doing something you wanted to do."

"Don't feel guilty," he said. "I like looking at the sky and showing it off, too."

"Well, thanks for showing me, anyway. Is there anything I can do to help repay you?"

He smiled. "If you don't mind being bored, I could use an extra set of hands. It's not difficult, but like grinding a mirror, it's just tedious."

He led her into the hanger, and turned on the lights near the wing. A large sewing needle hung on some heavy, stringlike thread from the wing. "It looks real straight forward," he explained. "It's not."

Starting the needle was easy, but it had to be guided blind through the thickness of the wing, to come out right next to the rib, at exactly the right place, on the other side. A strong light shining through the fabric of the wing helped, but the trick was to run the point of the needle through the wing fabric on the far side, then judge how far off from the proper place it was, then make adjustments. Then, the needle had to be guided back through the wing, with the same problem, and the seine knot tied off before moving on to the next stitch.

It soon became clear to Jackie that Mark had been optimistic; while it wouldn't be too bad a job near the trailing edge of the wing, in the center of the wing it might take a dozen trips back and forth around the wing for a single person to make one stitch.

Mark drug a shop stool over for her to sit on, and while their conversation continued, the pace slowed down a lot, since the friendly discussion was interspersed with a lot of directions on how to move the needle. "Left a little . . . the other way . . . now up just a hair . . . now push it through . . . OK, I've got it," she would say, pulling the needle and the string through, then starting the return stitch at the proper place, he would give her similar instructions. Then, once he had pulled the needle back through, it still took him a couple of minutes to knot the stitch off and go on to the next one. It was tedious, and although out of the biting wind, Jackie soon found out it was cold enough to see her breath in the hanger. At least, she could wear gloves; Mark mostly tried to make do without, sticking his hands in his pockets, or over the light bulb to warm them. Even then, they could only go so long before they had to retreat to the warmth of the space heater in the office.

It was on one of those warming breaks by the oil burner that she asked, "Why not just wait for the weather to warm up to do this?"

"I want to be done before the weather breaks," he told her. "The clock is running."

"I don't understand," she said.

Mark mentally flipped a nickel. His parents, of course, knew what he had in mind, but he hadn't told anyone else, not that it mattered. If it didn't work out, he didn't want to look like a fool. But then, no one else had quite asked what his hurry was, either, and it couldn't hurt to tell Jackie. "I want to fly out of here, just as soon as the weather gets a little nicer. I've got a trip I've been wanting to take."

"A long trip?" she asked.

"Yeah, I guess a long trip," he said. "While I still can. If I don't do it before I go to work for the phone company, I won't ever have the chance again, and this is something I've dreamed about for years."

"Where are you going?" she asked conversationally.

"Nowhere in particular," he said. "Just around. There's a few things I'd like to see, a few places I'd like to go, a few things I'd like to do. But mostly, I just want to go and see what's on the other side of the mountain."

Jackie smiled. "That could be quite a trip," she said. "What are some of the things you want to do and see?"

"Oh, nothing very special," he said. "Go to Stellafane -- that's a big star party in July in Vermont. Go to the Texas Star Party in May. I'm planning on taking the telescope with me. I'll take my backpack, too; there are a few places I want to go backpacking, like in the Wind River Range in Wyoming, maybe in the Colorado high country, too. There's places I just want to look out the window of the plane, places like the Grand Canyon. I don't have the money to put a lot of radio in this bird, so I'll pretty much stay away from big cities. I plan on camping by the plane, sleeping under the wing most of the time, and I don't want to waste any good camping weather. I want to be on the way by the middle of next month, end of the month at the latest."

Over the next hour or so, Mark told Jackie of his plans for the trip, and how it had come about. It had come to him in the army telephone school, at a post in New Jersey. It had been a long school, and a couple of times he had come back to Spearfish Lake on leave. Flying in an airliner into Camden, he had looked out of the window and realized that there was a lot more to the country that just the little part that he knew. He knew that there was going to be a good chance that he was going to go to Vietnam to fight for his country, and he felt like he'd like to know more about it.

Mark had grown up, of course, on stories of flying, and that included plenty of stories of the old barnstorming days, half a century before, when World War I veterans and their decrepit Jennies had flown around the country, landing in cow pastures, sleeping under the wing, taking people for rides at five dollars a head just to keep their sagging airplanes in the air. Mark had met a few pilots that had been barnstormers back in that era. While they all said it was no way to make a living, it was a heck of a lot of fun when they were young.

Mark had not hated his time in Vietnam, but had found it desperately boring, and the only thing that had kept boredom from overwhelming him was the thoughts of what he might do once he got out of the Army. Since he liked backpacking, he gave some thought to hiking the Appalachian Trail, but there were other things he wanted to do, too. Besides, he couldn't take his telescope along. Finally, he realized that what he really wanted to do was to relive a little of those barnstorming days that the old Jenny pilots still yarned about.

"Jackie," he said at one point while he was tying a knot, "It gave my life a focus, and there were times that it was the only thing that kept me going. For pretty close to three years -- more than that, now -- it's kept me going. This trip is all I worked towards. I smoke maybe a pack of cigarettes every two weeks, I had a couple of beers on payday. I can eat nearly anything, and don't mind if I miss a meal now and then, so I could survive the army mess halls, and virtually every cent I made I put in the bank so I could make this trip . . . OK, the knot's done, the needle's coming through to you again."

Part of the reason he had extended his tour in Vietnam had been the extra combat pay that he could bank, especially with the extra stripe on his sleeve. He had been willing to extend his tour again, except by that time he had not flown a plane in eighteen months, and he was getting worried about how rusty he was getting. Over a long leave at home he got a lot of practice in and his skills back to where he wanted them, flying his dad's old Stinson. He had hoped to be stationed somewhere in the states, where he could keep his skills current, but had been sent to Germany; two days before he left, he took his checkride for his Commercial Pilot license. He spent another eighteen months in Germany, managing to travel a little while spending little, but hoping his piloting skills didn't deteriorate too much.

While he was in Vietnam, he had done what he could do to research the trip. He did not have access to a good library in Vietnam, but he wrote letters -- mail was free from Vietnam -- and ordered catalogues and brochures, and dreamed a lot. Research was a little easier in Germany, and he had compiled a list of things he wanted to see and places to hike. For three years, he had been compiling a list of things to take with him, adding and deleting and agonizing, mostly over the weight. It was good therapy, if nothing else; he could always pull out his list and go over it once again, feeling that he was working toward the trip that had become such an obsessive goal to him.

It was clear from the beginning that he wanted to take his own plane, not his dad's Stinson -- his dad wouldn't like to be without it for six months or a year or whatever it took to work this trip out of his system. As a result, during his last months in the army in Germany, he had subscribed to a paper called "Trade-A-Plane". It was full of nothing but aircraft classified and display ads. As soon as Trade-A-Plane showed up at mail call, three times a month, Mark was lost to the world, studying prices of airplanes, studying what was available. By this time, he had about seven thousand dollars in the bank but wanted to save as much of it for the trip as he could, so he shopped hard for a bargain.

Thus it was that when the Army turned him loose at Fort Dix, New Jersey, the November before, the first phone call that he made was not home, but to a number in Indiana, and the first airline ticket he bought, still in uniform so he could fly military rate, was to Indianapolis, rather than to Camden.

Three days later, he was back in Indiana, driving a borrowed pickup truck and towing a flatbed trailer. He had already decided that a Cessna 140 was about what he was looking for, and it was a case of finding one at a good price. The one he found had recently had the engine overhauled, and Mark knew enough about aircraft engines to know that it was probably sound; it started easily and ran cleanly.

That was the good part. The plane already had fabric that needed redoing when it sat out in a hailstorm a couple of months before; the fabric on the wings hung in shreds. The owner had already put more money into it than he wanted to, and had a baby on the way; he asked $2000 for the bird, a good price. Even so, Mark managed to beat him down to $1800, and got him to throw in the materials to redo the wings at that price. He was satisfied with the deal.

Once he had the plane in the hanger in Spearfish Lake, Mark flew the Stinson down to Lordston and got Ken Sawyer, the tractor and aircraft mechanic, to fly back up with him to see what needed to be done to the bird. Beyond the fabric work, Sawyer gave Mark a long list of work that had needed to be done.

"I've chipped away at that list all winter," Mark told Jackie. "There were other things that had to be done, too. The interior looked like someone had been raising goats in it, so I had to redo that. I've got the fuselage about ready to put back together, and then give the fuselage a buffing and polishing. I can do that while we're doping and painting the wings. I put off working on the wings in hopes it might warm up some, and I guess it is better than it was in January. . . OK, the knot's done, the needle's coming through again."

Jackie looked back over what they had done; while she had been pulling the story out of him, they had made a lot of progress, although there was still a lot of wing, plus the other wing, to go. But then, they'd been at it a while. "Hey," she asked. "What time is it getting to be? I have to get up and go to work at five, tomorrow morning."

Mark looked at his watch. "I'd better get you home, then," he said. "You might be able to get five hours sleep."

"It's midnight?" she asked as Mark again tied a seine not. "Where did the time go?"

A little more . . . there. "Time flies when you're having fun," Mark smirked. "I hope I didn't bore you too much." He put down the needle and stood up.

On the opposite side of the wing, Jackie stood up, too, and looked across at him. "I did have fun," she told him as he turned to turn out a light. "It's been fun talking to you, and fun working on this with you. And, thanks for showing me M-31 and M-42 and Saturn and all that, earlier. I really enjoyed that."

"Well, you've been a big help tonight," he said. "I appreciate that. We've done more in a couple of hours than I could get done in a day, by myself. Any time you feel like helping out again, you're welcome."

They went out through the office, and Mark started to take the telescope down and put it in the Ford's trunk; it had stayed set up all the time they had been inside. "Didn't you forget to turn the heater off?" she asked.

"No," he said. "I'll be back out here after I take you home."

3.

Jackie hated working at Rick's on Sunday mornings.

Sundays brought the church crowd, and in Spearfish Lake, the church crowd was full of lousy tippers and complainers. The Saturday bunch was much more friendly, and the weekday crowds were, too. But, put ties on some of the same people, bring their wives with them, and the atmosphere changed completely.

It didn't help that Jackie had experienced two short nights of sleep in a row. She could barely drag herself out of bed a few short hours after Mark had brought her home the night before. The alarm had to ring for several minutes before she could pull herself together enough to sit up and shut it off. Fortunately, she'd had the presence of mind the night before to move the clock so that she couldn't reach it from the bed, or she would have slept all morning.

All morning long, as her feet began to ache from running back and forth with pots of coffee, she thought of Mark and his plans that she had heard about the night before. That would be quite a trip, she thought; it was quite a dream to have held. It would be a fun trip to take.

Except for some lunch business, the crowd died out about one, and Rick's normally closed at two. It had been a terribly long day, and she was glad to have it over with.

Outside, she saw that Mark had been right; some weather had moved in. It was still cold, more from the wind blowing than pure bitter cold, but it was overcast and it looked like there might be some snow in the air. Most of the snow around Spearfish Lake had disappeared early for once, except for some patches back in the shade of buildings or deep in the woods, but the sky looked like it could dump some more on them. For Spearfish Lake, spring was still a month or more off; winter usually hung on until everyone was thoroughly sick of it. By this time of year people were pretty tired of seeing bare trees and the winter gray and brown; the snow being gone just made everything seem more drab.

It was easy to understand why Mark wanted to be on his way to someplace else.

Jackie got into the car and started it up. As tired as she was, she thought that she would just go home and see if she could take a nap. Naps in the afternoon were hard, though; Johnnie made a lot of noise, and hadn't yet learned that there were times that people wanted to be let alone to sleep. Plus, the TV would be on, and besides a nap would put her schedule out of sorts.

As Jackie drove towards home she came up on the intersection of the state road. Going down the state road a short ways would take her out to the airport; she wondered if Mark were out there, working on the ribstitching of the wing. On a whim, she slowed and turned down the state road to see.

At the airport, she could see Mark's old Ford sitting in front of the hanger; apparently he was still there. For a moment, she thought that it would be rather forward of her to just barge in on him without warning, but decided to do it anyway.

Inside, she could see that he was intent on what he was doing. "Looks like you've made quite a bit of progress since last night," she told him.

"Dad was out this morning, and he helped me for a couple of hours before his hands got too painful," he said. "Every little bit helps."

"I just thought I'd see how you were coming. I can't really help you out this afternoon. Sarah needs to get her car back, and I'm not dressed for it."

"I could pick you up," he suggested. "You were a big help last night."

Jackie thought for a moment. She was tired, and she knew Sarah planned to go to Lynchburg right after she got home. If Jackie stayed home, then Johnnie would probably be left with her, and she was too tired for him right now. On the other hand, it would be pleasant to spend more time with Mark.

No contest. "Can you follow me right home?" she asked. "That way, I'm less likely to get roped into babysitting my stepbrother."

He stood up. "I can do that," he said. "I was getting about ready to get my hands into some gloves for a while, anyway."

Sarah acted a little disappointed that Jackie had something planned other than babysitting, but she wasn't about to say anything with Mark standing there, waiting while Jackie changed out of her white dress into something warmer, and pulled on the snowmobile suit once again. "She wanted to," Jackie told Mark in the car as they headed back to the airport, "She's got the idea that I should automatically be willing to be a free babysitter whenever she wants."

"Sounds like a real pain in the butt," Mark commented."

Jackie shook her head. "Most of the time, it's not, really. I don't mind Johnnie most of the time, but I just hate being taken for granted. Working at Rick's has helped. At least I'm not automatically free whenever she wants."

"You sound like you're not too crazy about her," he observed, swerving the car around one of Spearfish Lake's numerous potholes.

"She's OK," Jackie said. "We get along OK, most of the time, but I guess I've always felt that she took Dad away from me, a lot."

"You mean, compared with back when you were littler."

"Yeah," Jackie agreed. "I shouldn't really feel that way. I mean, Dad has to have his life, too. But, it seems like I'm on the outside a lot, kind of like a fifth wheel."

Perhaps it was the irritation with Sarah, or perhaps it was just being tired, or perhaps it was because talking over the wing, out of sight of each other, was sort of like being in a confessional; but as they worked on the wing in the waning hours of the afternoon, Jackie found herself telling Mark a lot about herself -- things that she had not been willing to talk about with a friend like Kirsten. It was good to have someone to talk to, who could listen, and perhaps understand.

For example, she had always felt awkward and freakish about her height. Always tall, she now stood an even six feet tall, taller by far than most of her friends, taller than most guys. She stuck out in a crowd, and she had always been self-conscious about it. But, in Mark, who was even taller than she was, although not by much, she found someone who could understand.

"It was tough for me, too," Mark told her. "That idiot Meredith, when he was the football and basketball coach, was always on my ass to go out for basketball. I could never make it clear to him that I can't play basketball, don't like basketball, and could care less about basketball."

"It's tougher for a girl, I think," she told him. "Six feet for a guy is just on the tall side. For a girl, it's awful tall. People were always making jokes about it, and that hurt. You know, 'Hi, how's the weather up there?' -- that sort of thing. It hurts. You can't do anything about it, but it hurts just the same. I felt like such a freak."

"The hell with the little people," he laughed. "You know and I know that one of the good things about being tall is that we can look down on them. When people laugh at us for being tall, it's because they envy us, not because they hate us. Be proud that you're so tall, not ashamed of it."

"That's easy to say," she said. "When you're a girl and there's no one that's anywhere near as tall as you, it's awful hard to do. Then, on top of all the tall jokes, there were always the stories about my mother. You know, my real mother, not Sarah."

"I know," Mark said. "At least, I know about the stories."

Jackie had been probing with the needle for the proper place on the far side of the wing, but now she stopped. "I haven't seen her for, six or seven years," she said quietly. "I just can't bear to look at her. There's nothing to see. She just lays there, staring at the ceiling, eyes open, humming the same note, all day, and they tell me all night. They're not sure if she's awake or asleep, and they don't think she'll ever get any better." She had never shared even this much with anyone, except for her father, not even Sarah, and she wondered even as she spoke why she was telling Mark now. "I'm not sure I care any longer, at least about her. I barely remember her when she was what you call normal, although

I don't think she was well, even then, but I didn't realize until later just how strange she was acting."

She probed with the needle again; Mark saw that it was in the right place, and pulled it on through without saying anything. Somehow, he couldn't think of anything to say.

As he tied the seine knot, she started to speak again. "You know, it's not the stories that people tell that bother me," she said. "It's just the fact that she's my mother. She's tall, like me, and I've worried for years, if maybe what she has is genetic." She was silent again, so silent that Mark stopped fiddling with the seine knot and stood up to look over the wing and see if she was all right. Sitting on the stool, she looked up at him and said, "God, I hope somebody has the good sense to kill me if I ever get like that. Frankly, Mark, it scares the hell out of me."

Mark found himself at a loss for words. Just what the hell do you say to something like that? "Well, I'm no expert," he said. "But, I would have to think that it's probably not genetic. Environment has to play a part, too." It wasn't the best thing he could have said, he realized, but he couldn't think of anything better. It would have to do.

"I hope you're right," she said finally. "I've had people that know more about it than you do say they don't know for sure, either."

"Like I said," Mark replied. "I'm no expert, but I'm pretty sure of one thing: worrying about it won't make it any better."

They were silent for a moment before Jackie nodded. "You're probably right. I guess I know that, but I can't help worrying about it. Let's get back to work."

Mark bent back over again, finished the seine knot, then started probing with the needle again. She had helped him work the needle into the right place and was pulling it through when he snickered a little; he couldn't help himself. "What's so funny?" she asked.

"Oh, the thought crossed my mind that the whole thing is something you could use to your advantage, not let it just get you down."

"What do you mean?" she said, a little suspicious.

"Well, take this trip. I haven't really told many people besides my family, and now you, what I'm up to. I mean, most people would think the whole thing is a little screwy, you know."

"I can see that," she agreed, "What's your point?"

"Simple," he smiled. "Me, people will say when they hear about it, 'What's got into that kid?' Now, if it was you that was doing something that's a little off the wall, people wouldn't think much of it. They'd just say, 'Aw, hell, it runs in the family.'"

She laughed along with him. "I never thought of it like that. It's probably something a guy could use, but it doesn't work the same for girls."

"Maybe we're not on the same wave length," he said, "But I think it works more for girls than it does for guys. I mean, guys have a little room to do stuff that's a little off the wall, anyway. Girls have to be pretty straight. You know, the double standard thing. I mean, it gives you an excuse to do something you want to do."

"I guess I see what you mean," she said. "I mean, when you stop and think about it, sitting out in a freezing hanger in a snowmobile suit sewing on a wing is kind of a screwy thing to do, but I enjoy doing it."

"Right," he laughed. "The best thing of all is that most people that you know, anyway, are going to be pretty nice about it. I mean, they're not going to say to your face, 'You're crazy to be doing that.' Let's take a break."

The space heater in the office felt good, and the warm cups of coffee tasted good, too, even though it was just instant coffee. They plopped down on the battered and broken old couch to let the warmth wash through them. Mark glanced at the clock on the wall. "It'll be getting dark soon," he said. "Don't guess we get to do any stargazing tonight. How long do you want to stay out here?"

"I'm in no rush to go home," she said. "I kind of like staying out here with you. It's so nice to be able to just talk with someone, and relax, and feel I'm doing something constructive, too. I know it may not seem like it to you, but I've really enjoyed last night and this afternoon."

"Well, I'm glad you're enjoying it," he said. "The thing is, I'm getting about ready to go get something to eat. Would you like to go out for a sandwich, or something? Maybe go out and get a beer?"

"No beer today," she said. "It's Sunday, and all the bars are closed."

He stopped for a moment, thinking. "Yeah, it is Sunday, isn't it? Well, we could just do what I normally do when I get hungry when I'm out here."

"What's that? Go without? Not on my account."

"Naw, I just heat up a can of stew on the space heater. You like a nice plate of canned stew to go with your coffee?"

"Would you think I was crazy if I said that having a plate of canned stew and a cup of instant coffee out here with you is better than having the best steak in town by myself?"

He nodded his head, and said, "It's nice that you think that way," but his mind was on something long ago and far away -- in Bangkok, to be precise. It had been years since he had been so comfortable and relaxed with a woman. The last time he had done something even comparable had been just walking through the city with Mei-Ling. He savored the memory while he opened a can and poured its contents into a pan. He hadn't told Jackie, but he had probably enjoyed being with her over the past twenty-four hours as much as she had enjoyed being with him. Maybe more.

He thought back to how often he had hoped and prayed for a girl friend, someone just to talk with, to joke with, to enjoy being with, and those dreams went back even further than the trip -- much further. As much as he had enjoyed the sex he had with Mei-Ling, it had seemed a touch artificial, which he knew it was -- but the companionship and the shared fun he had enjoyed with her had only proven to him what he had missed by not having a girl friend. He could tell that he was well on the way to having a girl friend now, perhaps not the stacked-up blonde or the sweet Chinese-Thai girl of his dreams, but perfectly adequate. In many respects, much better than adequate. Jackie might not have been Miss America, but she wasn't ugly, either; the worst you could call her would be "plain". And, she seemed interested in a lot of things he was interested in, and that, he knew, was even harder to find.

Why now? In a month, maybe less if things went well, he'd be gone. It was damn inconvenient timing, to say the least. But then, that was one thing he had learned from Mei-Ling: enjoy it now. It may not be there tomorrow.

All these thoughts blasted through his mind in a matter of seconds, and he was a little surprised at how briefly the image of Mei-Ling lingered. "To tell you the truth," he said, "I can't think of anything I'd rather do than share a plate of stew out here with you, under these circumstances."

Hours later, they got the last stitch in the wing. It was nearing midnight again, and both of them were tired, but they had been able to see how little was left, and it kept them both driving on. As he tied off the last stitch and clipped off the end of the string, he said, "That's one down, and one to go. I really appreciate the help you've been, Jackie. It would have taken me all week to do this by myself."

"I'm just glad I could help," she said. "Are you planning on starting on the other wing tomorrow? I'm off, and I could help you then, if you like."

"Look, I don't want you to think you have to do it," he said as he picked up tools and turned out lights, "But if you'd like to help out again, I'd really appreciate it. It's not just getting this wing done, but I've really enjoyed having you here."

"I've enjoyed it too," she said. "More than you might think. What time do you want to pick me up?"

Jackie was a little surprised to find herself awake before the alarm went off the next morning. It had been set for nine, but at eight-thirty she was so awake that she knew she might as well get up. She pulled on a robe and headed downstairs to pour herself a cup of coffee. She didn't like it real hot; by the time she would finish her shower it would be just about right.

Her father was sitting at the kitchen table, nursing a cup of coffee, he must have made it home after she went to bed. Since she was running a little early, the shower could wait a few minutes. "So how was the run, Dad?" she asked as she poured a cup of coffee, then ran a little cold water into it to make it cool enough to drink.

"Not bad," he said. "About the same, except that coming back from Syracuse I had three units, and all of them kept running. First time that's happened in a while. Then, I just missed crunching a car, right outside Putnam yard."

"Close?" she asked. A railroader's daughter, she knew just how dangerous it was to run a crossing ahead of a train that couldn't stop within a mile or two.

Walt Archer shook his head. "Missed them by inches, horn going all the time. I've never killed anyone yet, but sometimes you wonder if someone that dumb or that careless doesn't deserve to die."

"You have to wonder about people like that," she agreed, sipping her coffee.

"I don't want to think about it," he said. "God, I close my eyes and see that guy's taillights right under my feet. But anyway, Sarah tells me that you've been out late on dates every night."

"Not really dates, Dad," she explained. "Well, Friday night was a date." She blinked. Was it only Friday night that she had been out with Hjalmer? It seemed like months. "The last couple of nights, I've been helping Mark Gravengood work on his airplane. You remember Mark, don't you?"

"Sure," Walt said. "He just got out of the army a few months ago, didn't he? What have you been doing with him on his airplane, anyway?"

Jackie explained the ribstitching process she had been helping Mark with. "I can see it goes really slow when it's only him doing it, but it really works well with the two of us. He's picking me up in an hour or so, so we can start on the other wing."

"Well, I guess it doesn't sound like a date," he said.

"It's really kind of far from it," Jackie told him. "You ever hear of bundling boards? Back in the old days, when houses weren't heated, people used to court by climbing into bed with this board fixed between them so they'd keep their hands off of each other. It's kind of like that. We've got this fifteen foot bundling board, about four feet wide, between us. We talk a lot, but we hardly ever see each other."

"You like Mark? I hadn't seen him since before he joined the army, but he always seemed like a pretty level-headed kid."

"He's a nice guy, dad. I enjoy being with him. When I was out with Hjalmer, it seemed kind of like boy-girl. With Mark it seems kind of like brother and sister."

"Well, have a good time," he said. "Just don't let it get out of hand and you find yourself doing something you really don't want to do."

"I don't intend to let it happen, Dad," she said. "I kind of thought that it might have been heading that way with Hjalmer Friday night, and I knew I'd walk home if I had to. I just don't get that kind of feeling with Mark."

Walt sipped his coffee. "Well, I've always been able to depend on you to do the right thing," he said finally. "It's going to have to be up to you to do it." He sighed, and looked at the ceiling. "I've realized, the last two or three years," he said, "That sooner or later you're going to go off to college, or go off with some young man, and whether you do right or do wrong is something Sarah and I really can't do much about. We'll just have to depend on you to know what's right, and hope we've raised you to know to do what you're supposed to."

"You're saying, be a good girl, and don't go to bed with everybody I meet, right?"

"Yeah," Walt said. "I just can't bring myself to say it like that, to you, anyway. I have to make myself realize that you're not my little girl any longer, and it's going to happen sooner or later. It's just that you're going to have to be sure it's right, that you're not making a bad decision. If you're not sure it's right, it's probably not."

"Well, I don't think there's any danger of that with Mark," Jackie said. "Not now, anyway. And, it might take a long time." Especially with him leaving on his trip, she thought. It might not happen at all. "For right now, I'm just enjoying being with him, and helping him out. It might develop into something, and it might not. But, it's fun, and he's a nice guy."

"I remember him as a good kid," her father said. "It always kind of struck me that he had his own list of things to do, but then, I guess we all do. What time is he picking you up?"

"Ten," she said, looking at the clock. "And, if I'm going to get a shower before he comes, I think I'd better get moving."

She took a cup of coffee with her stopped by her bedroom to pick up clean clothes for the day. As soon as the water in the shower was warm, she got in, soaped herself down good, rinsed off, and washed her hair. She had missed her shower the day before; her schedule had been just too tight. Her hair had gone several days, now -- too long, but it was such a hassle to get it dry that she usually tried to put it off as long as she could.

Feeling suitably clean a few minutes later, she shut off the shower and got out. The bathroom, which had seemed uncomfortably cool a few minutes earlier, now was cozy with the heat and the moisture of the hot shower. She dried herself off and turned to brushing out her wet hair. She was tempted to put on her robe, but it didn't seem necessary.

In the mirror, she looked strange without glasses; better perhaps -- who could say? Looking at the reflection of her naked body, she tried to imagine what longer hair than her current shoulder length would look like; it would certainly look different. Maybe she'd put off getting it cut for a while to see.

She continued to brush out her hair, but her mind went to what her father had said. She'd often wondered what it would be like to be with a man -- what it would feel like, how it would be. She knew what the mechanics of the situation were, of course, but what would it feel like? She wondered if she had a body that would appeal to a man. She was tall, of course, and thin, perhaps too thin. While she wasn't flat-chested by any means, she didn't have a chest like her friend, Kirsten Langenderfer, either. Boys had always sniffed around Kirsten because of her chest, she recalled, and she wondered if things would have been different if she'd had Kirsten's size, Kirsten's build. Would Mark like her body the way it was? What would it be like to be with Mark, anyway?

She put the hair dryer cap over her head, and set the hair dryer to running. It would take a while to get her hair dry, and she didn't dare go out in the cold with it damp. With the hair dryer roaring away, she sipped at her coffee and began to get dressed. As she pulled on her bra, she thought of the touch of Hjalmer's hand on her breast Friday evening, how exciting it had seemed. The little necking she had done with Hjalmer had been a lot of fun, too. It was strange, now that she thought about it, but Mark had never made the first move toward a hug, a kiss, or anything else. He had been the perfect gentleman, but perhaps he wasn't a touchy-feely type person.

She realized that Mark would be leaving soon. It might be a long time before he got back, and perhaps he didn't want to get anything going. Continuing to get dressed in jeans and a work shirt, she thought about that. It was going to be a heck of a trip; she envied him. Taking off in an airplane to bum around the country by yourself was just something that a girl couldn't do. A guy could get away with it, but a girl would be over her head in no time; maybe not safe, either. Strange things happened to girls that traveled by themselves.

It wasn't fair, she thought. She'd love to do something like that. Mark could do it, but she couldn't. About all she would be able to do would be to wait for his return, and hope they could get something going then.

If he returned.

Jackie was ready to go when she heard the rumble of the Ford's muffler, right at ten. As she went outside, she saw that a light snow had fallen overnight, an inch or two, perhaps; little enough that it hardly counted in a Spearfish Lake winter. Today seemed a lot warmer, although it was still overcast. It was clear that this snow wouldn't be around long; some of it was sloppily melting already.

The Ford left fresh tracks through the thin show as Mark drove up the airport driveway. While the heater was warming the office up, he and Jackie unfastened the wing from the cradle that had held it, and put the other one in its place. The wings were not heavy; the two of them could handle one of them easily.

"This is one of the fun parts," Mark said. "Getting the fabric on the wing in the first place."

The fabric was sewn in a long sleeve, that barely fit around the wing, and it took them a fair amount of shuffling the cradles around and working at the fabric to get it in place. "It looks kind of sloppy," Jackie protested. "How do we get it as tight as the other one?"

"We have to shrink it in place," Mark said. "You want to run out to the car? There's an iron in the back seat."

"An iron?"

"Sure. You iron shirts, don't you? We've got a wing to iron."

Working slowly and carefully, with the iron not very hot, Mark did just that. The heat of the iron shrunk the dacron fabric, but it had to be shrunk fairly evenly, and getting all the wrinkles out and the fabric acceptably tight was a slow process. "I've got an engine pre-heater here that could keep us a little warmer," Mark explained. "I mean, it would be possible to build kind of a plastic enclosure that we could get a little warm. But, the pre-heater would stink us out and maybe gas us, and worse, it might create a hot spot on the wing that would shrink more than we want it to. I'd rather be cold."

In spite of the fact that it was warmer today, they were cold by the time they had the wing ready for ribstitching. They retreated to the office, where they had lunch: some meat loaf sandwiches Jackie had made from the dinner that she had missed the day before.

After they ate they turned back to the ribstitching. After the practice they had, and with it a little warmer, things went well. On either side of the wing, they passed the needle back and forth, and sat talking -- not about anything in particular. Mark caught up on Spearfish Lake gossip he had missed out on for four years -- who'd gotten married, who'd gotten divorced, who'd gotten pregnant without benefit of marriage. He heard about the disappearance of Henry Toivo in Vietnam, and though he didn't say anything about it, was glad it hadn't happened to him. He heard about the riot at the school board meeting when the school board tried to extend the contract of the football coach, after the Spearfish Lake Marlins had gone three years without a win. The end result of the riot was that the coach was all but run out of town, and now the Marlins had a new coach that seemed to be doing some good.

The afternoon passed quickly, and they made good progress on the wing. With the weather a little warmer, fewer retreats to the office were needed. It was after dark before they realized the time, and realized they were hungry. Mark offered to take Jackie out to dinner but it seemed like too much trouble to both of them so they again made their dinner out of canned stew heated on the space heater and went back to work. It was late in the evening before they decided to call a halt, but they were more than halfway done with the wing. One more good day would have it under control.

"I'm not sure we've got enough cord to finish up the job," Mark said as he drove her home. "We'll hit it for a couple of hours, and see."

"Why don't we just get some before we start?" she asked.

"I don't think there's any in Spearfish Lake," he said. "I'll make a couple of phone calls in the morning, but we may have to go get some down in Camden or somewhere. Shall I pick you up around ten, again?

"You can make it earlier," she told him. "I'm not as dog-tired as I was last night. Say, nine?"

"Naw, let's make it ten. That'll give me time to make some phone calls. A couple of the places I need to call don't open until nine."

4.

Mark called her up a little after nine the next morning. "If I come right by, will you be ready to go?" he asked.

"Give me ten minutes," she said. Just as she was pulling on the snowmobile suit she heard the rumble of the old Ford's muffler pulling up outside, and went out to meet him. Though a brighter day, it was still overcast, but much of the snow from the day before had already melted.

"Well, did you find the cord we need?" she asked.

"Sure did," he told her. "Ken Sawyer's got a part of a spool of it, and we don't need much. We'll just have to go down and get it."

"Isn't he in Lordston?" she asked. "That's a long drive."

"It's in Lordston," Mark said. "But, it's not a long drive. What it is, is a good excuse to go flying."

"We can fly on a gungy day like this?"

"Well, it's not the prettiest day, but those clouds are up there pretty high, and we can get under them all right."

For once, Mark didn't park in front of the hanger doors. He avoided lighting the office heater, and went inside to the red, white, and black four seater Stinson sitting in the front of the hanger. While Jackie watched, half-mystified, Mark started the preflight routine, checking around the aircraft, draining accumulated condensation from the fuel, checking the oil, and things like that. "This old Stinson here is my buddy," Mark told her. "Dad's had it for ten or twelve years, now. I did most of my learning to fly in it. I feel kind of like a traitor, planning to make the trip in the Cessna. You ever been flying?"

"Your dad took me for a ride in that plane, once, maybe six or eight years ago," Jackie told him.

"Well, it won't be totally strange to you," he said. Preflight finished, he unlocked and opened the hanger doors, and with Jackie's help, rolled the big old taildragger out into the open. He closed the hanger again, and helped Jackie into the right seat.

"I guess I didn't notice before," Jackie said, "But this is all fabric, isn't it? Your plane has a metal fuselage."

"Where do you think I learned about recovering airplanes? Right here, back before I went into the service." He fiddled with some switches in the cockpit. "Well, let's see if we can get this thing started. The battery is getting old, and it could use a little more oomph."

He gave the engine a couple of good shots of prime. He had already thought to set the prop as far off compression as he could, so the starter would have time to get up a little speed before the engine hit its first compression stroke. He flipped on the mags and turned the key. The starter growled, the engine coughed, and a propeller blade went by in front of them, then another. The engine made three or four turns before a cylinder caught; the engine coughed, and two or three other jugs chimed in. In an instant all six were coming to life.

Mark left the throttle at a high idle while the engine warmed up. He turned to Jackie and said, "That was easier than it could have been. When it's cold, that engine can really be cranky." She smiled, just taking it in as he busied himself with a few things that needed to be done, like setting the altimeter, caging the gyro, and turning the radio on; things that did not make a lot of sense to Jackie. Tall as she was -- and her hair brushed the ceiling of the Stinson's interior -- with the tail of the airplane down she still could not see much over the nose.

After a minute, Mark let off the brake, and began to taxi out to the end of the runway. He kept it slow; there were puddles, and he didn't want to mess up the plane. At the end of the runway, he turned the plane into the wind, ran up the engine, checked the mags and the carb heat, and looked at the oil temperature gauge; the engine was warm enough to fly. "You ready?" he asked.

"Sure," she said. She had done this before; she knew there was nothing to be afraid of.

Mark turned the Stinson down the runway, and ran up the power. The old Franklin engine up in the nose of the plane bellowed, and the plane gathered speed. In only a few seconds, Mark could feel the tail getting light, so with a little forward pressure on the wheel he let the tail come up. The airspeed needle came off the peg, and in only a few seconds more, he could feel the Stinson trying to fly. Comfortable, he eased back on the wheel, and the plane left the ground.

Jackie could see the ground falling away. She remembered how strange it had seemed when she was a little girl, how suddenly it became a long way down. She could see the horizon come up as the plane climbed above the tops of the trees, and she wasn't alarmed when Mark banked the airplane a little and began a slow turn over the town. Curious, she followed the streets with her eyes, until she could pick out her house. How small it seemed! How small the whole town seemed, for that matter. The expanse of the lake spread out to the east, still covered with ice. She could still see the fish coops out on the ice, but knew that they'd be coming off soon.

In a few minutes, the Stinson was over the arm of the lake, heading southeast. "That's high enough," Mark said, loud enough for Jackie to hear him over the engine's roar, while leveling off the plane and easing the throttle back. He fiddled with the trim for a moment, to relax the pressure on the wheel, and set a course for Lordston. He figured he'd better keep near the state roads, just in case; besides, there wasn't much to see out over the swamp south of the lake.

It was very noisy in the cockpit, and it wasn't conducive to conversation, but that was all right: Jackie was fascinated with the scene out the window. They left the little world of Spearfish Lake behind quickly. She'd known all her life that Spearfish Lake was a northwoods town, but even with that, she hadn't realized just how much forest there was spread across the landscape. Here and there was a little farm, here and there a house, but she could see out of her window that they were mostly concentrated pretty close to the state road. Off in the distance, she could see Albany River, but she couldn't make out Blair, even further away. It was cold in the airplane, and Jackie was glad she had the snowmobile suit on. Although the heater knob was pulled all the way out, it didn't seem to be doing much good, but one foot was warmer than the other.

"You like it?" Mark asked over the roar of the engine.

"It looks different from up here," Jackie told him, feeling inane. She knew he had grown up with flying, and it probably wasn't all that special to him, but it was to her.

"It's like a different world," he told her back, in a loud voice to carry over the engine. The best part about flying to him had always been the looking out the window, at the way the land unfolded. It was a fresh wonder, always something new every time he got into the air, something new waiting to be discovered. He hadn't been able to fly all he wanted to since he'd been back from Germany -- the weather had been lousy, and he'd been busy, but still he wondered if he'd even get enough flying in to suit him on the long trip, which seemed a lot closer now than it had only a few days before.

It did not take them long to get to Lordston; in twenty minutes or so, Mark began to let the Stinson down towards the ground as the little town began to rise in the distance. He turned to Jackie, "I'll let Ken know we're here," he said. She thought that he meant that he was going to do it on the radio, but the plane kept getting lower and lower, pointed at a metal building with various machines and junk sitting outside. Mark got down so low that he roared by not much more than a hundred feet over the building, then pulled the nose of the airplane up and began a sharp turn. Down by the building, she could see a man come out an wave at them. Mark rocked the wings to signal that he had seen him, and pointed the Stinson off at a little airstrip Jackie could see a mile or more away. "Did I scare you with that?" he asked. "I should have let you know that was coming."

"That was fun!" she said. "I knew you knew what you were doing."

He eased the power back, pulled on the carb heat, and set up his approach for the airstrip. The plane sank lower toward the gash in the trees, and soon the wheels kissed the muddy grass.

Mark taxied the Stinson up to the end of the airstrip, the end by the road. He was still shutting the engine down when a muddy pickup truck pulled up alongside, and he and Jackie got out to meet the driver.

Ken Sawyer proved to be a man in his forties, wearing greasy coveralls, a good foot shorter than Mark. It looked like he hadn't shaved in several days, and it was a couple of minutes before Jackie noticed that he was missing his left hand; a hook was fitted there, instead. "How you coming on those wings?" he asked

"Oh, pretty good," Mark told him. "This is Jackie Archer. She's been helping me with 'em. We ought to be able to wrap the ribstitching up today, if nothing else goes wrong."

"I've got to go up to Spearfish Lake tomorrow and look at a guy's bulldozer," Sawyer said. "You want me to stop by and check them over so you can get on with the doping?"

"If you could, it'd be fine," Mark said. "Got a guy that's going to let me use a bay of his body shop to paint it, and he said he'd do the spraying, but I'm not going to be able to mess around."

"You're coming along pretty good, then," Sawyer said. "By the way, here's the cord."

"Thanks," Mark told him. "I don't think I'm going to need very much, but I don't think I have quite enough to finish. I'm glad you had it."

"No problem," the mechanic said.

"Hey," Mark asked, changing the subject. "You know who owns that 140 over there?"

Jackie looked across the field to a little plane, and realized that it was the same kind of plane she and Mark had been working on.

"Yeah," Sawyer asked. "The guy's in Florida."

"Darn," Mark told him. "I keep hoping I can find someone with a 140 so I can get a little dual before I fly mine for the first time. I've flown one two or three times, but it's been at least five years."

"No problem," Sawyer told him. "He told me I could fly it now and then to keep the oil up and the birds out of it. I can take you around the patch in it a few times right now."

"That would be great if you could," Mark said. "Jackie, would you mind sitting around here for a while?"

"No, go ahead," she told him. "I'll just sit here and watch."

Mark turned to the mechanic. "All right," he said. "Let's do it."

Mark and Ken walked over to the little Cessna, and untied it from the ground. Jackie watched as the two of them went over the preflight carefully, as the mechanic pointed out some things that Mark should watch out for. The two-seater seemed smaller than the four-seat Stinson, but she noticed that when Mark got inside that his head wasn't brushing against the ceiling. She stood back, as Mark started the engine; somehow, it didn't seem quite as noisy as the Stinson.

Once Mark and Ken finished the runup, Mark pointed it down the runway and opened the throttle. Though the little Cessna had only a little more than half the power of the big Stinson, it broke ground fairly quickly, although without the impression of the brute power that the Stinson gave off. It climbed more slowly, though; that was no surprise, but being smaller, it seemed livelier than the big, solid plane had had grown used to. The two of them flew out south of the airstrip a couple of miles, and Mark tried some turns, both steep and shallow; then, he slowed up to get an idea of how it felt approaching landing speed, and did some stalls, power on and power off. "About like I remember," he commented. "What do you want over the fence? About eighty?"

"Eighty's plenty," Sawyer told him. "Seventy's probably better, maybe seventy-five if you're heavy. Take her around a couple of times. These planes are pretty good about telling you what they want."

Mark turned the Cessna back toward the airstrip. Although there was not likely to be any traffic, he set up a landing pattern and began to shoot a few landings.

Jackie stood outside watching the little plane off in the distance for a while, then as her feet got tired, looked for a place to sit. She didn't feel like getting back in the Stinson, so finally she sat down on one of the airplane's wheels. After a while, she could see the little plane getting set up for a landing, and she stood up to watch. The plane straightened out along the grassy strip, sinking rapidly, and for a moment she thought it was going into the trees at the far end of the strip. She realized after an instant that it was just the angle she was looking; the plane sank onto the runway, and its tail came down. She heard the power come back onto the engine, and the tail came up again, heading for another takeoff.

The sight made her feel sad in a way, she realized at the plane soared over the road, climbing for altitude. She had enjoyed the last few days with Mark, more than she would have ever thought possible. She knew that it would not be very long before she would be standing beside the runway at Spearfish Lake, watching Mark fly his 140 for the first time -- and soon after that, he would be gone. She would miss him, she knew.

What fun it would be to go on that trip, she realized. She had envied him the idea of the trip ever since she had first heard about it, and had been sorry she couldn't do something like that. The flight this morning had only sharpened her taste for the trip; in the days they had spent together, Mark had told her of more of the things that he had planned, and it just seemed like a lot of fun. She could imagine a little, for instance, of what it would be like to see the Grand Canyon open under the disk of the propeller, to look down at it's awesome glory. She imagined sleeping under the stars next to the wing, in a farmer's field so black with night that she could see a million stars. Yes, it would be fun to make that trip, she thought. It was too bad that she couldn't. Even if she were to ask Mark, and he were to say yes, how would it look to her parents, to her friends, to go off on a trip like that with a guy she wasn't married to? Even if they were married, just supposing they were, it still wouldn't seem quite proper. As the plane flew around the airstrip, again and again, she found herself getting sad at the thought of losing Mark. Maybe he'd remember her, and come back for her, some day.

Up in the airplane, Ken Sawyer leaned back in his seat. He knew Mark was a good pilot, but he also knew that he hadn't had a lot of flying since he came back from the Army. But, his precise handling of the plane made him relax. Once Mark got the feel of the plane a little, there wasn't much to worry about. "Nice looking girl you got there," he said finally. "You taking her on the trip with you?"

"I didn't know you knew about the trip," Mark said.

"Your dad told me," Sawyer admitted. "Said he wanted me to make sure everything was as right with your bird as it could be."

"Naw, she's not going with me," Mark said over the roar of the engine. "She's just a friend that's been helping me out with the ribstitching."

"Kind of a shame," the smaller man said. "She looks like she'd be fun to have with you."

"I don't think I could take her if I wanted to," Mark said. "I don't think one of these things could take two of us and all our gear."

"You could push the gross weight a little," Sawyer said. "One thing you want to watch out for is your weight and balance, through. You get the baggage section full of baggage, even if you're not near gross, and just yourself up in front, and you might be pushing the edge of the envelope a little. The same weight, or even heavier, and a second person in front, and you'd be a lot better off."

Mark shook his head. "I don't think she'd go if I asked her," he said, more to himself than to Sawyer, and concentrated on his flying. He knew he was doing all right, but he also knew he could do much better. He would want some practice with his own plane before he took off on the trip -- short field and soft field takeoffs and landings, especially, but mostly just making sure he was comfortable with it. Flying this 140 made him sure that he'd made the best choice he could make for the trip, considering the money. It wouldn't be long before he left, now; Jackie's help had gained him a week, maybe two weeks.

Sawyer's comment opened a new train of thought in his mind. He imagined for a moment what it would be like to have Jackie along on the trip with him. It would be fun; she was a nice companion. Often as he had dreamed about the trip he had imagined in a vague sort of way finding some lonely girl in some town along the way, and taking her with him. This wasn't quite what he'd imagined, but . . .

He remembered, again, one night years ago, probably when he'd driven his old Chevy to New Jersey when he was in the army there. It was a long drive, and he'd driven all night, feeling terribly lonely. He passed by a medium sized town along the way, probably two or three times as big as Spearfish Lake, and the thought crossed his mind that somewhere in that darkened city there was a girl sitting staring at the wall, just as lonely as he was. All he had to know was which door to knock on, as if to say, "Hi, I'm Mark, and I'm here to love you."

The trick was in knowing which door it was. In the last few days, it almost seemed as if he'd found the door -- and now, he was going to be flying off into the sunset, instead.

He'd had to leave Mei-Ling behind; he had no choice, no future there. It had been great while it lasted. It was going to be harder than he realized to leave Jackie behind.

Maybe she would like to go on the trip. He thought about it for a moment, and decided it wouldn't hurt to sound her out a little.

They were back in the hanger in Spearfish Lake, ribstitching on the wing again, before Mark finally thought of a way to sound Jackie out about going on the trip without actually asking her to go.

They had been talking about what he was going to take with him on the trip. There were some things that were pretty logical, things like a tiedown kit for the airplane, a few tools, a backpack, a tent and sleeping bag; and a camera, clothes and things like that. There was a big selection of maps that he'd accumulated, enough to cover the whole country, and they had to go.

Other things weren't quite as logical; the telescope was going, for example. Mark had spent a few nights over the winter when it was too cold to do anything out in the hanger, down in the basement rebuilding the mounting, to make it as light and compact as possible, to fit in the plane. He had included both a note pad and a sketch pad, and even a small kit of water colors, as he wanted to try doing some drawings along the way as well. He calculated in his head; he weighed about 150, and he guessed that Jackie would go 130. The gear he had planned on taking weighed about seventy pounds. Allowing another ten or fifteen pounds for a supply of food and water, which would have to be frequently replenished, that left maybe forty pounds, fifty if he pushed it.

"Just for fun," he said. "Supposing you were to go with me on this trip. Do you think you could keep your stuff under fifty pounds or so?"

"I suppose I could," Jackie said. She'd been thinking about that very thing as he talked, what she would take if she were going on the trip. It was clear that it wouldn't be very much. "I suppose I'd want to take a tent, but we could share a tent, and you've already got one in. With the backpacking, I'd want to take my pack, and that would do to pack a lot of my stuff in."

"You've done backpacking?" he asked.

"Not for a couple of years," she said. "My dad and I went up and hiked through the Pictured Rocks, up in Michigan. That's quite a hike. He bought me a new Kelty just for that trip, but I've only used it a few times."

Without saying anything, Mark thought that was interesting. He hadn't really been aware that she'd been into backpacking at all. Camping, yes, but backpacking was much more critical of weight; she'd know how to keep the weight of her gear down, and make do with less. She'd probably have a lot of the gear she'd need, anyway. "Have you got a good sleeping bag?" he asked.

"A summer weight down bag," she said. "It won't do for real cold weather, but the idea is sort of to stay out of real cold weather, isn't it?"

"Yeah," Mark told her. "About the only real plan for my first day or two is to fly south to spring as quick as I can. Speaking of which, let's finish this rib and go have a warmup in the office."

A few minutes later, they were sitting in the office. Jackie had found a scratch pad, and was marking items down in a list. Mark gave her a copy of his list, and she cribbed a few items from it.

Some of the items on her list were a little surprising. "I'd want to get one of those little ultralight spinning rod and reel outfits," she said. "They only weight a couple of pounds. Take a few poppers, a couple of small spoons, and a few hooks for bait fishing. Mostly for fun, not with the hope of catching anything. It'd be too big a pain in the butt to have to get a fishing license in every state we visited."

The break stretched out as she worked on her list; many of the items they talked about to see if they could pare them down or do without. Her experience in backpacking and camping was proving to be a plus, Mark could see; she wasn't planning on taking the kitchen sink with her. Mark only had to make a few suggestions, and those minor.

"Let's see how we're doing," he said, after a while. Between them, they made guesses at the weights of the items on her list, and she totaled them up. "Comes to forty-two pounds," she said. "I can think of some things I could add, but then we'd probably accumulate stuff along the way." She shrugged. "It's fun to dream about," she said. "It's just too bad that I couldn't really do it."

"Why not?" he asked. So far, his idea had worked, and he could see that she was enthusiastic about the trip.

"Well, it just wouldn't be right," she said, a little sadly. "What would my dad and Sarah think if I ran off with you, since we're not married?. They'd think I was some kind of a tramp! Everybody else in town would think so, too. I'd love to go on the trip with you. I've been dreaming about it ever since I heard about it. But, there's no way I could do it."

It was after dark when they finished up the ribstitching. They had seen the end in sight, and without discussing it, they pressed on, skipping dinner. Jackie was as happy as Mark to watch him put the last knot into the cord. "That's it," he said. "I'll have Ken look them over tomorrow, then I'll take them over to the body shop."

Jackie stood up, saddened a little. The big, tedious ribstitching job had been fun for her, mostly because she had been with Mark. There probably wouldn't be that much opportunity again to spend time with him, working on the airplane or not.

Mark felt it a little, too; he had enjoyed being with Jackie, and it had been an interesting idea to think of taking her on the trip with him. It looked to him like she wanted to go, but that she wouldn't do it. He sort of hoped she'd still be waiting and available when he got back, next fall, or in a year, or whenever he happened to get to Spearfish Lake. "I think the grill is still open down at the Spearfish Lake Inn," he said. "What say I buy you a burger and a beer to celebrate?"

"I'm not really dressed for the Spearfish Lake Inn," she said.

"This time of year, no one will mind," he said. "We could go to the Pike Bar. The jukebox there is kind of loud, and nobody will care how you're dressed."

"Sounds all right by me," she said. They turned off the lights in the hanger, and turned off the heater in the office with a feeling of finality that was hard to overcome.

They walked into the Pike Bar a few minutes later, and got a table as far from the jukebox as they could manage. The waitress came over and got their order, reminding Jackie that she would be back at work the next day, not out at the hanger with Mark. It made her feel sad, in a way, but she resolved to spend all the time she could manage with Mark, while he was still around.

There were some great songs on the jukebox in the Pike Bar: the original Fats Domino "Chantilly Lace" was blaring as they sat down, and it was followed by others as someone in the room kept the quarters coming. After a while, somebody plugged in "Me and You and a Dog Named Boo." It was a song that both Mark and Jackie especially liked, and it had a certain significance, too: "Me and you and a dog named Boo, travelin' and livin' on the land; me and you and a dog named Boo, how I loved bein' a free man."

"Sounds like you," Jackie said. "I really wish I could go with you. I can't get the trip out of my mind."

"We wouldn't have room for a dog," Mark told her.

"The plane will have to do," Jackie said. "It needs a name, anyway. How about, "Me and you and a plane named Boo."

"Boo is a dog's name," Mark said. "If I were going to give it a name, that sure isn't the name I would give it. That plane is not going to be a dog."

Jackie turned to look at him. "What would you name it?" An intense smile was on her face.

"I've thought about it on occasion," he said. "This whole trip is like a dream, anyway. Maybe I shouldn't be doing it, but it's a dream to follow, like Don Quixote. If I were going to give the plane a name, I'd name it after Don Quixote's horse, Rocinante."

"Off tilting at windmills on your faithful steed, huh?" Jackie asked. "Who's going to be your Sancho Panza?"

Mark listened to the song for a minute. It had been too much to hope for, but he might as well make the offer. "You could be if you wanted to," he said.

She looked at him, almost with a tear in her eye. "I'd like to," she said. "Mark, God knows, I'd like to. But I can't, and you know why."

"I think you're wrong," he said. "But that's a decision you have to make, not me. Think about it. If you change your mind before I leave, the offer is still good."

"Thanks, Mark," she said. "I don't see how I could ever do it, but I appreciate your asking."

It was hard for Jackie to get dressed for work the next morning. She was up at eight, feeling that she ought to be getting ready to go out to the airport and help Mark with the plane, instead of pulling on the ugly white waitress dress and going to work the lunch crowd at Rick's.

It was still far too early to be going to work, but she decided to drive over to the airport, just on the off chance that Mark might be out there already. His car wasn't there, but there was a pickup truck and a long flatbed trailer sitting in front, as was the Cessna 140 that Mark and Ken Sawyer had flown the day before.

Jackie walked into the hanger, where she saw Mark and the mechanic inspecting the wings. "Hi, Jackie," Mark said. "Can't keep away, huh?"

"Just wanted to see them in the daylight," she said, knowing she was lying.

"Well, they look pretty good," Sawyer said. "There's no reason I can't sign them off."

"As long as you're here," Ken said, "I want you to check out a few things on the engine, so I can get started putting the fuselage back together. And, Jackie, as long as you're here, you can help us load the wings on the trailer."

It only took a few minutes to take the wings out to the trailer through the hanger door. Mark tied them down to the trailer for the trip to the body shop, using plenty of padding. "You going right over to the body shop?" she asked.

"No, there's a couple of things I need Ken's help on, and as long as he's got the other 140 here, there are a couple of things I need to look at to figure out how to do. Then, I think we'll fly around the patch a few more times. It'll probably take all morning, before I get the wings over to Bork's."

"Well, no point in my sticking around, then." she said, sadly; there wouldn't be much time she could spend with Mark, today. "I've got to be getting to work pretty soon, anyway."

Mark knew that he would miss her today, too. "Tell you what," he said. "By the time you're getting ready to close tonight, I should be getting pretty well tired of smelling dope fumes. You can only smell that stuff so much before you start getting light-headed and funny-minded, anyway. I'll stop over and have a hamburger and a piece of pie, and then maybe we can do something after you get off. It looks like it might clear off today; maybe we can get the telescope out."

It was a long morning for Mark. Sawyer checked the plane over pretty good, getting a lot of the inspection that would be needed for the annual inspection completed. After a while, they went out and shot some takeoffs and landings in the borrowed 140. With Sawyer back on his way to Lordston, Mark got into the pickup to take the wings to the body shop to paint them; the end of the job was in sight.

Mark didn't have a lot of experience with a spray gun, but Carl Bork had agreed to do the spray work for him if he got him set up. With some of the lumber he had brought he built stands for the wings in the paint booth, and he and Carl carried them in from the trailer. It took a while to get several places that he didn't want painted masked off to get Carl set up for the first coat, which was a type of fungicide. Carl looked at the instructions, and decided he'd better wear a respirator. Mark decided to wait outside the paint booth, and bummed first one, then another cigarette from one of the panel bashers.

The next step wasn't a spray job, but a brush job. He needed to put on at least four coats of thin, clear dope with a brush, working the dope deep into the fabric to help make it airtight, and there was nothing to do but get a big brush and start in.

One side of the first wing went fairly quickly, but that was all; by the time he got to the second side, he was bored and wanting someone to talk to. The afternoon was long and dull, duller still since he couldn't enjoy talking with Jackie. He had gotten used to having her around. It was kind of like Mei-Ling: he was comfortable being around her. By the time he got the last patch of on the last wing done, his head was spinning from the fumes, and the first wing side was ready for another coat.

Mark went outside into the cold, leaving the ventilator fan running full bore, and smoked a cigarette to clear his head. He felt better when he had finished, and went back in for the next chore. With one coat of dope on the wing, the next step was to dope reinforcement strips in place. These thin strips of cloth, pinked on the edges, needed to be placed over all the exposed rib cords and knots from the ribstitching, and doped into place. It was a slow job, and it took him most of the afternoon and on into the evening with frequent breaks for fresh air.

Along late in the afternoon, Carl stuck his head into the paint booth and said, "God, that stuff stinks. I think you've got everybody in the shop getting high. How much more of that stuff?"

"Well," Mark told him. "I kind of figured on going to dinner when I get done with these strips, and when I get back I should be able to get the second coat done. Then, two coats tomorrow, and then we'll be ready to spray."

"Well, I'm leaving," Carl said. "I'll leave the back door open so you can get in after dinner, but lock it up when you leave. Kick the heat back before you go."

It was after six before he was more or less done with the reinforcements. Rick's Cafe was only a block or so up the street; he decided to walk it to clear his head.

"God, you reek," Jackie greeted him as he walked into the little restaurant. "I mean, you stink to high heaven."

Mark took a table as far away from anyone else as he could manage, more to be kind to others than anything else. "I take that to mean you don't plan to help me out when you get off from work," he said.

"Oh, I'll help," she smiled. "But it means I'll have to wash my hair tonight, instead of tomorrow, so I don't want you keeping me out until all hours."

"Won't have time to do more than one coat tonight," Mark said. "But I'll be glad of your help, however long it takes. I swear to God, painting is duller than ribstitching."

As he ate, the other customers began to get up and leave; Rick's was a place that closed early, and Rick and Jackie began to close up while he watched. "You can follow me home and drive me back," she told him, "I can see I want to wear the oldest clothes I own, tonight."

"Might not be a bad idea," he said. "I get through with this doping, I'm not going to wash these. I'm going to burn them."

In a few minutes, Jackie was on her way home. Mark had told her he was going to drop off the pickup and trailer, and get his car, and that he would be along in a few minutes. Jackie walked in the front door, and noticed that her dad was home; she'd sort of lost track of his schedule. "Don't tell me you're going to be home tonight?" he asked.

"No," she said. "Just changing clothes." She went out into the kitchen, and searched through the rag bin. She found a hideous pair of stretch pants she'd always hated, and one of her dad's old shirts, with holes in it and some of the buttons missing. Perfect. Taking the rags, she raced upstairs, pulled off her waitress uniform, and pulled out the rags; Mark would not be long, she knew, and she didn't want to keep him waiting.

She was back downstairs in plenty of time. "Looks like you're dressed to paint the town," her father said. "Halloween, maybe?"

"Painting wings, actually," she told him. "Mark stinks so bad today I don't think the clothes would wash out, and I don't want to mess up anything good."

"Some date," her dad laughed, hearing Mark's unmuffled car pull up. "Well, have a good time."

Again, Mark helped her get into his car, although she thought she had the trick of the door, by now. It only took them a few minutes to drive back over to the body shop. "Well," she said. "I found out today that this is going to be my last week at Rick's. Marjorie's ready to come back to work."

Mark shrugged. "At least it's not as if you didn't know it was coming. What are you going to do, now?"

"I don't know," Jackie said. "Sit around the house, I guess. The Frostee-Freeze will be opening in a couple months, and I might be able to get a job there, for the summer anyway."

"You could still come along with me," he suggested.

"Don't think I wouldn't like to," she told him. "I mean, I want to do it, but there's so many things telling me not to. I mean, what are people going to think? What are Dad and Sarah going to think? For that matter, what am I going to think? I mean, I thought about it a lot, today. It's almost like we would be living together."

"Well, we would be, pretty much," he said.

"That's not what I mean, and you know it," she said. "I'm talking about going to bed together, and I don't think I'm ready for that."

"I'll go along with that," he said. "I don't think we're ready for it either."

"The heck of it is," she told him. "If I were to go along with you, we'd be living in each other's pockets, right next to each other, and we might find ourselves doing something we shouldn't be."

Mark was silent for a long time as he drove toward the body shop. In his fantasies about picking up some girl along the way and taking her with him sex was part of the fantasy, but somehow Jackie didn't quite fit the mold. He was aware that she was a girl, of course, and he had somewhere along the way imagined that they would wind up making love, but somehow, it didn't seem like an imperative. He was a little surprised to realize that he had never even kissed her yet. It was almost as if she were a sister, a buddy, not a lover. He was shocked to realize that, and realized that she wouldn't believe him if he told her that.

"I can't deny that it might happen," he told her finally. "If you go with me, I'm not going to promise you that we won't find ourselves making love. I'd be lying if I told you any different." He reached over, and pulled her over to him so he could put his smelly arm around her. "All I can promise you is that if it happens -- and it might not -- the time will have to be right, for both of us. I'm sorry, but that's the best I can do."

"I can live with that, I think," she told him. "If it happens, it happens, and hopefully, it'll work out for the best. But even if we're like brother and sister to each other, what will people think?"

"I told you about that," he told her, pulling into the parking area behind the body shop and shutting off the engine. "The hell with the little people, especially the ones with the little minds."

She nodded. "You also said, they'll say, 'Aw, hell, it just runs in the family.'"

"I told you," he said, getting out of the car to go open her door, "That it's the perfect excuse to do something you want to do, anyway."

She waited for him to open the door for her, and then said, "But what about my dad and Sarah?"

"That's a little tougher," he said. "You're going to have to be the one to deal with that one. About all I can suggest is that you sort of run it by them, without really committing yourself, and see what kind of a response you get. You might be surprised."

They got off the topic over the next few minutes, as Mark showed her what he was doing, and got her a large paint brush. "The general idea is to lay it on thick, so it soaks into the fabric," he told her. "But not so thick that it runs on you."

They took the opposite sides of a wing, and began to slap on the dope in silence, each lost in their own thoughts. With the two of them working, the work went more quickly than it had earlier, and soon they had finished the wing, and started on the other one.

After a while, they finished the second wing. Mark walked over to see if the first wing was dry yet. It wasn't, but it was tacky and well on it's way; they had made good time. "You know," he said. "If we were to wander over to the Pike Bar, we could have a beer and come back and get another coat on."

"I don't know that we're exactly dressed right for the Pike Bar," she said, pointing at the messy rags she wore.

"You're right," he said. "We may be overdressed, but let's go, anyway."

5.

They got the third coat of clear dope on the wing later that evening, before he took her home. It was late; not wanting to go to bed smelling of aircraft dope, she took a bath and washed her hair, resolving to sleep in the next morning. When she got up, it was close to time to have to go to work, but on her way to Rick's, she stopped off at the body shop, just to see how Mark was coming. The smell told her that he was deep into another coat of clear dope, and they made a date for supper, again. "I should smell better, tonight," he told her. "Silver dope doesn't smell as bad."

She was a little surprised to see him walk into Ricks a couple of hours later, to order a cup of coffee. "Carl's spraying a coat of silver dope on the wings," he told her. "There's nothing much I can do to help him. I don't know that he'll get another coat on yet this evening. I should go out and work on the fuselage, but there's not enough time left this afternoon to really get started on buttoning it up."

"What you're saying is that you've got a free evening, and don't know what to do, right?"

"Yeah," he said. "That's a little scary, when you put it like that. I guess I'm going to have to learn to slow down and enjoy free evenings."

A glimmer of an idea rose in Jackie's mind. "Dad had to work a double night last weekend, so he's got two nights off. He's going to be home tonight. Why don't I call up and have Sarah hold off on supper until after I get off work?"

Remembering their conversation of the night before, Mark thought he had a pretty good idea of where her idea was leading. It kind of smacked of bringing the boyfriend home for the parent's approval, but it did indicate that Jackie was still giving consideration to going with him on the trip. That was kind of a hopeful sign, and of course, he went along with it.

After he finished lunch, Mark went back over to the body shop. By then, Carl had a coat of silver dope -- containing aluminum particles -- on the wings. He eyeballed the paint as it was drying; it would need a little sanding before the finish coats of enamel could be applied. Once again, Mark went over his decision to paint the wings white. White enamel had been part of the paint and dope that had come with the plane, along with some red, for trim, but he had decided that trimming out the wings would look funny without painting the fuselage, too. With the trip coming up and weight at a premium, both the time involved and the weight of all that paint seemed excessive. Gray and white wouldn't look all that bad, anyway, once he got the fuselage buffed out. He was woolgathering, and he knew it. He was trying not to think about the upcoming evening with Walt Archer. He knew that the only thing to do would be to play it straight, whatever happened. If Jackie wanted to bring up the trip, then he'd talk about it. If Jackie wanted to talk about her going, then it was up to her. Perhaps the best thing to do was to make a good impression, and that meant a haircut and cleaning up. "You going to need me around here any more this afternoon?" he asked Carl.

"Naw, not really," the older man said. "I'll get another coat on in an hour or so, and the last one first thing tomorrow morning. It'll be tomorrow afternoon before you can start sanding, anyway."

With his hair shorter, he felt more natural. He drove on home, shaved again, and showered. There was a limit to how much he was willing to dress up for Jackie's dad, but it wouldn't hurt to have clean clothes.

Mark did not know Walt Archer well, and hadn't talked to him since before he went into the army, but he remembered him from years before, when his parents had played cards with Walt and Sarah many years ago. It turned out that Walt was an easy guy to talk to, and they talked about railroad engines and flying for a while before Jackie brought up the subject of the trip. Mark gave a brief explanation of what he planned, all things that Jackie had heard before, but he left out the idea of Jackie going along with him.

"Sounds like a hell of a trip," the older man said. "You take it easy, and take it as it comes, and you're going to have a good time. I just wish I was young enough and free enough to go with you. Back when I was your age, maybe a little younger, I spent a summer seeing the country, hopping freights, mostly. That was an adventure of a lifetime."

Jackie and Sarah had heard some of the stories of Walt's hobo trip, back about the time Mark was born, but neither of them minded hearing them again. Walt had a bunch of stories about the trip, and it kept him going for a while, with Mark drawing him out, only building up his desire to get going on his own adventure.

It had been a memorable trip for a young man. Walt had started for Texas, to go see an old school pal that had moved south during the war, and somehow, he never got to see the old school pal. He related the story of how he got on an empty boxcar in Minneapolis, thinking it was going to Kansas City, and was a little surprised to find it was heading west instead, so he rode along. He almost froze, sitting in the boxcar going through the mountains in Montana, but the views had been something to never forget. He wandered up and down the west coast, then worked his way back across the country. When he got back to

Spearfish Lake, he went down to Camden and put in his application with the D&O. Railroading had grown on him, and he'd been riding the rails ever since.

"I met a lot of good people out there, saw some great sights, and had a lot of fun. If your trip turns out half as good," Walt told him, "You'll remember it all your life. It takes a little courage to get up and do it, but it'll be worth it."

Jackie had seen an opening coming, and now was the chance: "Weren't grandma and grandpa a little upset at you taking off like that?"

"Well, yes, I guess they were," Walt said. "They knew that things can happen to you out there. But it was worth it, and they never held it against me afterward. I think Dad kind of envied me for taking the trip, and I never had any reason to be sorry about it."

Mark raised his eyebrows, and looked at Jackie, but her face was noncommittal, and she said nothing. They sat and talked for a while longer, and when the talk died down, they turned on the TV for an hour or two, and didn't say much of anything while it babbled away. Finally, it was starting to get late, and Mark got up. "Big day, tomorrow," he said. "If I can get a good day in tomorrow and Saturday, I might be able to get the wings finished."

"Will I see you for lunch?" Jackie wanted to know.

"Probably," Mark told her. "If I don't lose track of the time."

When Jackie came downstairs the next morning, she saw her father sitting at the kitchen table, having a cup of coffee. She had plenty of time, so stopped to join him. "That Mark is a nice kid," Walt said. "Seems to have his head screwed on pretty good."

Jackie nodded as she sipped her coffee. "I just hope we can get something going when he gets back from his trip."

"Yeah, that's going to be quite a trip. He's going to see a lot, have a lot of fun."

"I've been fascinated with the trip, ever since I heard about it," Jackie admitted. "It's too bad I can't go with him. That's one of those things a guy can do and a girl can't, at least without people getting ideas."

"Yeah, I suppose that's true," Walt said. "Boy, I'd sure go, though, if I had the chance." Jackie wondered if she heard an implied, "if I were you" in that sentence, but didn't know if she had or not.

"Well," Jackie said, taking another sip of her coffee, "I'm sure it would be fun, but it probably wouldn't be the right thing to do."

Her father nodded. "Yeah," he said. "Sometimes it's a little hard to figure out what's right and what's wrong, and sometimes it's not what you think it is. Sometimes you don't get a choice between right and wrong, but between bad and worse, and there are times that it's your decision." He changed the subject. "Are you going to be seeing Mark again tonight?"

"I suppose so," Jackie said. "I want to spend all the time I can with him before he leaves."

As Jackie drove Sarah's car down to Rick's, she didn't know what to think. She hadn't told her father she was thinking of going on the trip, but he almost seemed to be saying, "If the opportunity comes, grab it."

On the other hand, he almost seemed to be saying, "We can depend on you to be a good girl." It was hard to know what to think. She had wanted to tell her dad she had the opportunity to go with Mark, but couldn't bear to make herself say so -- perhaps from fear of being told she shouldn't go. Whatever the decision, she had to make up her own mind about it, and the safer course was certainly to stay home. If Mark came back, well, fine. If he didn't, well, there was always next time. Probably the best course of action was to not say anything to Mark, either way, and hope the idea died on the vine.

Donna greeted her as she walked into Rick's that morning, her last weekday there. "Hjalmer's over in the corner," she told Jackie. "He was wondering if you had come in, yet."

Jackie walked over to see what he wanted. "We still on for tonight?" he asked.

"I'm going to have to give it a pass for tonight," Jackie said. "I'm going to be busy for the next couple weeks. After that, I'm going to be pretty much free, though."

As the lunch crowd came and left, Jackie and Donna were busy, but all the while, Jackie thought about her brief conversation with Hjalmer. Picking back up with him was something Jackie could look forward to if Mark left, and she wasn't sure how much she looked forward to it. If she kept going out with Hjalmer, sooner or later it was going to come down to a wrestling match in his back seat, something she'd just as soon avoid. She had no doubts about the right and wrong of that. On the other hand, if she went with Mark, sooner or later it might come down to a wrestling match in a tent, somewhere, and that would be a whole lot harder to walk away from. On the balance, though, if it came down to having to have a wrestling match with either one of them, she found herself thinking that she'd rather it was with Mark.

Still, she couldn't get the thought of the trip out of her mind. Over the next hour or so, half a dozen times Jackie had made up her mind to tell Mark that she'd go with him after all, and half a dozen times, she talked herself out of it.

It was the middle of the afternoon before Mark walked in. "How's the silver dope coming?" she asked.

"Pretty good," he told her, as she set down a cup of coffee in front of him. "When the coat we just got on gets dry, I can start sanding, and it doesn't look like it's going to take a lot of sanding. Carl said he'd come in tomorrow and paint the wings, so probably Monday I could take them back out to the hanger and get them set up to hang on the bird."

"There's not a lot left to do, is there?" Jackie asked. In another week, or maybe a little more, he could be gone, she thought. "Are you going to get started on the fuselage tonight?"

"No," Mark said. "Last night reminded me that I need to spend a little time with my parents, too. Why don't you figure on coming over to the house after work, tonight."

On Saturday afternoon, Jackie stopped by the hanger to let Mark know she was off work, and to come over and pick her up. It was a fairly decent day, overcast but warmer than it had been. All the snow from earlier in the week had gone, but there were still patches of dirty white, hidden deep in the shadows.

"There's not really a lot you can do right now," Mark told her. "Maybe hand me a tool now and then, or something."

Jackie looked in the cockpit of the little Cessna. It was kind of a mess. "I think I'd better bring a vacuum, some rags and stuff, and clean this thing out," she said.

"I cleaned it up pretty good," he protested. "You should have seen it when I got it, before I put the new upholstery in."

By the time they decided to call it quits, it was after dark. The inside of the airplane was a lot cleaner, and it was beginning to look more like an airplane, anyway. As they stepped outside, Mark looked at the sky, and saw the moon looking back at him. "Hey, would you believe it? Clear skies!" he said. "Too bad the moon's out, but the moon's kind of fun to look at. You want me to get the telescope out?"

"Sure," she told him. It had been since last Saturday since the skies had been clear enough at night to do any stargazing, and she had hoped they'd have the chance to get the telescope out at least one more time before he left.

It only took him a few minutes to get the telescope set up. "It's a little hard to think of the moon as mysterious, any more," he said. "The guys walking around up there every few months have kind of taken it out of the class of being an astronomical object. But, it's still pretty to look at."

Jackie stared in the eyepiece, once Mark had the telescope pointed. "What you want to look at is the terminator," he said. "That is, the line between the lighted and dark parts. The shadows are long right in there, because the sun angle is low, and sometimes there's some really interesting things to be seen. Like, there's a place where there's a crater, where the top of the central peak is lighted, and the crater floor isn't."

"Oh, I see," Jackie said. She guided the telescope up and down, taking it all in.

After she had looked for a while, Mark asked, "What say we take a slide past the Pike Bar and have a beer or a Coke or something?"

"It's kind of late," Jackie told him. "And I really don't want to go into the Pike on a Saturday night."

"Yeah, I guess I don't either, now that you mention it," Mark said. "Well, when you're done, I'll put the telescope away and take you home. We've put in a good day's work today, and ought to be able to again tomorrow."

On the way home, Jackie realized that Mark had not brought up the subject of her going on the trip with him for days. Maybe he'd gotten the message. It was going to be hard to see him leave, but perhaps it was for the best that he left without her. "What are we going to be doing tomorrow?" she asked.

"Well, I'm planning on buffing out the fuselage before you get out there," he said. "It looks kind of gray and dingy right now, but a buffing and a couple of coats of wax will help it out a lot. Are you any good with a paintbrush?"

"Pretty good," Jackie said. "I liked art when I was in school."

"Well, that's something you could do tomorrow," he said. "After I get finished buffing the aluminum, the numbers will have to be repainted. I've got a can of red enamel, but I'll have to stop and get some brushes. I don't want to screw up good watercolor brushes with enamel."

"No problem," Jackie said. "I've got some oil brushes I haven't used in a while. They ought to be all right for lettering."

The next morning at Rick's was a long and slow one, the way most Sunday mornings there were, and knowing it was her last day of working there didn't make the morning go any faster for Jackie. In the course of a few days, she would be losing her job, what was de-facto her boyfriend, and a lot of things that had kept her interested. It was going to get boring, real soon, and she knew it.

Out at the airport, Mark had gone over the plane with a mechanical buffer, and now the fuselage looked a lot better than it had. Once Mark had told her what he had been doing that morning, she took a can of red enamel paint and her brushes, pulled up a stool and began to redo the registration numbers on the side of the plane.

At one point, Mark came over to check her work. "They look like factory numbers," he told her. "They don't look like you've just laid them on with a brush, freehand. That's good work."

"Glad you like it," she said. She finished the numbers on one side of the fuselage, and went around to work on the other side. The work moved along smoothly, and she lost track of time.

"Shit," she heard Mark say, from up in the engine compartment somewhere.

"What's the problem now?" she asked conversationally.

It turned out that a bolt head had broken off in an inconvenient place. "Now I'm going to have to take the whole fitting back to the house, drill it out, and retap it," he said. "It shouldn't take long."

"I think I'll just stay here and finish this up," she told him. "It's easier when you aren't shaking things, anyway."

"Fine with me," he said. A couple minutes later, she could hear the Ford start up outside, and drive away.

It didn't take long for Jackie to finish up the numbers, but it was obviously taking Mark longer than he had thought. She sat back on the stool, and with nothing to do, started to feel the emptiness of the building.

She would really feel empty with Mark gone. Perhaps there was something she could do that would make him think of her, to at least give her the hope that he would come back. An idea crossed her mind; she flipped it over for a few minutes, and thought it was a good one.

She moved up to the engine cowling -- it was on the left side, next to the hanger wall, the side away from where Mark had been working. She stared at the cowling for a moment, then went into the office and found a pencil and a ruler.

It only took her a few minutes to lay out her job. She didn't need to outline every letter; she could do it freehand, but keeping the letters and some of the longer lines straight called for guide marks. Hoping that Mark would not come back before she had completed, she took a stiff brush and the can of red paint, and started to fill in the lettering. That took the longest; the other part, also freehand, went quickly. Done at last, she stepped back against the hanger wall and looked at what she had done.

There on the cowling, lettered in red italics about an inch high, was the word "ROCINANTE". The word was underlined by a stylized medieval lance; by the "R" was a small silhouette sketch of a windmill, about twice as high as the lettering. By the "E" was a silhouette of the helmet of a knight's armor.

It was several hours before Mark discovered the logo on the cowling. "Hey," he called to her. "How can this be Rocinante if I don't have my Sancho Panza?"

"I thought you'd like it," she smiled. "Call it a good luck and come back present from me."

"I think it fits. I guess the plane's name is Rocinante," he said. "But we've still got work to do."

On Monday morning, they took the truck and trailer over to the body shop and brought back the wings. They were a dazzling white, and Ken set each up on a sawhorse and went to work on them. There was quite a bit of finishing work to be done before they could be mounted on the plane. Jackie could do some things, like removing masking tape and mounting navigation light lenses, but there was more where Mark needed extra hands. Several inspection holes had to be cut in the wings, reinforcing rings mounted, and cover plates fitted, and there was a lot of odds-and-ends work that took much of the day. "When does Rocinante get her wings?" Jackie asked at one point.

"Tomorrow, if the weather's clear," he told her.

Getting the wings on the next day proved to be a fairly quick proposition. It only took about half an hour a side to have them fixed in place, but there were control lines and gas lines and electrical lines to be hooked, fairings to be put in place, and the like, and it all took time. Mark and Sawyer worked hard at the final details, and Sawyer worked at a few things that Mark couldn't do. Finally, Sawyer completed his inspection of the plane, and signed the logbook.

By this time it was midafternoon of a bright day, although one on the cool side. The three of them rolled Rocinante out into the sunlight and over to the fuel pump, and Mark pumped a few gallons of gas into both tanks. He and Sawyer inspected everything for gas leaks; finding none, Mark pulled the propeller through by hand for a few strokes, then got into the plane. "Well, Ken, Jackie," he said. "Here goes nothing." He primed the engine a couple of shots, flipped on the magnetos, and hit the starter. The engine turned over a couple of times, and caught. Eyes beaming, Mark let the engine run at an idle for a few minutes, just to clear out the cobwebs. "Ken," he called, "You want to come along, or do you think I ought to do this solo?"

"Oh, hell, I'll come with you," the mechanic said, climbing in the right side.

Jackie sat on the fender of the Ford as Mark taxied the gray and white plane out to the runway. She watched as he and Ken ran the engine up, giving it a thorough checkout, then watched, with more than a little alarm, and it started to roll down the runway. She could see the tail come up; then she could see it break ground and begin to climb out. In but a minute or two, it was but a dot in the distance, and Mark and Ken began to feel it out.

They were back in only a few minutes. Mark landed, rolled to a stop, and taxied up to the hanger. "No question about it," he told the mechanic. "We're definitely out of rig."

"Is that something major?" Jackie asked.

"No, just an adjustment," the mechanic assured her.

Mark and Ken had to make several brief flights over the course of the next couple of hours, to work out all the bugs and make minor adjustments. "I think she's about as good as she's gonna get," the mechanic said. "Why don't you take Jackie for a ride, Mark? She's been aching for one, all afternoon."

"Yeah, come on, Jackie," Mark said. "We'll take a trip around the patch, then maybe go over and give the folks a buzz to tell them to come out to the airport."

In a few moments, Jackie was into the right seat of Rocinante, while Mark climbed in beside her. They were sitting even closer together than they had sat in the Stinson, if that were possible, but they had more headroom, and, amazingly, more legroom than in the four seater. It was as if the seat had been built for her. She was surprised to see that she could see over the nose much better than she could in the Stinson. Mark started the engine, which didn't have the growl of the bigger plane's either. A few minutes later, they were over Spearfish Lake, and Jackie found herself near tears.

She wanted to go on this trip with Mark so bad she could taste it, and riding in Rocinante's right seat only brought home to her what she could be doing if only she agreed to it. The country, the oceans, the mountains, the lakes and skies she could see from that seat, with only one word of approval . . . but somehow, it didn't feel right. As it was, she might fly with Mark again in the next few days, but it would not be long before he were gone.

When they got back to the airport, Mark's parents were there, and nothing would do but each of them taking a ride with him. After a while, Sawyer hopped in his plane and headed back to Lordston, and Jackie and the Gravengoods put Rocinante back in the hanger, and went over to the Spearfish Lake Inn for a well-deserved dinner and celebration.

After dinner, they went back to Mark's house. He got the telescope and tripod and the accessories out of the trunk, and set them up for a few minutes so they could have another look at the moon. Then, they took the whole rig down to the basement. While Jackie watched, Mark cleaned it, packed it away in the special box that would go in the plane. He took it over and set it next to a small pile of gear by the cellar stairs. "You're all packed, aren't you?" she said.

"Except for a few small items, like my razor and filling the water jug, I've been packed for weeks," he told her. "There were some bad days back there last winter when working on the gear was about all I could do."

Jackie stood looking at the pile in silence. It wouldn't be long now, she knew.

By now, Mark had pretty well given up hope that Jackie would be going with him. They had not talked about it for a week, except for his wisecrack Sunday. It was a shame; it would have been fun to have her on the trip, to share it with her, and perhaps let a relationship grow along with it; but if she couldn't bring herself to do it, there was no sense in pushing her. If he did, it probably wouldn't work.

The next day they did a fair amount of flying, allowing Mark to better get the feel of the Cessna. He was admittedly rusty, but the practice with the Stinson and the Cessna from Lordston had gotten him to the point where his skills felt adequate, although he knew he'd better not push his skills too far, at least for the first part of the trip. In the time left over, they cleaned up the mess in the hanger and swept it out. By the end of the day it was as if they had never been there at all. Rocinante sat in the front of the hanger, with the Stinson in back, and Jackie felt Mark's coming departure even more. Only a few more days . . .

The next morning, Jackie came downstairs to find the house empty. Her father, she knew, was off on a run; a note from Sarah was left on the kitchen table: "Johnnie is at Preschool. I'm going shopping, then will bring him home. If you're not with Mark, I'll leave him with you this afternoon."

Jackie shook her head. As soon as Mark left, she was going to be the automatic babysitter again, taken for granted. She was actually relieved to hear the rumble of the Ford outside once again. She grabbed her jacket and headed out to the car. Mark helped her get in through the tricky door, then started for the airport. "What's on for today?" she asked. "More practice?"

"No," Mark said. "There's going to be a front coming through tonight, and it's going to be crappy for several days later. I don't want to wait it out. Drive this home, and call Dad tonight, and he'll come and get it and do something with it."

"You're leaving today?"

"I'm leaving now. I told Mom and Dad goodbye before they went to work."

There just wasn't a lot to say the rest of the way to the airport. They parked next to the hanger door and opened it. Loading the gear did not take long; some of it had been loaded the day before, things like the tool kit and the tiedown kit that would want to stay in the airplane.

With that finished, they rolled Rocinante out of the hanger and over to the gas pump, where Mark carefully topped off the tank. He put the hose away, and walked over to where Jackie stood, next to the plane's left door. "This is it, I guess, isn't it?"

she said. "I mean, I know it sounds corny, but I'm going to miss you."

He took her in his arms and held her tight; she found her arms around his back, holding on to him, trying to hold him so close to her that he couldn't get away. After a moment, helpless to stop themselves, their lips met and their mouths locked together, neither of them daring to let the other go.

Finally, their mouths pulled apart, and Jackie lay her head next to his, still holding on for dear life. "I can't bear to have you leave me," she heard herself say. "Would you still take me with you?"

"How long would it take you to pack?" he whispered in her ear.

"Not long," she promised.

They hopped in the Ford and roared back over to Jackie's house. A mad half hour followed, in which she grabbed camping gear from the attic, clothes from her room, stuff from the bathroom. Fortunately, she remembered the list she had made days earlier, and it was still in the pocket of the snowmobile suit. She left a note of her own on the kitchen table, then they got back in the car, made quick stops at the bank and sporting goods store, then went out to the airport.

Her gear fit comfortably in Rocinate's baggage compartment, along with Mark's; they had figured it well. She got into the plane, and buckled her seat belt, while Mark climbed in the other side. He started the engine, taxied out to the end of the runway, and ran the engine up. Finally, he turned the plane down the runway, and brought it to an idle. "Still want to do it, Jackie?" he said.

"Yes," she said, wondering if Sarah had found the note yet. "No turning back. We don't come back until we're ready to stay."

"Good enough," he smiled, then, louder: "Sancho! My armor!"

They laughed, and then he pushed the throttle forward, to give Rocinante her spurs. The little Cessna raced down the runway, then rose above the trees. Mark dipped the wing slightly to turn south, toward the oncoming spring, but neither of them looked back at Spearfish Lake dwindling behind them in the distance.

*　*　*

Dad and Sarah:

I have decided to go on the trip with Mark, and we left this morning. Perhaps it's not the right thing to do, but I know I'll never have another chance like this, either for the trip or for Mark. I'll try to be good and not make you sorry that I did this, and I hope for your blessings and forgiveness.

I'll write often and call whenever I can, but I don't know when we'll be back. I love you,
Jackie

PS. Dad, Mark's car is out at the airport. The keys are under the seat. Would you see that it gets back to his dad, somehow or another? -- J

Part 2

Birds of the Air

1.

Mark and Jackie were a long way south of Spearfish Lake before the thrill of the moment began to wear off, and some of the old doubts began to rise in her again.

She felt like leaning over against Mark, close in the cockpit next to her, but thought better of it. Perhaps it would be better to keep what distance she could, just to keep them both from getting ideas.

Try as she could to look into the future, it seemed clouded. Mark had become a real friend in the few days that she had known him, and had always been the perfect gentleman. But what would it be like to be living with him?

That's what she would be doing, too -- living with him, sleeping with him, in the same tent. Those words implied a lot more than she hoped they would mean.

She'd drawn a lot of money out of the bank at their brief stop there. If things got out of hand she would have the means to go home, even if it meant going home in shame. She knew she would rather not do that, either, but she could if she had to. Hopefully, it wouldn't come to that.

Although it was quieter in Rocinante's cockpit than it had been in the Stinson, it was still pretty noisy for casual conversation, so she kept her misgivings to herself. The decision had been made; the note left behind for Sarah and her father sealed it. There would be no turning back now, she resolved; still, perhaps it would be better to wait a few days and see how things went, as well as giving her father and Sarah a chance to cool off, before she called home.

They were passing well to the east of Camden when the largely forested land below began to open up into more open fields. Below, Jackie could see that the snow was largely gone; spring was already closer. Mark had a map folded open, thrown up on the dash. For the sake of something to do, she took it and tried to make sense of it.

After a minute or so she realized that the town off to her right had to be Atlanta; there was the double-tracked main line railroad running across their course, and the branch line heading north. All of a sudden, a curious question arose in her mind. Over the roar of the engine, she turned to Mark and asked, "Where are we going, anyway?"

"South," he told her in a loud voice. "As far south as we can get by flying hard. The farther south we can get, the warmer it'll be camping tonight."

"How about tomorrow?" she asked.

"Farther south, I think," he said. "Unless you can come up with a better idea. I'd kind of figured on going right to Florida, and see if we can find a place to hole up for a few days. I've been pushing so hard for so long, I think I need to kick back and do nothing for a few days, and learn how to slow down and enjoy myself all over again."

"Sounds good to me," Jackie said. "I'm tired of winter. Let's get all the way away from it." It was a good idea, she thought; it would give them a chance to learn how to live with each other -- there was that phrase again -- to work out how they would operate; that was a better sounding way to say it.

They landed a little after one at a small airport well over three hundred miles south of Spearfish Lake. It was noticeably warmer, although still jacket weather. Mark had Rocinante gassed up, and they managed to borrow an airport courtesy car long enough to drive to a nearby restaurant for lunch. "I think if we want to save money, we'd better pack a lunch if we're going to be flying all day," Jackie commented as they sat down in a booth.

"I hope there won't be many days that we'll be flying all day," Mark told her. "We'll come across a few days that we'll want to get some miles on, but flying all day, every day, kind of misses the point. The trick is going to be to get away from airports, either with Rocinante, or on our own. I just sort of have a feeling that just stopping in some farmer's hayfield isn't going to work as well as it did for the old barnstormers."

"Maybe we'll just have to find out." Jackie commented as the waitress walked up. All of a sudden, she felt free as a bird. This little restaurant might as well have been Rick's, and the waitress might as well have been her, a week ago. How long ago and far away that seemed, now! "Do you have any idea of where we're going to hole up in Florida?"

"Are you two going down to Florida for the Apollo launch?" the waitress asked. "I've always wanted to see one of those."

Mark turned to look at Jackie, to see her eyes opened wide in obvious wonder. "I didn't know there was one coming up," he said. "I haven't been paying attention to the news. Do you have any idea of when it's going to be?"

"Next week, sometime, I think," the waitress said. "I saw it in the paper this morning. You want coffee?"

"Black," Jackie said absent-mindedly, thinking about watching an Apollo launch.

"Black," Mark agreed, thinking the same thing as Jackie was thinking. "And is there a copy of the paper laying around here?"

They made it as far south as a little airport in Kentucky before the day found itself waning. Mark got permission to tie Rocinante down out in the grass, and camp under the wing.

Mark had never gotten around to setting up the tent, which he had mail-ordered back around Christmas. It had the reputation of being a good tent, but it was complicated to set up the first time, with many mistakes and errors before they finally got it standing. "It won't be as bad, next time," Mark said as he and Jackie found places afterwards to sit and blow up their air mattresses.

"Once we know what we're doing," Jackie agreed, "It'll go better."

A little later, Jackie stuffed her air mattress into the tent. Mark handed his in to her, and then their sleeping bags and clothes bags, then crawled in after her to unroll his sleeping bag. As he crawled inside, Mark saw Jackie on her hands and knees, back to him, her pants tight across her fanny. "Boy, she's got a nice ass," he found himself thinking, and had to bring himself up short. This was Jackie, not Mei-Ling, after all. "A little on the crowded side in here," he commented.

"We're going to have to work out how we do this," Jackie said, turning around and sitting as best she could; the tent was a foot or more from being big enough for either of them to stand up in. "I mean, getting dressed and like that."

"It's going to be awkward," Mark agreed. "Maybe we should have brought your tent, too."

Jackie shook her head. "It's too late for that, now," she said. "Besides, you said we're pushing the weight limit."

"Well, if it doesn't work out, we can always get another tent," he promised. "I don't think it's going to matter tonight, anyway. It's going to be cold enough tonight that I think we're both going to want to wear our long handles. Let's get out of here and make ourselves some supper."

Mark had hunted high and low to find a camp stove that burned aviation gasoline, not white gas, since he didn't want to have gas in the luggage compartment. It seemed ridiculous to have to worry about stove gas when he would have two tanks of aviation gas close by. He'd been unable to find a two-burner stove that was light enough or small enough to go in the plane, but had managed to come up with two army surplus stoves that burned just about anything. He showed Jackie how to fill the camp stoves from the fuel sump drain, then spread a ground cloth under the wing and set the stoves to burning. Soon, there was hot water boiling on one stove, and stew cooking on the other.

"We're going to want to work together on the cooking, I think," he said. "How about if whichever one of us doesn't cook washes up, and we trade off?"

"Sounds fair to me," Jackie said. "But I think we want to eat more than just beef stew every night."

Mark nodded. "Yeah, I think I could even get tired of it after a while. Look, with two of us, this food thing is going to be tricky. We can't carry a whole lot, because of the weight. That means we have to hit a grocery store every few days, and there are going to be times that it won't be easy. I've got several freeze-dried meals in, but they taste like crap and are as expensive as hell, and there aren't going to be many places that we'll stop where we can get them. I had to mail-order the ones I have."

"I guess that means that we get to open a lot of cans," Jackie shrugged. "I guess we can do that. If it's OK with you, why don't we just make do with coffee and cereal for breakfast, and just kind of have snacks or sandwiches for lunch."

Mark got up and dug around in the plane's luggage compartment as he answered, "That's kind of how I planned it. We'll eat out, once in a while, and I wouldn't be surprised if we got asked home to dinner on occasion. We're just going to have to live a little grubby, that's all."

"It doesn't look like we're going to get a shower every night, either," Jackie commented. "We're going to have to take a bath once in a while, though."

"I can probably stand you longer than you can stand me," he said, sitting back down with the folder of maps in his hand. "But when it gets too bad, we'll have to work out something. Find a place to go swimming, or maybe get a motel room once in a while."

Jackie was silent for a moment. Somehow, the thought of sharing a motel room with Mark was far more distressing than the thought of sharing a tent with him. "I wonder how we register at a motel," she said finally, with more than a little accusation on her voice, "Mr. and Mrs. Gravengood?"

Mark shook his head, understanding her fully. He had, of course, realized that he and Jackie could wind up in bed together at some point, and if it were handled right he was sure he wouldn't mind. However, if it did happen, it might not be a long step until she really became "Mrs. Gravengood". That was a possibility he hadn't really considered. Having a girl friend, even one that he made love with, was one thing; marriage was another. Not that it would necessarily be unwelcome when the time came, but he just had not thought that far ahead. "No," he said, finally. "We'll use our own names. If anybody asks, you're my sister."

"I'd have to be your half-sister," Jackie laughed at his unease. "After all, our names are different."

"All right, Sis," he laughed with her. "You're my half-sister. I always wondered what it would be like to have a sister."

"That's fine," she said, feeling some of the pressure come off. "I always wondered what it would have been like to have had a brother about my age."

They studied maps while they ate supper, giving special attention to the area around Cape Kennedy. The launch of Apollo 15 was still a week off, so they had plenty of time, but if they could find a good place to camp in the vicinity it would be a good place for Mark to unwind and for both of them to learn how to be together.

After supper, while Jackie did the dishes in the leftover hot water for the coffee, Mark dug the telescope out of the baggage compartment, and they spent some time looking around the sky, dark now that it was past the full moon. Time passed rapidly, and even though they wanted to get an early start the next day, it was later than Mark had hoped before he realized the time.

"I'll put away the telescope," he told Jackie. "Why don't you get your longies on and get in the sack while I'm doing it?"

"All right," she said, heading for the tent. It seemed ages to Mark as he walked around Rocinante, checking the tiedowns, before he heard her say, "You can come in now."

She held a flashlight for him while he got inside, zipped the tent door closed, and got out his long underwear. "Why don't you kill the light while I'm doing this?" he suggested.

She turned out the flashlight and said, "I'll roll over so I can't see you."

"Not much to see in the dark," he said. "Besides, I wasn't planning on taking off my underwear. But, thanks anyway."

As she lay there with her back to him, she heard him thrash around behind her, with a little anxiety crossing her mind. She was zipped in her sleeping bag, zipped into the tent, unable to get out quickly. She made up her mind she'd scream if he touched her, although she realized that a goodnight kiss would be nice; the kiss they'd shared at the airport in Spearfish Lake had been wonderful, but under circumstances like these, who knew where it could lead?

Eventually, the thrashing around stopped, and she heard him say, "Good night, Sis."

"Good night, brother," she said with a little smirk, still tense, still awaiting a touch that she both hoped for and feared, waiting until she heard the soft, slow breathing that told her that he was asleep, then waited longer, half wondering if going on the trip had been such a good idea after all.

Light was filtering through the tent when Jackie awoke. Something seemed out of place, but she couldn't quite figure out what it was.

All of a sudden, she sat up with a start. She realized that she wasn't in her bedroom at Spearfish Lake, or even out camping with her father: the day before, she'd run off with Mark, and they were in a tent somewhere in Kentucky, on their way God knew where, and her bones ached from the cold of the night.

She rolled over, to see that Mark's sleeping bag was empty and wadded up into a pile. Hurriedly, she unzipped her own sleeping bag and crawled out partway, then unzipped the tent and stuck her head outside.

The sun was just coming up, and she could see frost on the grass in the shadow of Rocinante's wing. Mark was sitting on one of the plane's wheels; one of the stoves was set up and hissing, with a pot of water on top of it. "Ah, the dead awake," Mark said. "Did anybody ever tell you that you snore?"

"I don't snore," she protested, reflecting that she was a little surprised to wake up and still be a virgin; she wouldn't have bet a nickel on it the night before. "I didn't sleep at all last night, it was so cold." And I was so scared, she thought.

"It was a little chilly," Mark agreed. "That's why I want to get farther south. It's still April, after all. You like a cup of coffee to warm you up before you get dressed?"

"I'd love it," she admitted. In but a moment, Mark mixed a plastic cup of instant and handed it into the tent to her. It was very hot, hotter than she liked it, but the warmth of it coursed through her, making her realize how cold she had slept. She drained the cup and set it outside, then, not daring to expose her bare legs to the cold air, slipped her long handles off while still in the sleeping bag and pulled on her ice-cold jeans, wanting to scream at the chill. Getting her shirt from yesterday and her jacket on was not much better, but eventually she was able to clamber outside and stand up. "I don't think I've ever been so cold in my life," she said as he handed her a second cup of coffee.

"The sun will warm things up, soon," he said. "We can leave as soon as it melts the frost off the wings."

"Have they opened up yet?" she asked, nodding at the office.

"No," he told her. "If it's using the johns you're thinking about, I'd suggest the bushes on the far side of the hanger."

That was what Jackie had been thinking about, and she realized that she wasn't going to be able to wait much longer. She took a sip of her coffee, and realized that it was really too hot to drink, so she set the cup on Rocinante's cowling and traipsed toward the nearby hanger.

A few minutes later, she was back, and the coffee was just about right. "It's awful cold to be hanging my bare butt out in the breeze over in the bushes," she commented.

"Kind of em-bare-assing," he smirked.

"Yeah, that too," she said, laughing at the pun. "It probably won't be the last time I have to do it on this trip, though."

They each had another couple of cups of coffee, although cold cereal didn't seem appealing in the chill. While they sipped their coffee, they stuffed their sleeping bags, let the air out of their air mattresses, took down the tent, and packed everything but the stove and coffeepot in Rocinante.

By the time they had finished, the sun had stripped the frost off the Cessna's wings. "Might as well get going," Mark said, emptying the rest of the coffee water onto the ground. She took a rag and mopped off the windshield and the leading edges of the wings, then they both clambered into the cockpit.

"Before we get going, there's something I forgot about last night," she said, turning to him.

"What?"

"I kind of forgot to kiss you good night," she said, reaching over with her long arm, grabbed his far shoulder, and pulled him over to her. Their lips touched, and they kissed for a long time, feeling each other's warmth in the cold cockpit of the plane.

"I guess I'm just as glad you didn't kiss me good night last night," he said finally. "A kiss like that could get misinterpreted, real easy."

"Yes," she agreed quietly. "I think we'd better keep that out of the tent. For now, anyway."

They flew south all that day, stopping for lunch and fuel. They camped that night at a little grass strip in northern Florida, and it was a lot warmer -- warm enough that they didn't bother with long underwear. They could have flown on to Cape Kennedy that day, but Mark had suspected that the airport at Titusville was big enough and busy enough that they wouldn't have a good place to camp, so he wanted plenty of daylight to make other arrangements.

As it turned out, they could have camped at the Titusville airport, but it was already filled to the point where all the regular tiedowns were taken. Mark had to get out the tiedown kit to tie Rocinante down, far down the runway.

The airport manager was able to make recommendations, both on the best place to watch the Apollo launch, and the best place to camp; he'd been faced with this question before. Unfortunately for Mark and Jackie, without a car, it would involved a lot of walking. "This wasn't quite what I had in mind for our first backpacking trip," he told her, "But we're going to have to play it like we're backpacking."

The packs had not been set up for backpacking; hers had just had stuff thrown into it, two mornings and fifteen hundred miles before. It took them a while to sort and rearrange things for camping out for a few days. With their packs loaded, Mark locked the plane, took the telescope box in one hand, and they started for the airport gate.

It was a long hike along a busy highway to the area where the airport manager had told them might be both a good camping spot and a good place to watch the launch, still several days away. It was not really that hot -- only in the high seventies, or so -- but to the two of them, still conditioned fully to a Spearfish Lake winter, it might as well have been the middle of Death Valley. Both still had on long jeans; Jackie had on the one short-sleeved blouse she'd managed to throw in, and Mark had on a T-shirt, but sweat was still rolling down both of them. "As soon as we get camped," Jackie said at one point when they stopped along the side of the road for a drink and a breather, "I'm turning these jeans into cutoffs."

"Me, too," Mark agreed. "If we're going to spend the summer like this, there's no point in loading up on winter clothes. Did you think to bring a swimsuit?"

"Never crossed my mind," Jackie admitted. "You don't think swimsuits in Spearfish Lake this time of year. I probably ought to get one. Maybe we can hike back into town tomorrow and do some shopping."

"Tomorrow's Sunday," Mark told her. "Probably everything will be closed."

"Sunday already?" Jackie said, amazed. "I've lost track of time, already."

Finally -- it seemed like all day, although it had only been a couple of hours -- they found a suitable location, in some sandy scrub brush where they were concealed from the highway, overlooking a tiny bay with a beachy area that would probably do for swimming, although neither of them were too sure how much they wanted to get soaked in salt water and not be able to rinse off. Best of all, a few feet away from their campsite was a little hummock. From the top of the sand pile, they had a clear, though distant view, of the Saturn V being prepared for liftoff.

"It would have been nice to be able to camp by the ocean, instead of this backwater," Mark told her as they huddled in the shade of a bush, out of the midday sun. "That would have been a hell of a walk, though."

Mark had peeled off his shirt, by now, and Jackie wished that she dared do the same; then, comfort flying in the face of caution, she told him, "Don't get any ideas," and took off her blouse, but not daring to remove her bra, as well.

That was a little better, and after a while, they had cooled off enough to move ahead with erecting the tent. With it up, Jackie crawled inside and stripped off her jeans. With the tiny pair of scissors from her sewing kit, she chopped off the legs of the jeans and pulled them back on. She was a little surprised to find that she'd cut them off a lot shorter than she'd intended, but they'd have to do; besides, they'd be cooler that way.

After a while, they took the tent fly and with the aid of some sticks they found, managed to rig it up as a sun fly to get some shade. The afternoon was humid now, almost oppressive; thunderheads could be seen building up in the distance. They lay down in the shade of the fly; Mark told her, "I don't know about you, but I'm going to take a nap."

The idea sounded good to Jackie, and she lay down beside Mark, but sleep wouldn't come. She lay there, looking out across the water at the handful of boats out on the river, and at the far side of the tepid waterway, almost lost in the haze of the afternoon. Spearfish Lake seemed far away, almost in another world, distant and unreal. She wondered, not for the first time, what her father and Sarah and friends like Kirsten must be thinking, and found that it didn't concern her as much as she thought it would. So far, the trip with Mark had been fine, except for the sweaty hike this morning and the recovery from it, but she realized that this had to be part of the adventure, too.

She did find herself wishing that they had thought a little more clearly when they had been sitting in the hanger office not all that many days before, making out a list of things that she'd like to take on the trip. A swimsuit, of course, was one of the more glaring omissions, but it should have been more heavily oriented toward warm weather clothing, as well; otherwise, she wouldn't have to be sitting there in her bra and cutoffs. And sunscreen! Mark had an uncomfortable sunburn already, although luckily she had a complexion that tanned easily, rather than burning. It wouldn't have been a bad idea to have a book or two, or a portable radio, just to help while away slow, dull afternoons like this one.

She knew there ought to be something she could do, just to keep busy. All of a sudden, she had an idea. It wasn't perfect, but it would kill time.

The denim from the cutoff blue jeans wasn't a perfect material to work with; she could have done a much better job, in only a few minutes, with decent scissors and a sewing machine. But, it gave her something to do.

When Mark finally woke up some time later, she had finished the halter top. It wasn't a perfect fit; given the circumstances, there was a limited amount that she could do. Somehow, though, it felt better than wearing her bra in front of Mark; it felt more proper.

By then, the afternoon was wearing on, and the sun was down enough that they could come out from under the shelter and explore their domain, although there wasn't much to see -- just more and more of the scrubby brush poking up through the sand. They wound up on the beach below their camp. "I kind of wish we'd brought the rod and reel," she told him. "It'd be fun to tie on a spoon or something and just throw it around out there. God knows what a person would catch, though."

"You left it back at the plane?"

She nodded. "Yeah, I didn't think I'd want it."

"We could get it tomorrow or sometime," he told her. "I can see that our water is not going to hold out very long. Maybe tomorrow, early, while it's still cool, one or the other of us should hike back and get some more."

"That's pretty well a got to," she said. "I don't think we've got enough to get through tomorrow, but it must be a good three or four miles back to where we can get some."

He looked out at the little bay. "You know, a swim might cool us off."

She looked longingly at the water. "I'd love a swim," she said. "But all I've got that I could wear in the water is what I've got on, and I really don't want to get it wet."

"I suppose you're right. What do you say we set up the telescope and take a look at the rocket?"

It only took them a few minutes to set the telescope up on top of the little hummock. Mark kept the tripod legs pulled in, so they could sit comfortably and study the activity around the huge Saturn, miles away. With a medium power eyepiece, it was pulled in quite close to them, although it was difficult to make out much of what was happening through all the shimmering heat waves. "I think they keep it lit up at night," Mark told her. "Maybe after dark it'll settle down and we'll be able to see something."

They spent several minutes trying to make something out of the spectacle in front of them. Finally, Mark put the dust covers back on the telescope, and they went back to camp, and lay down under the sun shade. A little breeze had sprung up by now, cool and pleasant but not cold. They sat for some time, not saying much of anything, just looking across the bay.

"You know, I hate to admit this," Mark said, "But I'm just the least little bit bored."

"I guess I am, too," she told him. Somehow, this was one thing she hadn't expected on the trip.

"I know what the problem is," Mark said. "We're both people that have to be doing something, and the past few months there's been more to do than there's been time for. Now, here I am, camped out on what might as well be a desert island, with a beautiful girl at my side, just like it was a dream, and I hardly know what to do with myself. But, it's like I said, I need to slow down and learn to take it easy and enjoy myself."

"I don't think of myself as beautiful," she said. "Just sort of ordinary."

"You're beautiful, Jackie," he told her gently, "If for no more reason than you're here with me. Have I told you yet that I'm glad you came with me? If I didn't have you here with me, then I'd really be bored. I think you're taking to this trip better than I am."

She turned to him and smiled. "Well, I'm glad you brought me," she said. She wanted to kiss him so bad that it hurt, but she knew that a kiss just then would be the first step to going places that she didn't want to go just yet -- though she found herself realizing that the possibility of that happening bothered her less than it would have even a couple of days before.

Mark realized the danger, too. Calling Jackie "beautiful" was not a lie, for sitting there on the sand, in the late afternoon sunlight, she exuded a glow that he'd always suspected was there. It would have been fun indeed to liven up the afternoon with a little sex in the sand, and if Jackie had been like Mei-Ling, it would have happened long before. But, in Jackie, he recognized something more valuable, something not worth driving off over a brief fling, and he could feel that letting things get out of hand would scare her off for the long run.

He finally got an idea to defuse the situation. "Why don't you go over and sit on the side of the hill, there, and let me draw you. I need to get back in practice, if nothing else."

"Me?" she said as he crawled inside the tent for his pack, where he had a drawing pad and some pencils.

"Yeah, you. Don't know of any other pretty brunettes around here."

Rather reluctantly, with a little coaxing on his part, she went over and sat on the side of the hummock. "Don't worry about looking pretty," he told her. "Just look comfortable." He went back over into the shade of the tent fly, picked up the pad, and started to draw. Jackie felt very self-conscious for a few minutes, but as they sat and talked, she found herself becoming more at ease, while Mark worked away at the drawing.

Gradually she lost track of the time, and she had no idea of how much later it was before Mark put down the pad and just looked at her for a minute or two, then picked the pad up, and looked at the drawing. "Well, that's not too good," he said, "But we'll work on it. You make a good model, Jackie."

"Can I see?"

"Sure, come on over," he said.

She found that she had gotten a little stiff from holding still for so long, but it was good to get up and walk the few steps over to him. She took one glance at the drawing and said, "I'm not that pretty!"

"Sure you are," he said. "I'll admit, I could have done better. The shadow detail on your legs and your torso just isn't right, for example, but for a practice drawing, it's not worth fixing. I'll do better next time."

"But Mark!" she protested, studying the drawing of the long-haired, long-legged, well-built girl in a halter top and brief shorts half-sitting, half-laying on the hillside. "I don't have a build like that! It hardly looks like me."

He held the drawing up and compared it to her. "It looks a lot like you," he said. "I don't think I overemphasized anything. It just doesn't fit your mental image of how you look."

"Do you really think I look like that?"

"Pretty much," he said. "I'm no great artist, but it's a fair image, under the circumstances. We're starting to lose the light, but maybe tomorrow I'll do another one, just to show you I can do better."

As Mark turned to preparing supper, Jackie kept returning to the drawing. The girl in the drawing was pretty, and after a while, she realized that the girl was at least based on her. Could that be how she really looked to him? What a compliment if it was! She'd never thought of herself as being pretty, just too tall and too thin and rather mousy and shy.

Perhaps Mark really did see something in her that she didn't see in herself. It was an awesome thought, indeed. For an instant, she wondered how the drawing would have looked if she'd offered to pose nude for him, and she realized, surprised a little with her boldness, that sooner or later she'd make the offer.

Not yet. She wasn't ready for it, yet, but she realized that she was looking forward to the time when she was ready for it.

They took their time over supper, dragging it out until after the sun went down and they realized that twilight was falling rapidly, and they had to hurry around and get the dishes done and their air mattresses blown up before full darkness fell on them. Even after dark it was cooler, but still warm enough that they didn't bother getting more clothes on.

They sat around talking for a while after dark, and Mark smoked a cigarette, the first one in days. "We should have scrounged around and seen if we had enough dry brushwood around here for a little fire," Jackie suggested.

"That stuff wouldn't make for a big fire," Mark agreed, "But a little one would be nice."

"We'll have to do that tomorrow," she agreed. "Why don't we go up the hill and see if we can see anything more of the launch pad, now that the heat's settled down some?"

They trudged through the loose sand up to the top of the hummock, removed the dust covers from the telescope, and spent a long time looking at the rocket, brightly lit by floodlights around the base of the pad. "I can't imagine what it must be like to ride one of those things," Mark said, "But the view must be tremendous. I can't imagine what it would be like to look out the window and see the moon closer than you could ever see in an eyepiece."

The moon was down, just then, so when they got tired of looking at the Saturn, miles away, Mark turned the telescope on the sky and managed to hunt up Omega Centuri, the huge globular cluster that is one of the showpieces of the southern sky. "I saw this a lot better in Australia," he told her. "It was almost overhead, not down in the haze and the skyglow like this, but it's still a pretty sight. We should be able to see it better down in west Texas, when we're there a month or so from now. The air is a lot clearer and dryer there."

They spent perhaps a couple of hours, exploring the sky, both with the telescope and without it. Mark taught Jackie some of the constellations she didn't know, and showed her how to guide the telescope to some of the better things to look at. They explored space in the only way that was open to them, since they couldn't ride the huge skyscraper of lighted-up machinery a few miles away.

Eventually, they covered the telescope back up, and walked slowly back to the tent. As Mark unzipped the flap, he said, "I don't know if you're just too nice to say anything about it, or what, but I think I still stink from that walk in today. I'd sure like to clean up a little."

"Well, I don't think I smell too good myself," she said, "But we don't have fresh water to waste. Too bad we couldn't go for a midnight swim."

"Yeah, too bad we didn't think of swimsuits. Of course, it's dark enough, we could do without," he joked.

She felt herself blushing at the suggestion, no matter how dark it was, no matter how he meant it as a joke. On the other hand, the water would feel good . . . and she'd begun to feel just a little uneasy at herself for cringing at everything that might be considered a little suspicious. She was a little surprised to hear herself say, "Promise you won't turn on a flashlight?"

Mark was more surprised to hear Jackie's words than she was. He'd meant it as a joke, but apparently she was willing to take him up on it. Things could get out of hand, too soon, much too soon . . . "Great idea, but we'd better not," he said. "In the dark, we might not know if there's something there we wouldn't want to tangle with, like an alligator or something. I can stand you tonight, if you can stand me."

2.

Jackie started the night sleeping on top of her sleeping bag in her flannel pajamas, but somewhere over the course of the night she got cold enough that she slipped into her sleeping bag without waking up. In her dreams, Mark had not stopped the idea of a midnight skinnydip; they had stripped off their clothes, gone down to the little beach, frolicked in the water a little, splashed water on each other. After a while, in her dream, they'd walked back up to the tent, and he'd taken her in his arms for a long, heartfelt kiss, bare bodies pressing together, his manhood pressing hard against her, making her ache for what would come . . . and . . . and . . .

She found herself surprised and a little sorry on waking to be in her own sleeping bag, wearing her flannel pajamas. The dream had been so real, so wonderful.

Outside, she heard the hiss of one of the stoves. Mark was making coffee, already fully dressed. "Have a good night's sleep?" he asked.

"I think so," she said, still unable to shake off her dream. "Did we go swimming last night, after all?"

"Did you have the same dream I did?" he asked.

"I think so," she said shyly.

"God," he said. "That alligator was as big as a house. I'm not sure how bad I want to go swimming there today." Mark didn't say that his dream had ended up much the same as Jackie's, although it was a bit more adventurous getting there.

"I guess I'm glad we didn't go skinnydipping then," she said. "It would have been fun."

"We'll have to do it some time when we know there aren't any alligators around," he smiled. "You want a cup of coffee?"

"Of course," she replied. He poured hot water and mixed her a cup of instant.

While she lay there sipping it, half out of her sleeping bag, he busied himself around the campsite. "I've been thinking about it," he said. "That's a long walk into town, and I'm not sure we want to leave the campsite unattended. After all, other people are going to start showing up to wait for the launch. Why don't I make the hike today, while it's still early and cool for the first part, anyway? I can get water, anyway, although I don't know what else will be open on a Sunday morning. Then, tomorrow, when the stores will be open, you can make the water run and go shopping for a swimsuit and whatever else you want."

She thought about it for only a moment; his suggestion made sense. "Take what water you need," she suggested. "Leave the rest here, and I can take a sponge bath while you're gone."

"Sounds good," he told her. "I'll hold your coffee if you'll dump my pack out and hand it out here. I'll be long enough that you can sleep in a while if you want."

"Get sunscreen and sunglasses, if you can find them," she added as an afterthought.

There was perhaps a couple of quarts of water left in some pans when he put the canteens and water bottle in his otherwise empty pack, and headed for the highway. Jackie set the coffee cup out into the sand and snuggled back down into her sleeping bag.

The sun was barely peeking over the horizon behind Mark as he reached the highway and set out on the causeway toward the far shore. The dew was still heavy, and he was a little surprised that there was no fog; the air was quite heavy. He would have hitched a ride if he could. There was little traffic on the causeway, and virtually all of it was headed the other way; not surprising, as people would have to be getting to work over at the launch complex. While work had probably gone on all night, there would be people that would only be working days, even though this was a Sunday.

With the pack riding lightly on his back, he settled into an even, fast pace, not like the slow, heatbeaten trudge of the morning before. He hoped he would be able to hitch a ride coming back, when the sun would be up higher and beating down on him.

Although it was a good idea to leave Jackie at the campsite, it hadn't been necessary. But, he had wanted to get off by himself for a while, to be alone, to think about things. His dream of the night before had been all too real; Jackie had come to him willingly, although still frightened by the alligator she'd stepped on in the dark. While he had enjoyed having Jackie along on the trip, it was clear that having her along was going to include complications that he hadn't thought of when the offer had been made.

Damn it, did he want to marry the girl? That it would be an inevitable result of the trip was not a foregone conclusion, but it seemed like every day something happened that drew them closer. It was getting harder and harder to be like a brother to her; she had released things in him that had been bottled up since he'd said goodbye to Mei-Ling.

The thought of Mei-Ling startled him; he realized that it had been some time since he had thought of the little Chinese-Thai prostitute, and now, his mental image of her wasn't as clear as it had been even a couple of weeks before.

Clearly he was falling in love with Jackie.

There it was; he'd never admitted it to himself before, but once the word was out, it felt comfortable.

What would it be like to be married to Jackie? It would remove the barriers between them, barriers they themselves had set. He'd never really thought about what it would be like to be married, to Jackie or to anyone else, even Mei-Ling. Jackie was a nice girl, quiet and contemplative, intelligent and sensible, interested in many things he was interested in. He thought about several of his friends that had long since been married, and some of them divorced, and he thought of a few of the latter that he decided had never been as comfortable with each other as he was with Jackie.

But people change; clearly, this trip was going to change both of them, perhaps for the better, perhaps not. After all, marriage hadn't worked out for Jackie's mother, certainly not to her benefit, or anyone else's.

Mark remembered back to the cold of the hanger in Spearfish Lake, with Jackie on one side of the wing, himself on the other, when she had told him about her mother. Mark had no idea of what could have shoved her mother over the edge, but doubted that it had been her father; he was too nice a guy. It had to have been something inside. Was Jackie right to fear that it could happen to her, too? Where would that leave him?

He pounded on up the causeway with an even pace, thoughts heavy on his mind. It was clear to him that he and Jackie did not have a lot farther to go before turning back would be a lot harder. It would not have taken much of a suggestion last night, not much effort on his part, to have found himself making love to Jackie, whether she was ready or not, and he suspected that she was closer than either of them thought. How close neither of them would know, until some gesture, some remark, some touch would find themselves in each other's arms. Under ordinary circumstances he would have welcomed it, but it begged two questions: was she important enough to him to not risk losing her by doing something before its proper time -- but was she important enough to him to risk hanging on to her, in spite of an unknown factor of what could come?

He knew for damn sure that he'd better be able to give the right answer to both questions before he went too much farther. For the moment, the tentative answer to both of them was "yes".

Perhaps sex might come without facing up to a final decision about the second question -- but if it did, it would be awkward if the answer to the second question turned out to ultimately be "no" -- or if it turned out to be wrong.

If she hadn't been with him on the trip, then neither question would probably have come up -- but if he hadn't brought her with him, he might well have missed something worth the effort.

The thoughts churned over and over in his mind as he pounded his way across the causeway -- Jackie, her mother, sex, his own desires, marriage. Then, out of nowhere, came a thought that made him stop and sit down on a rock, looking out over the water.

Obviously, some kind of stress, whatever it was, must have had something to do with what had happened to Jackie's mother. The strain of Jackie living with him, with all the ongoing sex-related tension, had to be as stressful on her as it was on him.

Things bend before they break.

Perhaps how well Jackie stood up to the stress of traveling with him, living with him would give him a good idea of what he needed to know.

Oh, well. If Jackie couldn't take the stress, it was better to know now. If they wound up having sex, they wound up having sex. If it got awkward, it got awkward. The only thing to do would be to let nature take its course, without pushing matters, and see what happened.

If he could get along without a hard dick doing his thinking for him, so much the better, but if it happened, it happened.

Mark got back up and started toward the far shore, which seemed a lot nearer, now.

Jackie lay in her sleeping bag a while longer, but sleep wouldn't come. She knew she should have never had that cup of coffee; it had wakened her more than she would have liked. Finally, her aching bladder told her that she could wait no longer.

It was strange to go outside the tent knowing that Mark wasn't there. She did walk a ways away from the camp before relieving herself, but wasn't self-conscious about it like she had been before. She had only been with Mark a few days, now, but it seemed strange to have him away from her. She had grown comfortable with him, comfortable even with the thought that what she had dreamed might happen, could happen, and was even likely to happen, sooner or later. If it did happen, it would remove a lot of barriers between them; they could be even more comfortable with each other.

The question that she pondered as she started the stove going again, made some more coffee and brushed out her hair was whether to just go ahead and let it happen.

There wasn't a lot of water left, but with Mark gone and no one else around, it was too good an opportunity to take some sort of a bath to let pass. After giving it a good thought over coffee, while she sat on the sand in her pajamas, she realized that she would have a lot better bath if she went down to the beach and did her heavy washing, then came back up to the camp to rinse off in the fresh water.

It would have been better if she'd had a swimsuit, she knew, but the little beach was mostly out of sight of the highway, and even thinking about skinny-dipping with Mark had emboldened her a little. Without thinking about it too much, once she finished her coffee, she stripped off her pajamas, got a bar of soap, and walked nude down to the beach.

After Mark's remark about the alligator, she couldn't bring herself to go into the water very far, and she looked it carefully over before she waded in up to her knees, then sat down on the sandy bottom. The salt water didn't raise much of a lather with the little bar of soap, but she did feel a little cleaner after a while. Still, it seemed strange to be out there in the open, naked as a jaybird, and she made a quick job of it, then hiked back up to the camp.

A wet washcloth in what was left of the fresh water did a pretty good job of removing the stickiness of the salt water, and soon she stood under the sun shade, still nude, still a little surprised at her boldness. The sun was getting up a little now, putting a little warmth into what would obviously be a warm day, and the warmth of the sun and the gentle little breeze that had sprung up dried her off rapidly. It would be a long time before Mark got back, she realized, and the sun felt good, if still to early to add to her tan much, and feeling it some more would be nice.

Still nude, she picked up her as-yet unused towel and walked around to the sunward side of the hummock, where she spread the towel out on the sand and lay down on it.

She lay back and let the growing warmth of the sun course through her, stuck by the difference that only a few days could make. Even a few days ago, in the depths of a Spearfish Lake winter, she would have never dreamed of sunning herself naked, yet here she was, not thinking too much about it. A lot had happened in a very short time.

In the far-off distance, she could make out the top of the Saturn's gantry, just poking itself above the brush. Anyone on top of the gantry, with a telescope at least as good as Mark's, could get quite an eyeful if they were to happen to look in the right direction, she thought, although it didn't seem likely, and she wouldn't know if they did.

She thought about the rocket, and the pictures she had seen of it, thrusting itself up into the sky, and all of a sudden broke out laughing. She knew that some people saw the rocket at a phallic symbol, its powerful hard maleness thrusting itself up into . . . the thought lead inextricably to the dream she had had of Mark, thrusting his powerful, hard maleness up into her as she lay there, wanton and anxious for it.

The symbolism was so trite that she couldn't help herself. They had come close last night; very close, indeed. A word, a nod, the slightest advance on her part and it would have happened; her virginity, this morning, would have been in the past tense, and she didn't know whether she was happy or sorry that it was still intact.

She thought about Kirsten, her old friend, with her fiancée missing in Vietnam. Kirsten had been down that road, who knew how many times, out there on the top of Turtle Hill. She was paying for it now, in agony over her lost Henry, but she'd had a lot of fun with him before he left; she hadn't let the moment pass by. Dreams of Kirsten and Henry in the back seat on Turtle Hill brought her thinking directly to thoughts of Mark and herself, perhaps here on this very beach.

It would have been so easy . . . why hadn't she just kissed Mark, maybe let her hands wander a little, and let nature take its course? Was it because her dad and Sarah expected her to be a good girl? Was it because she had expected herself to be a good girl? Was it because she was supposed to be a good girl? Just what did her dad and Sarah think she was doing with Mark, anyway? They would have a pretty good suspicion of what was going on, and even though their suspicions were totally wrong, they wouldn't believe the truth. Perhaps, the next time the time was right, she should just let it happen . . .

Suppose she let it happen? Would they think any less of her? More important, would Mark think any less of her?

The thought surprised her. She knew she cared a lot about Mark, but ultimately, was he that important to her? Could she imagine herself married to Mark?

It was not hard to imagine. He was a nice guy, easily the nicest she had ever known. Unlike Hjalmer, she could see making a life with this quiet, intense man, and it didn't seem like an unpleasant life. Very likely, it had already started, and making it permanent didn't seem like such a big leap, now that she thought about it.

If everything went right, it could happen. If everything went right, they could make a life together . . . if everything went right.

It hadn't gone right with her mother, after all, and she had lived with the fear that things might not go right for her ever since she had been old enough to comprehend it. Was it fair to saddle Mark with a risk like that? Was it fair that she was saddled with it?

Worse, was it fair to saddle a child with it?

She lay back, amazed at the thought. Up to this point, she had only kissed Mark twice, once at the Spearfish Lake airport, and once at that airport in Kentucky, and here she was, thinking about having children with him!

Still, it was a fair question. Best answer it now, before things got too serious. Perhaps if she couldn't answer it now, she'd better get the money out of her pack and get a bus back to Spearfish Lake, before things got any deeper.

No, it wasn't fair to saddle a child with it. Whatever else happened, there would be no children, period. Deep in her gut, she realized that if she stayed on the trip with Mark, she'd better start taking precautions, just in case. It would at least put off the final answer to that question for a while, and it could wait a few years.

Was it fair to Mark? After all, it wasn't like he didn't know of her concern, although she should remind him if things got any more serious. Having fun wasn't a problem, even if the fun extended to sex when the time came. Marriage, though . . . perhaps she should try to keep the lid on, just in case.

The sun was getting up more, now. She didn't know how long Mark had been gone, or how soon he would be getting back, but she realized that she'd better get back to the tent and get some clothes on. It'd be best not to give him any ideas -- today, anyway.

Jackie had her cutoffs and halter top back on when Mark got back to the tent, carrying a full pack. "I got water," he said. "I got us sunglasses and sunblock. Best of all," he said, setting the pack down, and opening it, "I got this."

"What?" Jackie asked.

Mark pulled the pack open. Jammed inside, so tight that she couldn't see how he had gotten it in there, was a styrofoam cooler. Inside was an ice-cold six pack of Coke, the ice still rattling.

"Hey, that's great!" she said, impulsively putting her arms around him and giving him a quick kiss: number three, she counted in her mind.

"I was able to hitch a ride back," Mark said. "I wanted to get beer, but you can't on Sunday mornings."

"A beer would be nice," Jackie said, reaching into the cold water, pulling out one of the Cokes and opening it in one quick move, "But this is perfect."

It was still early the next morning when Jackie, dressed in blouse and cutoffs finished her coffee, picked up her pack with the now-empty styrofoam cooler and a small collection of both their dirty laundry stuffed inside, and started for the highway.

As much as she had sex on her mind while Mark had been gone yesterday, the afternoon and evening had been very low-key by comparison. She'd posed for another couple of drawings, that still came out making her more beautiful than she felt, but she was glad of the compliment. It turned out that he'd bought a book, but rather than curling up with it, suggested that they read it to each other. It turned out to be a good book, "Pilgrim at Tinker Creek" by Annie Dillard, and it led to a lot of discussion and not much reading. Still, it was nice to lay in the shade, with her head on his stomach, and read about life and nature along a mountain stream. They hadn't made it through the book, not by a long shot, and it looked like it would provide several interesting afternoons to come. She'd laid out in the sun a bit, too -- although not naked, like she had been earlier. In the evening, they'd looked through the telescope some more, and had built a little fire out of dead brush and driftwood. It had been an idyllic day, one to remember as she started out across the causeway.

She was used to walking, and liked it, although not in the extreme heat they had endured Saturday. Her long legs carried her along rapidly, although the causeway seemed to stretch out endlessly. She resolved to stop and take a break somewhere along the way, but never felt quite like stopping, so she made good time across the causeway and turned to follow the highway into town.

As luck would have it, she did not have to go far towards the center of town before she found a doctor's office: the highest priority item on her mental shopping list, the one she hadn't revealed to Mark. The office wasn't open yet, a sign said, although it would be soon; she sat down to wait.

It was more than a little embarrassing to explain to both the receptionist and then the doctor why she had come, but she was hardly the first girl that the doctor had met who had her request. After a brief examination and history, she was given a prescription for six months worth of birth control pills, and told of a drug store at a shopping center a half a mile up the road.

With thanks that her stop at the doctor hadn't been worse, Jackie set out up the road to the shopping center. The druggist, fortunately, was a woman, and didn't have any smart remarks; Jackie stuffed the little oblong boxes into the side pocket of her pack, and resolved to keep them a secret from Mark. Still embarrassed, and glad no one knew her, she bought some condoms at the drug store, too, since the doctor had told her it would be a while before the pills took effect.

There was a clothing store a couple of doors up from the drug store, and Jackie went there, next. She quickly picked out another pair of shorts, and a couple of t-shirts, one of them reading "Cape Kennedy, Florida -- America's Spaceport", the other one plain white. Then, she went looking for swimsuits.

With her long torso and slender build, Jackie was hard to fit for a one-piece swimsuit, which was what she really wanted, partly because it was what she was used to, and partly because it might not be so suggestive. She didn't see anything that she liked that showed a chance of fitting. Finally, a short, heavy-set salesgirl with a thick southern accent told her, "You ought to try a bikini. You really have the build for one."

"You think so?" Jackie said. "I'm too thin for one."

"Nonsense," the girl said. "I wish I could wear one, but I'm too heavy. Now, you have the perfect build for a bikini, and since you're so hard to fit for a one-piece, you really ought to try one."

It finally came down to a choice between a green terry-cloth bikini, held together with plastic rings at the hips and between the breasts, and a nylon number with a brown and gray paisley type print; it seemed even scantier than the green one. "Which one do you like?" she asked the salesgirl.

"I think I like the brown one," the girl said. "I think it would be a little sexier on you. Besides, the nylon will dry out in about fifteen seconds, while the terry-cloth one will take all day. I don't like laying around in a wet swimsuit."

The salesgirl's argument made sense; Jackie decided to take the brown and gray one, but wondered if she'd have the courage to wear it in front of Mark. At least it was lightweight, and the top could double as a halter top. Maybe when they were backpacking, the bottom could double as a spare pair of panties, too, she realized.

With that under control, she put her purchases in the pack and headed back toward the causeway. She had seen a convenience store not far from the corner, and decided to tank up the water jugs and get some cold beer there; there was no point in carrying the weight an inch farther than necessary.

She stopped at the store, bought a candy bar and surveyed the magazine rack, but didn't see anything she really wanted to buy. She bought some food and ice and beer and filled the jugs, then realized that she was going to have to walk with the load back across the causeway in the warming morning. The load would be at least as heavy as the load she'd packed over the causeway the first time. It would be hot when she got back; she didn't look forward to carrying the load, and wished that she dared hitchhike, as Mark had done the day before.

As she walked out of the store, a short, blonde girl about her age left a taller man beside a car with a home state license plate. Seeing the plate, so far away from home, made Jackie feel a little less far from home. "Hi, neighbor," she said, slinging her pack.

The girl came up to her. "Hi," she said. "Are you camping around here?"

"Over on the other side of the causeway," Jackie told her.

"Is your campground full?" the girl asked. "The woman inside said she doesn't know much about the campgrounds around here, and my husband and I are looking for a place to camp until the launch."

"We're not in a campground," Jackie told her. "My boyfriend and I are just tenting out in the scrub, just at the other end of the causeway. There's no johns or anything, but there's plenty of room."

The girl's husband came over and joined them. "All the campgrounds for miles around are full, and they aren't crazy about people tenting, anyway. They'd rather rent a site to someone with a motor home forty feet long."

"Well," Jackie said, "You're welcome to camp over around us, somewhere. I guess it's OK; we never asked. We just walked in off of the road a ways.

"Where'd you leave your car?"

"Didn't bring a car," Jackie said. "We flew in, and backpacked the rest of the way."

"You're walking?" the girl asked. "We'll give you a ride."

Jackie's new friends proved to be Roger and Kathy Griswold, from Arvada Center, perhaps a hundred and fifty miles south of Spearfish Lake; Jackie could remember flying over the little crossroads town while she had been following where she and Mark were going, their first day out of Spearfish Lake.

It only took a few minutes to get back across the causeway. A hundred yards past the little path into their campsite, Roger found a little-used two-rut path out into the brush, that stopped after a short ways. Probably a place where kids went to park and make out, Jackie realized, but a perfect place to leave the car where it wouldn't be noticed.

She lead the hometown couple into their camp, where Mark was standing, shaving, wearing a t-shirt and a swimsuit he'd bought the day before. "I brought us some company," Jackie told him.

"I didn't expect we'd be out here by ourselves forever," Mark said.

"This is Roger and Kathy Griswold," Jackie said, making introductions. "And this is my boyfriend, Mark."

"You like some coffee?" Mark said. "The water's hot."

They had to scramble to come up with four cups -- Jackie wound up drinking coffee out of a small cookpot as they sat and got to know each other. "I take it you're down here to see the launch, too," Roger said. "I've never seen one. It ought to be great, but as soon as we see it, we're about going to have to be getting home."

"Vacation's about over, huh?" Mark asked.

"No," Roger said. "I'm a farmer. I work about 800 acres of grain and dairy cattle with my dad."

"Seems like it's getting time to start plowing," Jackie commented.

"Well, normally it would be," Roger said. "But it's been kind of cold and wet, and when I talked to my dad a couple of days ago, he said we might as well stay over an extra week, since we're on our honeymoon and all."

Mark shrugged. "I guess, being a farmer, that June wouldn't exactly be the prime time for a honeymoon."

Roger snickered a little; Kathy set down her coffee cup and blushed. "Let's just say that our wedding was a little unplanned. I mean, we sorta had to get married," she finally stammered.

"We were going to get married anyway," Roger said, just a little shyly. "But it didn't quite come off like we'd planned. But, I think it'll work out for the best."

Mark looked at Jackie, who looked back at him, just as hard. Not a word was exchanged, but their faces carried all the communication they needed. Jackie was very relieved at her stop at the doctor's and her purchase at the pharmacy earlier that morning. "If that's what you think, then that's all that matters, I guess," Mark said diplomatically.

Now it was Roger's turn to blush a little. "It's just that this sort of thing isn't supposed to happen to Methodists."

"But it did," Kathy added. "It ought to work out in time, though."

Mark shook his head. "The best thing is to not let it bother you. If you want to camp here, let's finish our coffee and Jackie and I will help you unload. There's a nice little spot to camp around the bay a bit."

Camping out of their car Roger and Kathy had quite a bit more gear than the backpacking Mark and Jackie, and several trips were required through the brush to the little campsite fifty or so yards away. They had a large umbrella tent, and heavier sleeping bags, a cooler and a camp stove, another sun fly, and even a table that cunningly unfolded to seat four in only moderate discomfort. The day was warm by the time the Griswold's camp was set up. "You guys like a cold beer?" Roger asked.

"Love one," both Jackie and Mark chorused. The four of them sat down under the Griswold's sun fly and talked about their travels. It was clear that Roger and Kathy had tried to see everything there was to see in Florida in two weeks. The Griswolds, however, were fascinated by Mark and Jackie's trip. "I'm tired of traveling after two weeks," Kathy said. "I'm just looking forward to staying in the same place for a few days. I can't imagine being gone all summer, or even longer."

"Well, we're still getting used to it," Jackie said, sipping at her beer.

"You rebuilt this airplane of yours?" Roger asked.

"We rebuilt it, Jackie and I," Mark said. "In fact, we only finished it a week ago today."

"It does not seem that long," Jackie said. "It seems like it must have been a year."

"I just think you guys are going to have a wonderful time," Kathy said. "Me, I'm about ready for a swim. Is that beach any good?"

"I've only been out about waist deep, earlier this morning," Mark said, "But the bottom is pretty solid. You mind if we join you two?"

"Sure, come on," Roger said. "We'll get changed and meet you down there."

Mark drained his beer, but Jackie took another sip and brought the can with her. They walked around the hummock where the telescope sat, and down to their tent.

As soon as they were out of earshot of the Griswolds, Jackie said in a low voice, "Do you get the feeling of 'There but for the grace of God, et cetra'?"

"I don't know," Mark told her. "They obviously fit together pretty well. It might not be all bad. I've only got one question."

"What's that?"

"What happened to our brother and sister act?"

"I don't know," Jackie said. "I guess I'd just be more ashamed of lying than I am of the truth."

Since Mark already had his swimsuit on, he waited outside while she changed. She hadn't confronted the thought of actually having to wear the gray and brown bikini in front of Mark, yet, although she knew that sooner or later she would. Wearing it in front of total strangers made her want to hesitate even more, although there wasn't a lot of choice, now. She wiggled out of her clothes and pulled the tiny pieces of fabric on; there seemed to be very little cloth and an awful lot of her. She hesitated at the tent flap, a little scared to be seen as nearly undressed as she was. She was going to be so embarrassed . . .

She heard Kathy's voice float up from the water: "Are you guys coming?"

"Be right with you," Mark called back.

There was no putting it off. Mark would have to see her dressed like she was. For an instant, she thought of pulling on a T-shirt, but knew that only put off what was to come; then, she threw back the tent flap, crawled outside, and stood up.

Mark let out a low whistle. "Wow," he said. "You look great. You make me proud you're my girlfriend."

Having faced up to the inevitable, Jackie turned around so he could get a better view. "You like it?" she asked.

"No," he said. "I love it. Let's get down to the beach."

Before she could have any more second thoughts, he took her by the hand, and together they walked down to where Roger and Kathy waited.

The other couple was already frolicking in the water when Mark and Jackie arrived. It hadn't been quite clear before, but now they could see that Roger, though shorter than Mark, was considerably more muscled; with his hat off, they could see that he was already starting to go bald. Kathy probably weighed about what Jackie did, but that weight was packed into a frame that was nearly a foot shorter; she was a lot more rounded out than Jackie, and perhaps even a little heavy for her red and white bikini that was scanty even by Florida standards.

The next half hour was rambunctious; there was a lot of splashing and yelling and horseplay, but very little swimming actually went on. Jackie didn't have much time to feel self-conscious about wearing her new bikini; she was having too much fun playing in the sun and the water with Mark and their new-found friends.

After a while, the four of them wound up laying on towels on the shoreline, talking and letting the sun and the air dry them off. "This is such a great spot," Kathy gushed. "Jackie, I'm glad we met you. This is the best time I've had on this trip."

"You mean we haven't had other great times?" Roger said, joking.

"This whole trip has been wonderful, you big old dog, you," the little blonde said, rolling on her side to face her husband.

"That's more like it," he said, rolling over to face his wife. Mark and Jackie could see the other couple's arms around each other, with some heavy-duty kissing going on as two pairs of hands wandered over their partner's bodies nearly oblivious of the watching eyes.

"I'm glad you brought them," Mark whispered to Jackie, laying close beside him. "They've been fun."

Jackie rolled up on her side, mostly to look at Mark, but she couldn't help but see the scene a few feet away. She could see Roger's hands untie the back string of Kathy's bikini, and could not help but wonder how it would feel to have Mark's arms around her like that. "They seem to be enjoying themselves," she whispered back, then rolled over farther to kiss him.

In but an instant, she felt Mark's arms enfold her, and her arms went around him. She could feel the roughness of the sand sticking to his arms as they pressed on her skin, laid bare by the bikini, and could feel his hands as they groped up and down her body, and everything felt wonderful. Somewhere in there, she could feel Mark's hand on her breast, and she didn't flinch, like she had when Hjalmer had brushed her there; his touch felt warm and glowing, and she arched her back to draw herself closer to him.

How long they lay there, kissing and groping and nuzzling, they never knew. It seemed like an instant, and it seemed like forever, and neither of them wanted it to stop.

Looking over Mark's shoulder, Jackie could see Roger and Kathy get up. "Look," she whispered to her boyfriend.

Mark rolled over and broke contact to look over his shoulder, to see their friends scamper up the path to their tent, arm in arm; Kathy was carrying her bikini top in her hand. He rolled back over to face Jackie and whispered, "Now, is that inspiring, or what?"

Jackie pulled him tight and kissed him again. They kissed for a long time before she whispered in his ear, "Do you want to go up to the tent?"

Mark kissed her briefly and whispered back, "Do you really want to?"

Jackie pulled him tight, and was silent for a moment. "I guess not," she said, "But I'm willing to if you want to."

They pulled each other tight and held on for a while before he whispered back, "When you're ready, I'm ready." And he was ready, painfully so. "But if you're not ready," he continued, "Then I'm not."

"I want to say yes so bad it hurts," Jackie said, a tear coming to her eye. "But I don't think we should." Mark held her tight; she could feel his strong arms around her bare body. She stayed silent for quite a while, just trying to draw herself closer and convince herself she had made the right decision. "I mean, she's married and she's already pregnant."

"It's not like it's the same thing," Mark whispered back.

Jackie was crying a little more, now, and Mark could feel it. "She was pregnant before she got married, and I don't want that to happen to us," Jackie said. "I don't want to get pregnant and have you feel that you have to marry me."

"It seems like it worked out for them," Mark said quietly, "But I guess you're right. Maybe we'd better quit this and go get dressed."

"That's not it," Jackie said. "I don't ever want to have a baby and have it risk what happened to my mother happen to me." Jackie was quiet for a little longer. Mark could hear her sob a little, and then say, "Can we just lay here and hold on to each other?"

"Of course," Mark said, pulling her to him even more closely, and she held on as if the whole world would come apart if she let go.

Neither of them knew how long it was that they lay there, holding on to each other and kissing, but after a while, Jackie was able to realize just how much she enjoyed holding on to Mark, and having him hold on to her. There came a time that she was able to just rest her head on Mark's shoulder and enjoy the closeness. "Mark," she said finally, "Would it offend you if I told you that I'm falling in love with you, and I just don't know how to handle it?"

"Would it offend you if I told you the same thing?" he murmured.

"I mean it," she said, rolling onto her back, but keeping her head on his shoulder. "You've been so incredibly kind and understanding to me, and I just don't know what I should do."

"Well, just realize that I'm falling in love with you, too, and I don't know how to handle it," he said. "But I keep being afraid that I'll make the wrong move and blow it, and I don't want to."

"That's just it," Jackie said. "You're such a nice guy, I'm not sure that you should be falling in love with me. You could be letting yourself in for something neither of us can handle. I've had to live with it, but I don't know if I should ask you to live with the risk, too." She sat up, and looked at him. "I meant what I said about not daring to have a baby. I know I can't ask a child to live with the risk."

"Well, I can concede you that," Mark said, a smile that was inexplicable to Jackie growing on his face. "To be perfectly truthful, I haven't thought about it, but I'm not too crazy about kids, anyway. I mean, I was never very happy with myself as a kid. All I ever wanted to do was to grow up so I could get away from kids."

"I guess you're right. I mean, I've spent a lot of time with Johnnie, and I know what a pain he can be. It's almost like I've had a kid of my own, and why bother? But that's not the point, and you know it."

"Jackie," he said, "There's a risk that you'll get smacked by a drunken driver the next time you walk across the causeway. Or chomped up by an alligator the next time you go swimming. We have to live with risks. These things happen. I guess all I can say is that I can risk it with you, if you can risk it with me. I'm falling in love with you, and that's worth a fair amount of risk."

"I'm falling in love with you, too," she said. "And, I think we'd better go up to the tent and get a beer and relax, or we're going to have to go up to the tent and go inside."

"I'd just as soon lay here and look at you," Mark smiled. "If we go up to the tent, you're going to have to put your top on."

Jackie blushed and looked down at herself. Sure enough, her bikini top was laying in the sand; it had to have come off a long time before. No wonder Mark's hand had felt so warm on her breast!

She took the top in one hand, and pulled him into a sitting position with the other. "Let's go get that beer," she said. "At least you told me before Roger and Kathy got back down here."

3.

Jackie didn't get her top back on until after the beer had been opened, just to tease Mark for not telling her about it. "Well, it is a very nice view," Mark told her.

"I'm not that well built, and you know it," Jackie protested. "Now, Kathy, she's got a nice chest."

"She's got a nice chest, I admit," Mark said. "That bikini of hers shows it off real well. But I think yours is prettier, because I think you're a prettier woman."

"I still don't think I'm as pretty as you say I am," she told him, shaking the sand out of her top and taking another sip of her beer.

"And I still don't think that you realize how pretty you are," he said.

"Kathy's pretty," Jackie told him as she started to tie the top back on. "I'm not as good-looking as she is."

"Kathy's pretty, for a short woman," Mark agreed. "But you're prettier than she is, and taller, which make it even better. Don't argue with my taste, Jackie; I know what I like."

Jackie could not have had her top back on for more than a minute when they heard a voice from down at the beach: "Well, so that's where you went to."

They looked up; Kathy and Roger were walking toward them, hand in hand, each carrying a beer. They'd managed to get their swimsuits back on, but they had very satisfied looks on their faces. "Sorry we had to run out on you," Kathy smiled, with perhaps just the faintest trace of a blush on her face. "But we had some important business to attend to."

"Yeah," Roger said with just a trace of embarrassment as they walked toward Mark and Jackie, "You know how it is, I guess."

"When you gotta go," Mark smirked, "You gotta go."

"We came over to offer you a beer," Kathy said, and to see if maybe you wanted to get together for lunch."

"We don't usually have much of a lunch," Jackie said. "Maybe a sandwich or something. When you're backpacking, that's something you have to put up with."

"Well, come on over," Kathy told them. "We've got lunch meat and chips and like that."

No one quite remembered how the suggestion arose over lunch at the Griswold's camp, but it was a quick and unanimous decision for Roger and Mark to drive back across the causeway that afternoon and buy some charcoal and steaks for their supper. It took a while for the men to get around to leaving, as the four found they enjoyed sitting around the little table in the shade, just talking about whatever happened to come up.

In an era where four young people, ranging in ages from nineteen to twenty-four, sitting around in a lonely campsite could be expected to be passing around a joint or something stronger, these were not that kind of young people. The strongest drug passed around was a few cans of Budweiser, and that not enough to much more than cool off. Roger and Mark and Jackie and Kathy were pretty straight midwestern country people. Though Mark and Jackie were a bit less churchy than the Griswolds, the four had a lot in common, and before the men started for town to get steaks and bread and charcoal and more beer and pop, they found they'd become fast friends.

After the men left, Jackie and Kathy continued to sit in the camp and talk. "You know," Kathy finally said, "We're sitting here in the shade, when we could be out in the sun, working on our tans."

They found their towels, and spread out on the sunward slope of the hummock between the camps, on Mark and Jackie's side. They oiled themselves up and lay out to bake, still talking. Jackie knew that she would like to ask Kathy what it was like to be with Roger, what it was really like, but she knew she'd be to embarrassed to ask. Somehow, though, Kathy got to telling how she'd been engaged to Roger, and that they'd found themselves in the back seat of his car one night after choir practice, and things sort of happened. She had been shocked to realize that she was pregnant, but, as it turned out, not unhappy, either.

Their honeymoon had gone well, all in all. "It's like this bikini," she said. "I mean, I kind of got it for Roger to enjoy, since there's no way I'd ever wear anything like this around home, but he likes it, and there won't be much more time for me to wear it. So I better get the best use out of it while I can."

"It really makes you look sexy," Jackie assured her "But I know what you mean. "There's no way I would have worn something like this around Spearfish Lake, either." Feeling hot on one side, Jackie rolled over onto her belly.

Kathy did the same, reaching up and untying the strings of her bikini top. "Oh, I'm really a little heavy for it," Kathy protested. "I pop out all over. Now, you have got the build for a bikini like you've got. I'd really love to be tall and slender and sexy, and be able to look like you do."

"I don't know," Jackie said, deciding to untie the strings of her top, as well. "I think sometimes that I'm too tall."

"If I were as tall as you," Kathy said, "I think I'd wear high heels, just to make me feel even taller. But then, I've always been so short and dumpy that I'm surprised Roger ever took a second look at me."

While Jackie tried to hold up her end of the conversation, there was a lot of food for thought in Kathy's remarks. All her life, Jackie had envied short girls, normal girls; she had never dreamed that they had envied her, too! And, apparently, Mark wasn't just pulling her leg when he said that she was pretty, too; Kathy evidently thought so.

"Well, I think that you've got a great guy, there," Jackie said. "You were lucky."

"Well, I think you've got a pretty nice guy, too," Kathy told her.

They lay talking for a while longer. "You know," Jackie remarked, "I'm starting to wonder where the guys are."

"Kathy, cock your leg back up the way you had it," they heard Mark's voice say.

Both of them looked back over their shoulders, to see Mark sitting in the shade of the sun fly, drawing pad in hand, with Roger looking over his shoulder. "What the heck?" Kathy asked.

"We've just been volunteered to be models," Jackie told her new friend. "Prepare to become a sex object."

Kathy smiled, lifted her leg back up, and turned back to Jackie, "As long as it's Roger that's involved, I don't mind being a sex object. I kind of like it, in fact." She raised her voice and said, "Draw me pretty, Mark!"

"That shouldn't be any trick," Jackie said. "He always draws me prettier than I am, too."

"That's not true, and you know it," Mark said, not looking up from the pad where the drawing was rapidly taking shape; he'd already had a good start before the girls noticed their return.

"Did you get the steaks?" Kathy asked.

"Steaks and a lot of other good stuff," Roger said, fascinated at the drawing that was being created in front of him. "I don't know how you do it," he said to Mark, much more quietly. "I wish I had talent like that."

They picked up their conversation, while Mark continued to draw. Presently, Kathy began to feel her back beginning to feel a bit hot. "Can we roll over, now?"

Roger thought the chance was too good to miss. "Only if you don't put your tops back on," he told the girls.

A smirk came over Kathy's face. She whispered to Jackie, "I'll do it if you will."

"I'd do it if it was just Mark," Jackie told her. "I don't think I should do it in front of your husband."

"Yeah," Kathy sighed. "I guess I'm not ready for group sex, either."

"Just stay there another couple of minutes," Mark said. "There's some shadows I haven't got quite right. One of the things I want to do on this trip is to collect drawing and photos and watercolors that I can turn into paintings over the next few years, and this will make a good one."

"I hadn't realized you were an artist, too," Kathy said.

"I play with it," Mark said. "It's just something to do for fun. I plan to make a living as a telephone repairman, not an artist."

"When you get around to painting that picture," Roger said, pointing at the drawing Mark was still detailing, "Would you sell it to me?"

"If you want," Mark told him. "Just bear in mind that it may take me years to get around to it."

"I can wait," Roger replied.

"Actually, what we should do," Mark conceptualized, "Is work up a different rough, if we're going to do that. Jackie and Kathy need to change places, so Jackie would be the one with the back of her head to us. What probably would be even better would be something of Kathy, in a nice, planned pose."

"That'd make quite a souvenir of our honeymoon," Kathy said.

"There's no reason we can't do it," Mark said, then sketched for another couple of minutes. "I'm pretty well done," he told the women finally. "Get up if you want to."

Both of the women got up to go over and see what the drawing looked like. It was highly detailed, even though he was still working on it. Kathy was in the foreground, one ankle up in the air, with the back of her head showing as she talked to Jackie, who was more in profile. "That really does look like you, Jackie," Kathy commented, "But I think your boyfriend got me a little better-looking than I am."

"I don't think it looks like me at all," Jackie said. "I'm not that pretty."

"I'm tired of hearing that from you, Jackie," Mark said. "Now, you've got Kathy doing it, too. What do you think, Roger?"

"You can't really tell about Kathy with the back of her head showing like that," Roger said, "Although it does look like her body. But there's no doubt, that's Jackie."

"You know," Mark told Roger thoughtfully, "Now that I've got both of these women accusing me of dolling them up in these pictures, I ought to do one of them and really doll it up, just to prove I'm not bullshitting them."

"What do you mean?" Kathy smiled.

"Oh, something in a planned pose, something that's deliberately exaggerated," Mark said.

"I'm game," Kathy told him. "Just give me a few minutes to go potty, lay on another coat of suntan oil, and get another beer. How about you, Jackie?"

"I still think he's bullshitting me," she said. "I'd like to see what he thinks is exaggerated."

A few minutes later, Mark deliberately posed the two women. Again, Kathy was the closer of the two, but she was now sitting upright, hands in the sand behind her, with one leg drawn up. Jackie sat on one leg on the far side of Kathy, one leg sprawled out, supporting herself lightly on one arm. "Is that comfortable enough for you two to stay like that for a while?" Mark asked.

"It'll do," Jackie said, "But I'm going to get stiff, after a while."

Mark nodded. "We can take breaks, if we need to, but I'm going to work a little more quickly on this. After all, I'm just doing this to make a point." He went back into the sunshade, picked up his pad, stared at the two of them for a moment, and started drawing.

The two girls fell to talking again, while Roger continued to look over Mark's shoulder as he worked. Since both Kathy and Jackie were looking right at the men, they both noticed a few minutes later when Roger shook his head and looked up at them, and muttered, "My God, I see what you mean."

With a big smile, Mark asked, "How'd you like to have a painting of this one hanging over your fireplace?"

"We'd have the Methodist Men's Club meeting there every week, for sure," Roger laughed.

"Jeez," Kathy said in a voice low enough that only Jackie, behind her, could hear. "I wonder what he's doing to us?"

"Are you real sure that you want to find out?" Jackie whispered back.

"I'm not sure I'd want this painting hanging over my fireplace or not," Kathy told her. "But I am looking forward to finding out what it looks like."

"Hold still and be quiet, you two," Mark said. "I'm trying to work on your faces."

The four of them were quiet for the next few minutes while Mark worked. After a while, he told them they could talk again, but to keep holding still. He worked for a few minutes more, then said, "It would be possible to work on the detail more, but I think that's enough to make my point. What do you think, Roger?"

"Let's face it," he said. "That is the stuff dreams are made of."

"I've had a few dreams like that myself," Mark said.

"I'm kind of glad they don't look like that," the shorter man said. "I'd hate to spend my life with a baseball bat beating men off of my wife."

"Are you going to let us see this?" Kathy asked.

"I'm not sure you should," Roger told her.

With that, both the women had to get up and take a look. "Holy mackerel," Kathy commented. "I know I don't look like that. I just wish I did."

Jackie looked at the drawing. Both girls were still recognizably Kathy and herself, but much more sensuous. She was still tall, but a lot fuller in the chest, thinner at the waist and more rounded at the hips. In the drawing, her long hair, twice its real length, cascaded over her bare shoulder and down onto the ground. Her shoulder wasn't the only thing that was bare; in the drawing, both she and

Kathy were nude, and the only thing that kept the drawing of Jackie from being a full frontal was the strategic placement of Kathy's knee. Kathy was a little taller, a little thinner, and even more voluptuous. Her face was a little thinner, as well, and her blonde hair was much longer. "You've got to admit, that doesn't look like me," Jackie said.

"Actually, it's not that far off," Mark said. "Compare it with some of the other drawings I've done of you, and you'll realize I haven't exaggerated that much. Granted, I had to use my imagination to fill in a few details, but it's easy when you've got a couple of very sexy women to start with."

"Wow," Kathy said, shaking her head. "It's neat to even think of looking like that, but I've got to admit, I don't think I'd like to have a painting of that hanging over the fireplace for the Methodist Men's Club to leer at."

Roger broke out laughing. "Can't you just imagine the gossip if that painting were to show up in the Methodist Women's Rummage Sale?"

"I don't think Spearfish Lake would be far enough away to move," Kathy replied, laughing herself. "Maybe Argentina would be. I'd love for you to do a painting of me, Mark, but please, not that one. Something maybe just a touch more conservative, please."

Mark shook his head. "I'd be glad to," he told the blonde woman. "But not today. You've been out in the sun long enough today as it is, and we need to start to think about cooking some steaks. Tomorrow, I'll do a couple of drawings and take some photos, so I can get the details and the colors right."

"Are you going to do a painting of me, too?" Jackie asked.

"No, Jackie," Mark said, closing the sketchbook and standing up to stretch. "I'm not going to do *A* painting of you. I'm going to do a *LOT* of paintings of you."

That evening, they grilled their steaks, and drank some beer, and talked some more. After it got dark, they climbed up onto the top of the hummock, uncovered the telescope, and looked at the Saturn V a few miles away, then looked at some of the things in the sky. Then they went down and threw some sticks and dry, dead brush onto the dying coals, and had a little campfire. Eventually, all admitted they were tired, and Mark and Jackie walked back to their own campsite.

It was cooling off enough for Jackie to put on her flannel pajamas again; Mark let her change inside the tent, while he changed outside. When she told him she was ready, Mark came inside, and lay down on his sleeping bag. She slid her sleeping bag and air mattress over next to him, lay down on it, and said, "I bet we get to sleep before they do,"

"No bet," Mark said. "I wouldn't be surprised if we wake up before they get to sleep. They're good people. I'm glad you met them."

"Yes," Jackie said. "This has been a wonderful day."

"Glad you enjoyed it," Mark told her. "Well, goodnight, Sis."

"Hey, I want a goodnight kiss."

"I thought we agreed we were going to keep that outside the tent."

"That was then," Jackie said. "Now, I want you to kiss me, and go to sleep in your arms. Nothing more than that, but I just want to hold you tight. I meant what I said about falling in love with you."

"I meant everything I said, too," he said, pulling her to him. "When you're ready, I'm ready. I can wait until then."

There really wasn't anything to say after that. They kissed, and held each other tight, and kissed again, and eventually both of them fell asleep.

It would be possible to detail the next day that Mark and Jackie and Roger and Kathy spent together, but it really isn't necessary. They spent most of the day together, swimming, watching the black skimmers drag their bills in the water hunting for food, and just laying in the sun. Mark and Roger drove over to the airport to get Jackie's fishing pole and his water colors; while they were gone, Jackie and Kathy, feeling very daring, took the opportunity to sunbathe in the nude. After the men got back, Jackie took the opportunity to cast a spoon out into the shallows a few times, but caught nothing. Over the course of the day, they all had a couple of beers. Mark did several drawings of Kathy, and shot up a long roll of film with photos of Kathy, Roger, and Jackie; they even took a few pictures of him, for good measure. In the evening, they grilled pork chops, and looked at the stars, and had a campfire.

It was an absolutely idyllic day, and the next day was pretty much the same, although by afternoon they were no longer alone. People had begun to line their cars up alongside the road, waiting for the launch of Apollo 15, and there were other campers about, though none of them close by. About the only thing that changed was that Kathy and Jackie didn't dare to sunbathe in the nude again. By late afternoon, though, the anticipation of the launch was growing in them, and they started to get excited.

The morning of the launch of Apollo 15 dawned bright and clear, and the four were up with the dawn. By then, it had gotten crowded out on the highway, and even back in the brush a bit. The four took a camp stove up on top of the hill to brew coffee, and took turns looking at the Apollo in the telescope. The service gantry had been pulled back, and now they could see the white tower sticking high into the blue Florida dawn. Roger had a portable radio, and they tuned in a local radio station that gave them the play-by-play of the launch preparations.

The hours and minutes drug by as they approached 9:38, the planned time of the launch. The radio told them that everything was going according to schedule; there had been no holds or other delays. By about ten minutes before launch, even this far away the crowd had become tense and quiet.

Next to the telescope, Roger called the four together. "I'd like us to join hands and pray," he said. None of the others had any objection, and they clustered together, hand in hand, as Roger bowed his head and said, "Lord, we just ask for you to lay your guiding hand over this flight and these astronauts, and help them and all of the support people to accomplish their mission safely and successfully. Amen."

A chorus of "Amens" followed Roger's words.

"I've always wanted to see one of these," Jackie said quietly to Mark, standing next to the telescope. Mark had put the lowest power eyepiece in the telescope, and told Jackie to use it. He would use the finder, from the other side of the telescope. Jackie had loaned her backpacking binoculars to Kathy, and Roger would use his own.

With greater tension, the minutes drug past, the radio marking time. When it said, "Thirty seconds to ignition," Jackie bent over the telescope to get one last look at the rocket before it launched. It almost filled the field of view of the telescope, and she could see the tendrils of steam coming off of it from the evaporation of the liquid oxygen and the liquid hydrogen, and the frost glistening on the rocket. "Fifteen seconds," the radio said. "Fourteen . . . thirteen . . . twelve . . . eleven . . . ten . . . ignition sequence start . . ."

Hunched over the telescope and looking through binoculars, all of them could see the flash of light under the rocket as the five huge main engines lit off, and the billowing cloud of smoke that soon obscured the Saturn V. With the closest view, Jackie soon couldn't see the rocket in the eyepiece, and looked up for an instant to see what was happening with her naked eye. "Three . . . two . . . one . . . liftoff, we have liftoff at 38 minutes past the hour."

With stunning grace, though silently at such a distance, the towering white vehicle began to lift gracefully toward the blue sky. "Burn, baby, burn!" Mark yelled his encouragement. Mark twisted the telescope a little to follow its ascent in the finder, and Jackie followed along looking through the main eyepiece.

The Saturn was noticeably smaller in the eyepiece, although its engines were still bright, when the sound hit them. It rolled over them, an enormous popping roar, almost deafening, awesome in its power. The sound shook the earth beneath their feet, making leaves and even branches shake. The sound rolled on and on, kept coming and coming. They'd all heard the sound on TV, but it was nothing like being there and feeling its power beat over their bodies.

Jackie looked up from the telescope again, to see the vehicle in the sky. It was a lot smaller now, hardly a dot in the sky, but leaving a huge smoke trail behind it. It was incredible that such a tiny object could make such a huge sound. Slowly, the sound began to die away, and they all followed the departing vehicle with their optics for a surprisingly long distance, long after the first stage had dropped away. With her eye to the telescope, Jackie could follow it the longest of all.

One by one, they stepped back, to see the smoke trail of the departed rocket still hanging in the sky.

"That was worth waiting for," Roger said.

"Yeah," Kathy agreed. "It was almost better than sex."

Is sex that good? Jackie wondered to herself, but didn't dare say. "It's like standing right next to the tracks when a multiple-unit hotshot freight blasts past," she said.

"Yeah," Mark agreed. "But we're five miles away! What must it be like to ride that thing?"

"Guess we'll never know," Jackie said.

"I know," Mark said. "I wanted to join the Air Force, become an astronaut, but these damn glasses . . . " his voice trailed off.

The crowd that had come for the launch left rapidly. By noon, they were just about alone in their beachfront camp, once again. After talking it over, they decided to spend one more night together, after which Roger and Kathy needed to be headed back to Arvada Center and the farm. Mark and Jackie were ready to be on their way, too.

It was another lazy afternoon, tempered with sadness that their idyllic few days were over. In the few days the four had spent together, they had become good friends. "When you two get back towards home, make sure you drop by and visit us," Kathy said.

"How do we find you," Mark asked.

"We're five miles east of Arvada Center, on the south side of the road," Roger told them. "The barn's got GRISWOLD on the roof in big letters. You can't miss it."

Jackie noted the information down, along with their address, on the steno notepad she had brought to make sort of a journal on, even though she hadn't made an entry up till then.

That evening, as they gathered around the telescope on top of the hummock, the looked at the thin crescent of rising moon. "They're out there, somewhere," Mark said. "We'd never pick them up, but they're out there."

"God go with them," Roger said.

They sat around the table at the Griswold camp the next morning, lingering over coffee, wishing this day didn't have to come. After a while, it was time to break camp. It did not take Mark and Jackie a long time to tear down their little camp and get their gear packed away; then, they helped their friends with their gear, and carried everything up to the car. It was jam-packed with the four of them and the gear in the car, but the ride wouldn't be a long one. "Let's stop and get another cup of coffee for the road," Roger suggested.

They found a little restaurant. Jackie knew that she had been gone from home more than a week, although it seemed like a year, and she tried to call home, but there was no answer. While the four sat and talked, she opened her steno pad and dashed off a quick letter home.

They sat and talked a while longer, wishing they didn't have to go, and finally, the Griswolds drove Mark and Jackie out to the airport. Mark checked out Rocinante, and gave first Kathy, then Roger, a ride around the airport and over their campsite in the little Cessna. Then he and Jackie packed their gear in the plane, and it was time to say goodbye. They hugged each other, and promised to write; then, there was nothing to do but to get in the plane and leave.

"They were neat people," Jackie said once they were out of sight of the airport. "I'm really going to miss them."

"I am, too," Mark told her. "But just keep thinking of all the neat people we're going to meet."

*   *   *

Titusville, Florida
April 16, 1971

Dear Dad and Sarah:
I tried to call you at home just now, but nobody answered the phone, so I thought I'd drop you a note.

Everything is fine. Mark and I met some great people from Arvada Center, and we watched the Apollo Launch together. The power you feel even from miles away is incredible. We all camped together on the beach for a few days, and had a lot of fun.

Daddy, it's been awful tempting to not be a good girl -- I'm finding that I like Mark even more than I realized. But I've been a good girl. I'm sorry I left so quickly, but it was a last minute decision. I really wasn't going to go until just a few minutes before we left, when I realized that I had to go or miss the chance forever. So far, I'm not sorry I've come with Mark, and I don't think I will be, so long as you will forgive me for the pain and the anger I'm sure I've caused.

I'll try to call again in a few days. Mark and I are heading down into the Everglades to do a little canoeing. After that, I don't know, but I guess we'll be heading west. Mark wants to be in west Texas by the middle of next month.

I love you,
Jackie

4.

Mark had offered to do the laundry this time, but Jackie had some shopping she wanted to do, so she gave Mark first dibs on the shower. In spite of the powerful humidity in the laundromat, the air conditioning made it comfortable, and the heat outside on this oppressive midday Monday almost gave her second thoughts.

Outside, the small south Florida town baked in the midday sun. In a way, it was a rather shabby little town, that could have used a bit more paint, a bit more grass, and a little less junk in the yards. The same could be said for many cities, including Spearfish Lake, but here there was a tropical languidness among the flat, swampy land and the palm and palmetto and sand that indicated that the mosquitoes could take it back at any moment.

Fortunately, there was a small clothing store not far from the laundromat that offered the potential for what Jackie needed: a different pair of pajamas. The flannel pajamas had proven to be much too much for sleeping in the tent in the Everglades the past three nights, she'd slept in her bikini, on top of her sleeping bag. It had been so uncomfortable that she'd thought about sleeping without even that on, but had realized that there was a limit to how far she wanted to push temptation.

Tonight, temptation was going to be pushed pretty hard, too; they had rented a motel room, partly for the shower, and partly for the color TV, so they could watch the astronauts on the moon.

The only bed in the room was a double bed. Mark had offered to unroll his sleeping bag and sleep on the floor, but without thinking, Jackie had said that it probably wouldn't be a lot different than sleeping next to each other in the tent. Only later did she realize that sleeping next to Mark in a bed, wearing only her underwear or her bikini was only going to make things more difficult. A lighter set of pajamas might offer a little more propriety, and might make things a little less difficult.

Back in the sleepwear department there was a pretty good selection, in spite of the small size of the store. Folks in these parts must do an awful lot of sleeping, she thought, but then it was kind of a sleepy town, anyway. She cast a long look at a transparent little "baby doll" outfit, realizing from the instant she saw it that the nightie quite clearly signaled "Take me off! Take me off!" She wondered what she would look like in it, and wondered what it would be like to have Mark take it off her -- some day. Not now, but some day. On the other hand . . .

She tore herself away from the naughty lingerie and found something a little more like what she was looking for: a loose lightweight cotton job, light green. The top had short sleeves, and was fairly long; it might even do for a top to wear during the day, if necessary. There were shorts that would reach halfway to her knees. It definitely wasn't a sexy outfit; it probably would do for what she wanted it for.

After another long, lingering, wondering look at the baby-doll that had caught her eye, she took the pajamas to the front of the store and paid for them.

The heat hit her like a brick again as she went outside; it was hard to endure. She still had only been gone from a Spearfish Lake winter for a week and a half, and she had never been able to handle heat and humidity well, anyway; much as she enjoyed the warm weather, she was a north county girl at heart. "How miserable it would be to live here," she thought.

While she had enjoyed the last three days of canoeing in the Everglades, it had also been pretty uncomfortable, hot and sticky and wet with sweat most of the time. While the mosquitoes weren't as voracious as they could get in the spring in the woods around Spearfish Lake, they were pretty bad.

While she sat in the laundromat and waited for the washer, then the dryer to finish their cycles, she let her mind unroll over their canoe trip.

There had been no one at the airport when they tied Rocinante down, and they had to hike into town. A man at a gas station had known of a place to rent a canoe, and even had been nice enough to drive them over to the livery. Both Jackie and Mark knew their way around canoes, and had even camped from them on several occasions, so it wasn't like they didn't know what they were doing -- but their previous experience had been on northern rivers, not in a southern swamp.

Fortunately, the Everglades are a national park, and some one in the National Park Service had the intelligence to realize that there were people that wanted to canoe in the place that didn't want to get lost in the almost featureless terrain. They had provided a marked canoe trail, and even raised, permanent tent sites at various places along the way.

Jackie had always been a girl that tanned easily, and she thought that all the time she had spent laying out in the sun over at Cape Canaveral should have made her burnproof. Even the layer of sunblock she had put on as a precaution didn't keep her from getting a touch of sunburn as she spent hours on end in the open, sitting on one of the seats of the canoe. She hadn't quite realized the effect that the sun bouncing off of the water would have. The only thing that kept her from getting a really bad burn was Mark's less burn resistant skin; he had really suffered. They had used up all the burn ointment in their little first aid kits, and they stopped fairly often to dose him again with sunblock. At that, he had to wear pants and a long-sleeved shirt to cut down on further damage, despite the heat, and partway through the first day Jackie decided to forego her bikini for her remaining pair of jeans and a T-shirt, in spite of the heat.

That had only made it even more uncomfortable and sweaty. They had tried to rinse some of the stink out of their clothes in the brackish water, with only limited success, and the humidity was so high that they had never really gotten dry again.

In spite of the discomfort and the sunburn, it had been an interesting trip. They met very few people, but there was so much to see! There was a wide variety of bird and animal life, and they spent a lot of time with Jackie's little backpacking binoculars, watching some of the exotic birds to be found. Mark had sketched some of the birds they saw, and they had agreed that a bird book was going to be high on their list of priorities of things to buy. They didn't push hard, at least partly because of the heat, but partly because they wanted to enjoy the ever-changing panoply of nature that unfolded before them.

They'd learned to travel only in the morning and the evening, and stay quiet in the shade during the worst of the midday sun. During their long nooning breaks, they did more birdwatching, fished a little, and read to each other. Mark worked with his sketchpad and occasionally took photos. In the loneliness of the place, with virtually nobody else around even on the marked canoe trail, Jackie considered posing topless or even nude for Mark, but never could quite bring herself to make the offer.

They had originally planned to spend a week or so out in the Everglades, on a long tour, but midway through the second day there came a good place to turn back and return to their starting place by a different route. They had both agreed it would be nice to get a motel room, a good shower, and watch the astronauts on the moon. It was not much of a decision to turn back, though they agreed that some other time it might be fun to try again.

With the laundry done, Jackie loaded it into her backpack and started off down the road toward the motel. She walked slowly in the heat, to try to avoid working up a sweat, but it was a long time before she made it back.

The motel was a grubby little mom-and-pop place that had seen better days, but it had the essentials that they required: a shower, a television, and a bed. Fortunately, the motel also had an air conditioner, and it was working mightily to remove the humidity from Mark's long shower when Jackie walked in the door. Mark was sitting on the bed in his underwear cutting his toenails.

"Here, put on some clean clothes," Jackie told him, opening her backpack.

Mark took the clothes she handed him, and joked, "I was beginning to wonder. I could see you leaving me here, with nothing to wear but a single pair of undershorts."

"Come on," Jackie said. "You know I wouldn't do that to you. Did you leave any hot water?"

"As far as I know," he replied. "I didn't have it cranked up real hot, but man, it felt good."

Jackie grabbed some clean clothes, headed for the bathroom, and stripped. It felt good to get out of the grubby cutoffs and T-shirt and underclothes. If she got a chance, they would be washed before she and Mark left town, and since it was a cheap motel room and the astronauts planned several EVAs, they would probably be a couple of days.

How wonderful it was to use a flush toilet -- the first time in a week or more. How wonderful the shower felt! In the ten days she had been with Mark, she had been swimming several times, and had sponged herself off on occasion, but nothing made her feel cleaner than a nice, hot shower. She gave her hair a good wash and let the stream of water soak away the grime of days. She felt like a new person when she finally got out of the shower, toweled herself dry, and pulled on clean jeans. She started to pull on a bra, but her shoulders still stung from the sunburn. She decided to experiment with going without one, and just made do with a T-shirt. Her hair hung wet around her shoulders, but it would dry soon.

She came back out into the main room as Mark was turning the TV off. "Did you find out what time the EVA is?" she asked.

"They didn't say a lot, but it looks like it'll be in about three hours," he replied. "It'll probably be a fairly long one, so we probably ought to think about getting something to eat before it starts."

"Can we wait an hour or so? I'd kind of like to let my hair dry out a little before we go out."

"Sure," he said. "No reason why not?"

"By the way," she asked, just a little curious, "I'm kind of wondering how you registered us here. Under both our names?

"No, 'Mark Gravengood, two in party'," he said. "The question of being married never came up. I've kind of got a feeling that this is the kind of place where they don't ask too many questions that they really don't want answered. You got anything you want to do while your hair is drying? Maybe read some more 'Tinker Creek'?"

"We could, I suppose," she said. "But when we came in here and I saw that phone, I realized I ought to try to call dad and Sarah. I don't want to, but I know I should at least try."

"Scared?"

Jackie hung her head and collapsed onto the bed beside him. "Petrified," she said quietly.

Mark reached out and pulled her to him. "It's not going to be easy, I know, but it'll get worse the longer you wait."

"God, I know that, Mark. What do I tell them? The truth? That despite my best efforts, I'm still a virgin?"

"That's not quite the truth, and you know it," he laughed despite himself.

"Still, I'd rather you didn't tell them that despite MY best efforts you're still a virgin."

Mark's attempt at a joke fell flat. She just shook her head, and he could see that she was trying not to cry. It would not do to have her calling home if she was unhappy or upset; he wouldn't let her until she felt better.

"I never told my folks that we were thinking about you coming along, either, and I never even left them a note," he said, far more serious now. "If they know you're with me, it's only because they heard about it from your dad or Sarah. I guess I have to wonder about what they think about it, too."

"It's a little different for you," Jackie said quietly. "You're a guy, and you were away for four years in the army."

"Yeah, I suppose it is," Mark said. "But, I suppose it could be worse, too. Think about Roger and Kathy."

Jackie looked up at him. "I don't quite follow you."

"It had to be tough for them. Remember what Roger said? 'Things like that aren't supposed to happen to Methodists'? They're pretty serious about their church, and I got the impression that their folks are even more serious. Don't you think it was tough for her to say, 'Hey, Mom, I'm pregnant!' It had to have been damned embarrassing, at best."

"She never talked about that, even when we were alone together," she said. "But I kind of got the impression that they had patched things up with their families. I'd bet they spent a long time on their knees, praying about it, before they told them."

"I'd bet you're right," he replied. "Would it make you feel any better if we prayed about it before we call your dad and Sarah, and my folks?"

"I don't know," she said, sitting up. "I don't think like that. I mean, I believe in God, and like that, but I've never been much of a church person. Dad kind of got mad at the church back home, back when I was little and mom got sent away. He said he didn't get any help from them, just whispers and hypocrisy and gossip, and we never went to church after that. I was real little, then, and I've never gotten in the habit."

"I know what you mean," he nodded. "My folks were never real serious church-goers, and they kind of dropped out of the church years ago, back when they got into that squabble over the nudist camp. You know, when the bank cut off the credit of the church members, because the bank president was the founder of the nudist camp. But looking at Roger and Kathy kind of makes me think that we're missing out on something."

"It could be," she said. "You usually think of church people being pretty dull and narrow-minded and straight. Somehow, Roger and Kathy, drinking beer and racing up to their tent every chance they got, just don't fit into that mold. Maybe they've got something there."

"Maybe we ought to stick our noses into a church now and then on this trip, just to give us something to think about."

She thought about it for a moment. "I've never even read the Bible much," she said finally. "What do you say that when we get done with 'Tinker Creek' that we get a Bible and read it the same way?"

"Let's just hold it to the New Testament," he said, noticing that her attitude had improved a lot in the last few minutes. "At least to start off with. What I remember from Vacation Bible School is that the Old Testament is a lot of begets and only a little good stuff. Do you still want to call your dad and Sarah?"

"I'm still not looking forward to it," she said, more soberly. "I mean, let's face it. No matter what we tell them, there's no way they're going to believe that we're not . . . oh, hell, I'll say it anyway, that we're not screwing ourselves silly every chance we get, like Roger and Kathy. I'm not sure I believe it myself."

"You're right," he nodded. "Under the circumstances, anybody would think that." He reached out and pulled her toward him again, to cuddle her close. "And, they would have a right to think that, no matter what the truth is."

"It might be easier if it was the truth."

He reached up with one hand to raise her head, so he could give her a kiss. As she pressed up against him, Mark realized all of a sudden that she wasn't wearing a bra under her T-shirt, and the realization filled him with excitement. Several times, now, they had been so close to tearing down this final barrier between them that some little shove, the right word or gesture on his part or hers would have resulted in making love. They had learned to live with the limits they had placed on themselves, even though both realized those limits were only temporary. Was this the time for that little word or gesture, perhaps a gentle touch of the breast that was burning him through the thin cotton of her T-shirt? Life with Jackie would be a lot simpler; there would be no more of this bottled-up tension, no more of having to juggle around simple things like changing clothes . . .

But somehow, this didn't quite seem like the right time. In the mood she was in, there wasn't much to keep her from picking up and going home. She could go home, let on that he had made a pass at her and she had fended it off, and retain most of her honor. There wasn't much he could do to stop it, and he'd have lost her forever -- but the longer she stayed with him, the less chance she would have to do it.

They kissed for a while, and she rested her head on his shoulder. "If there's anything I can do to make it right," he said softly, "Then I will. If it comes down to getting married, then it comes down to getting married. I'm game."

"I'm not ready to get married, yet," she said. "Not that I won't be ready to marry you some day, but not yet."

"I'm not ready, either," he admitted, "But I've come to realize that the possibility is there, and I've kind of come to look forward to it. I think you and I know each other well enough now to say that if we did decide to get married at the point we're at, we'd stand a good chance of having a pretty good marriage.

Knowing that, if getting married is what it takes, then I'm ready."

"But Mark, you know I like you an awful lot. I'm wondering if I like you so much that I'm not willing for you to take the risk of marrying me. My mother . . ."

"We've been over that," he interrupted. "It's a risk, I know, but it's one that I'll take if I have to. What you're saying is that you'd rather be married to someone who doesn't respect you, that beats the hell out of you every other day, just because you don't like him as much? Seems to me that would increase the risk of something happening to you, not lower it! Come on, Jackie, that doesn't make sense."

"I'm glad you feel that way," she smiled. "It's not going to come down to getting married just yet, I think, but it's nice to know you feel that way."

"I'm not saying we're going to get married," he said. "Although there's a good chance that it's going to happen. But, if we ultimately don't decide to get married, that shouldn't be the reason. Good enough for you?"

"Good enough for me," she smiled.

"Are you ready to call home, now?"

She nodded. "As ready as I'll ever be. I don't really want to do this, but I can't put it off much longer."

Jackie got up off the bed and went over to the phone, on the desk next to the television, dialed the operator, and placed a collect call to Spearfish Lake. When she heard her father's voice on the phone, she was seized with an almost overwhelming desire to hang up, but she swallowed and said, "Hi, dad."

"Jackie," his voice came over the line. "We got your letter today. How are you?"

"Just fine," she said. "A little sunburned from being out in the canoe too much, but otherwise, I'm just fine."

"How was the canoe trip?" he asked.

"A lot of fun," Jackie replied, a little surprised. She had expected her father to fly off the handle at the sound of her voice, but he seemed interested, and not angry. She relaxed visibly and told him, "We saw alligators, and all kinds of birds. That's really an interesting place. We wanted to spend more time out there, but we were both getting sunburned pretty bad."

"Is everything all right with you and Mark?"

"Couldn't be better," she told him. "Mark's been a perfect gentleman, and we've had a great time. How's Sarah?"

"She's been a little worried about you," Walt said. "Hell, I've been a little worried about you, too, but I was pretty sure you were in good hands and weren't likely to get into any real trouble. You haven't, have you?"

"Except for the sunburn, no," she said, "And Mark got it a lot worse than I did."

Across the room on the bed, Mark let out an inaudible sigh of relief. From the trend of the conversation -- and he was only hearing Jackie's end -- things were going a lot better than either he or Jackie had feared. He hadn't expected any real feedback from his family about taking Jackie with him, unless the Archers had made some waves; now, he looked forward to a conversation with them, this evening when they were both home from work.

Jackie and her father talked for about fifteen minutes, with Jackie bringing him up to date on all the highlights of the trip, never intimating that she or Mark had been anything but perfect little angels. She was much happier when she hung up the phone.

"Sounds like it went pretty good," he said.

She shook her head. "I think that he thinks that we're sleeping together, I mean, the way most people would say that. But, I think he's made up his mind to accept it, since what's done is done and there's not much he can do about it."

"Well, it's not like we didn't know that people were going to think what we'd expect them to think," Mark said. "Hell, even Roger and Kathy figured we were shacked up together, but they never said anything about it."

"They wouldn't have believed the truth, either," Jackie said, still smiling. "In fact, when you get right down to it, I'm not sure I would believe it, either."

Mark glanced at his watch. "Well, it's like this," he teased. "We could either make what everybody thinks that's happening really the truth, or we can go get something to eat. We could get either one done before the EVA comes on, but not both."

"Let me brush out my hair, and then we'll go eat," Jackie told him as she got up and went to her pack for her hairbrush, then replied with her own tease: "We've got time to eat, but if we get started on the other thing, we'll be all night and we won't get to watch the EVA or have anything to eat."

"That's what I like about you," he said, looking for his shoes. "Always practical. Always first things first."

They had to walk nearly half a mile to a little greasy-spoon restaurant that was open, and they only barely got back to the motel room in time for the start of the EVA of the Apollo 15 astronauts. It was a long one; the astronauts had taken the little moon-rover with them for the first time, and they were away from the lunar module for hours. It was very interesting for both of them to watch the astronauts explore the lunar surface, and see sights that had never been seen by man before; it excited them both to be part of the exploration.

They got so wrapped up in watching the TV that Mark never did get around to calling his parents that evening. After a while, Jackie went to the bathroom and put on her new pajamas, and joined Mark on the bed where they continued to watch the astronauts on the moon. Mark made no comment about the pajamas, and any thoughts of doing anything more than laying there half-upright, with her head resting on his shoulder were forgotten about. They talked very little, and then only about what was happening on television, but were satisfied to just cuddle with each other.

In spite of everything, after a while Jackie fell asleep, still with her head resting on Mark's shoulder. As she lay there softly breathing, Mark felt a great sense of contentment fall over him. Sex with Jackie would be nice, when the time came, he realized, but with her, he had achieved almost everything else that he'd craved, and more. She was a friend, a companion, someone to share experiences with. Feeling very daring, he let his hand come to rest on one of the sleeping girl's breasts. It felt soft and warm and comfortable, and he just let it stay there.

It wasn't like being with Mei-Ling, he realized. This was better. Sex could come in its own good time, but this was exactly what he wanted.

After a while, he fell asleep too, with the TV still on, his hand on her breast, and his head resting on hers.

* * *

Everglades City, Florida
April 20, 1971

Dear Dad and Sarah,
It was so good to talk to you yesterday, Dad. I'm just sorry that Sarah wasn't there. I would have liked to talk to her, too.

Last Friday, Mark expected that we'd be here long enough to get some of the pictures from Cape Canaveral developed, and we got them back today. I'm sorry that we didn't get any pictures of the Apollo going up, but we were too busy watching to take pictures, and really, we were so far away they probably wouldn't have looked like much. But I am going to include a picture of Roger and Kathy and Mark and me at our little camp near Titusville. We had a really good time with Roger and Kathy, and I hope we can see them again some day.

I already told you about our Everglades trip on the phone. We're going to stay where we're at today, so we can watch the astronauts on the moon again, then tomorrow we're going to be on our way. Mark says that there are a few other places he wants to see in Florida, but that they'll probably pretty much be one-day stops. I'll let you know the next time we're going to be in the same place for a few days, so you can send mail to us then.

I'm so happy that you weren't angry with me about my going off with Mark. I've tried to be a good girl and not do anything that you would be ashamed of, and Mark has made it easy for me. So far, we've had a lot of fun, and I like him a lot, too.

I'll write or call again in a few days. Say "Hi" to Johnnie for me.
I love you,
Jackie

5.

Mark didn't like the looks of the sky in front of them. "Better take it to the left a little," he told Jackie.

Obediently, Jackie banked Rocinante to the left a little, and settled down on a course that would take them closer to the shoreline of the Gulf of Mexico and one that would hopefully take them around the huge thunderhead that was building in front of them.

Mark had let Jackie handle the controls as far back as the trip back from Lordston. He'd noticed that she wasn't scared of handling the Stinson on that trip, and at the same time, she didn't have any tendency to overcontrol. Flying straight and level is the first thing that any student pilot learns, and it can be one of the more difficult, since flying straight and level is a series of gentle turns and banks while keeping the airplane's pitch in adjustment by gentle correction. There's not a lot of difference between not enough and too much, but Jackie had instinctively seemed to understand it.

After he had Rocinante flying, it turned out that she had taken to the lighter airplane just as readily. Mark's own learning to fly had not come out of the textbook, since he'd been flying the Stinson since before he was old enough to see the horizon over the panel, and when the time came for formal instruction, he shot through many of the things that flight instructors normally have to take time with, thanks to the years of experience he already had. Still, he knew enough of the basics of presolo flight instruction to run Jackie through some of the paces while they were getting a few hours on the Cessna at Spearfish Lake. On the trip southward, Jackie had proven to be good at following a compass course, as well.

Just for fun, when they'd landed at Everglades City, Mark had talked her through the landing, even though he wasn't a flight instructor, and it had worked out pretty well -- so well, in fact, that he let her try the takeoff when they left after they'd had their fill of watching the astronauts on the moon. He didn't have to do as much to talk her through the landing at Orlando West, and it went so well, and the airport was so empty that they shot a few touch and goes, with Jackie doing the flying.

At Orlando, they had spent a day visiting the new Disney World. Both of them remembered how, as children, they had wanted to visit Disneyland, in California, but it seemed as if the chance would never come. Now, it seemed as if they had entered a dream world, but somehow, the reality seemed a little less fantastic than the dream had. They pretty well covered all the ground they wanted to cover the first day they were there, and it seemed pointless to go back for a second day to see the few things they had missed.

Still, Disney World was a thrill, and it seemed like they should have some memento to remember it by. They each bought Mickey Mouse T-shirts, and Mark bought Jackie a small transistor radio, and gave it to her. "Happy birthday," he said.

"It's not my birthday," she protested. "It's in August."

"Well, happy pre-birthday," he told her. "I figure we can listen to it when we're sitting around in camp in the evenings, or maybe in the plane on long, dull flights."

"That's sweet of you," she replied with a little kiss.

From Orlando, they flew up to Daytona Beach, to go into town and check out all the spring break activity. Had things turned out a little different for the both of them, they might have been among the drunken college kids rampaging up and down the beach, but somehow, now, it seemed a little pointless to them. They weren't escaping from a springful of classes on a desperate search for fun, and somehow it had seemed a little overdone. An hour of checking out the scene, with all the college girls in bikinis so scanty that they made Jackie's seem downright conservative to both of them, was all that they had needed.

Still thinking like tourists, they went back to Rocinante, flew up to St. Augustine, and spent the next two nights there, exploring the old town in the day in between. The next day, they flew across the state to Cedar Key, and spent another hour there letting Jackie shoot touch and goes at the almost deserted airport; her skill was rapidly improving, Mark could see, and he began to think that sooner or later he would have to find a real flight instructor to go over some of the things he was sure he had missed.

That evening, they camped on the deserted beach, cooking hamburger steaks from the meat they had bought in town, and filling it out with canned beans. As dark fell, they made a little fire, and spend some time looking out over the ocean to see the lights of the shrimp boats in the distant darkness.

They'd brought the telescope with them to the camp, a lot of trouble, but it was right around the new moon. It was thrilling to look up and see a great view of the southern sky out over the darkness of the ocean, and they spent quite a little time at it.

In the darkness, long after the fire burned out, they dared each other to go skinny-dipping, and with an indescribable thrill, they had each stripped off their clothes in the darkness and went splashing into the water for half an hour of giggling and cavorting before the thrill wore off, and they went back up on shore, got some clothes on, and turned into their sleeping bags.

They had enjoyed their stay at Cedar Key so well that they stayed there another day to enjoy the peace, after seeing nothing but crowds at Disney World, Daytona Beach and St. Augustine. About all they did that day was lay around, work on their tans, spend some time birdwatching with the bird book they'd bought St. Augustine, and listen to the radio. The last, they didn't do a lot; about all they could get was country music or religious programming of the loud and brainless type, and both of them agreed that a little of that went a long way.

That evening, they turned the telescope on the thin crescent of the young moon, and Jackie thrilled to see the tops of the lunar mountains hanging out in space, and the tremendous relief of the craters and mountains in the low angle light. It was quite a sight, and they wondered if it had looked as strange and as thrilling to the astronauts, who had splashed down in the Pacific a few days before. After they put the telescope away, they teased each other about going skinnydipping again, but somehow the thrill didn't seem to be the same, and both sensed that doing it again could lead them to places that they didn't want to go just yet.

The next morning, they packed up their gear, and went into town. They took the time to go grocery shopping, as they could only carry a little food with them in the plane, and it was getting low. While they were there, they took the opportunity to get their laundry done, and it was after noon before they'd gotten back to Rocinante and loaded the plane up again, to head toward Pensacola, where Mark wanted to see the Naval Air Museum.

They had gotten a little more used to the warmer weather by now. For days, the skies had been pretty clear, and the temperatures warm, but not oppressive. The afternoon skies had been filled with the puffy white cottonballs of cumulus clouds. There had been a small thunderstorm once, while they were exploring Disney World. Mark had worried about Rocinante at its tiedowns far away at the grass field at Orlando West, but when they got back there that evening, they found that the thunderstorm had missed the airport entirely.

There was no good way to check the weather at Cedar Key, but it looked like it was going to be another nice day, so Mark didn't think of it much. Between the Country-Western music on the radio blaring away in the laundromat, the announcer had said something about "possible afternoon thunderstorms," but the sky was benign, and Mark thought that he was talking through his hat; at best, if there were thunderstorms, he figured that they would be local, and they could fly around the edges.

The thunderstorm that loomed ahead of them, half an hour out of Cedar Key, seemed to fall in that category. They had been following the highway through the rough afternoon air across what seemed to be an eternity of pine forest, not unlike what they were used to back home, and Mark could see another buildup far off to the southwest. Dodging over toward the Gulf of Mexico to avoid the thunderstorm didn't seem like a big deal; they could follow the coast around just as well as they could follow the highway.

"You want to watch out for those things," Mark told Jackie. "They're something you just don't want to tangle with."

Jackie looked down at the pine forest below them. "I thought that the forests were kind of empty back home," she told him. "But there's nothing out there but trees."

Mark glanced out his window at the ground. "Yeah, there's not a hell of a lot out here," he said, and then went back to trying to figure out what they were going to have to go next.

They had reached the coastline before they could turn back to the right, and try to skirt the thunderhead. It hung dark and ominous off the right wing. Rocinante's high wing obscured much of the view directly toward the thunderstorm, but there was plenty to see ahead and to the right of them, and none of it looked particularly good. This was more than a "afternoon thunderstorm" Mark realized; this was a big, well-developed severe thunderhead.

Finally, they were able to turn to the north a little, to try and pick up the highway that they had been following earlier; they had gotten behind the thunderstorm. The air here was smooth and calm and a bit cooler than it had been before. Off in the distance, the could see the slash of the highway through the trees, and Mark told Jackie to turn back westerly, to follow the trend of the highway and the coastline.

Visibility behind the thunderstorm wasn't particularly good; things were dark and gray around them, with the high walls of the clouds shielding the sun from them. They only flew westerly for a couple of minutes before Mark could start to make out another ominous looming of darkness in front of them: another thunderstorm was following the first one. He looked to the north and south, trying to figure out how to pick a way around this one.

"I don't like this," Jackie said, a little edge on her voice.

"Me, either," Mark agreed. "I think we'd better go back where we came from and wait until this stuff blows through. Why don't you head us back to the southwest, and I'll take a look at the map and see if there's any place we can land."

Mark pulled the map from the pocket. He hadn't really been paying a lot of attention to it, other than to make a mental note that when the highway came out to the coast, and the coast turned westward, he would have to start paying a little attention to it. As a result, he wasn't real sure where they were.

A quick check of the map told him that he should have been paying more attention to his navigation. The airport at Perry had to be close by someplace, but he wasn't sure where that might be. If it was to the east of them, or to the northeast, they could follow along behind the thunderstorm to the east of them, and land before the next one hit, but if the airport were to the west or northwest of them, then there just wasn't a heck of a lot to the east of them for a place to land.

This wasn't the time to try and find a road and follow it until they got some hint of where they were. If they were going to Perry, then they had to have a pretty good idea of where it was. It was not the first time that Mark cursed for not having the money to put a VOR radio navigation system in the Cessna, but this time was worse than most.

As Mark studied the map, Jackie was turning the plane around. "Which way do we head?" she asked.

"South, I guess," Mark said, just not sure. They still should have been able to sneak back through the hole they had come through only minutes before.

"Out over the ocean?" Jackie asked.

Mark looked up from the map. Sure enough, they could see that the storm that they had just skirted now extended out over the ocean. They flew south for another couple of minutes, but there was no sign of the hole they had earlier passed through. Flying out over the ocean, without any idea of where they were, was a foolish idea, at best.

With a sinking feeling, Mark told Jackie to turn back to the north. Perhaps they could fly north a bit, and find a place to land. If they could find the highway again, and it was running in the right direction, perhaps they could follow the road into Perry after all.

As soon as they turned back to the north, though, the sky looked ominous indeed. In the couple of minutes they had been flying south, things had gotten a lot worse, and Mark wondered if they could even find the highway. "Oh, shit," he said, realizing that he was in trouble, now.

"What do we do now?" Jackie asked.

"Damned if I know," Mark said. "The only thing I can think of is to get down lower, and see if maybe we can find a way to pick our way through the one to the west of us. It looks a little lighter to the left, but this could be tough."

By now, Jackie was beginning to realize that Mark was worried. The air was still only moderately rough, no worse than it had been all afternoon, but she didn't like the looks of those threatening clouds any more than Mark did. "I . . . I think you'd better fly this now," she said.

"Fine," Mark said, taking the wheel and turning the plane roughly toward the west as he reduced power to let down. "Here, hang onto this chart. I think we're around here, someplace," he said, indicating an area of chart about three or four inches long along the coast -- a distance of about thirty miles. "If you recognize anything, let me know."

Jackie took a look at the chart in the rough air. In the thirty mile area, there were only the signs of a few small rivers coming out to the coast, and a couple of ill-defined points that probably would be difficult to pick out from the air. She looked out the window, and all she could see was pine forest and other green. They were a couple miles inland from the coast, and it was out Mark's side of the plane, so she couldn't see it very well. Up ahead, she could see the deeper green of a swampy area, and could vaguely make out a river in the distance.

Suddenly, she could make out a road below them, and a few houses, but there was nothing anywhere on the map that looked remotely like what she was seeing on the ground -- and then she saw something else. "Mark!" she yelled. "There's an airstrip down there!"

"There's nothing on the map along in here along the coast until you get way the hell west," he said. "Are you sure?"

"All I know is there's a T-hanger, like the ones at Spearfish Lake," she told him. "There's a windsock. It looks like an airstrip. That's all I know."

Mark stood Rocinante on it's wingtip to make a quick turn to the right, so he could see out his side of the plane. As Rocinante's left wing came up, he could get a good look out the side at the oncoming thunderstorm -- a huge one, bigger than he wanted to tangle with. He straightened out on a northbound heading and looked down. Sure enough, it looked like an airstrip. There was a single T-hanger, and no planes tied outside, but there was a pole with an orange windsock hanging from it.

"Any old port in a storm," he said, pulling on the carb heat. "I don't care if it's a private field or not. Let's hope we can find some tiedowns. If that ground is hard, then we're going to have a heck of a time getting the portable stakes in." The portable tiedowns, stuck under Jackie's seat, had to be screwed into the ground. They were a pain to use, and were not as solid as a block of cement or a deadman set in the ground, like permanent tiedowns. Worse, a lot of this Florida soil was sandy, and they might not hold very well. Maybe, just maybe, the T-hanger would be empty, and he could borrow it for a few minutes, hoping that whoever owned this strip wouldn't mind.

Mark didn't bother to fly a pattern; he made a parody of an approach, saw he was high, and stood Rocinante on its side an a steep sideslip to make it to the little slash through the trees. They almost fell out of the sky; at something that seemed to Mark like a reasonable altitude, and almost like crashing to Jackie, he stomped on the opposite rudder, straightening the Cessna up, and eased back on the wheel to kill off some speed.

They landed rather far down the airstrip, which was fine with Mark, as they would have less distance to taxi to get to the hanger, where there might be some tiedowns, and he rolled down the runway at a good clip, splashing up water from puddles left by the earlier storm. The windsock on the hanger in front of them hung limp, but beyond it, they could see the black wall of the thunderstorm approaching, lit by fast repeated flashes of lightning.

Mark turned off of the runway right in front of the hanger, which was only a few feet off of the strip. Inside the open front of it, he could see a tractor and wagon sitting. "Don't guess we get to use the hanger," he said. "There ought to be a tiedown around here somewhere. Look for some ropes laying on the ground."

"Out my side," Jackie replied, pointing. "About twenty feet over."

"Thank God," Mark said, looking where she was pointing. It was hard to tell how stout the tiedowns were, but there was good thick rope laying there. He stomped on the rudder to swing Rocinante around, to taxi over the tiedowns. "Use their ropes first," he told Jackie, the excitement running high in his voice. "Then we'll use ours over them. We don't know how good those ropes are."

More or less over the tiedowns, Mark pulled back the mixture knob and shut off the magneto switches. The prop was still turning as he opened his door, piled out, and ran for the tiedown rope laying on the ground.

On the far side of the plane, Jackie was hardly slower. Mark had long before shown her the tautline hitch that was used to tie the wings to the ground, and she started to thread it as she felt the wing come tight from Mark's side. She was just pulling the rope tight when she felt Rocinante surge backward a foot or two, and looked up to see Mark pulling the rope tight to the tail; he had move quickly. "Now our ropes," he yelled, running for Jackie's side of the cockpit as the wind started to rise and the first drops of rain started to fall.

It took a couple of minutes to get the ropes out from under Jackie's seat, and untangle them, and by then, the rain was falling in sheets. Jackie took one of the ropes, and clipped the snap hook at the end through the iron ring on the tiedown set into the ground, and threaded it through the ring on the wing, as Mark charged off through the rain to the far wing. In only a minute or two, he was back with her under the wing, soaked to the skin.

"It if weren't raining so hard," he yelled, "We might try going over to the T-hanger to keep from getting rained on so bad, but I guess this will have to do."

"You want to get back in the plane?" she yelled over the noise and the thunder of the storm. By now, she was nearly as wet as Mark, from all of the wind-driven rain that had blown up under the wing.

"We're so wet, we might get everything inside soaked," Mark said. "And besides, if these tiedowns don't hold, I'd rather be outside."

The storm was vicious, violent; heavy sheets of rain fell down, driven by wild turbulent winds that tossed the treetops around and even set whole trees to moving. The windsock atop the pole fluttered this way and that, and it was difficult to see very far beyond. "I'm sure glad we're not trying to fly through this," Jackie yelled after a minute or two.

"Yeah," Mark said, "I think we made it just in time."

In a minute or two, the wind and the rain began to die down just a bit. It was still raining hard, but now it was more or less raining straight down, and raining in buckets. They tried to stand back under the wind as best as they could, more to keep the rain from falling on them rather than for any futile effort to get dry.

After three or four minutes, the rain stopped, virtually all at once. There was still a lot of wind and noise from the storm around. "I don't think it's over with," Mark said. "Maybe we'd better get over to the T-hanger while we've got a chance."

"Good idea," she agreed. "I am soaked to the skin."

They were in no mood to run, but they walked quickly toward the T-hanger, perhaps fifty yards away. Halfway there, Jackie stopped. "That's funny," she said. "I'd swear I heard a heavy freight close by, but I didn't see any railroad tracks when we landed."

The hair stood up on the back of Mark's neck. Now, he heard the sound that Jackie was talking about, and they both turned to look.

The sight behind them almost froze them with horror: a huge funnel cloud, hanging down from the wall of the thunderstorm. The tornado was obviously on the ground; they could see pieces of debris picked up by the tornado, and tossed into the air. Was it moving toward them? Mark could see that it was getting closer, but was is also moving to one side a little? He couldn't tell in the few seconds that he stood there, jaw agape at the sight.

He knew -- they knew they should run for cover -- but what cover?

Jackie started for the T-hanger -- at least it was something -- but Mark thought it looked pretty flimsy. Behind the T-hanger, though, was a big cinder block barbecue pit. He couldn't tell at first glance if it was big enough to possibly crawl into, but at least it would be something substantial to hide behind. "Jackie, come on," he yelled, grabbing her hand and leading her away from her initial shelter selection. Now they were running, running as hard as they could go for the faint shelter of the barbecue pit. As he ran, Mark wondered at what possible reason there could be for having a barbeque pit at a little country airstrip, but at the moment, he was just glad it was there. In a moment, they were hunkering down behind it, in what little shelter it provided, peeking around the block at the approaching surly black funnel of the tornado.

From the faint shelter of their vantage point, Mark and Jackie could see that the tornado was moving to one side a little -- not much, but at least it looked like it wouldn't hit them directly. "Get down," he yelled at Jackie, his adrenalin pumping hard. "Get down, cover your head with your hands. There's going to be all kinds of crap landing around here."

Obediently, Jackie lay down, and covered her head as best as she could. Mark tried to lay down more or less on top of her, to protect her as best as he could with his body. He took a final glance at the tornado -- it couldn't miss by much -- and wondered for a second if Rocinante would ride it out. If the plane could, fine, but right now, their lives were more at stake. The sound and the noise from the storm was incredible; they could hear full-grown trees being snapped like matchsticks from the violent winds.

Mark snuggled up against Jackie the best he could and covered his own head.

The sound became greater, even more violent, and then started to drop as the tornado passed them by. They were starting to relax a little when there was a loud "whack" on the far side of the barbecue pit; Mark though for an instant that someone had fired a gun -- not a pistol or something, but something like a recoilless antitank rifle -- and they both squnched back down behind the barbecue pit as the roaring died away slowly.

It was a long time before they dared put their heads up again. It was extraordinarily quiet, or perhaps they had just been deafened by the roar of the storm. From their shelter by the barbecue pit, they could see the tornado moving away from them, some distance off now.

Cautiously, Mark stuck his head up, and looked off in the direction the tornado had come from. It was lighter off that way, now; in the distance, there was a ray of sunshine glowing down through the clouds. "I think we made it," he said as he picked himself up off of Jackie.

Their hearts were pumping hard from the excitement and the fear and the relief, and it was all they could do to pick themselves up. Mark wanted a cigarette, just then, more than anything in the world, but the cigarettes were back in Rocinante, and the sight of the tornado going off in the distance was even more fascinating.

When he did finally turn around to look at the Cessna, he was surprised to see it sitting peacefully at its tiedowns, seemingly little worse for wear.

"Hey, Mark, look," Jackie said, diverting his attention from the plane.

On the far side of the barbeque pit, upwind of where they had taken shelter, a board, a pretty good sized two by four, had hit the one of the blocks of the barbeque pit, punching through both layers of concrete in the block. If the board had gone through another layer of block, the next thing it would have hit would have been the two bodies sheltering behind it.

"Jesus, would you look at that," Mark said. "How fast could that thing have been going?" He felt himself shaking a little, needing that cigarette to calm his nerves more than ever.

Neither of them were thinking too clearly as they walked over to Rocinante. Mark opened the door, and rummaged in his pack. The pack of cigarettes there was new from Cedar Key; the last pack had lasted all the way from Spearfish Lake. His hands were shaking as he fumbled with the wrapper and ripped the top off of the pack. He pulled a cigarette out, and stuffed the rest of the pack into his shirt pocket. There was a lighter in the flap of the pack; he was fumbling for it when Jackie said, "Hey, Mark, look at this."

He pulled the lighter out and backed out of the luggage compartment, to turn around and look at where Jackie pointed.

On the bottom side of the wing, right in the center and halfway out, was an exit hole, that looked as if someone had thrown a baseball through the it. Mark felt his heart sink; without lighting the cigarette, he walked over and looked at the hole.

Even at the first glance, it was easy to see that something had gone clear through the fabric of the wing. He knew that the dacron Ceconite fabric was resilient, and looked down at the ground, where half-buried in the muddy grass he found a splintered, broken up piece of wood that looked like it had been part of the trunk of a pine tree until a few minutes before. It had to have come almost straight down, judging from the path it had taken through the wing.

"I'm glad we weren't standing under the wing when that thing hit," Jackie said.

"Yeah, me too," Mark agreed, remembering that he had an unlit cigarette in his mouth. He looked carefully; the hole didn't seem to be anywhere near the gas tank, and miraculously, it seemed to have missed all of the spars and ribs and cables that were beneath the fabric. Still, he stepped out from under the wing before he lit the cigarette, and Jackie stepped out with him.

The first impact of the smoke settled him down a little bit, and allowed him to think a little. He stepped back another couple of paces, to where he could look at the top of Rocinante's wing. There was a little dimple where the piece of wood had gone through the wing like a dud anti-aircraft round. Looking carefully, he could see no more holes in this wing, but even from far away, he could see where there was another hole far out toward the tip of the other wing. It didn't look so bad, but still he went over to look at it. "Damn," he said. "Looks like this one went right through the wing, too, but didn't hit anything underneath."

Carefully, he walked around Rocinante, looking the plane over. Almost miraculously, the two holes -- four actually, counting the entry and exit holes as separate ones -- were all the damage that he found, although he knew that he would want to be very careful about going over the plane again before they flew it next, after the holes were fixed.

Delayed reaction to the storm was starting to set in on Jackie, now, and Mark still had it pretty bad. He reached in his pocket, shook out another cigarette and lit it. "Can I have one?" Jackie said.

"I didn't know you smoked," Mark said.

"I had a cigarette with Kirsten, once," Jackie said. "But right now, I can't think of anything better."

"Sure," Mark said, handing her the pack and offering her a light.

Though the cigarette didn't have quite the same effect on Jackie that it had on Mark, it gave her something to do with her hands, something to think about besides the rain of debris that had fallen around them only minutes before. "Are we going to be able to fly this thing out of here?" she asked.

"If we absolutely had to, I suppose we could risk it," Mark said, exhaling a cloud of smoke and explaining, "The hole out on the wingtip we could tape over with no problem, and I think we might be able to tape up the other one well enough to get someplace else if we had to. But we might as well fix it here. It's nothing we can't fix if I can have dad mail me some of the stuff that's left over from the recovering this spring. Besides, we're going to be stuck here for a while, anyway."

"What do you mean?" Jackie asked.

Mark said nothing; he just cocked his head out toward the airstrip.

Jackie looked out where Mark was nodding.

Half of the airstrip looked pretty much all right; there was some scattered debris. The other half was a lot worse: toward the end, there was some downed timber, but there was scattered lumber and bits and pieces of trees and brush laying almost solidly across the runway. In the middle of the runway, broken and fanned out, lay what was left of a wooden roof; shingles scattered all over the place.

"My God," Jackie said finally.

Mark nodded. "Someone's going to have to put in a lot of work to even clear a path through that crap so we can take off, and I wouldn't be surprised if that someone's going to have to be you and me."

6.

Jackie took a drag on her cigarette and coughed. She looked at Mark and said, "Do you have any idea where in hell we are?"

"Beats the hell out of me," Mark said. "There was nothing on the map, unless we're way the hell away from where I think we are. I kind of think that Perry is more to the east of us than it is to the north of us, but that doesn't help much. We got ourselves turned around pretty good while we were looking for a way around that thunderstorm."

Mark looked in the cockpit, and pulled out the map. Jackie looked over his shoulder as they analyzed where they were. As Mark had said, there was nothing showing on the map at all, but here they were, on an airstrip that the map didn't show. As they landed, they had seen a town a mile or more off in the distance, and a few houses near the airstrip, but neither the town nor the airstrip showed on the map.

All of a sudden, Jackie tried to suppress a giggle. "What's so funny?" Mark asked.

"You ever see 'The Wizard of Oz', maybe on TV?"

Mark smiled. "You mean, 'Toto, somehow I don't think we're in Kansas any more'?"

"Yeah," she smiled. "There's a path out behind the T-hanger that I think leads to a road."

"I don't think it'll be paved with yellow brick," Mark smiled. "We may not be in Kansas any more, but we darn sure are still in north Florida. Somewhere in north Florida, that is. I suppose we'd better find your yellow brick road, and find someone that can tell us where we are, and find a telephone."

"What do we need a telephone for?" Jackie asked.

"So we can call my dad and have him get some of the leftover fabric and dope in the mail to us."

Jackie looked a little alarmed. "Is there any reason we have to tell him what really happened? If Dad and Sarah find out, they might get all upset again."

Before they set out, they decided to get out of the storm-soaked clothes they had on, and put on some dry clothes. They changed out in the open, under one of Rocinante's damaged wings, then set out on their way.

Mark was a little relieved to find that the road in front of the airstrip wasn't yellow brick, but sandy dirt, much like they were familiar with from around their Spearfish Lake home. "Which way did you think those houses were?" Jackie asked when they got to the road.

"To the right, I think," Mark said, and they set off down the road.

To step out on that road was to feel the eternity of the forests surrounding them; for as far as the eye could see from above, they had seen forest and swamp and a few shapeless scattered clearings. Longleaf and loblolly pines rose jaggedly at intervals alongside of them, and there was a faint smell of pine resin mixed with the faint smell of the salt sea of the Gulf. It was a very quiet woods; they could hear the whisper of the remaining breeze through the pine needles as they walked soundlessly up the road, already drying from the fallen rain.

They did not go very far before they began to see signs of the tornado's passage. Here and there a tree was down, or ripped off halfway up, but as they walked along, somehow, none of the trees had fallen across the road. They turned a slight corner, right in the center of the path that the tornado had taken, and came to what had been a little clearing in the woods. At the foot of the clearing, they could see a river beyond; wide and still, it rolled away in marshy grasses and occasional cypress trees with their wide, grotesque stumps; little patches of Spanish Moss still hung from some of them, despite the violence of the storm.

At the edge of the clearing stood what the tornado had left of a white-painted building, now surrounded in debris the storm had left behind. The roof was gone, and a handful of negros stood silently in front of the building, just looking at it.

Mark and Jackie walked closer to the little group. "Anybody hurt?" Mark asked.

Most of the group looked up, surprised to see Mark and Jackie approach. "Naa, thank the Lord," a big, burly man said in a thick accent, almost incomprehensible to Mark and Jackie's northern ears. "Lord created, and the Lord destroyed, and Blessed be the name of the Lord. Ethylene and me was sweepin' the church out, gettin' it cleaned up for the prayer meetin' tonight, and the Devil's Wind come and the roof come up off the top of our heads."

"This was your church?" Jackie asked.

The man nodded. "With the Lord's help, we'll rebuild it," the man said.

"Cain't believe the roof just disappeared," a boy said. Mark and Jackie looked around. In addition to the man, there were three women, and the boy, about ten. "I think your roof is sitting back up in the middle of the airstrip," Jackie said. "What's left of it."

"You come up from the airstrip?" the boy said. "I thought I heered a plane land jest before the storm hit, and didn't think Mr. Cowgill was a-goin' to have any quail hunters this time of year."

"We were kind of surrounded by the storm," Mark told the boy. "We saw the airstrip and we landed. We're not even sure where we are."

"This is Twillingate," the man said. "Just the edge of it. The rest of the town's over yonder."

"Do you know if there's any place around where we can made a phone call?" Mark asked.

"Phone line's down out here," the man said, "But maybe Mr. Thibodaux can get through from the phone company."

"How do we find the phone company?" Mark asked.

"I can show them, Brother Erasmus," the boy said.

"All right, E.J.," the man, who had to be 'Brother Erasmus', said. "You take them to Mr. Thibodaux' place, but don't you be beggin' no dime for no bottle of Dr. Pepper, then stoppin' in the juke joint."

"Aw, I won't," the boy said.

E.J. led Mark and Jackie farther down the sandy road. "You'uns really fly in here?" he asked, as soon as they got out of sight of the shattered church.

"Right in front of the storm," Mark told him.

"What's your names?" he asked.

Mark introduced himself. "This is Jackie," he added.

"Mist' Mark, what's you last names?" he asked. "Brother Erasmus'd cane me if he heard me call grownups by they first names, 'specially if they is white grownups."

Mark smiled. They might as well be in Oz, after all. It was a lot different than Spearfish Lake. "You can call me Mr. Gravengood," he said. "This is Miss Archer, but you can call us Mister Mark and Miss Jackie if you think you have to. What's your last name, E.J.?"

"I's E.J. Seasprunk. The E and the J don't stand for nothin'. You really have you own plane?"

"We rebuilt it this last winter, way up north, where it gets real cold," Mark told him.

"You take me for a ride?"

"Can't right now," Mark told him. "The tornado put a couple of holes in the wings, and we've got to get it fixed, first."

"Can I help you fix it?" the boy asked. "All the time I look up and see planes flying over, I wonder what it's like to look down and see Twillingate."

"We might just be able to arrange that," Mark said.

The town of Twillingate didn't prove to be very much. There were several houses, all of them pretty well scattered, so they couldn't get an idea of how many they were, but it didn't appear that they were very many. It turned out that they were walking along the main road into town; the streets were unpaved sand, just like the road itself. At the edge of town, there was an unpainted, dilapidated building, rather tumbledown; from inside, at earsplitting volume, came the recorded, familiar voice of James Brown. "That's the juke joint," E.J. told them. "Brother Erasmus would skin me alive if'n I went in there."

On past the juke joint were more houses, scattered and set back from the road. Some were as unpainted and dilapidated as the juke joint; some didn't even have glass windows, just screens and shutters, with chickens scratching around old junk cars left to molder in the yards. Others were a little nicer; they had paint, and the yards were cleaner, but nowhere was there anything that would qualify as a lawn -- just sandy, weedy soil. Here and there, a small garden struggled to grow.

The "downtown" proved to be only five stores, the biggest of which was a wooden, two-story general store, set up several feet off the ground on pilings, as were most of the buildings in Twillingate. In front of the general store was a gas pump -- the old-fashioned kind, hand pumped, with a glass top. The user pumped the gas up into the glass top of the pump, to measure it by marks set into the glass, and then let it drain by gravity into the gas tank. Mark had only seen one of them in his life before; there was an abandoned store in Hoselton, east of Spearfish Lake, that had one setting in front of it -- but apparently, this one was in regular use. There was what appeared to be a dry-goods store, an unpainted garage-appearing building that also had a hand-powered gas pump, a building that appeared to be a small market, and another building that had a sign on it: Post Office, Twillingate, Florida. The few signs on the fronts of the building didn't give much indication of what went on in them.

E.J. led them right through the middle of the "downtown" section, to yet another of the houses sitting up on pilings. This one was a little bigger than the rest, and there was a small handwritten sign on the door: "Twillingate Telephone." E.J. led them right inside through the screen door, without knocking. "Missus Thibodaux, you heah?" he called.

An immensely fat dark-haired woman stepped out from the next room. "Oh, it's you, E.J.," she said. "Land, you scared me."

"This is Mist' Mark and Miss Jackie," E.J. told her. "They needta be makin' a phone call. They landed they plane upta' the airstrip jest afore the Devil's Wind come through."

"You folks all right?" the woman asked, in an accent hardly less thick than Brother Erasmus or E.J.

"We're OK," Mark said. "That tornado came closer to us than I like to think about, but we're all right."

The woman shook her head. "We didn't even think that they'd be anyone up to the airstrip. You'd be needin' to call out of Twillingate, I 'spect?"

"Yeah," Mark said, and explained how Rocinante had taken a couple of hits from flying debris, and how he wanted to call home for repair materials.

"Well, come on back," Mrs. Thibodaux said. "I don't know if Paul has got the line to Perry fixed yet, but we can try and see. E.J., you best be gettin' on back or Brother Erasmus is goin' to be wonderin' wheah you are."

"'Spect so," E.J. replied. "Mist' Mark, Miss Jackie, doan forget, I want to hep you fix you plane so's you can take me for a ride."

Mark smiled, reached in his pocket, and pulled out a dime. "Thanks, E.J.," he said. "We won't forget. Why don't you stop at the store and get yourself a Dr. Pepper, but don't you go into that juke joint, now."

The boy beamed. "Why, thank you, Mist' Mark," he said, and turned to leave.

Mark and Jackie followed Mrs. Thibodaux into the back room, and instantly Mark's jaw dropped. In front of him was an old-fashioned switchboard, with plugs and sockets. The army used similar systems, for its field phones, and Mark had worked on them, but he hadn't known that there were any left in civilian use. He could remember them in Spearfish Lake when he was a small child, before the dial phones had been installed, years before.

Mrs. Thibodaux picked up a headset and put it over her ears, and gave a crank on the switchboard a twirl. "Still dead," she said. "We've only got but the one line to Perry, and Paul went out to see if he could fix it. All the lines out to the north are down, but we can still call around town."

Mark moved closer, to get a look at the switchboard. It was older than the ones he had worked on in the army, and had "Rhinelander" in a metal script fastened to the top of it. It had to be at least fifty years old. "How many lines have you got?" he asked.

"Twenty-four lines, two hundred eighty-three phones," Mrs. Thibodaux said. "Bout half the lines got took down by the storm, but I called around on the ones that was left, and found out that no one was hurt, thank the Lord," she went on. "The old teppentine camp was beat up pretty bad, but there ain't been nobody livin' there for years. Brother Erasmus' church had the roof taken off, but since you came in from the airstrip I 'spect you know that. Your plane hurt bad?"

"Just a couple of holes in the fabric, but nothing we can't fix once I get the stuff from home," Mark said. "Do you suppose it'd be all right if we camped up at the airstrip for a few days, till we can get the plane fixed?"

"Don't suppose Mr. Cowgill'd mind," Mrs. Thibodaux replied. "I'd give him a call and ask, but the line's down to the plantation, too." Just then, a battered old pickup truck pulled up outside. "Here's Paul now," she said. "If he's back, then there's more trouble with the lines than he can manage by himself."

Paul proved to be a tall, thin man, taller and thinner than Mark; He was in his fifties, perhaps; it was hard to say, from all the lines in his face. "Got a couple hundred yards of line down out by the teppentine camp, Bessie," he reported in a accent that was more understandable than Mrs. Thibodaux, although it carried a strange lilt to it that Mark couldn't place. "Busted lines all over the place, and it's more than I can do by myself. Guess I'll have to drive into Perry and see if I can get one of them young fellas from Southern Bell to come help me out, and it could take a couple of days to get one of them down here."

"What's the problem?" Mark asked. "Getting the lines spliced and back up?"

"That, and running continuity checks, and just sorting everything else out," the man replied.

"Let's go do it," Mark said. "I want to make a phone call."

"You know anything about splicing lines and climbing poles, young fella?"

"Spent four years working on Army systems," Mark told him. "A year and a half of it was working on field phones, and that's not much different from what you've got here. By the way, I'm Mark Gravengood, and this is Jackie Archer."

The man stuck out his hand. "Paul Thibodaux," he said, "Guess you've already met my wife, Bessie, here. I'm sure pleased to meet you."

"They was flying past," Bessie said, "and landed out to the airstrip, and their plane got hurt in the storm."

"Thought I heard a plane, just before the storm hit," Paul replied. "If you don't mind, I'd be glad of your help."

Mark and Jackie and Mr. Thibodaux squeezed into the front seat of the pickup truck. It was a tight squeeze; there were tools on the seat, and other tools on the floor. "I was a little surprised to see a crank system here," Mark said.

"They's not but half a dozen or so of them left in the country any more," Mr. Thibodaux said as they drove back up the road toward Brother Erasmus' church and the airstrip. "And I hope we're not going to have this one in another year or so. Mr. Cowgill has been helping me with a bank up in Tallahassee, and maybe by next winter we'll be converting to dial."

"Who's this Mr. Cowgill?" Jackie asked.

"Mr. Cowgill owns the plantation, and most everything else around here," Thibodaux explained. "He's the one whose airstrip you landed on. In the winter, they's Yankees that fly in to hunt quail on the plantation," he said. "They pay a couple hundred dollars a day just for room and board and quail hunting."

"Seems like a heck of a lot of money, just for hunting," Jackie said.

"'Spose so," Thibodaux said. "But Mr. Cowgill's like everybody else around these parts, he's got to make it where he can."

"What do people do around here?" Jackie asked.

"Oh, this and that. Lot of 'em work out to the plantation. Mr. Cowgill's got a little corn out there, and some shade 'bacca. He's still got a few people slashin' for teppentine, though not as many as they used to be. Teppentine's hard work, don't pay much, and even the coloreds don't want to do it if they can find something else to do, and I don't blame them. Mr. Cowgill's got the sawmill, and cuts a lot of lumber, and people work for him at that. A few people fish mullett and gather moss and try to get by the best they can."

They drove by the shattered little white church, still roofless. A few more people were around now, looking at the mess that the tornado had made of the church. A little two-rut track led off to one side; Mark and Jackie had missed it earlier; they looked, and saw that E.J. had made it back to the church.

Thibodaux stopped the truck by the crowd of black people. "Sure is a mess, ain't it, Brother Erasmus?" he said.

"The Lord's will," the black man said. "Guess he's tryin' to teach us to have faith in spite of everything."

"Got to get the phone lines fixed," Thibodaux said. "Then I'll come back and do what I can to help."

"Sure would 'preciate it, Mr. Thibodaux," the big black man said. "Lord take care of you, now."

Thibodaux drove on down the road. "Guess he's a little shell-shocked," he said. "Brother Erasmus'll talk your ear off normally, give him half a chance, but he's been good people to have around. Shows you that it ain't true that nothin' good never came from a teppentine camp."

"What's this 'teppentine' I keep hearing about?" Jackie said.

"Teppentine is the sap they get from the trees. They boil it out, and it's used to clean brushes, and like that," Thibodaux explained.

"Oh, turpentine," Jackie said. "The word kept getting lost in the accent. I know about turpentine. We're from woods country ourselves."

They drove for a mile or more down the two-rut, and came to the place where the tornado's path had crossed the trail and the telephone line. It was a mess. Trees were down all over the place, covering phone wires. By some miracle, only one phone pole was down, but the old-fashioned multi-wire party lines were a total snare of wire. Some wires were broken, and others not. "Thought maybe we could take that busted pole and wire it up to that busted-off loblolly snag," Thibodaux said. "We can run some new wire, but I don't have enough to replace all that what's laying under that timber, so we'll have to salvage some."

Mark counted a dozen wires buried under the tornado's litter. "It'd be better if we could put in a new pole," he said.

"Don't got any new poles, right now," Thibodaux said. "I don't want to put a lot into fixing up this old system, anyway. It just wants to be good enough to last a year or so. We'll salvage some of the old system for the dial system, but this part is all junk, anyway. I can sling a new pole in there when we get ready to put the new system in."

"Well, you're the one that knows what you want," Mark said, shaking his head.

It was well that they had several hours of daylight left, for they needed most of it to patch up the multiple breaks in the system. Mark and Mr. Thibodaux took the wires loose from the crossbucks of the broken pole, then the three of them drug the pole by brute strength a few feet over to where a broken-off pine tree stood. With a block and tackle, they winched the pole upright next to the pine stump, and wired the pole to what was left of the tree with some of the pieces of telephone wire that lay around.

From there on, it was mostly wiring and splicing. The work wasn't difficult, but it required several sets of hands, and even having Jackie there to help pull and tug on things, or carry stuff, was helpful. One by one, they spliced on a length of wire at the next pole, and cut the old length free. Then, they ran the wire down past the new pole to the next good pole, climbed up, and with the help of the block and tackle, pulled the wire as tight as they could before they spliced it into place. Then, they went back up to the pole in the middle and lifted the wire up to the crossbucks and fastened it to the insulator, and after calling Bessie at the switchboard to check the circuit, it was on to the next wire.

After a while, the spool of wire in Thibodaux's truck began to run low, and they had to resort to salvaging some of the downed wire, splicing it together in short lengths. The day was winding down before they had all of the circuits back up and running. "Sure glad you happened along," Thibodaux told Mark and Jackie as the three of them got back into the old pickup. "When I need help with the system that's more than just carrying things, I have to get one of the guys from Southern Bell over in Perry to come over on his time off to help out, and sometimes they can't get here right away."

"It's no big deal," Mark told him. "I'm a phone man, anyway." He explained how his father had worked for the Spearfish Lake phone company for years, and how he expected to be working there in another year, too. "It's just a little locally owned company," Mark explained. "A little bigger than yours, but then the town is bigger, too."

"Kinda thought so," Thibodaux said. "Phone people tend to stick together when things get tough. I 'spect Bessie will have called people out on each of those circuits to see if everyone's all right, but we'd better drive back to see. I want to stop off at Brother Erasmus' church and see if there's anything we can do to help them out, but after we're done with that, maybe you folks would like to come have dinner with Bessie and me after you make your call."

"Thanks," Mark said. "We'd appreciate that."

It was along in the evening, now, though the sun was still fairly high. As they came back out into the clearing where the church was, they found Brother Erasmus, Ethelyne and E.J. busy with a few other people, carrying hymnals and other things from the church into a little shack out at the edge of the clearing. "Anything we can do to help?" Thibodaux asked Brother Erasmus.

"Not much now, Mr. Thibodaux," the big black man said. "We've got most of the things that would get hurt if they get wet out of the church. We goin' to have to get some lumber to rebuild the roof, but the Lord will provide, somehow."

"The old teppentine camp is pretty much a mess," Thibodaux told him. "But I'll wager they's some boards there that could be salvaged. I'd want to ask Mr. Cowgill first, but I'll wager he'd tell you to take anything you can use. Phone line's back working out to the plantation, so you could give him a call."

"Shore will give him a call, 'fore dark," Brother Erasmus told them.

"If he says it's all right, I'll come out tomorrow and help you haul in some of the boards," Thibodaux promised.

Brother Erasmus nodded his head. "Shore would 'preciate it," he said.

"Your old roof is up at the airstrip, I think," Mark reminded Brother Erasmus. "At least, I think it's your roof. It's busted up a bit, but there might be something there you could use, too."

They rode back up the road into Twillingate. "He's been a good man," Thibodaux said. "None finer. I'd hate to see him have to leave over something like this. He's poor like any preacher, but we're all poor, here. Still, he'd give you the shirt off his back if you needed it. That E.J. of his, his daddy run off before he was born, and his momma run off not long after that, and Brother Erasmus has been raising him, since they ain't no one else." He shook his head as they drove into the edge of town. "Sure makes you wonder what the Lord's thinking about, sometimes," he said. "Wreck the church of a good man like Brother Erasmus, and leave the juke joint standing."

The truck squealed to a stop in front of the phone company, which they had learned was also Thibodaux' house. Inside, Thibodaux asked his wife, "Line to Perry working?"

"It's got some static on it," Bessie said. "I called the sheriff and told him that they didn't seem to be anybody hurt out here."

"Don't guess much got hurt 'cept Brother Erasmus' church, the old teppentine camp and the airstrip," Thibodaux said. "These two was a big help. You want to get the operator in Perry on the line? Guess we can stand them a phone call and supper for they help."

It took Bessie longer to get the operator in Perry on the line than it took that operator to make a direct long distance call to Mark's home in Spearfish Lake. "Didn't expect to hear from you again quite so soon," Mark's father said. "Walt and Sarah were over last night, and they brought the pictures that you and Jackie sent them from Everglades City. Too bad you didn't get a picture of that rocket going up."

"We were pretty far away," Mark said, thinking that it had to be a long time ago that they had watched the Apollo 15 Saturn lift off into the air. Twillingate had to be another world entirely. "We had to watch it through binoculars and the telescope, and we just never thought to get a picture, but it didn't show much."

"Sure would like to see that some time," his father said.

"Well, Dad, that's not the reason I called," Mark said. "We had a little trouble with the plane. Just a hanger rash kind of thing while it was tied down, but I've got a couple holes in the fabric. I know I've got some dope and stuff sitting down under the workbench, and I'd like you to air mail some of it to us so I can fix it."

"I can do that. What do you need?"

"I'll need about a square yard of Ceconite, but it doesn't have to be that big," Mark said. "At least three or four pieces at least a foot square would work just as well. I figure I'll need a quart of clear dope, maybe a pint of silver dope, and maybe a half pint or a pint of the white enamel. There's a quart can of the enamel that's less than half full, and it would do fine. I'll need a little acetone, too, maybe half a pint."

"Better let me get a piece of paper and write all this down," his father said. In a minute, Mark went back over the list slowly, as his father took it down. "Anything else?" his dad asked finally.

"Maybe you could throw in two or three cheap brushes. There were some laying on the workbench, if you didn't clean it up," Mark told him. "Oh, and my pinking shears were down there too, if you could throw them in. Ship all that stuff the fastest way you can, and I'll see that you get paid for the postage."

"Don't worry about the postage, son," Mark's father said. "That's only going to be a few bucks, either way. Where do I send it?"

"Send it to us, General Delivery, Twillingate, Florida. I don't know the zip code, just a second." Mark asked Bessie for the zip code; she told them, and he passed it along to his father.

"I'll have it in the mail first thing in the morning," Mark's father promised. "How's your trip been since Everglades City?"

"Pretty good," Mark said. "We've been to Disney World, and Daytona Beach, and St. Augustine, and it's been pretty interesting. I'll have to sit down and tell you all about it some time."

"Well, it's good to hear from you, son. You take care of yourself, and be careful."

"Will do, dad. We'll be seeing you."

Mark nodded at Bessie, who broke the connection. "That's a relief," Mark said. "This is what? Tuesday? Wednesday?"

"Tuesday," Thibodaux said.

Mark counted on his fingers. "Yeah, it would have to be," he said. "We went to church in St. Augustine two days ago, so this would have to be Tuesday. That stuff might be here by Saturday, first of the week at the latest. Then, it'll only take a couple of days, and we'll be able to go."

"I called Mr. Cowgill for you," Bessie said. "I told him about you landing at the airport, and your plane being damaged, and you wanting to camp there, and he said he guessed it didn't matter if you did, seeing as how you didn't have much choice."

"Thanks, Mrs. Thibodaux," Mark said. "I appreciate that."

Over dinner, they learned more about Twillingate, and about Paul and Bessie Thibodaux, as well. The dinner was corn bread and fresh fish -- mullet that one of the local fishermen had netted out of the gulf that morning, and while it wasn't exactly lake trout, it was good eating. It was the first dinner they'd had in a home since they'd left Spearfish Lake, and it turned out that they had missed that a little. Besides, the Thibodauxes were easy people to get to know.

It turned out that Paul Thibodaux really wasn't a Twillingate native; he was a Louisiana Cajun, and had met Bessie when he had been stationed at Eglin Field during the war. Bessie's father had started the Twillingate phone company thirty years earlier, but he had taken ill shortly before Paul got out of the service. They had returned to Twillingate to nurse him and keep the phone company going, and had just never left. "We ain't gotten rich at it," he said. "But we've had a decent living, raised our children and put them through college. We like the place. Most everybody here is poor as church mice, but most of them are good people."

While they talked, Mark and Jackie told them the story of how they came to be flying over Twillingate, how they had landed in front of the storm, and of the terror of the tornado. "One thing I'm curious about," Jackie asked. "Is why there should be a barbecue pit out at the airstrip. Not that I'm complaining, because we're both darn glad it was there, but just wondering why it's there."

"Mr. Cowgill put it in back before they cleared the airstrip, and they just never took it down," Paul said. "We used to have a hog roast out there every fall, back fifteen, twenty years ago, but after the airport was in, we just quit having them. Don't suppose it's been used in years."

They sat around the supper table talking until it was almost dark. "Guess we'd better get going," Mark said. "We want to go out and get our tent set up before it gets too dark to see."

Thibodaux offered to drive them out to the airstrip, but they declined. "That was such a good meal, we need the exercise to walk it off," Jackie said.

"Well, don't be strangers while you're here," Bessie said.

Mark and Jackie set off walking back toward the airstrip. They walked silently at first, through what passed for downtown Twillingate, past the juke joint, where James Brown was still blasting through the failing light, and on up the sandy road through the scrub pine. "I've been in poor towns," Mark said. "I've been in places in Vietnam that are worse than this. I didn't really expect to find people as nice as they are, but I guess there are good people wherever you go."

"I don't know of any place around home that's anywhere near as bad as this," Jackie agreed. "I mean, you think of, say, Hoselton, but it's a paradise compared to this. But you're right, there seem to be good people here."

"You hear something?" Mark asked.

"Yeah," Jackie said. "Sounds like singing."

The sound was up ahead of them. As they got closer, it proved to be singing, indeed. They were not surprised to come out of the woods in front of what was left of Brother Erasmus' church, to see thirty or forty black people standing in the yard in front of the church, holding a hymn sing.

They were both impressed. In their limited church careers, they had both attended churches that could take the liveliest hymn and turn it into a dirge; the Baptist Church they had attended in St. Augustine the previous Sunday had been the same way, and since they had only been dressed in shirts and jeans, all they had with them, instead of nice clothes, they felt that their reception had been rather cold, and they were just as happy to leave.

The music here was different: negro spirituals, sung with feeling and power. Some of the hymns they had heard before, and had even heard negro church music on television, but they had never experienced anything like this. There were a couple of men over there in the dark, gathering gloom that could sing a rolling bass, and this was a congregation that knew how to sing.

Not wanting to be seen staring, they walked on past, but once they were out of sight, up in the edge of the woods, they stopped to listen for a while. "It doesn't sound like their church got blown away today," Jackie whispered.

"No, it doesn't," Mark agreed as they watched from the shadows, impressed with the sight and sound in front of them.

Eventually the singing came to an end. They stood there, wondering if there would be more, and then they could hear Brother Erasmus' voice booming across the little clearing. "Brothers and sisters," he said. "The church didn't get blown away, today. The building got beat up a bit, but we all know that the church is more than just a building. A church is it's people, and as long as we've got our people, we've still got our church."

A chorus of "Amen, Brother," went up.

"Nobody got hurt or killed today, praise the Lord. That's worth feeling joyful over, and that's something we have to praise the Lord for."

"Amen, Brother," filled the evening air again.

"We can rebuild the building. The building is just handy. The building is just the place where the church meets. It's not the church. Even with the Lord's help, it won't be easy for us to rebuild the building, but at least we don't have to rebuild the church."

Jackie leaned over and whispered, "I guess I never thought of it that way."

"Yeah," Mark replied quietly. "Let's listen."

"Brothers and sisters," Brother Erasmus said loudly enough that Mark and Jackie could head them clearly. "We may be poor in money, but we are not poor in spirit. We have the faith that the Lord will provide for us, so we must have the faith that the Lord will show us the way to rebuild our building. The Lord creates, and the Lord destroys, but he does nothing without havin' some meaning for it. We must be open to the lesson that the Lord is teachin' us today, 'cause he does nothin' without a purpose."

"Amen, Brother" again sounded in the clearing.

"Makes you wonder," Mark whispered.

"Wonder what?" Jackie whispered back.

"Makes you wonder if he's right, or if it's just an excuse that covers everything."

"He believes it. He's got faith, if he's got nothing else. Maybe it would be nice to be able to believe that," she said, quietly in the falling darkness. She stood there silently for a moment, then said, "Mark, I think we'd better get back to the plane."

7.

The dew was heavy on the grass as they got up the next morning; it looked like it was going to be a hot day. They brewed up coffee under Rocinante's wing, where the dew on the ground wasn't quite as heavy.

It had taken them a while to get to sleep. Even at the distance that their camp was from the church, they could still hear the singing off in the distance late into the night -- not loud, and not oppressive, by any means, but enough to know that it was there. "They sure like their singing," Mark had said as they lay on their backs in their sleeping bags, once they'd gotten the tent set up.

The woods were quiet this morning, but there was a smell of pine and wood smoke on the air -- a sweet smell, and a familiar one, a smell that somehow reminded them of their home far away.

Mark sipped at his coffee, and surveyed all the debris on the runway. "I suppose we'd better get started at that today," he said.

"Mark, I don't know that the two of us can get all that cleaned up," Jackie replied quietly. She looked out at the mess; there was a lot of work there. Most of the debris was trees and bits of trees, branches, and the like, but there was plenty of sawn lumber and junk strewn about. "It would take the two of us all summer to clean that up."

"Probably so," Mark agreed. "But, I don't see where we have to clean it all up. If it's just for the one takeoff, we can get by on a narrow path, so long as it's fairly straight and it doesn't have to be the length of the runway."

"You're saying clear just enough to take off from, and the heck with the rest?" she asked.

"Yeah," Mark told her. "If we get Mr. Thibodaux or someone to take you and the gear over to Perry, maybe seven hundred or eight hundred feet would be enough. I'm pretty sure I can get it off that quick in still air, and maybe less if there's a breeze blowing."

Jackie nodded. "That does make it a little simpler," she said.

"First thing we've got to do," Mark said, "is figure out which seven or eight hundred feet we want to clear. In other words, what's going to be the easiest. With that roof out there, and those downed trees, it may not be as easy as I hope."

They finished their coffee and went out to look the situation over. The tornado had crossed the western end of the runway, and the situation there was hopeless; but back to the east, it looked more promising. There was still plenty of debris all over the place, but it was smaller, in sizes they could handle. After quite a bit of pacing off and checking sight lines, they settled on a promising line. While there was a fair amount of limbs and boards and trash along it, it was the least marred by larger trees. "Maybe we can borrow a chainsaw or an axe from Mr. Thibodaux or someone," Mark said. "If we can cut those trees up into three or four pieces, we ought to be able to move them ourselves. The rest of it's just going to be hauling stuff off of the runway."

They paced off the line they had chosen. Starting right at the end of the runway, there was about 900 feet until they reached what was left of the church roof. "That ought to be plenty, if I've got the plane light," Mark said. "We'll have to find a way to get you and the gear over to Perry, whatever direction that is, but that shouldn't be a problem."

"That's not going to be enough for the both of us and the gear to get off, then?"

"No," Mark told her. "If the roof weren't there, we could probably clear another three or four hundred feet on the other side of it, and we'd be pretty sure of being able to get off all right fully loaded, especially if we have any sort of a sea breeze."

Fortunately, they still had brown jersey gloves in the plane, left over from the cold weather in Spearfish Lake. They got the gloves on, went out to a point a few feet from the church roof, and started hauling debris.

They had been at it about an hour when they heard a voice call to them, "Good mornin', Mist' Mark, Miss Jackie."

They looked up to see Brother Erasmus standing over by the church roof. "Good morning, Brother Erasmus," Mark replied. "What brings you out here today?"

The black preacher shook his head. "I talked to Mr. Cowgill last evenin', and he said he didn't want me usin' them boards from the old teppentine camp. 'Devil's in them boards,' he said. So, I reckoned I'd better come over and start to get what boards I could off the old roof."

"Kind of a mess, isn't it?" Mark commented.

The preacher shook his head. "Devil's wind didn't leave much we can use, but we'd better use what we can."

"It's all stuff that's got to be moved so we can take off," Jackie said, not quite truthfully. "So we'll be glad to help you where we can."

"I'm much obliged for any help I can get, right now," the preacher replied. "I was a little disappointed in Mr. Cowgill last night. I know that lumber over there ain't much good, but everything counts."

Mark shook his head. "Afraid we haven't got much in the way of tools that'll do us much good, but we'll do what we can."

They set to work. The lumber was pretty broken up, and there wasn't a lot that counted for good lumber to be salvaged, Mark thought. In the back of his mind, the thought arose that two or three hundred bucks worth of good lumber would go a long way toward putting a new roof on the church, especially if it were locally sawn stuff, and Thibodaux had said something about a sawmill around here. Two or three hundred dollars was two weeks traveling, or so. In the long run, he wouldn't miss it. He wasn't ready to say anything about it just yet, but the guilt of being on the trip, just playing, really, was heavy on him.

"That E.J., is that your boy?" Mark asked, to make conversation as they worked.

"He is, and he isn't," Brother Erasmus said. "His daddy run off before he was born. He was a teppentine worker, over to the old camp before they closed it down. Then, his momma decided she had to go up to Mobile for a while, and she ain't never come back for him, and I don't guess she's ever gonna."

"He seems like a nice boy," Jackie said as she pulled a loose board from the wreckage and carried it over to the pile they were establishing at the edge of the runway. "Very polite."

"He didn't pester you none for a Dr. Pepper, did he?"

"No," Mark said. "He was just nice and helpful, and I gave him a dime and told him to go get one, just to thank him. You've done a nice job of raising him. Is he in school, now?"

"He'd be in school, down in the village," Brother Erasmus said. "He's a smart boy, gets good grades. I hope he can stay interested in school long enough to go to high school, so he could get some of the schooling I never could get in a teppentine camp."

"How far did you get in school?" Jackie asked.

"Sixth grade is as far as they had in the teppentine camp where I grew up. Not the old one here, but over the other side of Perry. I was already workin' in the teppentine when I got to the sixth grade, so I only went to school the last year when it was cold, and the sap weren't runnin'."

Mark's crowbar popped off a nail. He wanted to cuss, but decided he'd better not. "How'd you get to be a preacher?" he asked as he tried for a new bite on the stubborn nail.

"That's kind of a long story," Brother Erasmus said. "I worked in the teppentine camp till I was seventeen. Now, teppentine's hard work, and anybody that works teppentine wants to work at somethin' else. When I was seventeen, I run off to Jacksonville, and got a job on a construction gang. That was all right, the pay was good, but after work and Saturday nights, I spent my money in the juke joints. I was a young man, and I run a little wild, I guess. Well, one mornin', I woke up in jail after a fight in a juke joint, and I thought that weren't no place for me. I was ashamed of myself; I was a sanctified boy, I'd been saved when I was little, and the sins I'd made of my life was a sore in the eyes of the Lord. Preacher man come through, and gave me a Bible. I didn't read too good then, but the words on them pages come clear to me. Well, after I got out of jail, I quit goin' to the juke joints and started goin' to church. It was maybe four, five years later that the minister said they was going to be a lay preacher's course, and by then I was so deep in the Word of God I wanted to take it, and I guess the Lord was movin' my soul. Well, after that course was over with, the church felt the Spirit of the Lord on them, and decided to help me pay to go to a church school up in South Carolina. They was too poor to pay everything, and I had to get a job washin' dishes up there in South Carolina while I went to school, but they graduated me after a year, and the church in Jacksonville ordained me."

"How'd you wind up in Twillingate?" Jackie asked, levering a board free.

"They was a man from Twillingate went to the church in Jacksonville, and said there was some people here that had a little church, but they could only get a circuit rider but once a month, so I come over here, went to work in the old teppentine camp to feed myself, and took over the church. I met Ethylene over in the teppentine camp, and we been here ever since."

Mark shook his head. "Doesn't seem like a little church in a little town like this would pay you enough to live on."

"They pay me a salary," Brother Erasmus said. "They can't pay much, and I give most of it back to the poor. See, in the Good Book, you read about Paul, travelin' around Greece and what's now Turkey, spreadin' God's word and God's wisdom. Well, all the while Paul was spreadin' God's word, he was makin' tents so he'd have food on the table, even when the Romans had him in chains. See, Paul was a tentmaker, and he knew it wasn't right expectin' other people to support him for doin' God's work, so he stayed bein' a tentmaker. Now, Paul was a great man of God, so who am I to think I'm any better than he was?"

Mark was impressed. Previously, he'd thought of being a minister as being an easy job, one that didn't involve a lot of work. It took a lot of faith, a lot of motivation, to take on being a minister on top of doing a hard day's work for a living. "What are you working at now?" he asked.

"I worked at the teppentine camp till it closed," Brother Erasmus said, "But then, I decided that I'd better try to get along at other things, so if the Lord needed me, I wouldn't have to answer to the boss. I fish a little mullet, fix people's houses, work for Mr. Cowgill when it gets busy for him on the shade 'bacca. Just whatever comes along. Sometimes I don't know where my next meal is comin' from, but so long at the Lord has got it figured out, I don't figure it's my place to worry about it, and he's always provided for me. 'Have faith in me and I will provide,' it says in the Good Book."

"Brother Erasmus!" a man's voice called from behind them. All three of them looked up to see a short, thin man, with thin red hair and a red face, sitting in a pickup truck.

"Mist' Cowgill," the black preacher said. "I didn't expect to see you here today."

"Didn't expect to see you here at all," Cowgill said. "Been looking all over everywhere for you. Didn't find you there, so I knew you had to be here. Is this those people with that little plane over there?"

"This is Mist' Mark, and Miss Jackie," Brother Erasmus said. "They been helpin' me salvage lumber off our old roof."

"I told you I didn't want you using that old stuff," Cowgill said, shaking his head.

"I kin understand why you don't want me using that old stuff from the teppentine camp," Brother Erasmus said. "Devil's in them boards, sure, but this is different."

Cowgill shook his head. "Can't figure what you'd want to use that old junk for when I've got Samuel down at the church, unloading a load of new wood from the sawmill."

"Why, now you've shamed me in front of these good folk," Brother Erasmus smiled, with a big grin on his face. "I was just tellin' them to have faith that the Lord will provide, and I guess since I was out here my faith was a little weak."

"That'll be the day," the man in the pickup said. "Lord made me feel a little guilty last night, after all the good you've done around here, so t'wern't no reason I couldn't come up with a truckload of wood and some odds and ends."

"I'm much obliged, Mr. Cowgill. The Lord does provide."

"Well, let's go provide Samuel with some help unloading that wood. We loaded it with a fork truck down at the mill, but we're going to have to unload it by hand." He turned to Mark and Jackie. "If you'd like to come along, there's room in the back."

There was a lot of wood on the stake truck sitting in the churchyard, but with the five of them working at it, the work went quickly. "I throwed in a few other odds and ends I had laying around, getting in the way," Cowgill said. "Maybe you can use them." Mark smiled; the "odds and ends" included six rolls of tar paper and close to a hundred pounds of nails, all still in fresh boxes with the price tags on them.

The sun was up high, and all of them were sweating hard by the time they finished unloading the stake truck. "Ya'll want to ride down to the store, I'll buy us a Doctor Pepper," Cowgill said as the last board was stacked. "I wanted to talk to these folk, anyway, and they been a big help."

The cool breeze coming over the back of the pickup truck was refreshing as they rode into Twillingate. Brother Erasmus rode in front with Cowgill, and Mark and Jackie and Samuel, a young black man who didn't have much to say, rode in back. It felt good to sit in the shade of the porch of the general store, sipping on the bottles of pop.

"I know you young folk didn't have much choice about landin' here," Cowgill told Mark and Jackie. "And, I don't mind you campin' out there as long as it takes you to get your plane fixed. But I just want you to know that this is the busy season for me, and there's no way I'm going to be able to get a crew out there to pick up all that stuff until next fall, before quail season."

"We kind of figured that," Mark said. "We've already started work on clearing a path through there. If we can get a path twenty feet wide, maybe eight or nine hundred feet long, that'll be all we need."

"Kind of figured when I saw that little plane of yours that you wouldn't need every bit of the runway like those two-engine jobs those Yankees fly down here quail hunting," Cowgill admitted.

Mark nodded. "The only thing is," he said, "There's a couple of logs out there that are too big for Jackie and me to move, and we were wondering if there were some place we could borrow a chain saw for an hour or two."

Cowgill thought about it for a moment. "Well, pulp is pulp, I guess. I'll tell you what. There's probably a day's work for the pulp crew just cleaning up some of the bigger logs out there. I'll have them come out there tomorrow, rather than out to the woods. They'll leave a lot of slash laying around, but it'll be stuff you can move. That be all right?"

"Sounds great to me," Mark said.

Cowgill took a sip of his Dr. Pepper. "Sorta thought so," he said. "I can see you folks are people that don't mind getting your hands dirty, not like the Yankees that come down here and expect everything to be done for them, or them college kid hippie liberals that think they know everything and come down here to stir things up. You see some work that needs to be done, you don't mind doing it. I heard about you helping out Paul Thibodaux yesterday, and I realized you was working folk."

"I'm a phone man," Mark said. "I wanted to make a phone call, and that was what needed to be done. After yesterday, I was glad to be working at something, rather than thinking about the tornado."

"Thibodaux is a good man," Cowgill said. "Like everybody else in Twillingate, including me, he ain't got a pot to piss in or a window to throw it out of, but he keeps the phones going with chewing gum and bailing wire, somehow or other. What do you think of Twillingate, anyway?"

"It's not much to look at," Jackie admitted, "But everybody we've met here has been real nice. I guess it's not what I would have expected."

"You mean, like nightriders and civil rights demonstrations and like that?" Cowgill said, frowning.

"There's been an awful lot of it on TV," Jackie said, trying to be honest as well as diplomatic.

"That there has," Cowgill admitted. "But, there's been none of that stuff here. What you got to remember is that we're a real small town. That means everybody knows everybody else. We're a poor town, always have been. Everybody has to work together, or we all starve. You get into bigger towns, even towns up north, and it's niggers and honkies and trouble. In Twillingate, the colored folk and the white folk are friends. Am I right, Brother Erasmus?"

"Is any more," the black preacher said. "There once was a time when the teppentine camp was open that it wasn't quite like that, but mostly it was the teppentine folk that caused the trouble."

"That's part of the reason I got out of the teppentine slashing business," Cowgill said. "Got to the point where the only people you could get to slash teppentine for you weren't worth the trouble or the money. Why lose money and make trouble? We still grub out light stumps for teppentine, but that's with bulldozers, and it's a whole 'nother business."

Brother Erasmus agreed. "Black folk and white folk work together a whole lot better since you quit the slash teppentine," he said.

"That's only part of it," Cowgill told Mark and Jackie. "We've got along a whole lot better since Brother Erasmus has been here, and I don't mind him hearing me say it. Now, I'm a bidness man, and I care about the people I've got working for me. Since this is a small town, I have to care about them, since no one else will. I'd rather have my workers sober and getting food for their families than I would have them getting drunked up at the juke joint and letting they families go hungry. Brother Erasmus here can't keep 'em all on the straight and narrow for me, but he can help with some of 'em. That's why I don't mind donatin' a little lumber and a few odds and ends to rebuild his church."

"Like I told you," Brother Erasmus said. "The Lord does provide."

"Would you mind if I see if I can provide a few people to come to a raisin' Saturday?" Cowgill asked.

"I'd appreciate that," the preacher said. "Mist' Mark, Miss Jackie, I think what Mr. Cowgill is trying to say to you is that you shouldn't believe all the things you hear on TV about these parts. Now, they is nightriders, and they is Klansman, and they is places where they is trouble. But for every place that there is trouble there's a lot of places where there are people that are friends, people who don't like to see things like that on the television."

"That's right," Cowgill said. "They's been less of it since this Vietnam thing was going, but I pity the folks that had to go there."

"I spent eighteen months there," Mark said. "I didn't have it real bad, but I knew people that did. What you see on TV isn't like it really is."

"Same thing here," Cowgill agreed, upending his pop bottle. "Well, I got to get some work done today, but can I drop you people off back at the church or the airstrip?"

Mark and Jackie decided to get off the back of the truck at the church with Brother Erasmus. "You folk be havin' a good day," Cowgill told him as they got out, and Samuel went over to the stake truck. "Brother Erasmus, would you be tellin' your people that if they need any firewood, I'd be much obliged if they'd pick it up off the airstrip."

"I sure will, and I thank you, Mist' Cowgill," the preacher said.

"Good to meet you folk," Cowgill said to Mark and Jackie. "Knew you was northerners, but I kind of had a feelin' you weren't Yankees, and they's a difference."

"Good to meet you," Mark said. "And thanks for your help."

Cowgill drove off. "He owns what you call the plantation, right?" Jackie asked.

"He do," Brother Erasmus told her. "That, and a lot else around here."

She nodded. "That's not quite what I would have expected a plantation owner to be like, either," she said.

"The man may have a little more money than the rest of us," the preacher said. "But that give him more to worry about, too. I've worked in places where the owner ain't like that atall."

Mark shook his head. It was not what he had expected, either. "Is there anything we can do to help you this afternoon, Brother Erasmus?" he asked. "We've got to get up and work on cleaning off that airstrip, but I suppose it won't matter if we put it off a day."

"If we goin' to be havein' a raisin' Saturday, I s'pose we ought to be layin' out some rafters. Let's go back up to the old roof and get the measurements we need, and start layin' them out."

Mark wasn't exactly the world's greatest carpenter, but he had the basic knowledge of the subject and knew what to do when he had a hammer in his hands. It proved that Brother Erasmus was a pretty good carpenter, though; he knew what he was doing. Mark learned more than he'd ever known about laying out a roof that afternoon. "Where'd you learn this?" he asked Brother Erasmus.

"Picked it up here and there," the black man said. "Now, Jesus was a carpenter, and that work was good enough for him, so I learned it where I could."

They worked through the afternoon, and made good progress on building the rafters for the church. Brother Erasmus was an interesting man to talk to, and Mark and Jackie learned a lot about a kind of life they'd never dreamed of. They noticed that most of the stories that Brother Erasmus told somehow or another led back to a point from the Bible, and Mark and Jackie didn't mind listening to him talk about that, either. They soon learned that they'd had only the shallowest conception of what being a Christian was all about, and realized that they were learning a lot more than some carpentry and what it was like to be a black man in the south.

The black man was never pushy, but he soon was able to get Mark and Jackie to confirm that they never had really been church people. Mark told him that he and Jackie had agreed that they had made up their minds to start reading the Bible a little, but that they hadn't gotten around to starting yet.

"They's a lot that's in that Book," Brother Erasmus said as he sawed on a bevel with a handsaw. "They's a lot more in there than just the words, and sometimes Jesus has to speak to you to help you understand what they really meanin'."

As the afternoon went on, E.J. turned up from school, and started to help out. A little later, Ethylene also showed up; it proved that she also worked at the plantation. "Sure was nice of Mr. Cowgill to give this to the church," she commented.

"Reckon the Lord will provide," Brother Erasmus told her. "These folk have been a big help all day. Reckon they could have some supper with us."

"We don't want to put you out," Mark protested.

"Bible says, 'Don't bind the mouths of the kine that tread out the grain,'" Brother Erasmus said. "You been workin' hard when they's no need for you to, and I wouldn't feel right otherwise."

Brother Erasmus' house proved to be a little place up in the woods behind the church; somehow, they hadn't noticed it there before. It was small, but it was neat and well kept. Mark and Jackie both noticed the number of well-tended potted flowers surrounding the house, and noticed that none of the flowers needed to be cut back or watered. The house may have been small, but it was obviously a valued home. "I keep workin' at fixin' it up here and there," Brother Erasmus told them. "When I was a-workin' in the teppentine camp, I never reckoned that I'd have a house of my own."

Supper turned out to be mullet and corn bread again, the same as they'd had with the Thibodauxes the night before, and after supper, they sat out on the porch and talked some more, until the light was starting to fade from the sky. "We really need to be getting back while there's still some light," Mark finally said. "If that pulp crew is going to be out at the airstrip tomorrow, then I suppose we'd better hang around out there, but we'll come back down the day after and see if there's anything else we can do to help.

"'Fore you go," Brother Erasmus said, getting up to go inside the house. "I got somethin' for you."

"What's that?" Jackie asked.

The preacher came back outside after a minute. "You was sayin' that you wanted to get to readin' the Word," he said. "But I don't guess that you folks got a Bible to read. You remember how I told you that when I was in jail, the preacher man came 'round and gave me a Bible?"

"That was over in Jacksonville, wasn't it?"

"That was it," Brother Erasmus said. "This here's the Bible he gave me, and I figure it's got power in it. I'd like you folks to have it."

"We can't take that," Mark protested. "That has got to have an awful lot of meaning for you. It wouldn't be right of us to take it."

"You take it," Brother Erasmus said. "It had power in it for me, and I figure it'll have power in it for you."

Mark and Jackie protested a little more, but to no avail. "All right," Mark said finally. "We'll borrow it from you for a while, but we'll get it back to you, somehow or other."

"You don't have to do that," Brother Erasmus said. "You be needin' the Book."

"We'll get it back to you, sometime," Jackie promised. "We'll just borrow it for a while."

The next morning, they were still drinking their coffee when Mr. Cowgill's pulp crew showed up and started in on the downed trees that littered the airstrip. The crew cleaned up the two trees that had worried Mark in short order, and then started in on the much greater litter of trees toward the other end of the airstrip. Mark had a word with the black man that seemed to be in charge of the crew, and had the crew hook a chain from their tractor to what was left of the church roof, and drag it off to one side of the runway. As they worked, Mark and Jackie turned back to the tedious job of dragging and hauling slash and debris off of the section of runway that they'd decided needed to be cleared.

It was a hot day, but they made good progress in the morning. As the morning grew hot, their progress slowed down, and they decided to take a long break during the heat of the day, and they were just nicely getting back to work when E.J. showed up. "Brother Erasmus told me to come down and see if I could help you folks out," the boy told them. "He said he got to go out to the plantation to tend to a sick lady, but he'd stop by later."

The three of them worked on. It had only taken the tornado seconds to deposit all the stuff on the runway, but it was clearly going to take a lot longer to get it off again. After a while, both Brother Erasmus and Ethylene showed up, and pitched in on the clearing for a while, and by the time they quit, they were close to the point where Mark figured that he had the minimum needed cleared to take off when they got Rocinante fixed. "We'll take care of the rest of it," Mark said, and explained his plan to just clear off enough so he could take off light. "But now that the roof has been moved, and some of those logs on the other side of it have been taken out of there, we ought to have enough runway so that I don't have to bother finding a ride for Jackie and our gear over to Perry."

"You still goin' to give me a ride in your plane, Mist' Mark?" E.J. asked.

"That's the other reason I'd like to clear off more of the runway," Mark told the boy. "I can't take you for a ride unless I've got more runway clear."

"I'll come up tomorrow after school and help you with it some more," the boy promised.

"Tell you what," Mark said. "You and Brother Erasmus and Ethylene come up here about the time it gets dark tonight, and I've got something I'd like to show you."

The three were back just as it was getting nicely dark. The moon was only a few days old, and the air was still and clear and clean. Mark had the telescope set up when the three arrived, and showed them the moon at a moderate magnification. "Can you see where them Apollo men landed?" E.J. wanted to know.

"Afraid not, E.J.," Mark had to say. The moon is really a pretty big place, and that lunar lander is not a whole lot larger than a pickup truck. About the best we can make out here are things that are maybe a mile across. Besides, the place where the astronauts landed is dark, now. The moon is a round ball, just like the earth, and what we're looking at mostly right now is the part where it's night."

"Many's the night I've looked up at that sky with that big old moon hanging there," Brother Erasmus said. "I never thought people would be walking around up there. When I was a boy, I never thought I'd see the day it happened."

Mark showed them some of the other things in the sky as the moon sank lower. M-13 was up pretty good, and so was Omega Centuri. It was a little hard to express any idea of how far away either of them were, or just how big or old they are, but they were pretty, never the less. "Lord put some pretty things up there in the sky, didn't he?" Ethylene said.

It would have been possible to start a debate in response to her comment, and Mark had been in a few, but this time, he refrained from commenting. "He sure did," he said.

The next morning, Mark and Jackie were sitting under Rocinante's wing, drinking coffee and trying to get up the ambition to go out and clear more debris off of the runway when Paul Thibodaux drove up in his pickup truck. After they exchanged greetings, Thibodaux got right to the point. "I'm wonderin' if I can borrow you from Brother Erasmus for a while today," he said. "Had a snag go down last night. Must have been hangin' on since the storm, and it took out the line out to the plantation."

"Sure, what the heck," Mark told him. "I didn't really want to work on the runway again today, anyway."

What should have been a fairly simple job turned into one that was tougher than Mark had expected it would be. While only two wires needed to be spliced, the falling tree had pulled down a rotted phone pole, and this one had to be replaced. That meant digging a post hole by hand in the sandy soil, and then wrestling the pole upright with a block and tackle. "Got to do this more or less right," Thibodaux told him. "This is one of them lines that we prob'ly won't replace when we put the dial system in."

Once they got the pole tamped into place, restringing the wire and splicing in a connection was fairly straightforward. Still, it was coming up on midday before they got the job finished. Hot and sweaty, they sat down in the shade to cool off before heading back toward Twillingate. "So how you be likin' our little place?" Thibodaux asked.

"Everybody we've met here have been real good people," Jackie said. "I guess we really haven't met a lot of people, but we've liked the ones we've met."

Thibodaux smiled. "Everybody in town knows about you," he said. "'Course, stories travel fast in a small town like this. Some people was thinkin' you was Yankees down here to make trouble, but people have been seein' that you've been workin' hard and not sayin' much. Heard a couple of people say, 'They may be northerners, but they ain't Yankees."

"Mr. Cowgill said that," Mark said. "The way he used the word, it was like some people use the word 'nigger'."

"Ain't it the truth," Thibodaux smiled. "People always find it easy to hate people they don't know. You two make sure you come to the raisin' at Brother Erasmus' church tomorrow. There's a lot of people that's been wantin' to meet you that's been lookin' for an excuse, and a lot of them'll be there."

*   *   *

Twillingate, Florida
April 30, 1971

Dear Dad and Sarah:
I've been meaning to write to you for a couple of days now, ever since Mark called home Tuesday night, be we've been so busy that I just haven't had time to write.

I suppose Mark's folks told you that we had a little trouble with Mark's plane. It was sitting tied down on the ground when a wind came along, picked up some debris, and poked a couple of holes in the wing. Mark says it won't be any trouble to fix, once the stuff gets here from Spearfish Lake.

I don't know if you've got a map that will show Twillingate on it; we can't find it on any map that we have with us. It's a little town on the Gulf coast, not too far from Tallahassee. I suppose there aren't more than about 300 people that live here, and more in the surrounding countryside. It's just a little backwoods country town, but the people here are real friendly and interesting. It's a lot different from home in a lot of ways, but in some ways, it isn't a lot different from being in the woods at home.

We aren't much more than a mile or so from the ocean, but this afternoon was the first time we got a chance to walk down to see the ocean. One of our new friends, Mr. Thibodaux, who runs the phone company here, said that there was a little beach out there so we walked down to see it, mostly for something to do. It was a pretty walk, and we saw a lot of different birds, and when we got down to the ocean, we found that the beach was nice, so we went swimming.

The days here are very hot. I would think that it would get so hot and humid here in the summer that you couldn't breathe, as bad as it's been during the middle of the day.

Tomorrow might be an interesting day. We've been invited to a church raising, I guess kind of like the barn raisings that used to happen years ago. Mr. Thibodaux said that the women all get together and make a big lunch for everyone, and he says that it'll be the best chance we'll have to find out what real southern cooking is all about. I can't wait.

Hopefully, the package from Mark's dad will be here tomorrow, or maybe Monday, and then it'll only take us a day or two, and we'll be on our way. I'm not sorry that we stopped here, though, even if the plane did get damaged. Staying here for a few days has given us friends and experiences that we've never had gotten otherwise.

I'll try to give you a call about the middle of the week, to let you know that we're back on the move again.

Love,
Jackie

8.

Mark and Jackie didn't know exactly what to expect at the "raisin'" on Saturday morning, but what they found when they walked down to Brother Erasmus' church didn't quite match with their expectations.

When they talked about it afterwards, Jackie admitted that she more or less expected to see a handful of church members. She didn't expect to see the little clearing in the woods filled with fifty or more old cars and pickup trucks, and perhaps a couple of hundred people, black and white together, already handing up the rafters that she and Mark and Brother Erasmus had built in the preceding days, and building more besides.

But that was what greeted them as they walked down the sandy road from the airstrip.

Not all of the people that were there around Brother Erasmus' church were working, not even a majority of them. There were a lot of women and children there; the smaller ones were playing tag, running and laughing, and some of the larger ones had gotten up a ball game. A few of the children were attacking the weeds around the church with push mowers and weed whips. A charcoal fire had been built a ways away from the church, and there was a spitted hog roasting on it, turned by kid power. Tables had been set up around, and the white and black women of the community were busy pulling together what already smelled to be a great meal.

As fast as the rafters could be passed up, Brother Erasmus and Mr. Cowgill put them into place, and other men started nailing them off. Mr. Thibodaux was there, scrambling around up in the rafters, making sure they were square and level before other men nailed temporary battens in place that would keep them straight until the roof could be sheathed.

"Lord knows what I'm going to do in that crowd," Mark said. "But I suppose I'd better go and look like I'm lending a hand."

"Same here," Jackie said. She saw Bessie Thibodaux, and decided that she would be a good person to ask what to do.

"Lots to be done," Bessie told Jackie. "Why don't you lend a hand with peelin' these potatoes?"

Jackie picked up a paring knife, and started in, just listening to the conversation of the women around her. The talk was thickly southern; even a couple of days before, she would have had trouble making out what the women were saying through their thick accents, but she had started to get used to it. Several of the women there had seen the tornado, but no one but Ethylene had been any closer to it than Jackie had been, and mostly for the benefit of the others, Bessie drew Jackie and Mark's story out of her. That led to a discussion of how she and Mark came to be on the trip they were on, and some of the things they had seen, like the Apollo launch a couple of weeks before.

Time flew by; by the time Jackie finally looked over her shoulder to see how things were coming, she saw Mark and perhaps a dozen other men nailing boards onto the roof. Looking closer, she could make out that the same thing was happening on the far side of the building, and the hammer blows sounded like a hailstorm.

"Ain't that somethin' to see," Ethelyne commented. "They say many hands make light work, and don't you know it when you sees it."

Jackie and Ethylene stood there watching the roof take shape like a time-lapse movie. As fast as a board was handed up and put into place, it was nailed off; each man only had a couple of rafters that he had to nail on, and the men and boys handing up boards had to work fast to keep up with the men hammering. Down behind the men nailing down the boards, other men were unrolling tar paper and tacking it into place, and a course of shingles was already being started along the bottom of the roof. Another crew was busy slapping fresh white paint that had been produced from somewhere onto the weathered sides of the church. It kept them fascinated to watch.

"Land sakes, it's good to see that," an older white woman that Jackie didn't recognize said. "Wouldn't want to wish evil on nobody, but it's almost worth having that tornado come through to see this."

"It's good to see that people can work together," Jackie said, thinking of all the horror stories she'd heard about small southern towns and their race problems. There was no evidence of that here. When Mr. Cowgill had told Mark and herself that the people of Twillingate got along because they all knew each other, she thought that perhaps he had been pulling her leg, and Brother Erasmus had been unwilling to argue, but the sight in front of her told her otherwise. As she had listened to the women talk about cooking and babies, she had realized that if she closed her eyes, she couldn't tell if a woman talking were black or white. Twillingate may have been a small southern town, but Jackie wished that a lot of people could have seen the sight in front of her.

"You must the the Miss Jackie they talk about," the woman said. "I'm Elsie Sprague. Reverend Sprague, over to the Baptist Church, is my husband."

"Oh, please call me Jackie, Mrs. Sprague. I'm pleased to meet you. Is Reverend Sprague around here?"

"He's up there, nailin' down shingles," the older woman said. "We got a lot of people from our church over here, to help out our brothers in Christ. I'd been a-hopin' to meet you. Reverend Sprague and I would be mightily pleased if you were to come to our church tomorrow."

"I'd love to," Jackie said, "And I'm sure Mark would, too. The only thing is that we've kind of promised Brother Erasmus that we'd be his guests here."

"That shouldn't be a problem," Mrs. Sprague said. "Our church is at 8:30, and Brother Erasmus doesn't start his service till ten. You can ride over here with us or somebody, since a lot of people want to go to both churches tomorrow, after our little workbee today."

"I'm sure we'll be glad to come," Jackie said. "The only thing is, we don't have any nice clothes with us, no going-to-church clothes, anyway. Just shirts and jeans."

"That ain't no problem," Mrs. Sprague told her. "The Good Lord opened his arms to sinners and even to tax collectors, so he don't mind people that ain't got nice clothes."

It wasn't yet noon when the last shingle was being nailed into place, and the last board was being painted. One by one, the men came down from the roof, and stood back to look at the work they'd accomplished.

Brother Erasmus and Reverend Sprague climbed up onto the steps of the church, where they could look out at the crowd. "I want to thank all you good brothers in Christ for your help here today," Brother Erasmus said. "If it weren't for you all, we'd never have got done what we got done here today, and I'd like to invite all of you to come over tomorrow to help dedicate our new roof."

Shouts of "Amen, brother," rose from around the gathering, and Mark and Jackie noticed that the words rose from black and white alike, men and women.

After the words had died down, Brother Erasmus continued, "Now, Ethylene and Miz Sprague tell me that the hog ain't quite done yet. So, 'fore we eat and celebrate, I'd like to ask you to help me thank Mr. Cowgill for donatin' the materials for our new roof. You all know that the Devil's wind left slash and stuff all over the airstrip, and Mr. Cowgill is going to need it cleaned up 'fore the quail hunters come in. Since we're all here, let's just all go up there and spend an hour or so at it. If'n we all work as well up there as we worked here, we should be done just about the same time as the hog is."

Now Reverend Sprague spoke up. "Course, cleanin' up the airstrip is going to be a big help to Miss Jackie and Mister Mark, who you've all heard about. These young folk blew into town on the storm, and they've pitched in and worked like they've been one of us, and we've been mighty glad they been here. They've given of themselves a lot, and the only thing I've heard they've asked for is the loan of an axe. Mister Mark, Miss Jackie, I think I speak for everybody in Twillingate when I say that we're glad that the storm brought you here, and hope that you'll remember us when you leave. Let's go clean up the airstrip."

Only a few of the women and children stayed behind, to tend to the food. A lot of the people walked up to the airstrip, and others piled into cars and pickup trucks. Mark and Jackie shared the back of someone's pickup truck with Brother Erasmus. "You didn't have to do that," Mark said.

"Mist' Mark, I done told you, have faith and the Lord will provide," the black preacher smiled. "Course, some times you got to let the Lord know you ready to be provided for. That ain't in the Bible, but it's one of those things you just got to learn. Have faith, have patience, and the Lord, he do provide."

"'Cast your bread upon the waters and it will be returned unto you a hundredfold' also gets in there, too," Reverend Sprague said.

"I wonder what time the mail gets in," Mark said to Jackie while they were still getting dressed Monday morning. Their package hadn't come in on Saturday, or at least that's what Mrs. Highland, the postmaster, told them at the hog roads Saturday afternoon.

"Probably not real early," she replied, "But I suppose we can go down and wait for it."

With breakfast over, they walked slowly down the road toward Twillingate. It still seemed a little strange to see Brother Erasmus' church with a roof on it, and a fresh coat of paint. The front door was open, and the sound of hammering could be heard from inside, so they stopped to investigate.

They found Brother Erasmus on a step ladder, fitting wiring into an electrical box. "Buildin' a roof is one thing," he said. "Wirin' is somethin' you don't want fifty people all doin', on account 'a no one knows what's been done."

"Same way with phones," Mark agreed. "Anything we can do to help?"

"Not much right now, 'cept maybe you can hand me up that bag of staples there by your feet."

Mark handed Brother Erasmus the bag of staples. The black man took a couple, and stapled a wire into place. "So how was dinner over to Reverend Sprague's house yesterday?" he asked.

"Pretty good," Jackie said. "This was quite a weekend."

The black man stopped what he was doing and smiled. "One thing you got to understand, Miss Jackie," he said, "Every weekend in Twillingate ain't quite like this one was."

It had been quite a weekend. After the assembled workers made short work of clearing off the airstrip -- not just a path, but the whole thing -- they went back down to the church for the hog roast. Mark and Jackie were amazed at the food; there was a lot of it, some of it unidentifiable to their northern tongues, but virtually everything was good. After the eating was over, someone started a softball game among the adults -- not black against white, or church against church, which would have been the same thing, but plantation workers against everybody else. The plantation workers had a some good good hitters, but then so did the other team, which also had a young black man that worked on a fishing boat who had a deceptive dropping curve that virtually no one could get a piece of. There weren't exactly nine men on a team, and substitutions were wide open; even Mark was called to bat once, but fouled out on a short blooper to the right field.

After "everybody else" won 9 to 7, somebody produced a fiddle, and there was square dancing. Mr. Thibodaux proved to be a pretty good caller, and it proved that he could play the fiddle, too. There was hymn singing; and it proved that the Baptists could sing a hymn pretty good, too. As it was getting dark, Brother Erasmus suggested to Mark that people might like to have a look through the moon in his telescope, and a young white man offered to take Mark up to the airstrip to get it. As soon as Mark had the telescope set up out on the edge of the crowd, there was a long line of people of all ages to look through it, while the dancing and the hymn singing went on. It was late before the party died out.

About eight the next morning, as Mark and Jackie were still pulling themselves together, Mr. and Mrs. Thibodaux showed up at the airport in his pickup truck, and they rode over to the Baptist Church, where they were amazed to see how many people there were that they knew from the day before.

During the announcements, Reverend Sprague said, "I know a lot of people want to go over to the dedication of Brother Erasmus' roof this morning, so we'll keep this short today." Even so, it was a rush to get over to the other church for their second church service of the day. Judged objectively, Mark and Jackie thought that the Baptists ran a close second to the black church for the quality of hymn singing.

They had Sunday dinner with the Spragues, a dinner that kind of grew into an afternoon open-ended discussion with several people that dropped by the minister's house on courtesy calls. As Mark and Jackie walked back out to the airport later, they saw that the evening service was getting under way at Brother Erasmus' church, so they stopped off there, as well, and it was late before they finally got to bed.

"I think I see that," Mark said. "After working all week, a weekend like that every week would just about kill a person."

"Oh, these things happen ever' now and then," Brother Erasmus smiled. "Usually, it ain't a raisin', or somethin' like that, but somethin' like a weddin'. Town like this, we have to get our fun where we can. I don' know if you saw some of the young men sneakin' off into the bushes Saturday night to sip at the moonshine, and they was some of the young men and young women a-sneakin' off into the bushes for some other things. I s'pose I shoulda said something about it to my folk yesterday, about how it ain't proper to be doin' somethin' like that at a church raisin', but it wouldn't have solved nothin'. It wouldn't be the first raisin' or weddin' around these parts that's lead to a weddin' or two."

They heard the beeping of a horn outside, and Mark went to see what was going on. Outside, Mr. Thibodaux sat in his truck. "Thought you mighta been here when I couldn't find you out to the airstrip," he said. "I brung your package from Miz Highland."

"Hey, thanks, we appreciate that," Mark said. "Brother Erasmus, we'll be seeing you. We've got work to do."

"If you don't mind," the preacher said, "I'd kind of like to see how you do this."

Thibodaux joined Jackie and Brother Erasmus watching Mark as he opened the package. "Dad sent more than enough of everything," he said. "There's three times here over what I'm going to need, although I guess it's better to have too much, rather than not enough."

Mark worked slowly and carefully; this was going to be a patch on Rocinante's battered wings, but he wanted it to be a permanent one. He used acetone to remove some of the enamel on the fabric around the holes, then carefully washed off the remainder of the chemical. Then, using the pinking shears, he cut patches of Ceconite to fit. After doping both the fabric on the wing around each of the holes and the patches heavily with clear dope, he pressed each patch into place, working it as tight as he could. "This stuff doesn't shrink as well as the old cotton used to do," he said, "So you have to make sure that each patch is as tight as I can make it."

It was a couple of hours before he finished up. "Is that all there is to it?" Mr. Thibodaux asked.

"No," Mark said. "That's just the hard part. I'll have to wait for this to dry, and then put on another coat. It's going to take at least eight coats of one thing or another, clear dope, silver dope, or enamel, with some sanding in between, and it could go ten coats or more. It's going to take a couple of days."

While they were waiting for the first coat to dry, Mark and Jackie went back to the church to help Brother Erasmus with the wiring. It was the first afternoon since they had come to Twillingate that time had drug for Jackie; they had been busy most of the time, but there just wasn't much she could do to help.

Late in the afternoon, E.J. got home from school. "Remember, Mist' Mark," he said, "I want to help you fix your plane so's you can take me for a ride in it."

"Well, come on," Mark told him. "I'll let you help me with painting another coat onto the patches."

Mark let E.J. brush on some of the clear dope, and he was pleased with the neat and careful way the boy worked. The job didn't take long, but while they were working on the plane, Mr. Cowgill drove up in his pickup. "The missus and me would be pleased if you'uns would come to supper with us tonight," he said. "It's probably too far to walk back, so I'll bring you back."

"We're just finishing up," Mark said. "As soon as I clean the brush, we'll be ready to go."

Mark and Jackie had heard a lot about the plantation since they had been in Twillingate, but had never seen it. "Gone With The Wind" had colored their imagination, and they had pictured a big white house, with pillars and a wide porch, and were a little disappointed to see what would have been just a more or less typical house for Spearfish Lake. It was nicer than the homes in Twillingate, but nothing particularly special. There were a handful of smaller houses nearby, and several barns and outbuildings, but it was obviously a place where people worked.

Mrs. Cowgill proved to be nearly an invalid, getting around with a walker; the cooking and housekeeping was done by a black woman from Twillingate. Mark and Jackie could remember Ethylene talking about helping with the cleaning at the plantation.

Over dinner, Mr. Cowgill commented, "You remember what I said about that this is a small town and we've all got to work together."

"Yeah," Mark agreed. "I see what you mean."

"Ain't nobody here got much money, including us," Mr. Cowgill said. "But we all do work together, and we respect each other. You folks will be leavin' soon, and I'd just hope that you'll remember the folks of Twillingate bein' poor in dollars, perhaps, but rich with friends."

"We've been impressed," Jackie said. "We won't forget this place."

By the time they got back to the airstrip, it was too late to put on another coat of clear dope, but Mark was up early the next morning to get another coat on Rocinante's wing patches. "I suppose we could go back down to the church and help Brother Erasmus with putting the dry wall on the ceiling," he said. "That's a miserable job to have to do by yourself."

"I'll catch up with you," Jackie said. "This might be a good time for me to take a sponge bath. I'm just not up to sitting around watching you work."

Feeling cleaner for having freshened up, Jackie cleaned up the tent, and repacked a few things. The boredom of the afternoon before had impressed her, and she wasn't looking forward to another day of it. Then, she realized there was something that she could do.

Mark was holding a panel of dry wall into place while Brother Erasmus nailed it off when Jackie walked in, bringing a couple of bottles of pop she had gotten from the general store. "You two look like you need a break," she said.

"Right good to see you, Miss Jackie," Brother Erasmus said. "Let's just get this panel nailed off, Mist' Mark, and I'll be glad to sit down."

They sat down on the shady side of the building to cool off. It was already getting hot, and it looked like it was going to be a long day. "Brother Erasmus," Jackie said. "There's something I've been wondering about. We've just been calling this church 'Brother Erasmus' Church, and we don't know what the name is."

"I guess everybody calls it that," the preacher said. "This is the Twillingate Bethel Church, but don't nobody hardly call it that."

After a while, Mark and Brother Erasmus went back to work, leaving Jackie outside. Time slipped by, and the men had gotten several sheets of dry wall into place when Mark realized that it was long since time that the coat of dope should be dry on the patches. "I'll be back in a little while," he told the preacher.

Mark should not have been surprised at what he saw when he went out the front door of the church. Jackie was there, a silver-painted board in front of her. She was partway through lettering "Twillingate Bethel Church" on it in white enamel, freehand in old English lettering. "You said we had plenty of silver dope and enamel," she said, "So I didn't think you'd mind."

Mark shook his head. "Where did you learn how to do that?"

"Oh, I just picked it up," Jackie said. "I got to playing with calligraphy back when I was in school. Old English is one of the styles I can do from memory, but I can do almost any style if I have a sample in front of me. I just have to be careful when I'm working freehand."

"Brother Erasmus," Mark called, "Come look at this."

The preacher joined Mark, looking at Jackie work on the sign. "My, that's nice work," he said. "The Lord must guide your hand."

"It takes a little practice," Jackie said. "But I just wanted to leave a little something behind to thank you for what you've done for us."

"Lord gave you a talent," the preacher replied. "You want to put it to work."

It was Wednesday afternoon before the last coat of enamel on Rocinante's wing was dry. That morning, Mark and Brother Erasmus nailed Jackie's sign onto the front of the church. "We'll stay around until E.J. gets back from school," Mark told the preacher. "Soon as he gets home, tell him to come out to the airstrip if he wants a plane ride. Why don't you bring him down, and I'll give you one, too."

After that, they walked into town, to mail the unused repair materials back to Spearfish Lake, then went back out to the airport to wait for their friends. As they waited, Mark and Jackie walked up and down the airstrip, looking for nails or small debris that might have been missed during the cleanup on Saturday afternoon, but they found almost nothing. The job had been thorough; it was almost as if there hadn't been a tornado there a week and a day before.

E.J. was wide-eyed as they helped him into the plane. Mark fastened the seat belt, then got in the left side, and cranked Rocinante up. This would probably be the only time the boy would ever be in an airplane, he thought, so he decided to give him a good ride. Once they were in the air, they flew over the church and the town, over the plantation, and out over the ocean a ways. E.J. was glued to the window for a time, and Mark let him handle the controls a bit, just to give him a taste of what flying the plane was like. It was a while before they landed.

"Mist' Mark, that's fine, seein' like a bird sees." E.J. said when they were back on the ground. "You think I could learn to fly some day?"

"No reason why not," Mark told the boy. "You've got to work hard in school, and not throw away your time or your money, but when you get older, you can do anything you set your mind to."

Mark took the time to give both Brother Erasmus and Ethylene a ride around the area, too, and both of them enjoyed it as well.

Finally, it was time to go. Mark and Jackie loaded the last of their gear into the luggage compartment, said their goodbyes, and waved back as saw Brother Erasmus and his family waving goodbye to them. Once in the air, Mark turned north. He still wasn't too sure where they were, but he knew if he flew that way far enough, sooner or later they'd pick up the highway and be able to follow it west. They turned back to watch Twillingate disappear behind them, until it became invisible in the forests below.

"I kind of hate to leave," Jackie said. "That got to feel like home, real quick."

"Yeah, there's some good people there," Mark said. "Who knows? Maybe someday we'll go back, to return Brother Erasmus' Bible to him. That's as good a reason as any."

"That's not a reason," Jackie said. "That's an excuse. But it's as good as any."

* * *

Hazelhurst, Mississippi
May 8, 1971

Dear Dad and Sarah:
We've been gone from Twillingate for a couple of days now, but we really haven't had the chance to write. We flew up to Pensacola and visited the Naval Air Museum, and that's kind of an interesting place, although it meant more to Mark than it did to me.

Right now, I'm laying in the tent on this sopping wet airfield. It's been raining steadily, and it's wet all around, and we haven't been able to fly today, although I hope we will tomorrow. Mark says the weather reports show this stuff lifting. We're heading west from here; we're going to the Texas Star Party, which starts the week after next. That's one of those things that Mark really wanted to do.

Twillingate was an interesting town. We were there a little over a week, and we made a lot of friends. Both Mark and I agree that we'd like to visit there again. We're already learning that we have more fun, meet more people, and learn more, when we're in a place for a few days, rather than just making a night stop.

We've had a lot of fun on this trip so far, and we've met a lot of interesting people. We've only been gone for a month, now, and if the trip continues like this, it will be something to remember for a lifetime. Maybe I disappointed you by running off with Mark like I did, but I had to take the chance when I had it, and so far, it's been worth it.

Mark and I have just decided that we don't want to try cooking under the wing tonight, so we're going to get our ponchos on and go try to find a place to eat. Maybe I can find a place to mail this while we're out, so I'm going to wrap this up.
Love,
Jackie

9.

Texas came at them, and there was no way to go around it without going out of their way.

They took their time crossing Texas, making five night stops, all of them at small grassy airports. They'd given some thought to hiking down on the wilds of Padre Island, but when they got there and flew over it, it didn't look quite as appealing, not even for a night stop at the one airport that was open to them on the island. The weather was so snotty that they fled to the clearer skies of the west.

They wanted to stop at San Antonio to see the Alamo, but Mark realized that San Antonio had awfully busy skies for the mere 12 channels he had in Rocinante's radio, especially since none of the channels could do him much good, especially considering all the jet training traffic from Randolph and Kelly fields. So, they wound up giving San Antonio a wide berth.

The weather cleared as they got into the higher, dryer country to the west of San Antonio, and for the first time they were flying over country that seemed like desert to their northern boreal forest trained eyes.

Flying over this country was a new experience for them. Up until this point, their navigation had been pretty much "thumb-on-the-chart"; if they knew where they were going, Mark might draw a line on the map, just to give them some reference in where they were supposed to be. Very often, he wouldn't bother, since they would normally be following rivers, railroads, or highways. Rarely were they in a place that they couldn't figure out where they were from three or four checkpoints that could be found on one of the collection of aircraft sectional maps that Mark had collected over the years. Some of those were far out of date, but he had a complete collection of up-to-date WAC charts, although those were of a smaller scale, and weren't quite as good as the sectionals for navigating by looking out the window.

As they got out into the desert country, navigating by strict "thumb-on-the-chart" became a lot more difficult; when they came to an area where they couldn't follow a road or something, then Mark would lay out a line on the map and carefully work out the compass course that they would have to follow, making corrections for wind drift, compass variation, and deviations caused by Rocinante's own magnetic field. While they were successful in finding where they were going by this age-old method, called "dead reckoning," they soon came to agree that it was worth the trouble of going out of their way to follow a road.

In desert country, Mark figured that if something were to happen, they'd be better off if they were near a road, anyway. Still, he wished on occasion that he had gone ahead and spent the money on a better radio than the one that had come with Rocinante, one that had more channels and perhaps a receiver for an omni navigation system.

By now, Jackie was doing her fair share of flying the Cessna while in the air, and she was becoming progressively more comfortable with it. They were sharing the navigation, as well; Jackie had quickly picked up the rudiments necessary for the simple system that Mark used for "thumb-on-the-chart" pilotage, and he took the time to explain how dead reckoning was done, as well. For a while, when she was navigating from the sectional, he followed along with the appropriate WAC chart, until both of them gained confidence in their navigation.

It's perhaps best to say that there were times that they never quite knew where they are, but there never came a time when they couldn't find out where they were going if they had to.

They stopped at a little grass strip near Rankin one late one afternoon. They had thoughts of going on, but they could see thunderstorms in the distance, and figured that fighting with them late in the day, and then fighting to set up a campsite in the middle of a storm left something to be desired.

The airstrip was kind of a dismal place, smelling of crude oil from nearby oilfields; other than that, it was barren and empty, covered with scrubby, dusty brown shortgrass. It was hot, and the air was heavy, and even as they looked around for permanent tiedowns it looked like the line of thunderstorms was getting closer. In the end, they tied the Cessna down tight to the portable tiedowns, and set up the tent under the wing, where it might get a little shade from the still-hot sun. "Miserable place," Mark commented.

"If this is what the Texans talk so big about, they can have it," Jackie agreed.

"The heck of it is, we've got about four days to kill, and I don't want to kill it here," Mark said. "There's no point in getting to the Texas Star Party before about the 18th, but we can get there from here in one easy day. Less than that; we've got fuel enough in Rocinante already to get there."

"I sure don't want to kill it here," Jackie agreed. "You got any ideas?"

"The only thing I can think of is to try a backpacking trip down in Big Bend National Park," Mark said.

"What's there?" Jackie asked. "I mean, I've heard of the place, but I don't think I've ever heard anything about what's there."

"Me either," Mark said. "Desert and mountains, I guess. I've never done any desert backpacking, but I suppose we could do a couple of out and back overnights to get an idea of what it's like."

"We sure haven't been doing the backpacking that I thought we'd be doing," Jackie said, shaking her head. "But then, I guess it's been a little early for the kind of places that we'd like to go backpacking."

Mark pulled out one of the sectionals, and tried to figure out where they could land and have a reasonable access to Big Bend. "The only thing I can see," he said, after a while, "Is to fly into Fort Stockton in the morning, and ask there if anybody knows of what the best approach is."

"Maybe we could call the park headquarters from there and ask," Jackie suggested.

"That's kind of the square way to go about it," Mark said. "Other than that, it's not really a bad idea."

"Why don't we just pull up stakes and head into Fort Stockton yet this afternoon?" Jackie asked. "It'd be better than this dump."

"I kind of expect that Fort Stockton is going to be about as bad as right here, only a bigger airport," Mark replied. "Besides, the way the thunderstorms are building over there in the west, I'd imagine we'd have fun getting there. They ought to settle down by evening, and if we get going early in the morning, we'd still have plenty of time to fly down to Big Bend."

"Well, I guess you're right," she said. "You want to get out the books and read a bit?"

They had been keeping with their reading program right along. In the three weeks they had been reading the New Testament to each other, they had worked their way through Matthew, Mark, and Luke, and were now well into the Gospel of the Apostle John. "Kind of looking forward to getting into Acts," Mark said. "That's kind of fun, I seem to recall."

With their Bible reading for the afternoon completed, they turned back to "Pilgrim at Tinker Creek." They had almost gotten through it; only a few pages remained. "We're going to have to find another book," Jackie said.

"Got one," Mark told her. "Ever read 'Walden'?"

"We read a bit of it while I was in high school," Jackie said. "How about you?"

"I've read it and reread it and reread it again," Mark told her. "I think it would be fun to read with you, and discuss it as we go along."

"You brought a copy with you?" she asked.

"Wouldn't be without one," he nodded. "The copy I've got with me is kind of beat up from being annotated so much, but I've learned that old Henry was a sharp old cookie who bears a lot of thinking about."

They barely managed to get done with "Pilgrim at Tinker Creek" before the thunderstorms were threatening for real. "I was kind of thinking about supper,"

Mark told her, "But I suppose we'd better batten down the hatches and wait for the storm to blow through."

The storm came half an hour later, bringing lots of wind to blow the tent around and rock the Cessna at its tiedowns, but little rain, only a few drops. They could see the core of the storm go to the north of them, with lightning flashing and thunder rolling, and they could see that a real rain had fallen a few miles away. From a distance, they could see the cloud of rain falling to the ground; other clouds around had rain falling from them, called "virga", rain that evaporated before it hit the ground.

As the line of thunderstorms moved off to the east, it was clear and still behind them. They sat under Rocinante's wing cooking their dinner, looking at the thunderstorms off to the east, still roaring and banging away.

Before long, they had finished their dinner and the dishes. "Kind of a boring evening," Jackie said. "I suppose it's too late to go to Fort Stockton, now."

"Yeah," Mark said. "I suppose we could read some more. Or, we could shoot some touch and goes. We'd still have plenty of gas to get to Fort Stockton in the morning."

Jackie brightened. "I'd love to," she told him. "I'm tired of sitting around on my dead butt."

"Let's start from the beginning," Mark told her. "Right down to the preflight walkaround of the airplane."

Jackie had seen him do the preflight many times, and he had taken her through it step by step a couple of times. Now, it was his turn to look over her shoulder as she walked around the airplane, checking for holes in the fabric, loose hinges and bolts, and the like. She checked the oil, and made sure everything was in place in the engine compartment. Only then did they get into Rocinante's cockpit, Jackie sitting on the right, as usual. Mark had to help Jackie reach a couple of things that were inconvenient to reach from the right side, but in a few minutes she had the plane running.

Taxiing a taildragger is a little frustrating. Jackie had already learned that since she couldn't see close in front of the nose of the airplane, she had to be careful about where they were going, and sometimes it took a bit of zig-zagging. Down at the end of the runway, she ran the plane up, checked the mags and the carb heat, and then asked Mark, "Are we ready?"

"If you're ready, we're ready," he said.

"OK," Jackie said. "Here we go." A little uncertainly, she reached out with her left hand and shoved the throttle forward. Rocinante began to gather speed. There was a little swerve as the tail came up, but Jackie was quick to catch it and not overcontrol her correction. In but a few seconds more, a little backpressure on the Cessna's wheel lifted them off of the ground. Jackie climbed out straight ahead, until she could see that the altimeter had reached 400 feet above field elevation, then started a gentle climbing turn to the left. They reached 800 feet above the ground roughly opposite the center of the field; Jackie throttled back, and pulled on the carb heat.

Mark thought that the carb heat was hardly needed in this neck of the woods, as dry as it was, and it was good to get into the habit. Jackie was clearly going to be doing more flying; she was well on her way to being a good pilot. She had the touch, and Mark wished again that he was legally a flight instructor, because there was a limit to how much he could teach her.

Opposite the end of the runway, she pulled the power back to an idle, and let the Cessna glide straight ahead, losing a hundred feet or so, before she turned left, onto base leg. Mark commented, "Looks good so far," but kept his hand off of the wheel.

Her turn onto final approach was a little wide, but she corrected properly, lining herself up with the grass strip. Mark glanced at the airspeed: not bad, considering that Jackie couldn't see the indicator well. She was rapidly getting the feel of the airplane, how it wanted to act at various speed, and Mark knew that was more important than the ability to read a dial.

Still, she was a little high coming over the fence, perhaps a bit fast as she started her flare. "Hold it off," he said. "This isn't a tricycle gear, you don't drive it on."

Jackie increased the back pressure she was holding on the wheel, and felt Rocinante get sloppy, just at the time that the wheels hit the grass in a reasonable three-pointer. "How was that?" she asked as Rocinante rolled on the ground.

"Pretty good," Mark said. "Let's do it again."

Instantly, Jackie crowded the throttle forward, and reached up to push the carburetor heat on. In only a couple of seconds, she had the tail back up again -- they hadn't lost that much speed -- and soon they were climbing out again.

They did a half a dozen circuits of the runway, landing and taking off each time. "You're getting better," Mark said, making a mental note of the fact that he hadn't touched Rocinante's controls at any time in the session. "But, that's enough practice for today, or we might be a little tight on gas in the morning."

"Darn," she said as she let the Cessna roll out to taxi speed. "It felt like I was getting the hang of it, there."

"You are getting the hang of it," he reassured her as she turned the Cessna around and began to taxi back up to the tiedowns. "We'll do this again. Some one of these days, we're going to have to find you an instructor, so maybe you can see how good you're really getting."

"Oh, hell," she said. "I don't see how you can taxi up to the tiedowns, and I don't want to hit the tent."

"Easy enough done," Mark taught. "Come up on it so you can see where you're going out your side window, and then turn onto the tiedowns at the last second." She tried it, and it worked. The tent bounced around in the prop blast, but she idled the engine and it quietened down. Mark watched with a smile as she pulled the mixture back, to let the engine die.

"Not bad," he said, unbuckling his seat belt. "I think that calls for a kiss for your instructor."

She kissed him -- just a quick peck. "I'm glad you're showing me how to do this," she said. "I never thought I'd be able to do this."

"I don't know if you noticed," he told her. "I never touched the controls, the whole time. I guess I'm going to have to let you do more of the regular flying."

They got out of the plane, then tied it down. They dug the stove out again, and made themselves a cup of coffee to celebrate, and then sat and drank another cup as they watched the sun set. "I will say one thing about this place," Mark said. "I'll bet it's dark around here at night."

"You want to get the telescope out?" Jackie suggested.

"It's only a few days after the full moon," Mark said, "So we'd probably only have an hour or so before the moon comes up. But, yeah, what the heck, let's do it. We still want to get up early, though."

The moon was rising before they got the telescope put away and got into their sleeping bags, and they kissed each other goodnight before rolling over. It had cooled off a bit, and the warmth of the sleeping bags felt good; it made for a good night's sleep.

There was dew on the grass the next morning when they got up. "What do you say if we say nuts to the coffee, and just get on our way?" Mark suggested. "There'll probably be some in the airport office at Fort Stockton, that is if it's like any other airport in the world."

"Fine with me," Jackie said. "We had a better time here last night than I thought we were going to have, but I'd just as soon get on our way."

Mark let Jackie do the walkaround in the morning, and let her fly to Fort Stockton, not much more than a half an hour away. "We could have made it on into here last night," she commented.

"True," Mark said. "But the bigger the airport, the stickier they are about letting us camp out beside the runway. Besides, there's enough lights around here that it wouldn't have been as much fun to use the telescope."

As expected, they found coffee in the airport office; they also were able to get a bit of advice. "The best place to go is an little airstrip called Terlingua Ranch," one of the people at the airport told them. "Odds are that you can get a ride into the park from there. If you can't it's a hell of a long walk, and there's not a lot of cars that go by to hitch, since it's not on the main road. There's a private field that's closer, but they get sticky about people dropping in without warning."

"Sounds reasonable," Mark said. "If we can't get a ride, we just won't go into the park."

"That's probably the best way to play it," the man said. "You want to have all the water you can carry out there. In fact, any time you fly around this part of the country, you want to have a pretty good supply of water with you. It probably wouldn't be a bad idea if you were to fly around the place and check it out before you land. You want to stay up above 1500 feet above ground, though. That's a national park, and they do get a little upset at low flying."

They were amazed at how bleak and empty and rugged the place seemed, even though the countryside on the way down there was not a lot less bleak. Terlingua Ranch proved to be a dude ranch of sorts, and they were able to slip one of the ranch hands a few dollars to drive them down into the park, and up into the hills to the park headquarters. Since the ranch hand's girl friend wanted to go along for the ride in his pickup truck, Mark and Jackie rode in the back along with their packs, getting dusty and letting the sun beat down on them, and the wind blow their hair. He looked as Jackie as they were carried along, and thought about how pretty her hair was, blowing in the wind.

At the park headquarters, they explained to a ranger what they had in mind: a couple of easy out-and-backs in different directions, just to get the feel of backpacking in desert country.

"Ever hiked in the desert before?" the ranger asked.

"No," Mark said. "Always in northern forests."

Even though it was a fairly busy day -- a Saturday -- the ranger took time to explain some of the things that they had to think about. As the man in Fort Stockton said, water was precious, and they wanted to husband it. Even in May, it was hot enough in midday that they ought to think about finding some shade, even if it was a tent fly, and sitting out the heat of the day. Otherwise, take it easy, and don't overexert themselves.

The ranger also told them a bit about the park: "This is probably the most isolated area in the National Park System. The Rio Grande, cutting deep canyons through desert mountains, forms the Big Bend of Texas," he said. "It's wild and rugged back there, and there are five different type of ecological zones, from the Rio Grande flood plain to the Chisos Mountains. Mostly, it's part of the Chihuahuan desert, but there are some pine forests in the Chisos Mountains. This area was a stronghold of the Mescalero Apache, and never really got civilized. It was used for grazing, and they overgrazed it heavily. There was also mining around here, before the Big Bend became a National Park in 1944."

"What did they mine?" Jackie asked.

"Cinnibar," the ranger said. "They smelted mercury out of it, but it was mostly mined out half a century ago."

They settled for a short hike through the steep countryside the first day, to an old mine; they explored it a bit, then set up camp. It was a dry camp; there was no water for miles. As the evening fell, they watched the sun go down, and read a little more from John and from "Walden."

It got dark quickly, and Mark was amazed at how clear the skies were -- even better than back at the airstrip at Rankin, the night before. Other than the few lights at the park headquarters and the lodge, around the corner of the ridge, there were no lights for miles. "I don't think I've ever seen the stars like that," he marveled.

"Don't you wish we'd brought the telescope?" she replied, in similar awe.

"It would have been a lot to carry," Mark admitted. "But it shouldn't be any worse up at Fort Davis next week, and we'll have progressively less moon each night."

They were up early the next morning, and hiked back to the park headquarters, getting there by midmorning. "There's a loop hike you might want to take, if you want to stretch it out to a couple of nights on the trail," the ranger told them. "The countryside is pretty, but you'll have to keep an even closer eye on your water."

Mark and Jackie studied it carefully on the map, and decided to go ahead with it.

It was a long hike, and a dry one, but they were careful and took it slow. Much more than they had the day before, they were amazed at the amount of life that they found inhabiting this oppressive, forbidding countryside. This was true desert, and deep desert at that, but still there were patches of green that would have been easy to overlook from the seat of an overflying airplane. In fact, the desert was fairly alive with life of various sorts, and here and there were green spots among the greasewood and cactus and scrubgrass, where there might have been the hint of a little more water than elsewhere.

What had seemed drab to them only a couple of days before had become beautiful and fascinating. There was no one thing that stood out among their experiences along this relatively short, two-night loop hike, during which they were entirely alone, but it was a peaceful, relaxing, rewarding time. They weren't exactly old desert rats by the time they hiked back into the Park Headquarters on Tuesday morning, but along the way, they had gained a lot of respect for the desert, and had learned that there was more there to see than met the first glance. It gave them a whole new perspective.

Before they left to go back to the plane, they hunted up the park ranger that had befriended them. "I'm glad we came here," Mark told him. "You gave us a whole new insight on an area that I thought was mostly drab and ugly, and we have to thank you for it."

"I appreciate hearing that," the ranger said. "That's my job, after all, but it's nice to hear it."

They were able to get a ride as far as the park boundary easily enough, but when they came to the side road from Panther Junction that would take them back to Terlingua Ranch, the traffic died out. Fortunately, they had filled their water bottles at the park headquarters, and they rather wearily started hiking up the road to the airstrip where Rocinante waited for them.

Walking down the dusty road was not nearly as fascinating as hiking down the trail through the park had been. This was ranching country, but thinly populated, even by cattle, which had to scrabble for water along with everything else. It was a long and dusty trudge, and the miles drug by, one after the next. They stopped for a long break, and hit on their water, then began to walk again, hot and sweaty.

They did finally get a ride, but it was only about a mile from the airstrip. The driver was going on by, but agreed to take them up the side trail to the ranch, where they were overjoyed to see Rocinante again. They offered to pay the driver for rescuing them, but he waved them off, saying, "We try to go out of our way to be nice to strangers around these parts."

It was a fairly short flight up to the town of Marfa, less than an hour, and they were almost cooled off again when they landed. The heat on the runway was intense, and they were glad to find a place to tie down.

They knew that they were going to be away from Rocinante at the Texas Star Party for several days, so they packed their packs a lot heavier than they had before, taking most of the stuff from the luggage compartment, including the telescope.

It was a long way from the Marfa airport to Prude Ranch, north of Fort Davis, where the Texas Star Party was held. Fortunately, one of the men at the airport had a friend who was willing to drive them up to Prude Ranch in an old '56 Ford Victoria that looked like a twin of the old clunker that Mark had driven around Spearfish Lake. The right hand door was sprung the same way, and Jackie found that she remembered the trick of opening it.

Though still pretty much desert to their northern forest eyes, the land around Fort Davis was a little greener than it had been down in the Big Bend country. As they drove on up the valley of the Davis Mountains toward McDonald Observatory and the Prude Ranch, they began to see even more trees and more greenery, and realized that they would be seeing more greenery.

Their driver, who hadn't said a word on the entire trip up to the Ranch, let them off at the headquarters building for the star party. The Texas Star Party was a fairly new thing at this time, but it had already gained national prominence as the place to go for serious dark-sky observing; there was little ground lighting within miles, and the west Texas skies were clear and bright. That was why the Universities of Chicago and Texas had combined forty years before to build McDonald Observatory only a few miles away, and put a 82-inch telescope -- for years, the second largest in the world -- on the peak of Mt. Locke, which was in view from the campsite at Prude Ranch. It was argued by many that Mt. Locke was the best observing site in the continental United States, at least for deep-sky observing with a large telescope, and it was with a feeling of reverence that Jackie didn't quite understand that Mark went up to the registration desk.

"Oh, you're Mark Gravengood and Jackie Archer," the silver-haired woman at the registration desk said. "We were wondering when you were going to show up."

"I'd had a package sent here for me," Mark said. "Did it get here?"

"You got two, and Jackie got two, as well," the woman said.

"Boy, am I glad to see those," Mark told her. "The big one is observing gear. We've been traveling, and I've only carried the stuff I absolutely had to have with me. The rest of it is mail, I guess. We haven't had any mail from home for a month."

"More than that," Jackie said. "Six weeks, anyway."

They found a campsite under the edge of some trees, one that would also make a fair observing site to the south. The telescope, and the supporting gear, could be carried if they wanted to look off in other directions. They downed their packs, and even before they set up the tent, they opened the boxes to see what they had brought.

Mark's large box he knew about; he had packed it the week before they left. It included such things as his favorite old Skanate Pleso star charts, extra eyepieces, a higher and more solid tripod than the one he had been using, and an equatorial mount and drive for the telescope. With some of the fittings he had put in the box, he would be able to do some astrophotography.

"Around this place, a six-inch f5 telescope is going to be really in the small potatoes department," he told Jackie. "There's going to be plenty of big stuff here, and we'll probably spend a lot of time wandering around checking out some of the big telescopes, rather than piddling with this little thing. But, this is probably going to be the best sky I've ever had this under."

Jackie was barely listening; one of her boxes, the small one, proved to be mail -- several magazines she hadn't seen yet, a few letters, and a nice, long one from her dad and Sarah. She resolved that she'd read them slowly and carefully, spreading them out. It had been a long time since they had gotten mail, and it could be a long time again before they would be able to predict that they would be in one place long enough to receive it.

The other box had her puzzled, though. There was only one way to figure it out: she opened it. "Cookies!"

"Say what?" Mark said, opening his other box, to discover mail of his own.

"Cookies!" Jackie repeated. "Sarah must have gone out of her way to make them. There's sugar cookies, and chocolate chip, and oatmeal, and I don't know what all. Have a cookie!"

"Tell you what," he said. "I'll trot up to the headquarters building and get us a couple of cold cokes, and that'll go even better with those cookies than warm water from our packs."

He was back a couple of minutes later carrying cold cokes, dripping already with condensation. Jackie was munching on a cookies, and reading a letter. Mark sat down beside her, popped open a coke, and handed it to her. She took it absent-mindedly and sipped at it, intent on the letter. He opened his own coke and took a sugar cookie, and began to paw through his box of mail. There were some letters there, and a couple of new copies of "Sky and Telescope" that had come out after they left home. He was leafing through the letters, trying to find the ones that seemed to want to be opened first, when she said, "Well, I guess we can go home again."

"What do you mean?"

"It means that I'm not going to have to be ashamed to walk in the door at home again," she told him. "Listen to this, it's from Dad: 'We've been waiting for the mailman every day since you've been gone, in hopes that we'd get another letter from you. It certainly seems like you're having a dream of a trip, the kind of thing that I did all those years ago, and I envy the both of you the youth and the freedom that it takes to just head out on a trip like that.

"'When you first left, I was a little surprised, and didn't quite know how to feel. I wished that you had let us know that you were planning on going, but then I realized that you hadn't planned on it, it came as a whim. Maybe I was a little disappointed in you, but then I realized that in a way, you were doing what your heart told you to do, and I guess what my heart was telling you to do, too. My parents were never too happy with me when I went hoboing around back after the war, but I've never been sorry that I made the trip, and I feel pretty sure that you will never be sorry that you've done what you've done. So, I can't be angry with you for leaving, although I probably would have tried to stop you had I known about it ahead of time. But that would have been my head talking, and not my heart. I suppose that I would have said that it's not right, not safe, for you to go off with Mark, so I guess I'm just as glad that you took the bull by the horns and went and did what you wanted to do.

"'Both Sarah and I think highly of both you and Mark, and we know that you won't let us down, that you'll be careful and stay out of trouble and have a good time. You are both adults, and I believe we can trust in your good judgement. We're both looking forward to the time that you can come home and tell us stories so that we can enjoy them. We know that you're going to see a lot of new places and make a lot of new friends, but we're waiting until you can come back and be with us again, too.'"

"Man," Mark said, shaking his head. "I can hardly believe that."

"Me either," Jackie agreed. "I mean, even after the way we've talked on our phone calls, I kind of figured that he'd be madder than hell, and maybe he was until he had a chance to think it over. But, Mark, you just can't ask for a letter that's better than that."

Mark took another sip of his coke and tried a chocolate chip cookie. "I don't know. I guess I kind of expected to get some static from my folks when we've called home, but there's never been any word of it, just 'We hope you and Jackie are having a good time.' Do you suppose they know something we don't?"

"I suppose they suspect a little more than the truth," she said. "I mean, it's not like we've eloped, or something."

"For a while there, I kind of had the impression that we thought that it would have better if we had eloped," he nodded. "That's sort of respectable, in a way, but we've been away from Spearfish Lake long enough that it doesn't bother me as much, any more."

"You're right," she said. "Spearfish Lake seems so long ago and so far away, it's like we're in another world."

* * *

Texas Star Party
Prude Ranch, Ft. Davis, Texas
May 18, 1971

Dear Dad and Sarah:
We just got to the Texas Star Party a little while ago, and got your letter and packages. The cookies are wonderful! Mark and I have agreed to try to stretch them out as far as we can over the next week, rather than be like little pigs and eat them up as fast as we'd like to. They taste of home to both of us.

It was so good to hear from you, especially, Dad, and to let us know your thoughts about Mark and me being on this trip together. So far, we have had a lot of good times, seen a lot of places I would never have seen if I had stayed in Spearfish Lake, and done things I would never have dreamed of doing if I had stayed home. I'm glad that I came on this trip, and knowing that you don't hold it against me helps me enjoy it even more.

I really am looking forward to coming home again, and sitting down in the living room, and telling you all that's happened and showing you the pictures we have taken. However, it won't be any time soon, probably. I don't expect that we'll be home before fall, and Mark's original plan was to be gone for a year.

It really makes me sorry that we have not been able to be in one place long enough, or know where we're going to be far enough in advance to get mail from you, but the wait was worth it. Getting mail was all the sweeter for waiting for so long.

We are going to be here for a week, so I suppose if this letter gets right to you, we could get more mail here. I'm writing this in the middle of the afternoon, and we just got here, but I think I'll try to call home tonight to tell you that you could send more mail if you send it right away.

Since my last letter, we've come quite a long ways, clear across Texas, but I'm going to be honest and say that the first half of the trip across Texas was not one of the better parts of the trip so far. The weather was lousy, and a couple of places that we wanted to go didn't work out. Once we got into west Texas, the weather was better, and we just today finished three days of backpacking in Big

Bend National Park. I never thought I would enjoy hiking in a desert -- so dry and barren -- but it proved to be a lot more interesting than we thought. The worst part of the hike was getting back to the plane from the park. We had to walk six or seven miles on a dirt road, and it was not fun. I'm still dirty and grubby, but as soon as I finish this letter, I'm going to go over to the rest rooms and have a nice, long shower. It will be so good to be clean, again!

I'm writing this in the first rush of getting mail from you, and I just wanted to let you know that we got it and appreciate everything. I'll write to you a little later in the week, again, and let you know more about Big Bend, and about what's going on here. It looks like it's going to be interesting, even though we've just barely gotten here.

Love,
Jackie

10.

When Mark and Jackie arrived at the Prude Ranch, there weren't a lot of people around, but more kept pulling in during the day with little fanfare, and soon there was a pretty good crowd congregated in the little meadow in the Davis Mountains.

After a while, they set up their tent and their campsite. They both took the opportunity to take showers, the first time in days. While Jackie started her letter home, Mark began to set up the telescope. It was a little different than he had become used to; this was his original equatorial mount, where the telescope could follow the stars as they moved across the sky by a movement in a single axis, rather than two. The equatorial mount was a lot heavier than the simple little altazimuth mount he had built to take in the plane with him, and it wasn't easy to use, but if he was going to use it for photography, he needed it.

As darkness fell, the place came alive. All over the field, dust covers and tarps came off of telescopes that had been set up earlier. As much as Mark wanted to mess with his own telescope, the temptation to explore a bit and see what others had brought overwhelmed him, and Jackie wandered along with him.

Mark had never seen such a profusion of telescopes, of all shapes and sizes. As he had predicted, his own telescope was one of the smallest present; at least, there were few smaller. Most, however, were not a great deal bigger.

Of course, they stopped and looked through many of the telescopes. Several of them were pointed at Omega Centauri, the big southern globular cluster that Mark and Jackie had seen through the Florida haze. Even in Mark's telescope, they were able to see it a lot more clearly in the Texas sky.

But in bigger telescopes, it was even better. The advantage that a bigger telescope has over a smaller one is that not only do the larger ones collect more light, they allow smaller objects to become point sources, not just mere fuzzballs. In Mark's telescope, it was possible to resolve the stars at the edge of a globular cluster like Omega Centauri or M-13, but in a 12-inch telescope they looked through, it was possible to resolve stars nearly to the core.

With their eyes adapted to the dark, it was easy to walk around the field, lit only by starlight. Occasionally, they would have to use their red flashlights. Mark warned Jackie that using a white flashlight was a major no-no, as even a glimpse of a bright white light could ruin someone's hours of dark adaptation. In the darkness, Mark could see a group of people gathered around what had to be the biggest telescope he'd ever seen.

In the dark, it was hard to get a feel for how big it was, but Mark guessed that it had to be nearly twelve feet long, and with a mirror that could go as big as 24". Never having looked through a telescope that size, they got in line.

As the line moved slowly ahead, Mark could see that this telescope was not on an equatorial mount, but an altazimuth mount built close to the ground. Even as tall as he and Jackie were, and as low in the sky as Omega Centuri was, it took a stepladder to get up to the eyepiece. Mark let Jackie go first. "My God, you can see all the way to the core," she exclaimed. "This is such a fantastic view!"

"That's Omega Centuri," a tall, thin man standing next to the stepladder said in a thin, high, reedy voice. "But I suspect that you know that already. If it starts to get out of the field of view, just push on the telescope until it gets back in."

Jackie stood on the stepladder studying the globular cluster for a long time. She knew that Mark and other people were waiting for a look, but she couldn't tear herself away from the view of the huge ball of stars that filled the eyepiece. It was as if she was standing at the porthole of a starship close by, studying the millions of tiny points of light -- most of them white, but she could make out pinkish and yellowish and bluish ones.

Eventually she let Mark have a look. "Wow!" he said at the sight. "That is just absolutely incredible." He, too, stood there looking at it until he started feeling guilty about the other people that were waiting.

"Come back a little later," the man said. "After a while, we'll have a look at Jupiter. The view you get is very good. You can see all sorts of detail, and the red spot really stands out."

Mark stepped down from the stepladder, and another eager looker climbed up it. "That's quite a mirror," Mark said. "Did you grind it yourself?"

"Oh, yes," the man said. "It's a 24 inch mirror, made from porthole glass."

"I'll bet it took you a while."

"Yes, but I had very little but time when I ground it," the man said. "You see, I was a Bhuddist monk at the time, and I was living under a vow of poverty, but I've found over the years that working glass is very good for meditation."

"You're not a monk any longer?" Jackie asked.

"No," he man said, a bit ruefully. "The master decided that my telescopes were a distraction, and threatened to throw them into the bay, so I left the monastery. Even at that point, I'd had to hide my telescopes around the neighborhood. I often set up a telescope on the sidewalk after dark, and let people look at the stars and planets, and almost every night, a child would say, 'Hey mister, what's that?', and I would answer, "A telescope. Would you like to take it home with you?'"

They laughed, and the man went on, "You see, I have felt over the years that if everyone could see sights like Omega Centuri, like you have just seen, that we would all have a better picture of our place in the universe. Since I've left the monastery, I've mostly traveled around, introducing people to the universe."

"That's quite a telescope," Mark said. "I don't want to bother you now, but I want to come over in the daylight and get a good look at it."

Mark and Jackie walked away, to wander on and see what else there was to be seen. "Now, there's a strange man," Jackie commented. "But he's a very nice person. And what a telescope! I can see how a look though that can give you a different perspective on the universe."

"I can, too," Mark said. "I mean, we're already used to the concept of such things. But can you imagine some city kid on the sidewalk, seeing something like that for the first time, and what it would do to his view of his place in the universe? I mean, we think of ourselves as being pretty big and important, and even flying across the country, looking out Rocinante's window, we begin to realize how small we really are."

"Wouldn't it be nice to have a telescope like that?" Jackie said. "I think I would enjoy doing just what he's doing, showing off the sky to people."

"I would, too," Mark said. "I don't think I would want to make a life of it, but when you look at it from his viewpoint, I can see how it would be rewarding."

They slept late the next morning, but not too late, because there were things to do during the day. They sat in front of their tent brewing coffee when a tall, thin, gray-haired man walked by. Mark thought he might be the man from the big telescope of the night before, and spoke up, "So how late did you stay out last night?"

"The moon was long up before the crowds died out," the man said. "I was rather tired after the long drive, but I don't like to put things away while there's anyone waiting. It must have been two or three in the morning before I crawled into the telescope tube for the night."

"You sleep in the telescope tube?" Jackie exclaimed.

"Oh, yes, I've spent many a night there," the man said. "It keeps the rain off quite nicely. You see, I only have to loosen a couple of bolts to take the mirror out. It travels in its own special case, since the cell is not strong enough to hold it in the tube while I'm traveling."

"Well, sit down, have a cup of coffee," Mark offered.

"I'll pass on the coffee, thank you," the man said. "I don't drink it, since it's a stimulant. Is this your telescope?" he went on.

"Yeah," Mark nodded. "I'm afraid it's nothing special. I built it myself, back when I was in junior high."

"Why, that's wonderful," the man said. "By the way, my name is John. May I have a look?"

"Sure," Mark said, getting to his feet, out of courtesy, more than anything else. He helped John take the plastic tarp off of his little telescope.

"Very nice workmanship," John commented. He looked around for a minute, then something off in the distance caught his attention. "Perfect," he said, and pointed the telescope off at it. Mark could see him fiddle with the focus. "Very nice mirror," he said finally. "A bit overcorrected at the edges, but certainly not objectionable. I don't see any sign of stress from the cell."

"How can you see all that?" Mark asked, incredulous.

"I never had the money for a testing bench, so I learned how to test the mirrors right from the light of the stars. When you get used to looking at the disk you see when it's out of focus, you can learn quite a good deal about a mirror."

"There's no stars out, right now," Jackie said.

"Yes, but all you need is a point source of light. There's a raven sitting on a post over there a few hundred yards away, and I tested the telescope on the glint in his eye."

Mark and Jackie's mouths both fell open with awe. "I can't believe it," Mark said finally.

John was used to his star tests amazing people, so he broke the silence. "You were in junior high when you ground this mirror?"

"Yes," Mark said. "It was quite a job."

"You did an excellent job," John said. "You have every reason to be proud of yourself. You could do a very good job with a much larger mirror."

"Yeah, I keep thinking about a larger telescope," Mark admitted. "I guess I've got aperture fever, like everyone else. But, it never seemed worth it to go from a six to an eight or a ten, and once you get beyond ten, an equatorial mount really gets to be a handful. But, you seemed to have cracked the problem. That's simple, but it really seems to work well."

"I had no choice but to keep it simple," John said. "Aside from the natural beauty of simplicty, I didn't have to tools or the shop to do anything too complex."

Jackie smiled. "You mean, like, '"Life is too complicated. Simplify, simplify?"'"

"You've read your Thoreau, then," he said. "Yes, that's it exactly. That man had a lot of wisdom that gets overlooked in his message of simplicity."

"Well, I want to come over in the daylight and see just how simple that is," Mark said. "I mean, I like the idea of a big mirror, but that tube seems like such a big hog to have to deal with."

"It is big, but simple," John told them. "Again, I didn't have the facilities to do anything more complex, but it works well, too. I can think of ways that someone could keep the sheer size of it down, if that was important to them. You don't really need a big tube, when the purpose of the tube is mostly to support the secondary and the eyepiece, and to keep light out. A simple frame of small tubes could provide the support, and a black cloth could keep out stray light."

Mark tried to picture it in his mind. Yes, it could work, he realized, and wouldn't be much more complicated than the big, simple tube. "It all wants to be thought about some," he said. "But I think I'm going to be looking for a piece of big glass."

For the next week, Mark and Jackie's biggest problem was that there just weren't enough hours in the day to do everything they wanted to do.

The problem was pretty simple: in the meadow on the Prude Ranch, there were about 100 telescopes, of which Mark's was one of the smallest. Even on the first night, the moon wasn't rising until after midnight, so there was much to see -- but perhaps more important than looking through their little telescope was the visiting around to other, larger ones, traipsing around that kept them going until after the moon was up.

That wouldn't have been so bad; in a normal situation, they could have slept in the next morning. But, the organizers of the event didn't want anybody to get bored; so all day long, there were seminars, discussion groups, presentations, and field trips. When those weren't going on, there was always someone to stand around and talk to.

Some of the seminars were rather on the technical side, and Jackie, at least, skipped a few of them, in order to try to keep the sleep deficit from getting too out of balance, and she tried to spend at least some time each day laying out in the Texas sun in her bikini, trying to work on her tan.

Jackie still made it to many of the seminars; sometimes, they weren't totally greek to her, and she found that she understood more than she thought she had.

Some of the field trips were fun, too. One day, they got aboard a van and rode the few miles over to McDonald Observatory, which stood on the hill overlooking the field of telescopes.

Touring the observatory was lots of fun. Mark had never been inside a big dome, or seen a big research telescope close up. The 82-inch was by now relatively small potatoes as a research instrument, though still on the list of the biggest ten telescopes in the world. Somehow, it seemed old and a little outdated, next to its younger and bigger brother, the new 107-inch telescope that had only seen first light a couple of years before.

"Now think about it," Mark said. "Think of how much better the view is between my six-inch and John's 24-inch. That's about the difference between the view in John's 24-inch and the 107-inch."

The week sped by rapidly, a maze of days and nights, busy all the time. Mark spent a lot of the time talking telescopes, and Jackie knew that in his sketchbook were some drawings of various ways to do larger telescopes. "I'm getting a lot of good ideas," Mark said at one point. "I guess when we get home again, I'm going to have to find a big glass blank and start in on something a little bigger than what I've got now."

Though they were busy, they had a good time, and met lots of new people, all of them avid astronomy people. There were plenty of new friends, people to stand around and talk with, people to have a lazy cup of coffee with. Given the common interest, it was easy to meet people, and the conversation wasn't limited to things astronomical; topics ranged from politics to religion, from sex to sports cars, from birds to fishing. It was a refreshing week, and it came to an end all too soon.

A week after they arrived, the new moon came; the sky was free of the moon all night, and the observing ran on until the wee small hours. They got a good night's sleep, then got up, took a final shower, and tore down their tent and packed up. Among the packing was the box with the extra observing gear, including a few new things that Mark had picked up; another box was filled with some extra odds and ends they had accumulated in Rocinante, and decided that they would not need again on the trip.

Jackie managed to cadge a ride for them back into Marfa from some new friends from Oklahoma they had met, and along toward the middle of they day, they loaded their things into the back of an already full pickup camper, and the four of them squeezed into the front seat of the camper for the ride to the Marfa post office, then back to the airport.

It was good to get back to Rocinante again; it sat there, faithfully waiting for them like a long-lost friend. It had been the longest time that they had been away from the little Cessna on the trip. It was hot inside the cockpit, where the plane had sat in the sun for days; they opened the doors wide, to let it air out a little, and carefully packed their things back in the luggage compartment. In a week, they had forgotten some of the tricks, but soon they were ready to go. "Where are we heading?" Jackie asked.

"Now that you mention it, I don't know," Mark said. "Ever since we left Florida, we've been kind of heading for the Texas Star Party. Now that it's over with, I really don't have any plans. You got any ideas?"

"Let's head for another part of the country," Jackie said. "Maybe someplace like Yellowstone National Park. That ought to keep us going for a few days, until we can made other plans."

"Sounds good to me," Mark said, reaching into the briefcase behind Rocinante's right seat where he kept the maps, and laid out some WAC charts.

It took parts of four different charts, laid out on the concrete of the Marfa airport, to work out a general plan. "Well, if we head more or less north to about Cheyenne or Casper, in Wyoming, and then turn west, we can stay out of the real high country," Mark told Jackie. "I don't have any experience in mountain flying, and I kind of would like to ease into it, rather than start out in the really high country, and we'd be facing some real high country if we head there direct. Not that we're not going to see some high country, but let's ease into it."

"You're the captain," Jackie said. "I'm only the co-pilot, but it sounds pretty good to me. What's north of here that we might want to check out?"

Mark traced his finger over the WAC chart in the general direction of north. "Not a heck of a lot on this chart," he said, starting to put it away.

"Hey, look," Jackie said. "Right here on the edge. Carlsbad Cavern."

"Yeah, that's a possibility," Mark agreed.

"We've spent the last week looking up," Jackie said. "I've always heard that Carlsbad Cavern is pretty spectacular. Maybe we need to look down a bit."

A few minutes later, they had Rocinante in the air again. They flew north, up over the Prude Ranch, where they had spent their last week. It was in the middle of the Davis Mountains, so they were up fairly high. The white domes of McDonald Observatory, which held the telescopes that seemed so large, were just tiny below them, and the field where they had spent so much of the time lay very small. They could see, even from the altitude that they were at, that only a handful of campers and astronomers were left at the ranch. "I sure would like to go back there, some time," Mark said.

"Maybe next year, if we're still traveling," Jackie agreed.

It was only about an hour and a half flight to the north to Carlsbad Cavern airport, but after they left the Davis Mountains, there was very little beneath them, although they could see the Guadalupe Mountains off in the distance to their left. There were but a handful of landmarks to steer by for most of an hour, but their navigation was good; the airport came up almost right over the nose.

At the airport office, they called the park headquarters, and learned that they would have to have reservations for the cave tour, and the earliest they could get reservations for was the next day. They got a rather reluctant permission from the airport manager's secretary to camp under Rocinante's wing, then pitched their tent and had a late lunch.

After Mark made a couple of sketches of Jackie, they killed the rest of the afternoon getting back to their reading program, which had been more or less put on hold during their busy week at the Texas Star Party. Their reading was more "Walden" again, and the New Testament. They had finished the Gospel of John at Big Bend, and were now deep into the book of Acts, and they read on and on about the adventures that Paul and other apostles had as they spread the word of Jesus all around the eastern Mediterranean centuries before.

"I'm impressed with the depth of their faith," Jackie commented at one point. "They had to be interesting people. I just wonder what it would have been like to meet one."

Mark leaned up against Rocinante's wheel, deep in thought. "You don't have to wonder," he said finally. "After all, we met one, just the other day."

Jackie looked puzzled for a moment, then said, "You're talking about John, aren't you?"

"Sure," Mark replied, still mentally exploring the idea. "An apostle, wandering the world, preaching the gospel of . . . no, that's not right, he's a Bhuddist, after all. Wandering the world, preaching enlightenment through understanding of the universe. Sharing his message with all who would come and listen to him. I don't think Paul or Barnabas would have been very different from the apostle we met."

The next morning, they hiked several miles down to the cave, proper. It turned out that they had signed up for a long tour of the cave, one that didn't get started until the middle of the morning. Mark had not realized that he was a touch claustrophobic, and he was uneasy all through the tour, but that didn't keep him from enjoying the wonders they found underground, some of the huge rooms filled with flowstone, stalctites and stalagmites, and other rooms filled with various crystal gypsum in intricate forms too difficult to describe. Carlsbad Caverns were an awesome spectacle, and they were both glad they had come to check it out, although Mark, and to a lesser extend, Jackie, were happy to see sunlight and clear skies above them again.

They were lucky to get a ride back to the airport. By now, it was late in the day, and as they walked up to their campsite, the airport manager's secretary waved at them. They went over to talk.

"I caught hell for letting you camp there last night," she told them. "I don't mind, but I hope you aren't planning on staying again tonight."

"We had kind of planned on it," Mark said. "It's kind of late, and we're tired."

"Well, I'd rather you didn't," the woman said.

"How about if we load up our packs and hike a mile or two out into the desert?" Jackie suggested. "That way, we wouldn't be around to bother anybody, and we could get on our way early in the morning."

"I'd have no objection to that," the woman agreed. "Be sure you take some water with you, though. It's awful dry out there."

They quickly loaded their packs, keeping them light with the idea of only spending a single night in the desert. They made a fairly short hike, only a mile or two, off in the opposite directon from the airport, toward a little ridge that looked like it might make for a shady camping spot.

They found one, fairly shady under some scrubby trees. It was not a great campsite, but it would do for the night. By the time they got their tent set up, and had some supper from a can, it was getting dark, and stars were starting to pop out overhead. To the west, they could see the thin sliver of a very new moon setting into the mountains, and they only got to read a little bit from "Acts" before it was too dark to see the fine print.

"Might as well turn in," Mark yawned. "It'd be nice to get an early start in the morning. Maybe we can really get some miles on."

They were no sooner than in their sleeping bags when the moaning started. It was low, at first; they had to strain to figure out if they were really hearing something, and they asked each other if they heard the sound, just to prove that it wasn't their imaginations.

As the evening went on, the noise increased. It was almost as if there were some animal caught in a trap, crying out in pain; or, perhaps, a ghost.

"You don't suppose it could be a ghost, do you?" Jackie said, as the sound of the moaning increased to the point where it was about as loud as a spoken word between them.

"I don't believe in ghosts," Mark said. "But, I don't know what it could be. It almost sounds like wind blowing through a pipe, or something like that."

The sound came and went, sometimes higher in pitch, and sometimes lower; sometimes louder, and sometimes softer, but loud enough that neither of them could sleep, wondering what it might be. Once, Mark and Jackie both got out of their sleeping bags and went out into the night, trying to figure out where it was coming from, what it could be, but after a while, they were no wiser, and they went back to their sleeping bags and tried to sleep. "I still think it's a ghost," Jackie said.

Though neither of them thought that they slept much, they must have gotten to sleep sometime over the course of the night, for when they awoke bleary-eyed in the morning, driven out of their sleeping bags by the heat of the sun on the tent, the moaning had ceased.

"I don't think I slept an hour," Jackie said. "Do you want to make coffee, or do you want to see if we can get some at the airport?"

"Oh, the heck with making any," Mark said, realizing that it was a tough decision to make. "Let's just pack up and get back to the airport, and get the heck out of here. Maybe we can make a short flight today, and find a good place to stay tonight. I don't know about you, but I'm getting about ready for a night in a decent bed."

"I don't know that I need a decent bed," Jackie replied, yawning again, "But I sure need a decent night's sleep."

Their exhaustion was evident when they walked into the airport office and got a cup of coffee. "You don't look like you had too good a night," the secretary said.

"Didn't sleep much," Jackie said, explaining about the moaning that had bothered them all night.

"Oh, you must have been out around Misery Hole somewhere," the woman said. "It sounds like that a lot. It's not only at night; it can happen at any time. Sometimes, on a quiet day, you can here it from here."

"What causes it?" Mark asked.

The woman shrugged. "Nobody knows," she said. "I've heard a lot of stories, and some of them are pretty weird. Some say that it's the ghosts of some Spaniards that Apaches tortured to death."

"Weird, right," Jackie agreed.

They gassed up Rocinante after they finished their coffee, and set out to the north. The New Mexico countryside to the north of Carlsbad Caverns in empty indeed, and they had to go far out of their way to find roads to follow in their trek northward.

On that May day of 1971, both Mark and Jackie yawned as Rocinante carried them northward following an empty road across a nearly featureless desert, with mountains far off in the distance. After a couple of hours, they landed at the little town of Santa Rosa for fuel; in country as empty as this was, there was no point in flying with less than half a tank. It was the hottest part of the day, and the heat was stifling. They were pretty well done in, but the airport manager said there was no motel nearby, and even the one in town was nothing to write home about. "I think there's a good motel near the airport up at Raton," he said.

Raton was a hundred miles and more further north, but over more settled countryside; they decided to push on for another hour or so, and make a short day of it. Perhaps they could get an afternoon nap. It was with some reluctance that they got back into Rocinante's cockpit and flew on to the north.

Mark tried to figure out a compass course to take them over the next empty wasteland by dead reckoning, but it hardly seemed worth the trouble. In the end, he picked out a compass course a little to the west of north, knowing that in fifty miles or so they would come up on Interstate 25; once they found that, they could follow it northward.

As they came up on the Interstate, they were angling in on a high mountain range. Off in the distance, they could see snowcapped peaks. "It looks like it might be fun to go hiking up there," Jackie said. "I'll bet it would be fun, up in the high country."

"Maybe later," Mark told her. "Looks like it's still a little cold up there, right now."

At Raton, they found that the airport was unattended. "It doesn't look like we're going to be able to get fuel here, anyway," Mark said. "Maybe we ought to fly on north."

"I saw some motels off by the interstate interchange when we landed," Jackie said. "But that's farther than I want to walk, right now."

They were almost ready to leave, when they saw a sign on the hanger wall: one of the motels offered a courtesy car. That settled it. "We can get gas somewhere north of here tomorrow," Mark yawned. "Let's see if we can find a place to tie this thing down."

The courtesy car came for them within a few minutes of being called, and it proved that the motel wasn't very far away. Mark and Jackie noticed a pool and a restaurant as the car pulled in, but at the moment, they were too tired to care.

The motel was more expensive than they wanted, but they were in no mood to argue. They carried their packs to their room, not far away, but when they went inside, they discovered that it was hot; while there was an air conditioner, someone hadn't turned it on.

"Damn," Mark said. "It's too hot to sleep, until that takes hold, and that's going to take a while."

"I know we had showers only a couple of days ago," Jackie agreed, "But right now I feel too grubby to want to mess up clean sheets. Why don't we go jump in that pool for a few minutes, while the air conditioner is cooling this place off?"

"I'm almost too tired to care," Mark told her. "Besides, it might wake me up. But, what the heck, I don't think I could sleep in this heat, anyway."

In a few minutes, Jackie was in her bikini, and Mark was in his cutoffs, and they were in the pool. The water was quite warm, and it stank of chlorine, but the water felt good, anyway; it was fun to splash around and dive.

The motel room was still warm when they got out of the pool, although the air conditioner was gaining. They each took a quick shower, more to wash the chlorine off. It was too warm for pajamas, still, so Jackie decided that sleeping in her bra and panties was no worse than wearing a bikini. Besides, she was too tired to care. By the time Mark got done with his shower and pulling on his undershorts, Jackie was asleep on the bed, and he lay down beside her.

They slept soundly for several hours. Perhaps it was his pure exhaustion, or perhaps it was the smell and feel of Jackie laying beside him, but he found himself dreaming of Mei-Ling, the first time in some time. In his dream eye, they were back in the hotel room in Bangkok, with the heat and the humidity surrounding them, both of them peacefully asleep. In his mind, he reached out and pulled her to him, and caressed her, and kissed her, and . . .

"Damn it, Mark, what are you doing,?" Jackie said quite loudly in his ear.

Somehow, he pulled his mind together from a deep sleep. It wasn't Bangkok, but Raton, New Mexico, and the girl he held in his arms wasn't the little Mei-Ling of his dreams. He looked down, and realized that in his sleep he had unfastened Jackie's bra, and was caressing her bare breast.

Embarrassed, he pulled his hand away. "Sorry," he said. "Just a dream, I guess."

"I thought it was a dream, too," she said, squirming around to get her hands behind her, to refasten the bra. "I guess maybe I was dreaming, and I was really enjoying myself, and then all of a sudden I realized what was really happening."

"Well, I hope you won't mind it if I say that I was enjoying my dream, too." He pulled her close to him, and kissed her.

"Yes," she said a while later, "It was such a nice dream, I'm almost sorry it wasn't real."

* * *

Raton, New Mexico
May 28, 1971

Dear Dad and Sarah:

I'm writing this to you from a restaurant. Mark and I had a rather sleepless night last night, so we took a nap this afternoon, and just got up.

Last night, we were camped out in the desert, down near Carlsbad Cavern, and we kept hearing the strangest noise. It was kind of a moaning, or a howling, and it kept us awake most of the night. The lady at the airport this morning said that the locals down there think that it's the sound of ghosts of old Spaniards that were murdered by the Apaches, centuries ago. I don't think it was a ghost, and I don't know what it was, but I do know that we were awful tired when we got here this afternoon.

The Texas Star Party turned out to be a lot of fun! We had a busy week, and met a lot of nice people. The only problem is that we were up most of the night, and then all day following, and we kind of got behind on our sleep.

By rationing ourselves very carefully, we managed to make the cookies last all the time we were at Ft. Davis. Thank you again for them; we really enjoyed them. It was nice to hear from you, and we thought of you every time we ate some.

We flew over an awful lot of desert today. It's so empty, it's unbelievable, but at the same time, it's pretty in its own sort of way. Most of the way, we followed roads, but there were a couple of places that we got away from them, and out away from the roads, there is absolutely nothing. It's totally empty, except for maybe a scattered windmill, or a bunch of cattle here and there -- really, darn few cattle for all the land we flew over. I've seen a lot of westerns, and even then you don't realize how empty the land must have been for the cowboys -- and this is now. What must it have been like a hundred years ago?

I guess we're heading north and then west for Yellowstone National Park, now, but you'd better not send any mail there, yet, since I really don't know if and/or when we're going to get there, and, for that matter, I don't know where you'd send it that we'd find it.

As soon as we finish dinner, I guess we're going to try and catch up on our sleep some more. Right now, I feel so groggy from lack of sleep that I'm really looking forward to conking out again.

Love,
Jackie

When they left Colorado Springs heading northward, they were a little unsure how to get through the Denver area. There were a lot of control zones and areas ahead of them. The choice was not very clear; either they could go well out of their way to the east, out into the nearly desert-prairie, or they could hug the mountains, really, up in the foothills, to circle the city from the west. The foothills route was clearly going to be prettier, and Mark had very little experience flying in mountains, so this seemed like a good chance to get a taste of it.

They were still climbing out of Colorado Springs, with Mark flying and Jackie navigating, when she noticed something on the chart. "Here's a place we could stop," pointing at a red dot on the map. "Black Forest Glider Port. It's not very far ahead."

"We just got started," Mark said. "Would be fun to try some time, though."

"Have you ever flown a glider?" she asked.

"No, but it's on the someday list. I wanted to solo one when I was fourteen. They'll let you do it that young, but I could never talk dad into it. Spearfish Lake is not exactly what you call glider country, anyway." Mark looked out the window, and then got Jackie's attention. "Take a look over there," he said.

Off in the distance, she could see a white building, small on the ground, but even at a distance of several miles the building had a striking appearance. "What is it?" she asked.

"Chapel at the Air Force Academy," Mark told her. "It wasn't so long ago that my greatest desire in life was to spend four years there, but . . .."

"The glasses, huh?"

"Yeah, the Goddamn glasses. I guess I was supposed to be a phone repairman, not a fighter pilot. I think I've gotten used to that now, most of the time, anyway."

They flew on in silence. Mark turned to the left, to fly as close to the Air Force Academy without getting into the nearby control zone. This is as close as he would ever get to achieving that dream he'd had for years, until it had become clear that his eyes weren't going to be any better. In his mind's eye, for a moment he wasn't in a Cessna 140 that was older than he was, but in some sleek supersonic fighter, where he could cut in the afterburner and break Mach I going straight up. Yes, the Goddamn glasses, he thought; there was an experience he'd never have the chance to have.

With a shrug, he tore his eyes away from the dream of long ago, and wheeled Rocinante to the right, to pick up the interstate highway that they would follow to the north.

Probably they should have stopped at the gliderport, he thought. After all, what the hell was the hurry? He came close to turning back, but knew that if he did he'd have to look at the Air Force Academy again. He realized that he didn't really want to do that; it would open a part of his mind he thought he'd been able to close.

Oh, well, there would be other chances, he thought. He flew on to the north, between the interstate and the foothills, edging to the west to stay out of all the control zones and whatnot near Denver.

They were nearing Boulder before he was able to ease his way back out over flat countryside, with the mountains rising far above them to their left. There's got to be some beautiful country back there, he thought, even though it was awful high. Perhaps he and Jackie could poke their nose into a few places like that, but maybe there would be some places that weren't so high up.

They were high enough that the Denver smog was trapped in an inversion below, but above it, they could see for miles. How clear this western air was! It was not like back home, where the smoke and the haze from the trees and the moisture from the air made a day when you could see ten miles from this altitude a rare one indeed. Mark guessed that they could see a hundred miles ahead of them, at least.

He could see Jackie fold up the Denver sectional chart and put it away in the pouch by her ankle, and pull out another one, the Cheyenne sectional. It only gave a hint of the north part of Denver, and she had to fold it this way and that to get to the right area, and hunt around to see where they were.

Mark looked over her shoulder for a moment. They were passing Longmont, but ahead of them, there were not many places that they could stop for gas for a while. There was Cheyenne, but that was another controlled field, and an Air Force Base, as well. There was Laramie, but that wasn't quite on their route. There were still a couple of airports not too far ahead of them that looked big enough to have fuel pumps; perhaps they'd better stop.

He turned the radio back on and tuned it to 122.8, the Unicom frequency, to check and see if one of them had fuel. The channel was filled with the talk of a lot of traffic, off to the east at Greeley, and he wondered a bit at what the reason could be. When he got a brief break, he called ahead to the nearest field,

Loveland; they responded quickly, with the wind and active runway, and confirmed that they had eighty octane.

"We'll be with you shortly," Mark replied, then hung up the microphone. "You want to try to land it?" he asked.

"Well, I think I can," Jackie said.

This would be the first time that Jackie would have landed at a strange airport, one that Mark had not already flown them into; a good test, to push her learning, he decided.

They were flying out of the smog, now, and Jackie was able to pick out the runway from far away, and set up a pattern entry that Mark had no reason to complain about. At 5800 feet, she set herself up for the pattern, and began her approach using the runway as a cue, just as she had already learned.

Flying on the right side, Jackie didn't have a good view of the airspeed indicator, and she was a little fast. Mark realized that she would be until he decided to start making her fly on the left side, or until she got more familiar with flying, but realized that it was good to not depend on gauges too much.

With the extra speed, Jackie's landing was a little long, and she had a little bounce, but not enough to matter. "Good landing," Mark said as she let the plane slow, keeping it going straight; she'd long since got past overcontrolling on the runway. "Some one of these days, we're going to have to find a real flight instructor to take you around a few times, and maybe turn you loose."

"I'm in no hurry," Jackie said. "It's just good to know that I could fly this if I had to."

The attendant acted as if the few gallons of 80 octane they bought was hardly worth the effort, one of the few unpleasant people they had met at an airport along the trip, and they were glad to be on their way. Mark let Jackie do the takeoff, too; they climbed out to perhaps 1500 feet above ground level, and turned to parallel the interstate, still several miles to their right. Mark wanted to edge even further away from it, to avoid the Air Force base at Cheyenne. To their left, the mountains flattened out a little, revealing tortured brown foothills. It was a shame the attendant had been so nasty, he thought; it would have been nice to stay around here somewhere and explore the vicinity.

In the distance in front of him, he could see some aircraft activity; there was a white plane, perhaps three or four miles ahead, crossing from right to left in front of them. He looked again; it was closely followed by a second plane.

All of a sudden, he realized that it was a glider and a towplane. He stole a look at the map, and sure enough, only a few miles ahead was a red circle symbol, lettered "Waverly West Soaring Ranch".

"What do you think about a glider ride after all?" Mark asked Jackie, who was still flying Rocinante.

"Sounds fine to me," she said. "I kind of wondered why you didn't stop earlier."

"Better let me have it," Mark said, letting her comment go unanswered. He looked off into the distance for the gliderport; it didn't stick out like a paved strip would have. He glanced at the map again; it had to be there, next to that reservoir. "Keep an eye out for gliders," Mark told her. "They have the right of way."

As they got closer, he could pick out the runways, mere places where the grass showed signs of wear. Part of one runway showed signs of having been oiled for a part of its distance, and there were white spots that marked its outlines; another runway ran almost corner to corner of what had to be a square mile section. The wind sock seemed to indicate that the slightly improved runway was the one in use; there were a couple of cars sitting off to the side near the end of the runway, and two or three people standing around. A glider and a towplane sat on the runway; as they watched, the towplane gave off a cloud of dust, and both started to move.

Mark set up his pattern, checked the skies once again for gliders, and turned to land. Rocinante touched down not far beyond the beginning of the runway and rolled out quickly; Mark turned to the right, and taxied back in the grass to where the cars and the people were gathered, then turned into the wind and shut the Cessna off.

A tiny man with a neat Van Dyke beard walked up to them as they got out of the plane. "How you doing today?" he asked.

"Oh, pretty good," Mark said. "Can we get a glider ride, by any chance?"

"Sure thing," the little man said. "Jack is just starting with a student, but this should be Fred's last flight with the student he's got now. I don't think he's got anything after that. If you want to wait a while, it won't be any problem. There's some tiedowns about thirty feet behind you, if you want to tie that down."

"Thanks, we'll wait," Mark said. The three of them pushed Rocinante back to the tiedowns, and walked over to the group clustered around an orange and white sailplane.

The sailplane wasn't quite what Mark had expected, a sleek piece of fiberglass with immensely long wings. It still had the long wings, but it looked like something out of the twenties, with a fabric structure and strut-braced wings. There was only a single wheel, far back under the belly; it sat resting with one wing down. As they watched, a man sat in the cockpit, while a bearded man stood next to the cockpit, talking.

While they waited, an old dog sauntered up to them, wagging it's tail. Mark had to look again; it may have been the homeliest, scraggliest mutt he had ever seen. Jackie bent over and patted his head, and the dog sat down beside her.

In a minute, the man outside opened a door hidden under the wing and squeezed into the back seat. He was a big man, maybe Mark and Jackie's height, but wider; he looked like he might have been a football lineman. "Hey, Bruce!" he yelled, "You want to hook us up and run the wingtip?"

"Sure thing, Jack," the little man yelled back. "Here comes Paul now."

Mark could hear an airplane approaching; he looked up to see a Super Cub, trailing a rope, in a deep, deep sideslip, dropping toward the runway like a rock. Only feet above the runway, the pilot straightened it out, touched it down on the numbers, and stood heavily on the brakes, coming to a stop almost where the plane hit. "Back in a minute," Bruce said. He ran out onto the runway, grabbed the end of the rope, and ran it over to where the glider lay waiting. He attached it somewhere on the front, and put tension on the line. They could see the pilot pull a knob, and the towline released; then Bruce hooked it up again. He went out to the wingtip and picked it up, signaling the pilot to take out the slack in the towline.

The slack came out with a little jerk, pulling the glider ahead a couple of feet. Bruce looked back, to make sure no other aircraft were approaching, then waved his arm in a big circle. In an instant, the Super Cub's engine bellowed, and the dog next to them began to bark. They could see a cloud of dust being raised, and the glider rapidly began to move forward. Bruce could only stay with it four or five steps before it was shooting down the runway. Not too far away, they could see the sailplane and the towplane rise above the cloud of dust. All in all, the towplane could not have been on the ground more than a minute.

Bruce came back over to them. He bent over and petted the dog. "You've learned your lesson, haven't you?" he said. "Barking is all right, chasing them, no."

He looked up at Mark and Jackie. "We've had a tough time teaching Cumulus here to not chase gliders. He's kind of a hard-headed dog. He's been hit by gliders at least three times, but I think getting hit by a prop this spring cured him."

"He got hit by a prop?" Mark asked, incredulous.

"Just dinged him," Bruce said. "Knocked him ass over teakettle, though, and it may have taught him a lesson."

Mark looked back down the runway at the towplane and glider. He could still hear the bellow of the Super Cub, and could see that both were climbing rapidly. "That's got a little more power than Mr. Piper intended," he commented.

"It's got a 180 Lycoming," Bruce said, "And the tow pilots complain that it still isn't enough."

Mark shook his head. That was three times the power of Wally Byer's little yellow J-3 that shared the hanger with the Stinson, back home. That was a little putt-putt; the towplane wasn't.

"Here comes Fred," Bruce said. They looked back down the runway; another sailplane was approaching. It was similar to the trainer that had just taken off, except for being green and white, but only a gentle whisper of air across reaching wings heralded its approach. It touched down at the end of the runway and rolled for a short distance, before turning to roll off of the runway. All of a sudden, it's nose came down, and it came to a stop, perhaps fifty yards from them.

Bruce and Cumulus started to slowly walk toward the glider, with Mark and Jackie following along.

The canopy of the glider opened. "It'll be ten minutes or so before Paul gets back," Bruce said. "Is it still flat out there?"

"There's a little bump or two below a thousand feet," the man in the back seat said with a slight accent of something European. "But it's still dead flat above that. I think this inversion is just capping thing off, but it might be better this afternoon."

"We've got a couple of rides for you," Bruce told him. "These folks just flew in for a ride. Can we work them in now?"

"Might as well," the man in back said. That must be the Fred that Bruce was talking about, Mark and Jackie realized. He turned to the student, who was unbuckling himself from the front seat. "Marty, if you stick around, maybe things will pick up this afternoon," he said to the student.

"Yeah, what the heck," the man said. "It looks like too nice a day to go home and mow lawn."

"All right," Fred told him. "Which one of you wants to go first?"

"Why don't you go ahead, Jackie?" Mark said.

She was in the cockpit and was being buckled in before she began to have second thoughts. In Rocinante, they just wore a lap belt, but here there was a five-point harness to buckle around here. What was the point of a five-point harness unless it was going to be used, she wondered. On the other hand, it made her feel safer in a way.

While they waited for the towplane to return, they stood and talked for a minute. They learned that Fred was the owner of the gliderport, and he'd been flying gliders for a long time. "How'd you get into doing this?" Jackie asked.

"That's how they taught us to fly in the Luftwaffe," Fred told her. "Before I became a fighter pilot."

The words didn't mean much to Jackie, but they did to Mark, with a certain degree of amazement. He had never met a German fighter pilot before. There was a question or two he wanted to ask, but the towplane was approaching; the time would come later.

Bruce closed and latched the canopy. While Mark stood back out of the way, Bruce ran to get the towline again, much as he had before. In a minute, they were watching the green and white sailplane disappear down the runway.

As Mark, Bruce, and Cumulus watched them fly away, Mark could not help but ask, "Is that true what he said? About the Luftwaffe?"

"That's about all Fred ever says about it," Bruce told him. "Don't you dare tell him I said so, but we had a tow pilot here one time that spoke German, and Fred didn't know it. An old buddy of Fred's showed up, and they got to telling war stories in German, and the tow pilot said they were some wild ones. He said he got the impression that Fred had over a dozen kills."

Mark let out a long, low whistle. Cumulus perked up his floppy ears at the sound. "I won't tell," Mark said. "I can see why that might be something he might not want to talk about, under the circumstances."

"Nice looking Cessna you've got there," Bruce said to change the subject.

"I rebuilt it this last winter," Mark said, and explained a little bit of how he and Jackie were touring the country as Cumulus lay down at their feet.

They talked about flying for a bit. Mark was surprised to learn that the little man didn't work at the gliderport, but was a college professor that liked to hang around out there. Flying was one of his passions, he explained, although he wasn't too good at it. Their conversation was broken up by the return of Paul and the other trainer, which sat on the ground for only a few minutes before the towplane returned and towed the other sailplane off again. "When it's flat like this," Bruce explained, "And all we're doing is training or rides, it's about all one towplane can do to keep up with two gliders."

A few minutes later, Fred, Jackie, and the green trainer returned. "It's great!" she said. "So smooth and quiet! Fred let me fly it some."

Jackie climbed out of the cockpit, and Mark climbed in and strapped himself in. He looked at the panel in front of him, nearly devoid of instruments: an altimeter, a couple of rate-of-climb gauges, and that was about it; about the only thing he couldn't figure out was a piece of yarn taped to the canopy in front of him. Fred explained for a minute what was going to happen, and then Bruce closed the canopy. Mark could see the towplane pull in in front of them, and come to a stop. Bruce ran out to get the rope, and bent down under the nose of the sailplane. "Pull the red knob in front of you," Fred said. Mark did as he was told, and saw Bruce's hand outside the canopy ball up into a fist, and realized that that must be the signal to let the knob go. He saw the little man stand in front of the nose, and pull on the rope.

"Pull the knob again, to check that it releases," Fred told him. Again, Mark pulled it, and the towline fell away. In a minute, Bruce had the towline hooked up again, and went to level the wing. Bruce signaled the towplane to take out the slack in the rope, and when it came tight, Fred asked, "You ready?"

"I guess so," Mark replied.

"Wag the rudder." Mark stepped on one rudder pedal, then the other. Mark didn't see Fred give Bruce a hand signal, but Bruce saw it and began to make the circular motion with his arms. Inside the canopy, Mark couldn't hear the towplane well, but could see the dust cloud raise behind it. The glider began to move forward, accelerating rather quickly, and Mark was surprised to see that Fred had it in the air, skimming the runway, while the towplane was still on the ground.

They were not very far above the ground before Mark realized how much better the view was outside the sailplane was. The cockpit was so narrow that he hardly realized it was there; it was almost as if they were a bird on the wing.

After they were a ways above the ground, Fred said, "You want to try to fly it?"

"Sure," Mark said.

"All right," Fred told him. "Flying on tow is probably the most difficult part. You want to keep quite a bit of forward pressure on the stick. Try to keep the tip of the towplane's rudder right in the center of the window on top of the fuselage."

It took Mark a minute or two to get the feel of it, a little surprised at how stiff the controls were and how sluggish the sailplane banked. Fred explained the need to stay clear of the disturbed air coming off of the towplane's wingtips, and stuffed the sailplane down into one of the vortices for a moment to demonstrate, before pulling back up into a normal tow position to let Mark continue to fly it.

"We'll get off at 8000 feet," Fred told him. "When we release, we'll do a climbing turn to the right to get away from the towline and burn off speed. The towplane will turn left and dive away from us."

"We're coming up on 8000 feet now," Mark said.

"Then put on just a little bit of skid to the right to put a little more tension into the towline, and pull the red knob," Fred told him.

Mark did as he was told, and pulled the release. With a loud "Bang" that startled him a little, the towline shot away. He could see the towplane bank away and leave them.

Climbing a little, the sailplane slowed. Mark let the nose drop until the pressure came off of the stick, a little astonished at the low reading on the airspeed indicator. The Cessna wouldn't even fly this slow, and here the sailplane seemed comfortable.

"We can just sit up here and sightsee," Fred told him, "But since you're a pilot, why not get the feel of this? You'll find it rolls a little slow, but it's very well-behaved."

Mark started a turn to the right. "You're coordinated pretty good," Fred told him. "You can check your coordination with the yaw string taped to the front of the canopy." He pressed on the rudder a little, to demonstrate how an uncoordinated turn caused the yaw string to flutter to one side or the other.

Satisfied, Mark tightened the bank some more. The stick seemed a little weak in his hands, so he dropped the nose a little to pick up some speed. Fred suggested that they straighten out, and try some stalls.

Stalls in the old Schweizer trainer weren't hardly worth of the name. The plane barely broke over a stall from a normal attitude, but dropped rather naturally and kept on flying. The air was still, and they were slowly sinking, but much more slowly than he had expected. "You've been flying a while," Fred said.

"I started flying my dad's Stinson before I was old enough to see over the panel," Mark told him. "It's so quiet, and the view is great."

"Your girl friend liked it, too," Fred said. "Has she been flying long?"

"She's technically not supposed to be flying at all," Mark said. "I've been teaching her a little. She's been flying with me enough that she's learned quite a bit, but I'm not a flight instructor. If I was, I'd think that's she's close to soloing."

"I thought she'd been flying longer than that," Fred said. "I talked her right through to a landing, and she did fine."

"Yeah, we need to find a flight instructor some time," Mark said.

"I'm not a power instructor, but Jack is," Fred said. "Maybe he'd be willing to fly with her. He'll do just about anything to get another hour in his logbook. He flys students over at Greeley six hours a day, five days a week, then comes over here and flys every chance he can get on the weekend. He thinks if he can get 2000 hours picked up by the end of the summer, he can get a job at a commuter airline back home."

"We just stopped to take a ride," Mark said, "But I'd kind of hoped to get to fly one of these things when there's some thermals in the air, to see what that's like."

"It might pick up this afternoon if you want to stick around," Fred told him.

Mark asked how much it would take for him to get a license in sailplanes; he remembered hearing somewhere that it wasn't difficult, and flying the trainer didn't seem difficult.

"A couple of hours of dual," Fred told him, "And then a few solo flights. You could do it in a couple of days if you were in a hurry, three or four if you wanted to take your time."

As the Schweizer slowly sank, Mark gave it some thought. The gliderport probably wouldn't be a bad place to camp for a day or two, and if this Jack were willing to fly with Jackie, so much the better. Mark had not felt intimidated in teaching Jackie a bit about how to handle the Cessna, but worried that perhaps she was picking up some bad habit that he couldn't realize. A couple of hours with an instructor seemed like a good idea. "How much would it cost?" he asked Fred.

The answer he got was higher than he wanted, but their money was holding out well, and, after all, the idea was to spend it before they got home. This could be fun, he thought. "I'll talk it over with Jackie," he said.

"You want to land this?" Fred said. "Now, in a sailplane, we always fly a right-hand pattern, with turns to the right. The towplanes always fly a left-hand pattern, so they can see if there's any sailplanes about to turn in front of them. Now, we want to enter the base leg at about 800 feet above ground level; that's 6300 feet on the altimeter . . ."

The air was still pretty dead a couple of hours later, when they gathered up in the office for lunch, mostly sandwiches and the like brought from home. Mark and Jackie limited themselves to bags of peanuts and cans of pop from the styrofoam cooler in Rocinante.

Mark briefly had second thoughts about having Jack fly with Jackie in the Cessna. After all, it was a taildragger, and flying taildraggers was getting to be a lost art. His second thoughts evaporated a little later in the morning, when another couple of sailplanes were rolled out of the hanger, and Jack rolled a second towplane out to help deal with them. Another taildragging Super Cub, like the first, it told Mark all he needed to know about those qualifications. As Fred had said, Jack was willing to take Jackie out in the Cessna, after Mark had explained what was going on. "The only thing is, I want to go around the patch with you a couple of times, first, to make sure I know how you fly and how it flies."

"We can do that," Mark said. "When do you want to get started?"

"As soon as we put the sailplanes away this evening."

"Fred," Mark asked. "You got any problem with us camping here overnight? We can go into town and get a motel or something, if you'd like."

"No problem," Fred replied. "The only thing is, it'd be best if you camped out on the edge of the property, maybe over by the gully off the end of runway 34, and don't come around the office. Cumulus is the friendliest dog in the world in the daylight, but he knows his job is to guard the office and hanger at night. I let him run loose, and I don't even like to come out here at night. He might tear my arm off first and ask questions later."

"Cumulus?" Jackie said, looking at the grungy old dog asleep at her feet. "He's just an old softie."

"Only in the daytime," Fred repeated. "I came out here one day last spring, and found the hanger doors open a couple of feet. Someone had pried the lock off. I got out of my truck and looked in the hanger. There was blood and pieces of clothing all over the place, and Cumulus sitting right in the middle of it, with a very satisfied smile on his face, just like he was saying, 'Hey, boss, I done my job.' He must have waited until they got the hanger door open, then nailed them. I called the police, and they found someone in the hospital with massive dog bites. The clothing matched, and the guy is still in jail."

"How'd you get him?" Jackie asked.

"He just showed up here one day," Fred said. "Just a stray. He saw that there was a job to be done, and that he was just to dog to do it."

"We used to have to keep him chained up," Paul, the towplane pilot said. "Then after I hit him with the prop last spring, he decided that chasing planes wasn't as much fun as it used to be, so we let him run loose."

"Speaking of cumulus," Jack said, "I see a couple popping up in the mountains. Maybe things are perking up a little."

"Could be," Fred said. "Jack, why don't you fly with Marty again, and I'll fly with Mark."

It was almost half an hour later before the trainer with Mark and Fred aboard released from tow high above the gliderport. The air was more lively, now; Fred found a thermal, and showed Mark how to work it. In hunting around, they found the other trainer circling a spot above a ridge to the west of the gliderport, and flew over to join them. "Watch yourself," Fred warned as they joined in below the other trainer. "We may have a visitor."

With the sailplane in a tight circle, the rate of climb indicator showed a steady, if slow climb, and the altimeter slowly wound up. After a while, they were higher than they had been when they had released from the towplane.

Mark could not get over how peaceful it was, how good the view was from the cockpit of the slow-flying glider. It was almost as if he were a bird . . .

"There he is," Fred said, pointing over Mark's shoulder from the back seat. Mark looked out in the general direction Fred was pointing, and saw a little black dot, seemingly far in front of him.

"A hawk?" Mark asked.

"An eagle," Fred told him. "He's got a nest over on the ridge somewhere. "He's gotten so used to the sailplanes that he apparently thinks we're just big birds, too. He'll find lift for us on days when we can't find anything else, and he doesn't mind when we come over and join him. Of course, he comes over and joins us when he's scratching for lift and we've found something."

Flying with an eagle, Mark thought. Now, that was one to remember . . . that was the kind of thing that this trip was all about. If nothing else, that made this stop worthwhile.

They were up about an hour before Fred suggested that they go in to land. They could have stayed up longer, but he had another student scheduled for the afternoon. As they landed, Fred showed how easy it was to land the trainer right where they wanted to. They normally carried quite a bit of speed down the approach, and the trainer would float quite a bit in the ground effect, with it's long wings. The trick was to float around, just above the ground, until you came up to the spot where you wanted to land, then pop the spoilers. "We've had bets on spot landings," Fred told him. "It usually comes down to inches."

As the afternoon wore on, Mark and Jackie learned from Bruce how to run towlines and wings, and about the various signals involved. After a while, there weren't any more sailplanes left to launch, and they wandered up to the office and the cooler of water there. Fred was already there; the trainer he had been flying was off on a solo flight, and he was telling Mark and Jackie some of the special things about flying sailplanes when the phone went off. "Waverly West," Fred answered.

He listened for a moment, then said, "No, he's out flying . . . I see . . . yes, I see . . . well, I'll see if I can get him on the radio." He went over to the portable radio, mounted in a yellow box. "Golf Echo," he called, "Are you on tow?"

"Just landing," Paul's voice came back over the radio.

"You want to land it up to the office?" Fred said. "You've got a phone call waiting."

Mark looked out the window. He could see the towplane on short final; he saw it straighten out, heard a burst of power, and saw it point more or less at the office. Paul rolled the plane to a stop just short of the fence outside the office, shut it off, and came inside; it could not have taken a minute from when Fred called him.

Paul picked up the phone, and listened in increasing agitation. "Yeah, I'll be there as quick as I can," he said. "Early in the morning, probably. Des Moines General, right?" He listened for a few more moments in silence, then said, "Right, just as quick as I can."

He hung up the phone and turned to Fred. "My Dad's in the hospital. He's in real bad shape. His car got hit by a train. Look, I hate to run out on you but . . ."

"Don't stand here apologizing," Fred told him. "We'll work out something. Just don't kill yourself driving like a maniac." In thirty seconds, Paul was in his car, heading out the driveway.

"That's how it is from the other side," Jackie mumbled.

"How's that?" Bruce asked.

"My dad's a railroad engineer," she said, a little more loudly, but still subdued. "You don't stop a train inside of a mile or two, if it's moving fast. He says he's never killed anyone, but he's had nightmares about the close calls."

"Des Moines," Bruce commented. "He's probably not going to be back for a while.

"Jack and I can handle the towing for tomorrow," Fred said. "But I've got students Monday, and no tow pilot."

Mark only had to think it over for a second. "We're not going anywhere in particular," he said. "I could probably tow for you for a few days, if you can show me how."

Fred thought for a moment. "That's right, you do know how to fly a taildragger. You got a commercial license?"

"Over two years," Mark told him.

"Our insurance says you have to have over fifty hours in taildraggers. Have you got that much?"

"Fred, I've got about eight hundred hours," Mark said. "I don't have fifty hours that ISN'T in taildraggers."

"Come on," Fred told him. "Let's see how well you can fly a hot-rod Super Cub."

12.

Mark knew that he would never fly a fighter plane, never ride a rocket, but he learned in only a very few seconds that a Super Cub with a 180 Lycoming and a long climb propeller was almost the next best thing. With Fred and himself on board, and no glider in tow, they were off the ground in fifty feet. "Climb at about sixty," Fred told him, and Mark was awed at how far up the nose of the plane had to be to hold it down to sixty miles an hours. The rate of climb indicator on the dash of the plane was pegged at more than a thousand feet per minute, and the altimeter's needles almost blurred at the Super Cub raced skyward. Mark had flown planes with more power, but never in one that had anything like the Super Cub's power-to-weight ratio; it was a different world.

In spite of all the power, it was an honest airplane; turning precisely, with good control response, and a stall that was sharp but docile. Over the noise of the engine -- it had no mufflers, and was LOUD -- Mark got the indication from Fred to try a landing. Still getting the feel of the airplane, Mark set up a pattern and pulled the power back for the descent. With the engine idling, he and Fred could talk. "Just do a normal landing, don't worry about that steep approach stuff," Fred told him. He floated in over the fence, with the plane telling him it would be just as happy if it were going a little bit slower, and touched down on what passed for the numbers.

"Take it around again," Fred said as they rolled down the runway. Mark cobbed the throttle forward -- that was a little unfamiliar, the throttle was on the left, rather than the right that he was used to, but he figured he's get used to it -- and the plane was in the air almost before he could think about it. He was at pattern altitude and heading downwind even before they'd passed the boundary of the gliderport. "What a powerful beast," Mark mumbled to himself over the roar of the engine.

On this landing, Fred told him to roll it to a stop. "You can fly it," he said. "You're going to have to learn a little bit about flying it with a glider. He talked for a few minutes about the airspeeds to fly, about signals and such, and explained that the engine got hot after a long, full-power climbout, and it wouldn't do it any good to let it get shock-cooled. The normal procedure for a letdown, he was told, was to run the engine at 1800 RPM, in a deep slip.

"The other thing to remember is that you're pulling a two-hundred foot rope behind you, and it dangles about fifty feet below you," Fred said. "So you want to be at least fifty feet over the fence, or you're going to rip out the fence and we're going to have sheep all over the place. You've seen Paul do that steep approach of his. That's to keep the rope out of the fence and still be able to stop so there isn't a lot of towline chasing and you don't wear the towline out dragging it. He's learned how to do that with a lot of practice, so don't you worry about it. If you have to taxi back, you have to taxi back. I see we've got a glider waiting, so let's tow it."

Making the Lycoming do the work for two airplanes settled the Super Cub down a lot, but Mark was still amazed at the power it had. It broke ground a lot better than the Stinson did, and with the glider in tow, there was just no problem with controlling the rudder on takeoff; the plane wanted to go straight whether Mark wanted it to or not. It turned out to be a long tow, to 3000 feet above the gliderport; Mark broke off the tow, and began his letdown, learning very quickly that he wanted to sideslip to the left; to the right meant he leaned up against the door, which didn't seem too substantial.

Fred made one more tow with him, and Jack took a couple along with him. Jack also warned him against doing Paul's steep approaches, but said, "It's not that difficult, but it does take practice. Work up to it, a little at a time. You're also coming down pretty fast, which is good, but you need to plan your pattern entry while you're descending, or you can waste a lot of a time in level flight. Remember, you're an elevator operator."

The day was dwindling down when Mark made one last tow, this time solo. "Anything left?" he radioed to Fred.

"No," he was told. "Take it up to the pump, fuel it up, and we'll put it away."

Mark was a little surprised to find Jack waiting at the fuel pumps for him, a wheelbarrow with a generator sitting beside him. "I don't know if you noticed or not," Jack told him, "But there's no power out here, so you have to get the generator out to pump fuel." Starting the generator was tricky, but once it going the pump worked easily. Mark was surprised at how much fuel the tanks took.

"On a busy day, you have to fill it twice, maybe three times a day," Jack told him. "These things use fuel like it's going out of style. Keep an eye on your fuel level. The way we fly here, there's no reason you can't glide back to the airport if you run out, but it is rather embarrassing."

After flying the Super Cub, Rocinante seemed positively puny when Mark flew with Jack a few minutes later. They went around the pattern a couple of times, mostly to make sure that Jack knew where the switches and controls were. "I don't know if it makes any difference," Mark told the bearded instructor, "But

Jackie's done all of her flying on the right side, and you'll have to make up your mind whether to let her stay there, or put her on the left."

"If she's going to solo it," Jack told him, "She probably ought to be on the left, where she can see the gauges better. We'll try it that way and see."

Jack started Jackie right out from the basics, showing her how to do the walkaround. Right away, Mark noticed that Jack explained a couple of things that he had forgotten to mention to Jackie, and realized that having her fly with an instructor was a good idea. It probably would work out well; Mark could tell that Jack was a good instructor.

While they were doing the walkaround, Mark took the packs and the camping gear out of the luggage compartment, and with Bruce's help carried them over to a place near a brushy gully that led down to the reservoir to the west of the gliderport. It obviously would make a good place to camp.

As he and Bruce were setting up the tent, Mark watched as Jackie and Jack started Rocinante, taxied it out onto the runway and ran it up. It was a little strange to be standing there watching. It was the first time since he had owned the little Cessna that it would be flying without him on board. He wondered if this was such a good idea after all . . .

With nothing of the sort of power that the Super Cub exuded, Mark could see the little gray and white Cessna begin to roll down the runway. He stood up, holding onto a tent stake, and watched as the tail came up, and it broke ground. He watched until it was far away, a mere dot in the distance to the south.

As he was standing there, Fred drove up in his old brown pickup truck. It was a Chevy, old enough to have running boards, and it was in top-notch condition; somehow, Mark realized that it must have taken a lot of hours to keep it that way. "I'm going to take off out of here," Fred told the two. Bruce, would you or Jack make sure the office and the gate are locked when you leave? And, Mark, remember, don't go near the office after dark."

"Sure, will do," Bruce said. "I probably won't be here too much longer, but I'll see that Jack gets the message."

"Well, have a good evening," Fred replied, waving as he dropped the truck into gear and rolled away.

"Interesting guy," Mark said. "I think I'll light up a stove and make some coffee. You want some?"

"I'd have some. I've got some beer in the car," Bruce said, "But we operate on the rule that we never break out the beer until the airplanes are put away."

"Sound rule," Mark said, digging in the pack. Making coffee gave him something to do rather than think of Jack and Jackie, out there in Rocinante somewhere. It was a strange, disquieting feeling. He lit the stove, and set a pot on top of it.

"Hey, look," Bruce said, pointing at the sky.

Mark looked up, to see the eagle circling overhead, not far up -- a hundred feet or so, he guessed. "He's hunting," Bruce whispered. "I think he's found something."

They leaned back to watch. The bird flew in a tight circle, not far away from them, and Mark could sense that it was looking for an opening.

All of a sudden, the bird folded its wings back and dropped like a dive bomber on some unseen target in the grass below. Down, down he came, like a streamlined rock. Just at the moment when it seemed that he would crash headfirst into the ground, the bird opened its wings wide and extended it's claws. It gave one powerful flap to break it's fall, and in the same instant pounced with those huge talons at something in the grass, a mouse perhaps. With another powerful sweep of its wings, it was gaining altitude, and in a few more flaps, was high in the sky again, heading back for its secret aerie somewhere on the ridge.

"Wow," Bruce said. "I've seen him do that before, but never that close."

"Wow," Mark agreed. "That was something else." It was the second time this day that the eagle had treated him to the sight of a lifetime, and, he realized, the second time today that Jackie hadn't been there to share it with him. He felt sorry about that; she would have enjoyed it as much as he had.

They stood there in awe for a couple of minutes, until Mark became aware of the sound of an aircraft engine. It was far off in the distance, but it was heading their way.

The coffee was made, and Mark and Bruce finished a cup and worked on their second while Jackie and Jack shot landings in the fading light. From Mark's experienced eye, it didn't seem like Jackie was having any problems. After what seemed like hours, the little Cessna rolled to a stop, swung around, and taxied back to the tiedowns. Mark and Bruce got up, and went over to help tying it down, getting there just as Jack and Jackie got out of the airplane. "How'd it go?" Mark asked.

"Pretty good," Jackie told him. "It took a little getting used to being in the left seat, but it went OK."

"You guys done for tonight?" Bruce asked.

"Yeah, might as well call it a night," Jack said.

"Well, I'll hike up to the office and get my car," the short man said, "And we can talk about it over a beer."

"Been looking forward to that," Jack said.

Back at the tent, while they were waiting for Bruce to return, Jack summed up the last hour or so. "Jackie, you're pretty good," he said. "You've got a few points that need some work, and I'd like to see you get a little more practice in the left seat. I want to at least touch on everything in a normal student program, although you're not going to need the normal amount of practice. We can fly again tomorrow night, and if you can slide into town next week and get a medical and a student permit, I ought to be able to solo you next weekend. You got a logbook?"

"No," she said. "Should I get one?"

"Yeah, then I can sign you off," Jack said. "I'll pad out your hours a bit so it doesn't look like I'm soloing you with three or four hours, or like you've got all the bootleg time you've got."

It did not take the four of them long to polish off Bruce's eight-pack of Olympia, but dusk was falling when they did. "Suppose I'd better get a move on," Jack said. "It's a long drive back to Greeley, and if I wait much longer, Cumulus might not let me get in my car."

"I'll drive you up to the office," Bruce offered. "See you tomorrow."

They said their goodbyes, and in a minute or two, Mark and Jackie were alone. From their campsite, they could see the foothills of the mountains rising to the west, spread out in a golden brown light above the flatlands below. Both of them were famished, and they turned to making supper as they talked.

"We are in the middle of nowhere," Jackie said. "Did you see when we were flying? There must not be a house for a couple of miles, anyway."

"How was the flying?" Mark asked.

"It was really strange to be sitting in the left seat, with Jack next to me, rather than in the right seat, with you," she said. "For a while there, it didn't seem right at all."

"I'll tell you what seemed strange," Mark said, leaning over to put his arm around her, as if to make sure that she were really there. "Seeing you and Rocinante flying away from me, while I just stood there watching."

"We're going to stay around for a few days, then?" she asked.

"I guess," he said. "You've got to figure that Paul won't be back until the middle of the week, at least. I wouldn't mind tacking on the rating to my license, or at least getting you through solo. You've got solo cross-countries and stuff like that to do to get your license, but that shouldn't be any great trick to pick up when we've got an instructor around."

"I'm in no rush," Jackie said. "Just knowing something about flying the plane is fine with me."

"Well, getting you a license may have to wait until we get back to Spearfish Lake," Mark said. "That is, of course, if we get back to Spearfish Lake."

"What do you mean?" she asked.

"I keep thinking that sooner or later, we're going to come across a place that we like a lot, and people that we like a lot, and a job good enough to stay," Mark said. "I don't think this is the place, but it's close. We might just say the heck with going home."

Jackie shook her head. "Well, I guess I'd kind of figured that we'd get home eventually, but I guess I'm not ready for all the gossip and stories about me running off with you so we could live together."

"That's part of it," Mark said. "Although, in the long run, I don't suppose it would matter much, especially if we decide to get married. It's just that on days like today, I have trouble accepting the idea that I'm going to spend the next forty years as a phone repairman."

"It's been quite a day," Jackie agreed, stirring the pot of stew in front of them. "I never thought it would end up this way. I thought we were just going to have a long, dull day of looking out the window at brown while we flew up toward Yellowstone."

"To tell you the truth, I wasn't really looking forward to it, either," Mark admitted. "I guess this will be a good place to spend a few days."

They finished their dinner in the last rays of the dying twilight; it was dark before they had the dishes washed, by the light of a flashlight, the flame of the stove, and the light of the gibbous moon hanging in the sky overhead. With the slight hiss of the stove off, the silence of the empty landscape crashed down even harder on them. At their campsite, down by the gully, they lay back and looked at the sky. "Would you look at that moon," Mark said. "It's so clear that it looks like you could reach out and touch it."

"You want to get the telescope out?" Jackie asked.

"Naw, it's going to set too late to want to look at any of the faint stuff. If we're still here a week from now, though, and we can catch a night like this, it'll be neat to look at some of that stuff down in Sagittarius again. Besides, I'd just as soon sit here and look at the moon and hold on to you."

"Funny," Jackie whispered, not wanting to break the stillness of the night. "That was my idea, too."

It was so clear and dry that they decided not to sleep in the tent, but drug their sleeping bags and air mattresses out under the stars, the better to lay back and enjoy the night. Each in their own sleeping bag, they hugged each other a final time and kissed goodnight, then fell asleep under the huge dome of the sky.

They were sitting up, making coffee for breakfast, when Fred drove up in his pickup. "Have a good night?" he asked.

"Yeah," Mark and Jackie both chorused.

"Have any trouble with Cumulus?"

"Never saw him," Mark said.

"Good," Fred said. "I didn't think you'd have any trouble with him, but you never know for sure. I brought you some doughnuts, if you want them."

"Hey, great," Mark said. "We've got some coffee hot, if you'd like."

"I'll pass," Fred said. "It'll be a busy day, but it'll be a while before it gets started."

Half an hour later, Mark and Jackie walked up to the office and hanger, and helped Fred roll out the towplane, Golf Echo; the nickname came from it's registration number, N824GE. "It used to be 'GF'," Fred explained. "It belonged to the Wyoming Game and Fish, and they used it to plant fish in mountain lakes. When we got it, it had a big fish tank in the baggage compartment."

"That must be interesting flying," Mark commented.

"Yeah, bombing with fish, tiny little ones. That's got to be a little different," Fred agreed.

Mark had not taken a good look into the rather small hanger the day before. It was no larger than the one in Spearfish Lake, but there were three sailplanes in the hanger, as well as Golf Echo, and another towplane back in the back. The sailplanes sat sideways in the hanger, with wings down, and it was easy to see that it was a complicated and precise puzzle to get everything in so it fit.

The three of them turned to rolling the sailplanes out. Once they had the two trainers and a smaller single-seater outside, and the single-seater tied down, Mark ran a preflight on Golf Echo. He was just finishing up as Jack arrived, followed by two other cars with students.

"OK, Fred, what's the drill?" Mark asked. "Do we haul the sailplanes out to the runway by hand?"

"No need," Fred said. "We'll just take off from here." He pointed at a thin track on the far side of the driveway that ambled a short distance out across the shortgrass prairie.

"You're kidding," Mark said.

"No, we do it every day if the wind will let us," Fred said. "No reason not to today. Give the plane a good runup and let the oil temperature come up a little, and it will be fine."

A little unsure, Mark got into Golf Echo, started it up, and did the runup, while Jackie laid out a towline. Runup complete, Jackie fastened the towline to Golf Echo's tailhook, and then hooked up the glider, the way Bruce had taught her the day before.

Mark let the slack come out of the line gently; it didn't even take goosing the engine, as there was a little hill on his side. In the rear-view mirror above his head, he could see Jackie's arms go up to signal him to stop; then, a moment later, she swung her arms around in the "Take her away," signal.

Shaking his head again, Mark looked at the short length of the alleged runway, and shoved the throttle forward. Presumably, Fred knew what he was talking about.

Even with the heavy trainer on tow, they were all flying before they ran out of track. As they climbed out, Mark could see little puffs of cumulus clouds building back in the mountains; it promised to be a great day.

The next couple of hours were busy. Mark no sooner had one sailplane to altitude and off tow when he could see another one waiting along side the runway; sometimes two or more were waiting, as sailplanes began to appear from some of the other hangers around the field. At some point, either Fred or Jack rolled out the other towplane to help Mark with the backlog, but even so, Mark had only a minute or so on the ground before he was away again. He began to see what Jack meant by calling the towplane pilot "the elevator operator".

Mark had lost track of time when he heard Fred's voice on the radio, through the big, padded headphones he wore over his ears to deaden some of the sound. "Golf Echo, how's your fuel holding out?"

Mark pressed the button on the stick to key the boom microphone in front of his lips. "Still got some," he radioed back.

"Better top off," Fred told him. "I'll have Bruce get the generator out and meet you by the gas pump. This is going to have to just be a pit stop."

Bruce had the generator running when Mark taxied up to the gas pump. He'd brought a stepladder with him; at what Mark later found out to be 4'11", Bruce was nowhere near tall enough to reach the top of the wing without it, but as soon as the prop stopped he was scampering up the stepladder, fuel hose in hand. Mark hopped out of the cockpit, and stood on the tire on the other side, where he could reach the filler; Bruce handed him the hose, and he started to fill the other tank. "God, doesn't it ever let up?" Mark asked.

"When you get everything in the air, sometimes they stay up for a while," the little man said, looking at the sky, which was now filled with puffy white cumulus clouds. "It looks like it ought to be a great day, but it could get interesting later." He pointed off to the west.

Mark glanced back in the hills, where Bruce was pointing. There in the distance were some cumulus clouds that had grown beyond the puffy little cloud stage, into what he knew to be "towering cumulus". If they kept growing, those clouds could develop into thunderstorms. "I see what you mean," Mark commented.

"They're a ways off, yet," Bruce told him. "Maybe fifty or a hundred miles, so it'll be a while before they get here."

"I just can't get over how clear the air is out here," Mark replied. "The murk we've got back home, you're lucky to see ten miles."

"I can't get over it, either," Bruce said, "And I know what you mean. I'm from Pennsylvania, myself."

Mark could hear the tank getting full. He shut the nozzle off, and handed it to Bruce, who took it back over to the gas pump as Mark was getting back into the cockpit. There were now two sailplanes waiting for tows, so there was no time to waste. Mark started the engine and took off right from the gas pump; as soon as he was up a little ways, he began a wide left circle that would take him back to the end of the runway faster than taxiing would. It seemed like a natural thing to do, to fly out to the end of the runway for takeoff.

Sitting out at the end of the hanger was the big Schewizer 2-32 that hadn't flown the day before. This was two-place, a larger, sleeker glider than the trainers. It also had a radio, which the trainers didn't; Fred was in the cockpit. "You want to tow this a little faster than the 2-33s," Fred warned. "Around seventy is fine."

"Seventy, fine," Mark replied, but when he was given the signal to go, it was like the tow line was tied to a fence post. The tautness of the towline lifted Golf Echo's tail into the air, but even the 180 horse engine barely set the tow moving. They gathered speed only reluctantly, but once Golf Echo's Lycoming had gotten the tow moving fast enough for Fred to get the skid off the ground, things improved a little. Still, the towplane was far beyond the marked end of the runway before Mark could get it flying. They cleared the fence at the edge of the field by perhaps fifty feet, and it was a long, slow climb to altitude. Fortunately, Fred found a good patch of lift fairly low, and released from tow; Mark thought they might have been all morning getting to 3000 feet. "With that thing on tow, this thing could use more power," he thought.

It had warmed up as the morning went on. Mark and Jackie had both started out wearing jeans and flannel shirts in the cool of the morning, and it was uncomfortably warm in the cockpit on the rare instances that they were on the ground. In the rear-view mirror as he took out slack for the next tow he could see that Jackie had discarded her clothes from earlier, and was wearing the cutoffs and the halter top she had made back when they were at Cape Canaveral. It seemed like those days had been a long time before, but it wasn't two months, yet, but it seemed like much longer. In the rear-view mirror, he took a good look at Jackie and her now-deep tan. "God, she's beautiful," he thought. He was still looking and enjoying the view when Jackie gave him the signal to "Take her away."

Jackie had gone through a busy morning herself, though not as busy as Mark's had been. It turned out that moving sailplanes on the ground was a two, or sometimes three person job, sometimes involving a car to tow the sailplane around on the ground. Between hauling gliders around, hooking up tow lines, running wingtips, and talking with Bruce and some of the other people that hung around where the sailplanes were clustered at the end of the runway, she had a busy time -- but it was a fun time, too.

There finally came a time when Mark got every waiting sailplane into the air, and they were staying up. He landed on the runway and rolled off to one side, to wait for another tow. He strolled over to the campsite to get a drink of water, then returned to the end of the runway, where a cluster of people awaited. He sat in the shade under the wing of the towplane and talked with Jackie and Bruce for a few minutes, thankful for the break.

Just about that time, Fred's voice came up on the radio. "Take the towplane up to the office and tie it down," he said. "Then get ready to pitch in. In a few minutes, it's going to rain gliders."

With a quizzical look, Mark got up to get to the microphone, so he could answer Fred. As he did, he could see a dark, glowering wall building beyond the ridge to the west. "Where the hell did that come from?" he asked, looking off at the gathering thunderstorm.

"They get started early and blow up quick," Fred said.

Mark told Jackie to check Rocinante's tiedowns, and to button up the tent for a blow; then Bruce hopped into the back seat as Mark taxied Golf Echo up to some tiedowns near the office. Since it had to be the last plane in the hanger, it would have to sit out the storm unless the gliders could be gotten into the hanger first.

"We'd better get the other towplane in," Bruce said. He'd been through this drill before.

They no more than got the towplane in when the first glider arrived -- not down on the runway, but landing up the little track up to the gas pump. Jack was in the back seat, and he touched down a ways away, then let it roll up to the hanger, bringing it to a stop right on the ramp, its wing tip only a few feet clear of the door. Bruce rolled a dolly in front of the single wheel as Jack and the student got out, and the four of them pushed the sailplane inside.

It was wild for a few minutes. Two other sailplanes arrived in the next few minutes, but the single seat 1-26 had to be the next one to go in, and it was still in the air. Jack started to tie the second 2-33 down to tiedowns outside, and was halfway done when the 1-26 arrived; Bruce, Mark, and the pilot, who was no more than 15, wrestled the little sailplane into the hanger while Jack backtracked on the tiedowns. In a few minutes more, they had the second 2-33 in the hanger, and Mark went to get Golf Echo.

As he had been busy around the hanger, he hadn't seen what had been happening elsewhere, but there were several other sailplanes down on the ground and being tied down or put into some of the other hangers around the property. Mark looked out across the reservoir, and had second thoughts about trying to untie the towplane and move it; not half a mile away, the storm was kicking up whitecaps on the water, and moving toward them quickly. "Button up the hanger," he yelled to Bruce, then looked around to see if anyone else needed help, or if all the sailplanes were down.

It appeared that all were down but one -- the 2-32 was on final approach. It went into a single hanger down by the main runway, Mark knew, and he could see Jackie running for the hanger to help Fred put it away. Mark took off running, too, then stopped when he saw Jack shoot by in his little red Rambler Hornet, bent on the same mission.

A teacher to the last, Fred touched the big 2-32 down on the numbers at the end of the runway, the storm not far behind him -- then closed the spoilers, and let the sailplane float a couple of feet back up into the air again. It drifted across the field a couple of feet up, heading for the hanger, burning off the excess speed it had. Finally, it wasn't going fast enough to stay airborne, and it touched down, still rolling toward the hanger, which Jackie had reached by now.

Right in front of the hanger, Fred yanked hard on the brake and shoved the nose down, to let the skid drag it to a stop. Before Fred could get the canopy open, Jackie had grabbed the tail of the big sailplane, swung it around and was dragging it into the hanger. Just at that moment, Jack exploded out of his car and ran over to grab a wing to help push, even as Fred was getting out of the rear cockpit.

The storm hit at the hanger only seconds later. Mark realized that he was going to have to hustle to get inside the office, or he was going to get wet.

Mark got into the office just as the storm hit, to find several people there, including Bruce. Cumulus was there, too, hiding underneath a table, scared at the sound of the thunder. "This sort of thing happen often?" he asked.

"Maybe once a week," Bruce told him. "When it happens during the week, it's no big trick, but every sailplane on the field must have been up, and then it's a little more interesting."

Mark looked out the window. Rain was coming down hard, and the wind was blowing in big gusts. Golf Echo seemed to be riding out the storm all right, at its tiedowns right outside the office, but only rarely could Mark see through the storm far enough to see how Rocinante was doing. As far as he could see, the little Cessna was riding out the storm all right, but at a distance it was hard to tell. He hoped it wouldn't turn into a hailstorm; he'd spent most of the winter repairing the damage that a hailstorm had done to the Cessna, but the fresh Ceconite ought to be able to take more of a beating than the aged linen had been able to.

Down in the sheet metal hanger where Jack, Jackie, Fred, and the student were waiting out the storm, the noise was incredible. The temperature dropped fifteen or twenty degrees in a matter of seconds, and Jackie felt herself getting cold in her light clothing, not that there was anything much she could do about it. "You moved quick, and that was the right move," Fred told her. "I shouldn't have cut it quite so close."

The storm didn't last long; perhaps twenty minutes passed before the rain and the wind slacked off. Off to the west, there was a patch of blue. From a distance, Mark could see that Rocinante was still sitting there, apparently undamaged; although a gentle rain was still falling, he walked out to see for sure. Jackie met him part way there, on her way to get some warmer clothes. "I couldn't believe it when you grabbed that big potlicker and drug it inside by yourself," Mark said.

"I knew they didn't have much time," Jackie said. "I could see the storm coming, and all I could do was to take off running."

Mark walked around the Cessna carefully, but could see no sign of damage. He went over to the tent and checked it out, as well, but everything seemed all right there, too. He found the flannel shirt he had taken off earlier and put it on, and then, with Jackie, walked back up to the office. Other people were coming outside, now, to enjoy the clean, cool smell of the storm washed air; even Cumulus danced around excitedly in the mud, glad to have the storm over with.

Mark was checking Golf Echo out when Fred came out of the office. "That thing OK?" he asked."

"So far," Mark told him.

"Finish your checkout, gas it up, and then bring it around," Fred said. "We'll roll out one of the trainers."

"With all this rain, it's going to be dead out there," Mark protested.

Fred smiled, "Great for tow and landing practice."

Mark spent most of the rest of the afternoon playing elevator operator. Jack got the second trainer out for a while, and made half a dozen flights, but most of the flying was taking Fred with students to a low altitude, dropping them, then racing them back to the ground. Still, it wasn't quite as frantic as the morning had been.

After a while, Jack ran out of students. They put the glider away, and then he and Jackie fired up Rocinante so she could get her flying in. They flew around the pattern, making touch and goes for an hour or more, while Mark hauled Fred and the remaining trainer.

It was getting along toward evening, now; Fred finished up with his last student, then he and mark stood alongside the end of the runway, with the trainer and the towplane sitting nearby, and watched Jack and Jackie shoot practice landings. "She handles it well," Fred commented.

"I think so," Mark told him. "I just hope she's not having to unlearn any bad habits I've taught her."

"We all have bad habits," Fred said. "I tend to cut things a little too close, for example. There was a time . . . well, that's neither here nor there, now. It was a long time ago. You saw what I mean this afternoon, anyway. I should have had the 2-32 on the ground fifteen minutes earlier, and I knew it when I called you. But, it worked out in the end, at least partly because Jackie was on her toes. But, I like the way you fly. You're careful, and you're smooth. If they decide to quit flying pretty soon, how'd you like it if Jack gave you and me a tow, and then I'll turn you loose."

"Sounds fine to me," Mark said.

It wasn't much longer before Jack and Jackie landed, and taxied back to the tiedowns. Mark and Fred went over to help tie the plane down, and in a few minutes, Mark was in the front seat of the trainer, with Fred in back, Jackie running the wingtip.

It was a brief flight, just long enough to satisfy Fred that Mark hadn't forgotten much about flying the trainer since the day before. They touched down on the runway, and Jackie brought the towline over for another flight. "Land it on the runway," Fred said, and got out of the back, and almost before he knew what was happening, Mark was on tow alone behind the towplane.

He didn't tow up very high; he was tired, and it had been a long day. Besides, this solo flight was more ceremonial than anything else. It was over in ten minutes or so; then, they put the sailplane and the towplane away.

With everything over with for the day, about six or eight people gathered in the office to break out a cooler of Olympia. "Tomorrow's Monday, isn't it?"

Mark asked.

"Yeah," Fred said. "We won't be anything like as busy. It'll be just you and me and Jackie."

"I might be out later on," Bruce said.

"Do you think we'll get started real early?" Mark said. "We need to get into town, get some groceries, get Jackie her flight physical, get some gas in the Cessna, and some stuff like that, and we need to figure out a way to get there. I thought maybe we could borrow a car or something."

"Fly right down to Fort Collins Valley Airpark," Jack suggested. "You can do everything you need to right within walking distance."

"I don't really care if I go near that place again," Mark said. "They were pretty snotty, and I didn't see much of anything close by."

"Oh," Jack said. "You stopped at Loveland-Fort Collins, not Valley. Yeah, they're a bunch of pricks, all right."

"Mondays always get started slow, and we probably won't get very busy anyway," Fred told them. "If you're back by ten or eleven, then it ought to be all right."

*   *   *

Waverley West Soaring Ranch
Fort Collins, Colorado
June 11, 1971

Dear Dad and Sarah,
It was so nice to get that package of mail from you today! It seems so long since I last got mail and stuff from you, down in Texas, that I was really anxious to paw through it when Fred brought it to work with him this morning.

We heard from the guy that Mark is filling in for this morning, too. He still doesn't know how long it will be before he can get back to work. His dad is still in real bad shape, but getting better. I don't think he's going to race a train to a crossing again. I think we'll probably be here another week or so, but it's hard to be sure, so you'd better not send us any more mail after you get this letter.

It's a lot slower here during the week than it is on the weekends, so I'm just sitting here in the office, writing you this letter, while Fred is in the shop working on something and Mark is out in a glider. Mark has made several solo flights in the 1-26, the little single-seat glider, and Fred said he's ready to be signed off for his license when we have another tow pilot here. Jack will be here tomorrow -- he's a flight instructor over in Greeley during the week -- and he can give Mark and Fred a tow for Mark's checkride.

It's been very hot here all week. Mark and I discovered a path down to the reservoir, and a little sandy beach there, and we go swimming most every day after work, and that helps some. A couple of nights after work we've flown into Fort Collins for dinner -- they have absolutely the best Mexican food I've ever had -- but we have to leave early so we can be back before dark, as the field here doesn't have any lights.

It's been a lot of fun to be here, and Mark says he's learned a lot; but I think that we are both a little anxious to get moving again. It's very hard to stay in one place when we know that this trip is going to come to an end all too soon. I see Mark is landing, so I guess I'd better wrap this up.

Love,
Jackie

13.

"Hey Mark! Jackie! You guys gonna sleep forever? There's daylight in the swamp, so unass them sacks!"

Reluctantly, Mark gave up his dream, one that involved he and Jackie and not a lot of clothes. The morning was lighting the tent. What was Jack doing here? He dug out his watch. "Good God, Jack," he yelled back, "It's 6:30 in the morning, after that day we had yesterday! Don't you ever get enough?"

"I thought Jackie might like to get in a little flying time before we get busy," Jack said, a little quieter. "I brought you some coffee and doughnuts."

"Give us a few minutes to get around," Jackie told him.

"You go first," Mark whispered. "I'll roll over."

By now they had gotten used to dressing and undressing in the tent with the other present when they had to, although it had been several days since they'd last had to do it. Jackie slid off the top of the short pajamas she'd bought back in Everglades City and looked for her bra. It wasn't easily findable, so she settled for her halter top; she'd probably want it before the morning was over, anyway. She pulled on a flannel shirt over the top of it, then slipped the rest of the way out of her sleeping bag, pulled off her pajama pants, and struggled into panties and her cutoffs; it was probably a little too cool for them yet, but she might not get a chance to change, later. She gave her hair about four strokes with a brush, then, grabbing socks and shoes, she unzipped the tent and crawled outside to put them on. She sat on the bare ground to do it.

Jack got out of his car, carrying a bag and a cup of coffee. "It'll have to wait a minute," she said. "I've got to make a visit out in the bushes."

"Thought you might like a little coffee to prime the pump," Jack said, smiling.

"The pump is primed enough already, thank you," she said, getting up and starting for the cathole back in the bushes that Mark had dug earlier in the week. "Bruce brought his cooler out again last night, after you left. I sometimes wonder if he lives on Oly."

"That Tumwater will stunt your growth," Jack commented. "It stunted his, anyway. You ready for your coffee, Mark?"

"Give me a chance to get my pants on," Mark replied. "I'm half tempted to roll back over and sleep for a while, but you're probably just going to shoot touch and goes and keep me awake."

"Something like that," Jack said.

Mark was outside the tent by the time Jackie got back from the bushes. She had a sip of coffee and reached for a doughnut, and took both with her as she and Jack went over to Rocinante to start the preflight. In but a few minutes, they had the plane started, and were taxiing out onto the runway.

Mark scratched himself a couple of times, drank about half of his coffee, and decided that a cigarette would taste good. He hadn't had one in several days, and had to hunt through his pack for what was left of a pack of cigarettes. It wouldn't hurt to get another pack the next time they were near a store, he thought.

He sat down on the fender of Jack's car and watched the little Cessna fly around the pattern in the early morning light. He finished the cigarette, and finished the coffee, and just sat there, taking in the morning. It was a beautiful day; the sky was a cerulean blue, the kind of blue it only gets in Colorado on the kinds of days that from a plane you can see to Kansas. It was hot already; he'd noticed that Jackie had already taken off her shirt before she and Jack started flying. It probably would be a heck of a day for soaring.

A few minutes later, Fred showed up in his pickup, bringing Bruce with him; Cumulus had hopped in the back, and he gave an obligatory bark at the Cessna's takeoff.

"What happened to your car, Bruce?" Mark asked, listening to the Cessna take off and climb out.

"Got it in for a tune-up," the little professor said. "So I asked Fred if I could ride out with him."

"Thought we'd bring you some coffee and doughnuts," Fred said. "It's going to be a long day."

"Just had a cup," Mark said, "But I'd be willing to have another."

"Yeah, I'll have one, too," Jack said from behind him.

Mark must still have been a little sleepy; it was interesting for Jack, Fred, and Bruce to see how long it took him to put two and two together. "What the hell are you doing here?" Mark said as comprehension began to roll over him.

"Is your old lady always that pissed off when she gets up?" Jack asked. "I told her that if she was going to be that cranky, she could damn well leave me out of it."

Someone pressed a cup of coffee into Mark's hand, but he wasn't aware of it; his eyes were turned skyward, off to the south, where the gray and white Cessna was turning onto the crosswind leg. He couldn't take his eyes off of it, and wondered how Jackie must be feeling. He remembered his own first solo, nearly eight years before. He'd had vastly more flying experience than Jackie, had grown up with it, but he had still been so excited that he could hardly remember what he was supposed to be doing. Nothing in his life had matched it; the first time he had made love with Mei-Ling back in Bangkok sometime in another life hadn't even come close.

He could hear Jackie cut the power back on Rocinante's engine as she started her approach. The white wings that he and Jackie covered slanted and glistened in the sun as she turned onto the base leg of her approach. Was she a bit high? It looked like it from where he stood, but it was hard to tell. It had been hard enough to watch her fly with Jack, but now that she was up there by herself. He could see Rocinante's shadow sweep across the ground toward them as she approached the end of the runway, and far in the distance he could make out her head in the cockpit. Was she nervous? Relaxed? How did she feel?

Even watching Rocinante touch down dead solid perfect did little to take his own case of nerves away, for she let it roll for fifty feet or so, then he heard the engine's power come back on again; the tail lifted into the air, and she was gone again for another flight.

The coffee grew cold in his hand as he stood there watching, never taking his eyes off of the little Cessna. Her next landing was perhaps a touch longer than the first, but there wasn't any trace of a bounce, and she was off again.

"Pretty good," Fred commented, but Mark was hardly aware of what he said.

The last landing was the best of all; laid right on the numbers, a perfect power-off approach, with hardly a puff of dust as the tires hit the runway. Mark watched as she let the Cessna roll out; then she swung it around, taxied back up to the tiedowns. Mark set the coffee down on the car and raced over to the plane, getting there just as she shut the engine off. With a steady demeanor that was belied by the broad smile on her face, she opened Rocinante's door and stepped outside into his arms. "You did it," he said. "I'm so proud of you."

"Mark, that was wonderful," she said. "Why didn't you tell me?"

"It's different," he said. "You just can't know unless you've been there."

"I know," she said, and kissed him. They kissed each other hard, clinging to each other in joy and happiness, and the kiss went on and on, even though Mark and Jackie both knew that Jack and Bruce and Fred were standing there watching; somehow, this time, it didn't matter.

Finally, they broke apart, and Jack and Fred each gave her a hug, too; even Bruce, although he had to stand on Rocinante's wheel to get high enough for it to be a good hug.

"How'd it go?" Jack finally asked.

"It went wonderful," Jackie said. "I thought I was a little high the first time, but I slipped it a little and it seemed to work out all right."

"There's only one problem that I can see," Jack said, smiling and looking at Fred.

"You see, Jackie," Fred said. "There's a certain tradition that's normally followed at times like these. It's traditional to cut off someone's shirt tail and label it with the date of solo, and those who witness it get to sign it." Jackie blushed, and broke out laughing, while Fred continued: "However, with that halter top, you don't have enough shirt tail to say so."

They all joined in laughing, and Jackie offered them the flannel shirt she had been wearing before they started flying. Prepared for the occasion, Fred pulled out a pocket knife and cut off the shirttail, then took a felt pen from his pocket, and all of them signed it, each making a joke about sneaky girls that thought they could save a shirttail by wearing a halter top.

A few minutes later, with Rocinante tied down, they clustered around the vehicles, with fresh cups of coffee. "When we set this up," Fred explained, "Mark, we wanted to get out here early enough to get this done, and give you a chance to get in your glider checkride before we get busy," Fred told them. "So let's drink this up, and roll out Golf Echo and a 2-33."

It was probably twenty minutes later before Jack towed Mark and Fred off the short strip in front of the hanger. Fred told Mark that the checkride was going to take two or three flights, since there were a few things that he hadn't had a chance to demonstrate yet.

"Fine with me," Mark agreed.

"OK," Fred said, and pulled the towline release from the back seat.

They were maybe a hundred and fifty feet up. Mark took a quick look to his right; it might have been possible to turn back to one of the cross runways, but perhaps they were a little low. There was a field on the other side of the fence, but the fence was still a long way away. Really, the only choice was to land straight ahead. He yanked the spoilers wide open, and sideslipped the trainer hard, since the fence was getting closer rapidly. The trainer dipped down into a little valley, and Mark touched down on the gentle rising slope, and came down hard on the brake. "Let it roll," Fred said. "See if we can get up to the top of the hill."

They just barely made it. "I think you could have made it to the field on the far side of the road," Fred commented. "But this was just as good. I thought you could do it."

"Well," Mark told him, "I thought if someone was coming up the road we'd scare the shit out of them."

"Wouldn't be the first time we've gone over that road ten feet up, although usually it's with the 2-32 on tow on a hot day," Fred said. "I wouldn't pull a simulated towline break like that on just anybody. That was a good job." He looked around, then up to the windsock by the office; the towplane was landing across the grass in front of them, far off the runway. "Still dead. No reason Jack can't pull us off this hill northbound. We can take off without a wingrunner, but we're going to want a lot of aileron to get that wing up as soon as the tow begins."

On the next tow, Mark kept waiting for a simulated towline break, but it never came. They towed up high, and Fred put Mark through the various maneuvers around the towplane's slipstream. They got off tow high, and did several maneuvers such as stalls and steep turns before entering the pattern for a landing. Fred told him to touch it down on the white line limed across the runway, and Mark hit it on the nose."

"Well, no point in going again," Fred said. "There's a couple of things we missed, but they're not important. Let's tie this thing down and go do some paperwork."

It wasn't 8:30 in the morning, and they weren't open yet, and already Mark felt so drained that it seemed he'd put in a full day. Jack tied down the towplane by the office, and by the time Fred and Mark walked up there, they found Jack and Jackie immersed in paperwork. "I've signed you off for solo," Jack told her. "You've got quite a bit else to do before you can get a license, but you'll pick up a lot of it flying with Mark, and before you two leave, I'll give him a list of things to work on with you. You're going to have to demonstrate all of that to an instructor, and you've still got ten hours of instructor-supervised solo cross-country flight you'll have to get. All your solo flights are supposed to be instructor-supervised, while I'm thinking about it, but that's a rule that you can bend a little, so long as you don't get caught at it. While I'm at it, I'm going to sign you off to take your written examination, but you're not ready for it, yet. I've liberated a set of the books we use at the school for you. Work your way through them, and ask Mark if you have any questions, and we'll save you the several hundred bucks we'd charge you over at Greeley for ground school."

He finished signing the certificate, and handed it to her. She took it and read it carefully; it was an achievement that she'd never dreamed would come to her, a statement that she could do things she'd never dreamed she could do. She almost wished she could frame it . . . "S. S. Daniels?" she said. "I thought your name was Jack."

"I was hoping you wouldn't notice that," the instructor said.

"Well, what is your name?" she asked.

"Do you really want to know?"

"Come on," Mark said. "After the way you kicked us out of bed this morning, we really ought to know."

"Sylvester Shamus Daniels," he said, sheepishly.

"They why do they call you Jack?" she asked.

"If your last name was Daniels, and you wanted a nickname, what would you choose?"

They all had a laugh at that.

"Come on, Sylvester," Fred said. Let's you and Mark and I roll out the other sailplanes."

"Hey, it's not funny," Jack said.

"I know," Fred said. "After all, I've had to live with Frederich."

Jackie sat and stared at the student certificate for a minute, still amazed that it had her name on it. When Mark had her start flying with Jack, she'd never dreamed this would happen to her. She started to put the certificate in her pocket, then realized it would be better to have it with the aircraft papers down in Rocinante, so started out the door toward the Cessna.

She found Bruce standing at the fence, staring across the field. "I wondered what happened to you," she said. "I thought you'd be over at the hanger."

"Didn't feel like it," Bruce said, looking down. "I guess, right at this moment, I'm a little ashamed of myself."

"Why's that?" Jackie asked, leaning up against the fence to talk.

"Oh, it's nothing, I guess," he said. "I ought to be used to it by now. It's just that this morning you did something that I've never been able to bring myself to do."

"You mean, solo?" she asked. "I thought you were a pilot."

"Oh, I've flown a lot," Bruce said. "I've probably got a couple hundred hours in power, all dual. I've got maybe a hundred flights in sailplanes, all dual. I go flying with Fred every few days, and he always says that I can solo whenever I want to, but I've never been able to bring myself to do it. I guess I'm what you call a coward."

"I guess it would have been hard for me this morning if I'd have to think about it," Jackie told him. "I mean, Jack said he was going to solo me this weekend, but I never really believed it would happen, even when he got out of the plane. And then, I just went ahead and did it."

"That's what I mean," he said, looking up at her. "I've had plenty of opportunities to just go ahead and do it, and when the time came, I've never been able to do it." He turned and stared back across at the sailplane tied down near the end of the runway. "I suppose it's because I'm so short," he said. "All my life, I've been told, you're too little for this, you can't do that, you're too small."

"You think it's any easier to be a girl that's six feet tall?" she said. "I've gotten over the worst of it, but I was always too big for my muscles, tripping over my own feet. Everybody always laughed at me like I was some kind of freak. It's not like that with Mark. He's the first guy I've known that's taller than me that's not some prick of a basketball player. He's always told me, 'To hell with what other people think.'" Jackie caught her breath; she'd almost said "little people," like Mark did, but she'd caught herself in time.

"It's not what other people think," Bruce said. "It's what I think."

"Maybe you're thinking about it too much," Jackie told him. "I mean, hell, you're a college professor, you're supposed to be able to think. I'm just an unemployed waitress that barely made it through high school, and I guess I just go ahead and do things. Why don't you just quit thinking about it and do it?"

"That's easy for you to say," he said. "You knew you could do it."

"I think you know you can do it," she told him, watching Mark get into Golf Echo to taxi it around in front of the hanger. She put her hand on Bruce's shoulder and continued, "In fact, you know you can do it better than I can. Just say the hell with your fears and do it."

He was silent for a moment, then looked up at her and asked. "Will you run the wingtip?"

"Of course I will," she told him. "Let's do it now before you change your mind."

It took a few minutes to get the extra cushions for the trainer, and to put ballast under the seat so it would balance with Bruce's light weight. It wasn't until he was strapped into the cockpit of the trainer that he started to have second thoughts, but somehow Jackie sensed what was on his mind; she shook her head and whispered to him, "You know what you really want to do. Let's not put this off any longer." She closed the canopy, and signaled Mark to take the slack out of the towline.

The line came taut. Bruce looked up at Jackie and shook his head, but she shook her head back at him, and signaled Mark to take it away.

The surge forward caught Bruce half by surprise. For an instant, he thought about releasing from the towline and letting the glider roll to a stop, but he couldn't quite make himself take his hands off of the stick to reach for the release, and in the cool morning air, Golf Echo and the trainer were soon above the ground and climbing fast.

"By God," Fred said. "There's something I never thought I'd see happen." He had stayed back from Bruce and Jackie, not wanting to break whatever spell it was that she had managed to cast over the little man. "What did you say to him?"

"I told him that if an unemployed waitress was smart enough to solo, then a college professor ought to be," she said.

"Let's get down to the runway," Fred said. "I want to be there when he lands."

Jackie got into the right side of the pickup, while Jack and Cumulus hopped into the back. They got down to the end of the runway while the glider was still on tow, and stood and watched as the sailplane released. Mark landed the towplane and joined them presently, but there wasn't much to say.

In the still of the morning air, the glider sank steadily, and in a few minutes it was entering the pattern over the reservoir. They watched Bruce fly around the pattern and touch down at the end of the runway. As it rolled to a stop, Jackie pointed at the towplane and waved her arm over her head, signaling Mark to wind it up.

Bruce was opening the canopy as they got there. He had a big smile, and there were tears rolling down his face. "I can't believe I did that," he told Fred and Jack and Jackie.

"I told you that you could do it better than I could," she said. "You've proved it to me, but now you're going to prove it to yourself."

"Hey, that's not necessary," he said, as Jack bent over to hook up the towline. "I know I can do it. I just did it."

"Then prove it to me that you can do it again," she said. Jack put tension on the towline; she reached out and pulled the release to check it.

"I don't need to do that," he said.

"Bruce," she said, "I think you do, and you're going to do it for me, if nobody else." Before he could protest, she closed the canopy and signaled Mark to take up slack. She went over to the wingtip and picked it up, leveling the sailplane. Bruce smiled and pointed his finger ahead, and she signaled to Mark.

Bruce made still another flight before he quit, but Jackie didn't have to urge him for the last flight. At the end of the last flight, he let the sailplane roll off the runway, and Fred and the rest of them were waiting for him, scissors in hand. "Now, this is going to be one to tack on the wall," Fred said as he trimmed Bruce's shirttail while Jackie hugged him. "It's too early to break out the beer, but we can save that for tonight."

"Hey, Fred," Bruce asked, "Do you think I could fly the 1-26?"

Before long, flight operations began in earnest, although it had already been an eventful morning around the gliderport. Two students showed up within ten minutes of each other, and both Fred and Jack were busy flying with them, while Mark was back to being an elevator operator. It wasn't long before the sky started to perk up, and the flights became soaring flights in the rising air, rather than gentle sled rides earthward.

Other people began to show up; the day looked promising. Bruce and Jackie were busy for a while, helping to roll sailplanes out and launch them, and before noon, most of the sailplanes on the gliderport were in the air, both the gliderport's rental ships and the privately-owned ones. It was a while before Jackie got a chance to sit on the tailgate of the pickup truck and try to put it all together. It was wonderful to have soloed Rocinante, of course; three months ago, even two weeks ago, it would have been the furthest thing from her mind. But somehow, it was Bruce's solo, and what she had told him, that hit her even harder. It needed some thinking about . . .

It proved to be a busy day, the busiest they'd had since they'd been at Waverly. Mark made 27 tows before the day was over with, and even had to eat lunch in the plane while he was towing.

Both Mark and Jackie were glad to have the day over with as they sat down in their camp to eat supper by the light of a spectacular sunset that reddened much of the western sky. "Actually," Mark said, "We've accomplished everything we set out to accomplish here. As soon as Paul gets back, there's no reason why we can't get on the move again."

"It's sure been fun here," Jackie agreed. "I'm going to hate to leave, but I almost feel like it's time to be moving on, too. I've been thinking about it. Rather than head on to Yellowstone, I think I'd like to see some of the higher country in Colorado."

"I'll talk to Jack about it," Mark told her as he started in on the dishes. "He was talking about messing around in the high country last night, and I get the impression that he knows what he's talking about. I've never done any mountain flying to speak of, and that's kind of a tall order to start with."

"I kind of think that a backpacking trip in the high country might be fun."

"I do, too. That's one of the things that was on the list for this trip. But, we're probably got a few days yet to think about it, before Paul gets back."

Even though the sun had set by the time that Mark had finished the dishes, there was still a lot of light left of this long summer evening, not far from the solstice; it was much too early to go to bed, even considering how early they had gotten up. "Let's go for a walk," Jackie suggested.

"Fine by me," Mark told her, getting to his feet. "I'm stiff from sitting in that cockpit all day."

They started down the now-familiar path to the reservoir. It was an easy walk down through the gully to a two-rut lane, which came to an end at a small sandy spot. "Now that we're down here, I can't help but think that a swim would be nice," Jackie said.

"Yeah," Mark agreed, looking at the waters of the reservoir. "I feel all sweaty and grubby just thinking about it."

"I didn't think about swimsuits," Jackie admitted.

Mark shook his head. "Want to go back and get them?"

Jackie stood for a minute looking at the water. "By the time we got back, it wouldn't be as appealing," she said finally. "Want to just go without them?"

From the tone of her voice, it was hard for Mark to tell if she was teasing or not, and he was still too exhausted from the day's flying to play mind games. "I will if you will," he told her.

"Why not?" she said, reaching up to untie her halter top. In seconds, she was naked in they dying light, heading for the water.

It took Mark longer to join her there; he had shoes to untie.

Much of the tiredness of the day drained out of them in the next few minutes, as they played in the water, splashed each other, and laughed and joked. It was almost as if they were not naked with each other for the first time.

They'd never managed a long swim in the reservoir; it was mountain water, carried there by aqueduct, still cold from the winter snows, and a few minutes of it was about all that either of them wanted. It was not long before both of them collapsed on the little sandy spot that passed for a beach, to let the air and the remaining heat of the day dry them off a little. In the fading light, Mark took the opportunity to study Jackie's nude body. Her lack of self-consciousness about their lack of clothing surprised Mark a little, considering the lengths both of them had gone to in preserving their modesty over the past couple of months.

Still, he didn't want to act as if he were staring at her -- which he was. He lay back on the sand, still warm from the sun, and looked up at the evening sky, now dark enough that the stars were coming out. He could see the summer triangle, his old friends Altair, Deneb, and Vega as they started to fill the blue, the precursors of a glorious skyful of stars.

She lay down beside him, on her side, her head resting on his shoulder. Her wet hair was cold on his skin, but her bare body was warm where she pressed up against him. "It's been quite a day, hasn't it?" she commented.

"Quite a day," he agreed.

"I've been thinking about Bruce a lot, all day today," she said. "Do you know what I told him?"

"Not really," he murmured, enjoying the sensation of her body next to his.

"I told him to forget about his fears, and go ahead and do what he really wanted to do, before he had time to change his mind. I've been thinking about that a lot."

He rolled on his side to face her. "And?" he said, letting the question hang.

She pulled him tight and kissed him for a long time before she whispered in his ear, "I think you and I have had enough solo time. It's time for us to get some dual."

It took a second or two for him to understand what she was saying. "You want to go up to the tent?" he asked.

"This is better," she said. "Out under the sky."

It was a scene that Altair and Deneb and Vega have witnessed billions of times over the eons that their light have shown down on this battered orb, but down on the sand of the Colorado reservoir, it was the first time for this pair.

It could have been awkward, except for what Mei-Ling had taught him, what seemed a lifetime before. Jackie told him that it hurt her a little, but that she'd kill him if he stopped.

The last barriers between them now down, they stayed in the tent rather late in the morning the next day, exploring their new world. Eventually Fred had to drive out in the truck and yell from it's window, "Wake up, sleepyheads, we've got a tow!"

Mark and Jackie hurriedly threw on what clothes they could find; it was the first night they'd spent in the tent that they hadn't been wearing any. "Sorry, Fred," Mark apologized through the tent fabric, trying to cover things up a little. "You know how it is when you don't have an alarm clock. Once in a while, you sleep in, and after the day we had yesterday, I'm not surprised."

"You should have come to town with us," Fred reported. "I had the good sense to leave early, but I don't know if Jack made it to work today. I think he slept on Bruce's couch last night."

They rode back up in the truck to discover that Fred and a student had already rolled Golf Echo and the orange 2-33 out of the hanger. Mark looked around at the sky; it was clear overhead, and all the indications were that there was little thermal activity yet, but it looked like it could be a pretty good day. Back off in the mountains to the west, though, the clouds were already building rapidly, and thunderstorms seemed like a good bet.

Jackie had some coffee waiting for Mark down on the runway by the time he finished the second tow, but it took Fred and the student a while to get down, so there was time to drink it in peace, with just a little kissing and hugging to sweeten it.

It was a fairly lazy morning. Fred finished with the student, and flew with another over the course of the morning, and then after a while they all went up to the office to have lunch. By the time they finished eating, they looked outside to see the black wall of a thunderstorm building off to the west. It was not yet near, but obviously was heading their way, so Fred and Mark and Jackie rolled the 2-33 and the towplane back into the hanger, and Mark drove Fred's pickup down to the camp to check that the tent was watertight and that the tiedowns on Rocinante were solid.

The storm was just about to hit when a car drove in. The driver proved to be a student named Kent, who had been scheduled for the afternoon. "No flying today, huh?" he asked from his car window.

"We can maybe do some up and downs after this storm goes through," Fred told him.

Kent came inside and joined the other three, just as the storm hit. It was a louder one than the one a few days before, with more lightning, more thunder, including a flash and a bang so close it make their ears ring; it may have hit the lightning rod on the windsock pole, right next to the office. But, in twenty minutes it was over, except for some light rain that continued for a while after the violence was over.

Once the rain stopped, the four drifted outside, to enjoy the fresh, clean smell of the air. The sky was totally overcast, except for a bright patch far to the south. They knew from practical experience that it usually clears up quickly following summer thunderstorms in Colorado, and there was no real desire to fly under an overcast, rather than in clear skies.

But the overcast went on for a while. "What do you think, Mark?" Fred asked.

Mark shrugged. "Back in Spearfish Lake, I'd think that we'd had a frontal passage," he said. "This is Colorado, and things work a little different."

"I think you're right," Fred said. "But there's something about this that I don't like. Why don't you roll out the towplane and fly around the area to see what's going on. Get out to the west, especially."

It had been days since Mark had taken off with the towplane, without a sailplane, with the intent of gaining some altitude, and had forgotten how quickly he could get to 3000 feet above the ground. He flew a couple of miles to the south, then perhaps ten miles to the west, back over Owl Canyon, far beyond the first ridge. He turned and flew north a ways, then east again, starting his letdown for the gliderport. "Smooth as a baby's butt," he reported on the radio.

By the time he got back to the gliderport, the orange 2-33 had been rolled out onto the runway, and Jackie had a towline laid out. Mark stopped the towplane next to the glider and idled the engine; Fred came over for a talk. "I went maybe ten miles west," he told Fred. "There's nothing happening."

"I still don't like it," Fred said. "But it probably doesn't mean anything. We'll be going to 3000 feet, two, maybe three times."

It only took a few minutes to get the tow up to where Fred released; Mark dropped off, cocked the nose of the towplane up and began his practiced sideslip. By now, he was getting pretty good at the steep, slipping approach to a landing, and this was one of his better ones; Golf Echo only rolled a couple of hundred feet before he turned off the runway. Jackie came over and stood next to him as he sat in the Super Cub's seat, waiting for the next tow.

A few minutes later, Fred and Kent were down. It was only a matter of a couple of minutes to get them on their way again; again, the sky was smooth and the air was dead.

Until they hit 1500 feet above the ground.

All of a sudden it was if the whole tow had been thrown in a cement mixer. No, worse than that; God's own cocktail shaker, perhaps. Mark had never seen such turbulence in his life; it went in an instant from dead smooth to a desperate and failing battle to keep the Super Cub upright. Instantly, he realized that they'd all blown the decision -- this was a thunderstorm, and a bad one at that.

They were a little to the northwest of the gliderport; Mark started a turn to the southeast, in an effort to fly out of the wave of turbulence, but as he turned the ground seemed closer than it had before. Somehow, he stole a glance at the altimeter; they had lost a thousand feet in just a few seconds, and the rate of climb was buried at more than a thousand feet a minute down. It had to have been well over that; Mark was still trying to climb, and in smooth air, they should have been climbing at 700 feet per minute.

He pushed hard at Golf Echo's throttle, though it was still all the way forward, trying to squeeze a little more out of its engine, with the prayer that it could somehow help. He could tell from the jerks on the towline that he still had the glider on tow, and once he even got a glimpse of it in the rear-view mirror, wallowing and struggling to stay upright just as he was doing. He glanced at the altimeter again: 200 feet, as if there could be no stopping. The plane gave a lurch, and he could see the glider disappearing behind him; it was off tow.

Whether it had been released or the line was on broke, Fred and Kent were on their own.

Mark kept the throttle all the way forward, just trying to keep the plane upright. He knew in his heart that it was going to hit, and wanted to hit on the gear, if possible; it was his only hope left, but even that was a a struggle, with the plane rolling sixty degrees and more either direction. He could see the windsock flash by, almost at a level with him, but miraculously, he didn't go any lower, merely because the air taking him down couldn't go any lower, either. Feet above the ground, he kept the throttle wide open, running for that patch of daylight, far to the south.

As soon as Fred saw Mark turn toward the daylight, right after the thunderstorm turbulence hit them, he'd realized what Mark was up to; turn away from trouble and try to tow them away from the turbulence, even if it meant towing them away from the gliderport; but at 200 feet, Fred realized that it wasn't going to work. If Mark could tow them away at all, it was going to be just above the treetops, and the glider might have trouble staying above them. Making the best of a bad deal, he decided to risk a landing.

Jackie had been watching, had seen the storm hit them, right at the beginning, and had watched in shock as the towplane and the glider almost fell out of the sky. She lost sight of the glider after Fred released; her eyes were only on Mark as he shot over her head and beyond her view behind the office on the top of the hill. Sure he was going to crash, she started running as hard as she could go for the top of the hill when all of a sudden the orange and white glider got in front of her.

Under normal circumstances, Fred had set up a good landing. He had the wind on the nose, and saw the sink break up as they neared the ground. The might not even hit too hard; once they got on the ground, if he kept the spoilers open and the nose to the wind, they might have been all right. But, just above the ground, the wind switched on them; in an instant, they were being blown sideways, at perhaps 40 miles an hour. A lifetime of flying behind him, Fred mashed the rudder, trying to get the nose in the wind, and popped back on the stick, trying to give them a few seconds more in the air to make the turn, but it was not to be. The sailplane hit sideways, its tail low; it cartwheeled off one wingtip, then spun around it, coming to rest with the wingtip into the wing.

"Get out!" Fred yelled. Kent popped the emergency canopy release; the canopy flew off downwind somewhere. Kent tried to get out of the five point harness while Fred tried to hold the wing down with the ailerons. If the wind got under it, they could be rolled down the runway into a little ball.

"Get out!" they could hear Jackie yell over the wind. Fred could see her throw herself over the wingtip, to try to buy them seconds to get free of the glider. Kent clambered out of cockpit and ran to join Jackie on the wingtip; Fred had somehow managed to get out of his harness while holding the stick over, and he tumbled backwards out the door to the back seat. He picked himself up, and ran to join Jackie and Kent when the wind shifted yet again, clear around this time. It got under the wing that was up in the air, picking it up in an instant, before Jackie and Kent could react. Fred could see the glider being picked up and up in an instant, until it was standing on the wingtip . . .

And the wind stopped as suddenly as it started.

With a bang!!!! the empty glider crashed back down onto its single landing wheel and came to rest. Fred ran to Kent and Jackie, yelling "You all right?"

"Yeah, thank God," Kent said.

"What happened to Mark?" Fred yelled back. "I didn't see him after we released."

"The last I saw him he was going down on the other side of the line shack," Jackie said, remembering her mission that had been interrupted by the glider crashing in front of her. Scared to the depths of her soul, she took off running for the top of the hill, Fred and Kent puffing along behind.

When she got to the top of the hill, what she saw only gave her a little relief: nowhere in the mile or more she could see was there the crashed and burning wreckage of a Super Cub. She stood there in confusion for a moment, trying to carefully study the landscape, fearing that he must have hit somewhere beyond view. How could she find the wreck?

The idea of running for Rocinante to search for Mark was just beginning to enter her mind when she heard the sweetest sound she had ever heard: the hum of an unmuffled short-stack 180 horsepower Lycoming, heading her way.

*   *   *

Waverly West Soaring Ranch
Fort Collins, Colorado
June 11, 1971

Dear Dad and Sarah:
We'll probably be on our way again by the time you get this. The guy that Mark has been filling in for called today, and will be starting on his way back tomorrow. His dad is out of danger, and there's hope that he will eventually walk again.

It's been kind of a slow week, and the weather has turned chilly. One of the gliders got banged up a bit in a windstorm last Monday, and Mark and Fred and I have been working on it in the shop. It seems strange to be working on aircraft fabric again.

We're planning on heading up into the mountains and going backpacking by ourselves for a few days. Mark and I just feel the need to get away from other people and be by ourselves for a while, just the two of us. We've really gotten close to each other. Still, I'm really going to miss this place; it holds some very good and special memories, and we've met some really great people. Mark says that maybe we'll drop back by here some time.

I don't know when we're going to be in one place long enough for you to write to us, but we'll let you know when we find out.
Love,
Jackie

Part Three

The Prodigal Children

1.

It was a particularly nice morning when they packed up their tent and their gear, and loaded it into Rocinante, even before Fred arrived in the morning. When his old brown Chevy pickup pulled in the front gate that morning, Mark and Jackie and Rocinante were gone, on to other adventures, he was sure. "Well, Cumulus," he said to the bedraggled old dog that came out to greet him, "Our friends have left us, yes?"

In the few days that Mark and Jackie remained at Waverly West, most of the remaining barriers that had lain between them came down. Fred had seen the change, but had not been quite able to put his finger on what had happened; they'd been a close-knit couple when they'd arrived, but somewhere along the way, they'd become even closer. Possibly the crash had something to do with it, he guessed, but he wasn't sure his guess was right. Not that it would matter at all, but he'd probably never know.

The air was still laying flat and still as Mark and Jackie detoured far to the east of Denver to avoid the smog and the busy skies there. They could only tell that the mountains were there by seeing their tops, still white with snow, far off in the distance beyond Rocinante's right wingtip. Below them, a nearly feature-less prairie spread wide; there really wasn't much around in the semi desert, except for the occasional farm or ranch, the occasional fence row or windmill. Mark let Jackie fly the plane, since it was a good morning for her to get comfortable with it, while he sat back in the left seat to reflect on some of the things that he'd learned in two weeks among the glider pilots. No longer would he think of a bump as a bump, of rough air as rough air. It was now lift or sink; the air mass was alive, and could be used by someone who knew how to use it. Mark didn't know when or where he would get the chance again, but sometime again he would fly a sailplane.

South of Denver and Colorado Springs, Mark gave Jackie a new course to follow, one that would take them to Canon City and the gas pump. As always, it was too loud in Rocinante's cockpit for much serious discussion beyond an occasional, "Oh, wow, look at that," or a suggestion to approve her piloting, or other comments of such deep nature. Mark did have his arm around Jackie much of the way, and a couple of times, he told her that he loved her.

It really had not taken much discussion in the tent the night before, when they had made up their mind to leave Waverly. It seemed like a good time to get off by themselves, to explore the new worlds they had found in each other. Backpacking in the Colorado high country seemed like a good way to get away from people, and Jack had told them about Leadville, right in the heart of the highest of the high country. "The airport is up there pretty good," he'd said as they sat out a storm in the line shack, "But you can get there without crossing any high passes by flying up the Arkansas River Valley." It had seemed like a pretty good idea.

Rocinante took her own sweet time taking off from the runway at Canon City, making Mark wonder in the back of his mind if going up to Leadville was such a good idea after all, but thought that after all that he had flown Golf Echo in the past couple of weeks that he had perhaps just forgotten about how the little Cessna flew. After all, the sectional chart around there was the brownest he had ever seen one, brown indicating high altitude. The airport elevation for Leadville was 9927 feet, just short of ten thousand, but Jack had told them the airport had a long runway and clear approaches. Still, Mark had rarely flown an airplane as high above sea level as Leadville's airport elevation, so the prospect of landing there seemed a bit exciting.

The valley seemed very narrow below them as they flew up the river, following the river and the railroad beneath them. Miles to the west, the valley turned to the north and broadened out. Mark was flying now, keeping Rocinante in a gentle climb, and working patches of lift as they rose from the warmed sunward slope. Rocinante's altimeter slowly but steadily wound up, until it was nearing 11,000 feet. "How about that," he told Jackie. "That's the highest I've ever flown a plane, and the peaks are still way above us."

The valley narrowed beneath them a bit, then broadened out into a more open area, perhaps a thousand feet below them. They finally spotted the airport on the side of a mountain off to their right. The town was on the far side of the airport, and above it.

Mark flew over the airport, to get a look at the wind sock, which was hanging limp. The airport's approaches were wide open, although it didn't seem like a good idea to fly a pattern from the town side. "Looks like the place," Jackie said.

Mark swung around to land on the wide, paved runway. He let Rocinante roll down to the taxiway turnoff, by a small hanger. He taxied up onto the ramp, and noticed that the hanger doors were open; inside, a couple of men were working on an old green and white Cessna 182.

"Might as well get some gas," Mark said, taxiing up to the gas pumps and stopping.

He and Jackie opened the Cessna's doors and got out. The air seemed chilly, after the warm days at Waverly and the hot ones in Texas and the south. The chill air felt good, more like home, but was enough to want jackets. Jackie dug theirs out of the luggage compartment, and handed Mark his.

"Can I help you?" one of the men from the hanger said. He was tall and gaunt, fifty or so; his skin looked like he had spent years out in the open.

"Got eighty octane?" Mark asked.

"Got it if you want it," the man said. "But you guys are flatlanders, right? Ever been here before?"

"First time," Jackie told him. "It's really pretty."

"Then just a word to the wise," he said. "When you get set to leave here, you don't want any more weight than you have to carry, especially with a little airplane like that." He pointed at the airport door, where there was a sign that read, "ELEV 9927".

Now the other man joined them, still wiping oil from his hands. He was short, and a little heavy-set, and kind of reminded Jackie of her father. "This is the nation's highest airport," he told them. "There's only one paved runway in the world that's any higher, and it's only a little higher."

Mark started to get a sinking feeling, like he might have made a mistake. "It handled pretty good getting up here," he told the two men.

"But it climbed like a sick dog, right?" the taller man asked.

"I've seen it do better," Mark admitted.

"You gotta remember, up this high, a little C-85 like this engine is only putting out about fifty horsepower," the man that looked like Jackie's dad said. "Plus, your true air speed is higher than your indicated, so you've got more speed you have to pick up."

"You've got a mile of runway here," Mark said. "At home, I can get this thing off in 800 feet if everything's right. A mile ought to be plenty, I thought."

"Might not be," the tall man said. "You got much gas in there now?"

"An hour, maybe an hour and a half," Mark told him.

"I wouldn't put any in, if I were you," the shorter man said. "Fly right straight down to Salida and gas up there. They're half a mile lower, and they've got a longer runway."

"Well, all right," Mark said. "I won't put any gas in. But, we came up here to go hiking, so we might as well go hiking before we try to take off. Thanks for the advice."

"Welcome to Leadville," the shorter man said, putting out his hand. Shorter was relative; he was still a big man. "The name's Duke. This is my buddy, John. You two aren't the first flatlanders to fly into Leadville and wonder if they're going to be able to fly out."

Mark introduced Jackie and himself, then asked, "Duke, has anybody ever had to have a plane leave on a flatbed?"

"Naw," he said, "But we got a gal in the flying club that weighs about 85 pounds wringing wet, and sometimes she's had to fly people's planes out of here for them, while we take the people and their stuff down to Salida in Dirty Thirty, there," he said, pointing at the Cessna in the hanger.

"You got any idea where we could go hiking?" Mark asked.

"Well, gee, I don't know," John said. "It's still pretty cold up on the peaks, there's a lot of snow left up there." He pointed across the valley at a huge rock wall. "Along in the summer, a lot of people like to hike from Hagerman Pass up across Mount Massive and Mount Elbert. Awful pretty up there. I've never hiked up there, but I've flown the ridge, and it's a nice view. You guys do much mountain hiking?"

"Never done any," Jackie admitted. "But we're northerners, we're used to cold."

"It's still winter up here," Duke told them. "We just had snow last week."

"Yeah," John said. "Summer here doesn't last long. Six weeks, two months at the most between snows. Besides, that's awful high to be hiking if you aren't used to it. Besides, I'm not sure there's enough snow off to do any good."

"John, how about Mosquito Pass and the old mine?" Duke asked. "It's not quite as high, and it's a heck of a lot easier to get down if the cold or the altitude is too much."

"Don't know if the jeep trail's open yet," John said, then turned to Mark and Jackie. "What Duke is saying is that there's this old stagecoach road up the side of the ridge east of town. You get up on the other side of the ridge and and down a ways, and there's these little ponds. It's awful pretty in August, but they're still frozen over."

"Aw, hell," Duke said. "Let's finish the oil change, then take these kids and go see. I've been thinking about doing some trout fishing anyway, and they bite real good right after the ice is off. We needed an excuse to go flying, anyway."

Half an hour later, Mark and Jackie were in the cramped back seat of the Cessna 182 that Duke had called "Dirty Thirty". It wasn't dirty, and in fact, was rather clean, but it showed signs of use. John taxied the plane out to the end of the runway, running the engine up on the way, then turned around and ran the throttle up.

It had been several years since Mark had flown in a Cessna 182, but he remembered it as a powerful airplane. Though the engine roared, it seemed as if their speed built up rather slowly. They were still far below flying speed when they passed the taxiway. "Come on, bitch," John muttered, and eased back on the wheel, to lift the nose of the tri-geared airplane. Much farther down the runway than Mark would have expected, the wheels rather reluctantly broke ground.

"A little heavy, today," Duke said. "We usually don't fly this thing with four people, but we don't have much gas."

John turned the Cessna across the valley, and found some rising air along the sunward slope. It still took several minutes to climb up as high as the ridgetop. Duke took the wheel, and flew around the north side of the mountain they had called "Mount Massive." Nope, still all frozen in," he told John and Mark and Jackie. "Catch them right after they thaw out, and the fishing's pretty good. They're hungry, after being cold all winter."

The airplane turned south, to follow the ridge along the top of Mount Massive and the mountain to the south. "Awful lot of snow out there," John said. "Slip and fall and you wouldn't stop sliding until you got down to the river." Mark and Jackie looked out the window at the ridgetop; while there was bare rock in spots, there was a lot of snow. They glanced at each other, and shook their heads.

"Let's have a look at Mosquito Pass," Duke said. John turned east, and headed over town. On the far side of the little village was another rock wall, but through the shine of the propeller's disk Mark could see the faint trace of a road zig-zagging up the ridge. John had a lot of altitude as they approached the ridge, but as they approached it, there was a lot of sink, and it rose toward them alarmingly.

John took on the ridge in the way that Mark had always heard about, but had never had to do; he approached it at an angle, so that if the sink got too bad, they could turn away. Only when he was very close to the ridge did John turn towards it and race through the sink. The top of the ridge shot past them, quite closely, but Mark could not see any trace of the old stagecoach trail. "The snow's still ass deep," John said.

They were over a little valley, that opened out to the east. John circled the 182 in the rising air; below them, they could see the old mine he had talked about, and the ponds. These had big patches of ice floating around in the center, but were clearly melting out. "Any day, now," Duke said. "But, with the road still snowed up, you'd have to come up the Fairplay side, and that's a hundred mile drive."

He built up a little more altitude, and headed north. "Here's something that's kind of neat," Duke explained, turning around in the seat to look at them. "The Glory Hole. For half a century, they've been tearing this mountain down. It's a molybdemum mine, and there's not a lot of mountain left." Duke told them that he was a railroad engineer, and his job was to haul concentrate down from the mine to the switchyard.

They looked down; Jackie had to lean over Mark to see out the side, clear down to the bottom of the pit. It was a huge hole.

On the way back to the airport, Jackie put her mouth close to Mark's ear and whispered, "I don't know about you, but I've got things I'd rather do than be alone in a sleeping bag, freezing my butt."

Mark took her by the hand and squeezed a reply.

Back at the airport, they helped John and Duke roll the 182 back into the hanger. "I don't know," Mark said, "But I think hiking in the high country is still just a bit too cold for my taste."

"There's places lower down that are just about as nice. There's a little valley over the other side of Granite that's no higher than this, and it's the prettiest place in the spring. Wouldn't be a great place for a long hike, but I've often thought it would make a great place to go and camp for a few days."

"How far away is that?" Mark asked.

"Oh, maybe twenty miles," John said.

"That's a lot of walking on the road," Mark said.

"Too bad you didn't get here a month later," Duke said. "Along about the end of July, first of August, is the best time to get back up on the ridges."

"Too bad," Mark agreed. "There's some awful pretty country around here, I can see that. I'd love to explore some of it, but I think it's too darn cold. I suppose Jackie and I ought to get something to eat and then see if we can get out of here."

Duke looked at his watch. "Well, I can run you into town, but I've got to make a run up to the Glory Hole this afternoon. Work calls."

"Yeah," John said. "I've got some work to get done, too. You kids take it easy."

They stood and talked for a few minutes more, then John got in his car and left. Mark and Jackie got into Duke's pickup with him, and rode into town; it was only a mile or two. The town was interesting; a mining town, with the mines more or less played out, except for the Glory Hole, Duke told them. It was shabby and rundown. The Main Street wasn't bad, but up the side streets Mark and Jackie could see a lot of shacks; it was obvious the place had seen better days.

"Nice meeting you," Duke said when he let them out of the pickup. "If you want a haul down to Salida, our numbers are there on the hanger. You might want to figure on just staying over here in town tonight, and then trying to take off at first light tomorrow, when it's cooler."

Alone at last, Mark and Jackie found a restaurant called "The Golden Burro". They found seats, and a waitress brought them menus.

"Well, it was a nice idea, anyway," Mark said, "But let's face it, it's still too damn cold to go spend a week in the high country. You got any ideas?"

"We could head for Yellowstone again," Jackie said. "It seems to me that's what we were doing when we stopped at Waverly."

"Based on what we've seen today, I'm not so sure that I'm all that crazy about Yellowstone right now, either. It's not a hell of a lot lower than we are now, and it's farther north."

"Well, maybe this is the time to go see the Grand Canyon," Jackie said, "But I hate to give up the idea of our hiking trip up in the mountains."

"So do I," Mark said. "Let's see if we can find some lower mountains, farther south, where it ought to be warmer. We've got to go south a little, anyway, to get gas, so we could fly south to someplace down in New Mexico like Sante Fe or Taos, and see if the weather's a little better. I don't mind going south; We can do Yellowstone and the Wind Rivers in a month or so. I kind of wanted to visit Kitt Peak and a couple places like that, anyway."

"What's Kitt Peak?" Jackie wondered.

"Oh, a big observatory. It's one of those places I've read about in Sky and Telescope and like that, and I've just wanted to see it."

They ate lunch and wandered around the town a bit. Not far from the restaurant was the local historical museum, and they spent half an hour there, learning that a hundred years before the town had been a wild and rowdy mining camp, with fortunes won and lost on the turn of a card or the choice of where to dig in a spade. It had to have been an interesting place back then, Mark thought.

Eventually, they finished up with the museum. "I suppose we had better hike back out to the airport and see if we can get down to Salida and get gas before they close," he said. "If we can get out of there early enough, we might be able to get a good flight to the south yet tonight."

It was only a couple of miles back out to the airport, and downhill at that, but they were surprised at how hard they were breathing, just to walk fairly slowly alongside the road. "I'm sure glad we didn't decided to go hiking in the high country," Jackie puffed as they stopped for a minute. "If the air is this thin here in town, what must it be like over on the top of that ridge?" she said, pointing at Mount Massive, hulking over them on the horizon.

Mark shook his head. "People that live up here like John and Duke, they've got to be so used to it that it's no big deal to them. But, I tell you what, it's a big deal to me."

"It sure was nice of Duke and John to take us up behind the ridges," she said. "It would be fun to hike up there, maybe in a month or so."

"It sure would be," he said. "Maybe someday."

They walked on out to the airport. Along the way, Mark found a white rag laying alongside the road, and on the way into the airport, a stick about three feet long; he picked both of them up and brought them along. Jackie wondered what they were for, but he didn't say.

She still wondered when they got to the airport, which was now deserted in the midday of the afternoon. Mark took the rag and stick and went out to walk down the runway to the north. The wind was dead calm, and although it was still cool, about fifty, the altitude had her puffing so much that she sat down next to Rocinante on the ramp and waited for Mark to return.

He came back about fifteen minutes later without the rag and stick. Her curiosity would hold no longer. "What was that all about?" she asked.

"Maybe Duke and John got me a little scared," Mark said, "Or maybe the takeoff in the 182 did, but I put out a marker a thousand feet from the end of the runway, so I'd be sure I have room to stop if we can't get off."

"Oh," Jackie said in a small voice. She was beginning to realize that Mark was more worried about the takeoff from Leadville than he had let on; perhaps that was why he had been so quiet all afternoon.

It was no great trick to get into Rocinante; they hadn't unpacked, except for their jackets. The engine started right off, and Mark taxied out to the end of the runway -- a little beyond the end, in fact; there was a flat gravel area about a hundred feet long, and he realized he'd better use all he could. He turned to face the little Cessna towards the far end of the runway, which seemed a lot closer than it had when they landed, only a few hours before. He sat there looking for a minute, then turned and looked at Jackie. "Are you ready?"

"I guess so," she said quietly.

"Jackie, I love you," he said, taking her hand for a moment and squeezing it tight with a message that was louder than anything he could say. If something went wrong, it might be his last words.

"I love you, too," she said. "Let's do it."

Mark let down ten degrees of flaps, then locked the brakes and ran the engine up to where the brakes wouldn't hold any longer. It was ridiculous, he thought, a short-field takeoff on a mile of runway, but there it was, and that was what he was facing.

The little Cessna gathered speed slowly; Mark was amazed at how sluggish it was. They were a long way down the runway before he had enough speed to get the tail up, to where the prop would work more efficiently. Jackie wished she had something to hold on to, to make her feel less nervous. With her limited flying experience, even she could tell that things were not going right.

With the tail up, Rocinante gained speed a little more quickly. From looking out the window, Mark thought that their speed was about acceptable, but both the feel of the wheel in his hands and the airspeed indicator on the panel told him that things weren't going well at all. Not far ahead of him, he could see the stick that he had leaned up against a runway light, rag hanging limp in the still air, getting closer and closer. He stole one more disappointing look at the airspeed indicator just to reassure himself that his fingers weren't lying to him, then yanked the throttle back, stood on the brakes, and held back on the wheel to keep the little Cessna from nosing over.

Where their speed had seemed agonizingly slow only a moment before, now the far end of the runway was rushing toward them. Rocinante shuddered under the heavy braking pressure from Mark's feet, and Jackie balled her fists even tighter as the plane slowed. Helplessly, Jackie thought of her father, and how he must feel when he saw someone run a crossing in front of his train, knowing it would take him a mile or more to stop . . .

By the time Mark got the plane slow enough to turn around, they were at the bitter end of the runway, and there wasn't room enough between the runway lights to turn around. He had to taxi out into the gravel beyond the lights in order to get Rocinante heading back the other way.

"Not a chance," he said, breathing again. "We needed another ten knots at least, maybe fifteen to be sure. I'll be damned if John and Duke didn't know what they were talking about."

"I wasn't sure you were going to get it stopped," Jackie said. "It seemed like we were going fast enough, from looking out the window, but even I could feel that we weren't."

"We were going more than fast enough, at a lower altitude," Mark said, "But the indicated airspeed is what tells you if we were going fast enough, and we just didn't have enough in this thin air." He braked for the taxiway, and turned back toward the ramp.

"Well, what do we do now?" Jackie said.

"I don't know," Mark said. "I guess maybe we call Duke or John tonight, and tomorrow we can have one of them fly you and the gear down to Salida. If I can't get this thing off without you or the gear, maybe . . . well, this eighty-five pound gal they know isn't going to make that much difference, I don't think.

"I'm twenty pounds lighter than you are," Jackie said. "Maybe I could try it."

"Thanks for the offer," he told her. "But twenty pounds isn't going to make that much difference. Besides, you're still learning what your limits are, and I can push those limits closer than a twenty-pound difference would account for."

They tied Rocinante back down to the cables on the ramp, then went up to the pay phone to call Duke. "He's not home," his wife told him. "He's up the hill and won't be back till after dark."

"Try John," Jackie suggested, but the phone at John's house just rang and rang.

"It looks like we're stuck here for the evening," Mark said. "We might as well get the tent set up."

Jackie shook her head. "At least I'm glad we didn't ship the long handles back home. Cold as it is, we're going to need them tonight."

They managed to find a place to camp up in the pines behind the hanger. The ground was soft enough there to get stakes in, and the outhouse was only a few steps away. The sun sunk slowly in the northwest, but slid behind Mount Massive early; still, on this high summer evening, twilight was long. They got out their cooking gear and opened some cans for supper, then sat, drank coffee, and agreed that however much they'd like to slip into the tent and make love, it was too cold to be rolling around in bare skin on the sleeping bags. "We'll be someplace warmer tomorrow night," Mark promised, "Even if it's a motel here in Leadville."

They never did get an answer at John's, and the light was failing when Duke answered the phone. Mark explained what had happened.

"Look, try it first thing in the morning, at first light," Duke told Mark. "You'll get a little bit better break on the density altitude."

"Duke," Mark protested. "The airspeed was so low that I don't think a few degrees is going to do much good."

"All right," the older man said, "I'll come out about eight. If you're gone, so much the better. If not, well, then we'll do what we have to do."

With the sun setting late, the night wasn't that long, but it was cold; they had not spent such a cold night since that night in Kentucky months before, the first night that they had camped together, the night that Jackie had lain awake for hours in her sleeping bag, half in fear that Mark would come to her. Now, when she wished that Mark would come to her, she knew that if he did, it was too cold to enjoy it, and she lay awake in frustration. How much things had changed in the two and a half months they had been together! Could it have been that short a time? It seemed like they had been gone much longer than that, and here, on an early summer's night, they had caught back up with the winter that they had raced south to enjoy.

Probably it was the coffee as much as the frustration and the worry about the next day that kept Jackie awake. It was long after dark before she fell into a fitful sleep.

It was certainly the coffee that woke her up not too many hours later. She lay shivering in her sleeping bag in sheer pain from her aching bladder, listening to the whisper of the breeze in the pines, before she finally pulled enough courage together to unzip the sleeping bag, take her flashlight, and slip out of the tent for the short walk to the outhouse.

There was the merest sliver of twilight to the northeast, but she paid it little attention as she stumbled to the outhouse. The seat was so cold that she could barely stand to sit on it for the few seconds it took her to relieve the pressure, praying that her butt wouldn't get frozen to the seat.

Feeling much better, she pulled her long johns back up and went back outside. It was almost bright enough to see without the flashlight, and was so chilly that she longed to get back into her sleeping bag. It would be warmer, if not warm. The smell of the pines and the whisper of the breeze through the needles made her think of home . . .

"Mark!" she yelled.

He came awake with a start. What could be wrong now? "What is it?" he yelled back, still half-awake.

"There's a breeze blowing! A good ten or fifteen knots, if I'm seeing the windsock right!"

"What direction?" he asked, still not fully comprehending Jackie's discovery.

"Right down the runway!"

They tore the tent down in record time, stuffed their sleeping bags the best they could in the half-light and their flashlights, and cursed again at how long that it took them to get the air out of the air mattresses. Usually, they were pretty careful about how they packed Rocinante's luggage compartment, but this time they just stuffed things as best as they could, and the luggage was stuffed to the ceiling before they were through, and they could not have made it at all if they weren't still wearing their long underwear. Mark did the walkaround with a flashlight in hand, since it was still only barely light enough to see anything at all. He took a long look at the windshield and the wings, and noticed that no frost had formed on them.

Rocinante started right off, and Mark began to slowly taxi out to the end of the runway, hoping the engine would warm up enough if they took their time, but that the breeze would hold out, only a few minutes more. It was just barely light enough to see down into the valley, and see where the mountains were.

"I'm not sure I'm going to be able to see the marker," Mark told his lover. "You keep an eye out for it, tell me when we're coming up on it, tell me when we pass it. Yell it out, I want to make sure I hear you."

"I will if I can see it," Jackie told him.

Again, he pulled out into the gravel to swing the little Cessna around. "Be a good girl, Rocinante," he said. "This is the best chance we're going to get." He took a final look at the windsock, up at the hanger far down the runway; it still indicated a steady breeze. The gauges on the panel looked good. He turned to Jackie, smiled and said, "Sancho, my armor!" Mark lowered the flaps and shoved the throttle forward, giving Rocinante the spurs.

Looking out the window, to Jackie it seemed that the little Cessna was gaining speed even slower than the afternoon before, but into the teeth of the chilly breeze, it wasn't surprising. Still, even she could feel that the airplane was more lively; Mark had the tail up in half the distance of the last attempt to take off.

The speed built slowly, agonizingly slowly. When they passed the taxiway, at the midpoint of the field, it still seemed to Jackie that she could run faster than Rocinante was going. She began to look off to the left, across in front of Mark for the rag marker he had put out the day before, and the end of the runway was rushing toward them before she saw it. "There it is," she yelled. "A hundred yards!"

"Got it," Mark yelled. "Come on, Rocinante."

It didn't seem to Jackie that they could be going fast enough, but Mark had a better look at the airspeed indicator . . . maybe, just maybe . . .

"Passing the marker," Jackie yelled.

Mark kept the throttle on. They were committed, now; he knew, after yesterday's experience, that there could be no stopping. Either they were going to fly or there were going to be a ball of aluminum and flesh on the highway down below the end of the airport . . . but the airspeed indicator still seemed to be saying "maybe," and he could feel Rocinante come alive in his hands. He eased back on the wheel a little, and the plane gave a little hop. Not quite yet . . .

The end of the runway rushed down on them, and Mark held the Cessna down as long as he dared, thanking God or John and Duke or whoever had the good sense to give the airport wide-open approaches, so there would be no trees or power lines to clear. They were almost up to the runway numbers before he tried to life Rocinante off again.

Looking out her window, Jackie could see them flash between the runway lights, but the wheels were off of the ground over the gravel overrun.

The ground fell away beyond the end of the runway; not a lot, perhaps a couple of hundred feet, but it was enough that Mark could let the nose down a little to gain something resembling a comfortable airspeed. He couldn't keep going straight forever, and didn't have enough airspeed for much of a turn, but banked slightly to the west and the lower ground beyond, where with the nose down he might be able to gain a little more airspeed.

Somewhere not too far below them, a car ground up the hill with its lights still on in the morning twilight, but the needle on the airspeed indicator was still climbing enough to where Mark could sit back in his seat. It wasn't until then he realized he had been leaning forward, tense, trying to lift Rocinante into the air on sheer will. A scene flashed through his mind, from the movie, *"The Spirit of St. Louis"*, where Lindbergh's wheels brushed through the top of the trees at the far end of that runway so long ago. Now, he knew how Lindbergh must have felt . . .

Next to him, Jackie realized that she was breathing again. "I didn't think we were going to make it," she heard him say as he leveled the wings and set course for Salida, to the south.

"Why didn't you stop when we passed the marker?" she said. "I didn't think we were going to make it, either."

Mark let out a deep breath, still not quite believing what had happened. "Rocinante was telling me she thought she could."

* * *

Salida, Colo.
June 29, 1971

Dear Dad and Sarah:

Just a quick note this time. I'm writing this sitting on the steps of the airport office, waiting for them to open, so we can get some gas. From here, we're going to head on south for a ways.

We stopped in Leadville, but decided not to go hiking up in the high country, after all. It's still pretty cold up there; the mountains are still snowcapped, and here it is the end of June. It's awful pretty up there; maybe we can get to go back up there in a month or six weeks, when it's warmer. We flew over some places that look like they'd be a lot of fun to fish in.

While we were in Leadville, we met a Burlington railroad engineer that reminds me a lot of you, Dad -- except that he's a real homeguard, but what a run he has -- from 9500 feet elevation to 11,000, in twelve miles. I didn't ask, but I bet he knows a lot about braking.

Here comes the airport manager to unlock this place, so I'm going to wrap this up. We want to get going before it gets too warm. I don't know when I'll call again, but I'll write in a few days.

I love you,
Jackie

2.

It took a while for Rocinante to work up enough altitude to get over Poncha Pass south of Salida, but once they squeezed over the trees at the top of the pass, the valley opened up before them. To their left, the Sangre de Christo range stretched out as far as the eye could see. The mountains were snowcapped and jumbled, but in a line so straight that it was almost unbelievable. The valley below them was almost uninhabited; it was nearly desert, with only a lonely, straight road stretching out for miles ahead of them.

They flew south across the empty valley for nearly an hour before coming to the first real town, Alamosa. For a while, there were fields below them in the now-wide valley of the upper Rio Grande, but as they approached the border for New Mexico, again the land became barren and desertlike, with only the brown streak of the little river giving some green to its banks.

To their left, the Sangre de Christo range began to ease in toward them again. Mark let Jackie fly the plane while he studied the Denver sectional. "It's like this," he said finally. "Either we stop in the next hundred miles or so, or else we're going to have to go clear down to Alamogordo if we want to do any mountain hiking. We're only a couple hundred miles south of Leadville, but the country around here is lower, so it ought to be at least a little warmer."

Jackie looked over at the map. "We could stop at Taos, get some fuel, and get an idea of what the weather's like on the ground. If we're going to go to Alamogordo, we're going to need fuel, and I don't think we want to stop at Sante Fe. They've got a control tower there."

Mark studied the map in the Taos area. "There's this field called 'Angel Fire' over on the other side of the mountains," he said. "It looks like it's long enough and low enough that we shouldn't have any trouble getting off again. It looks like a pretty short walk to get up into the high country. Everything else around there looks like it would be a ten mile walk or more."

"Sounds like a possible," Jackie replied. "Maybe we ought to check it out before we get fuel, just to keep the weight down."

"We'll have to have another thousand feet or so to get over this pass," Mark noted. "It's about as high as that one we came over an hour or so ago."

"Don't we want to stop in Taos, anyway?" Jackie wondered. "We ought to maybe have a better map than a sectional, maybe something that shows trails on it."

"Hell," Mark said. "That would take out all the fun. Besides, I'm not looking for a long hike, just something to get up in the mountains and away from people. If that means away from trails, so much the better."

"I guess you're right," Jackie said, adding a little power to Rocinante and easing back into an easy climb.

There was about 10,000 feet on the altimeter when they crossed Palo Flechado Pass. The mountains on either side of them had peaks above them, but not very far above them, and there was only little snow showing on the tops. The countryside seemed a little dryer than the Colorado valleys hundreds of miles to the north. From the seat of the plane, they could pick out a couple of interesting areas to investigate on foot, places that seemed easy enough to reach.

It was a fast letdown into the airstrip at Angel Fire. They found a place to tie down Rocinante, then repacked their bags for the trip into the high country. It seemed warmer than it had been at Leadville, but it still wasn't as hot as it had been at Waverly not all that long before.

"I always wondered what this country was like," Mark said as he helped Jackie into her pack. "When I was in Boy Scouts as a kid, I always wanted to go to Philmont Scout Ranch. It's right across the valley there, around that next range. It always seemed like the neatest thing that could be done as a scout."

"Never got to go there?" Jackie asked.

"Nope, never did," Mark said. "We're not going there this time, either, although I guess it's pretty much the same sort of countryside."

Hiking back up to the top of the pass seemed like the easiest route into the high country, and would give them access to some appealing countryside they had seen to the west of the road. It was not a fast walk; it was mostly above 8,000 feet, and the air was thin indeed. It took them more than two hours to walk the three miles or so uphill to the top of the pass, where they plunged off into the roadless countryside beyond.

There was a hint of a trail leading on up the ridge. It was a sunny day, warm and with the scent of pines on the air. The path was rocky, here and there carpeted with pine needles, occasionally damp and mucky where tiny springs or rivulets trickled across. Birds flitted quietly into the trees; tiny white moths sprayed off from under their feet. In sunlight and in shadow, the trail led sharply upward.

Jackie led the way. It had surprised Mark that she liked to lead on a hike, and he didn't mind, because it gave him a good look at her thighs, her butt. He had been tense ever since the first attempted takeoff from Leadville, this time the day before, but now as they slowly worked their way up the flank of the mountain, he felt the tension ooze out of him.

They took five in a grassy spot among aspens. While Jackie peeled an orange and the smell of it prickled his nostrils, Mark lay on his back, head resting on his pack, facing up into the airy green aspen foliage.

As the day wore on, they came to a little cul-de-sac where there were a couple of small ponds, one in a meadow, the other nearly surrounded by pine trees. They were up near timberline, and the edge of the meadow was filled with scrub oak stubble and majestic boulders. Even as they stood there, they could see the circlets of rising trout dimpling the clear, flat water. "Looks like a good place to camp," Mark commented.

"Looks like a good place to fish," Jackie replied. "But let's save that for later. I want to climb that mountain."

They dumped their packs, pitched the tent, and resumed the climb. At first there was a grassy slope, then a thin sheep trail zigzagged up a shale slide and through some mammoth gray boulders. It was getting colder now; they carefully crossed several snow fingers a few yards wide, and then walked up through flowing brown grass that seemed to be crushed flat against the mountainside by invisible, recently-departed snow.

At the top, some mottled red boulders provided some shelter from the wind, and between them grew more of the thick, brown grass. Below them they could see the little ponds and their tent, each of the ponds dimpled with the rings of the rising fish. In the other directions, the brown grass sloped gently into forested mountains, and they could see far down them. Taos was nearly at their feet, only a few miles away; off in the distance, they thought they could see Sante Fe.

"Can you think of a better place to make love?" Jackie said.

"It's pretty cold," Mark opined. "The view is tremendous, though, and I'd hate to pass up the chance."

They stripped the minimum that they could under the circumstances. She tugged off his boots and jeans and underwear while he worked on her books and jeans and underpants, and then, up among the boulders in the flattened brown grass, still wearing their socks and shirts and jackets to keep warm, they made love, with their bare butts gathering goosebumps all the while.

Feeling much better, both to have their pants off and for getting them back on, they lay back out of the breeze for a few more minutes. "You know what would really be strange?" Jackie mused.

"What?" Mark murmured.

"I keep thinking that we've made love in the sand, in the grass, on a mountaintop, in sleeping bags and on them, in the daylight and under the stars, and we haven't yet done it once in a bed."

"We're more than overdue for an honest to pete shower," Mark said. "Lets keep that in mind."

After a while, they hiked back down to their campsite. Hoping that a game warden wouldn't show up out of nowhere, Jackie got out her collapsible spinning rod, tied on a rather nondescript little popper, and cast it out over the lake. Something took the little feathered lure almost as soon as it hit the water; after a brief tussle, she pulled in a ten-inch cutthroat trout, the first fish she had caught on the trip, even though she hadn't attempted a lot of fishing. She carefully took it off the hook and threw it back into the pond. She cast again, and caught another fish, of about the same size. Over the course of the next hour or so, she caught a dozen or so more, keeping none, but just enjoying the perfect day.

After a while, she asked Mark if he'd like to try, and he caught a couple before they put the pole away. "You know, Jackie," he said, "This is kind of what I had in mind."

Afterwards, they took a nap, and lazily made love again. As they afternoon wore on, they read to each other a little -- the New Testament, and some of Walden; in the weeks at Waverly, their reading program had fallen behind somewhat.

After a while, the shadows grew long. They scrounged around in among the pine trees for some sticks, enough to make a small fire that lasted until well after dark when the stars came out, even clearer and more steady than they had been at Waverley, the last place they had used the telescope.

"Makes me wish you'd packed the telescope up here," Jackie said.

"Yeah, me too," Mark agreed. "But that's a heck of a lot to be packing up in this country. There'll be other chances."

While they went to bed early, they stayed awake late, holding and caressing and loving each other between their opened sleeping bags until it became too cold to continue. They pulled on their long underwear and retreated to their sleeping bags, but continued to snuggle together through the night.

They slept late the next morning, but awoke to see the pond and the meadow still giving off smoke as the morning sun dried off the dew from the night before. They got dressed and fished for a while, then decided to climb another one of the mountains. It was a longer walk, though not a difficult one and at the top of the climb Mark pulled a small sketchbook out of his pocket, took a pencil, and began to sketch some of the scenery.

"It's been a while since you've done any sketches," Jackie said.

"I did a few at Waverly," Mark told her. "Mostly while I was sitting in Golf Echo, waiting for another tow. We were just too damn busy there to sit down and take an hour or so on a sketch, to really do it right."

It was too cold on his hands to do a really decent job, so he finally put the sketchbook away and took some photos.

After a while, they walked back down to the campsite at the ponds and began to make some lunch. Down off the ridge, with the sun beating down, it was a lot warmer, warm enough to strip off some clothes and enjoy the sunlight. As Jackie minded the water warming for coffee, not that it took a lot of minding, Mark pulled the larger sketchbook from his pack, and chewed on a pencil a bit, trying to figure out what to draw and how to do it.

"Would you like me to pose for you?" Jackie offered as she poured the water for coffee.

"Yes, if you don't mind," Mark replied. "It seems like it's been weeks since I've done a drawing of you."

"All right," she smiled. "I think it's warm enough to try posing nude."

As Jackie took off her clothes and let Mark coach her into a pose on a small flat rock on the shore of one of the ponds, somehow it seemed more natural than she had imagined it would be. She was less self-conscious than she had been when she had first posed for Mark, in her shorts and halter top, back at Cape Canaveral, but a lot of water had gone under the bridge in the two months that had passed since then. Mark worked on the drawing in some detail, and Jackie had no objections to his taking photos of her as she posed there for him.

Never the less, she was glad to get her clothes back on; the afternoon was cooler than she had thought, and the breeze had a little bit of a bite to it.

It was another lazy afternoon. They fished some more, and read to each other again, and took a nap. Mark drew another picture of her -- clothed this time, on his insistence, mostly because they had learned that even the warmest part of the day was still a little on the borderline of being too cool for sustained nudity. They fished some more in the evening, and had a fire in the twilight, and made love after they went to their tent again.

The next day was much the same as the day before. They didn't hike to a mountaintop, but up onto a high ridge. Later, they fished and read, and Jackie again posed nude for Mark. They made love, and wished their sojourn at these quiet mountain lakes where they had not seen another soul could go on forever -- even though they knew it couldn't. This would have to be their last day; they were running out of food. They could have killed some fish and eaten them, but they couldn't bring themselves to disturb the peace of their little hideaway in such a manner.

"Well, I suppose it's getting to be time to be moving on, anyway," Jackie commented as they opened their last can of stew.

"Yeah, we've been getting spoiled," Mark agreed. "This is as perfect a place as we've been in on this trip. If it was ten degrees warmer, I think I'd just want to stay here until we starved."

"That kind of quits being fun after a while, too," she said. "Starving, I mean. Do you have any firm plans on where we want to go next?"

"Well, Taos is supposed to be an interesting town," Mark said. "I don't suppose it would hurt to land at that little strip out at the edge of town and walk into the place to check it out. We've got to get some groceries and film and stuff."

"There's another interesting place not too far from here," Jackie said, looking at the sectional. Over northwest of here a hundred, maybe a hundred and fifty miles. Durango."

"What's there?" Mark asked.

"An old narrow-gauge steam railroad," Jackie said. "They make these tourist trips up through some really pretty country, I'm told. Dad said he always wanted to come out here and make that trip."

Mark shrugged. "No reason we can't do it, outside of the fact that it looks like the airport is a hell of a long way out of town. Maybe we can hitch a ride, though. You got anything you want to shop for there, or in Taos?"

"I'd kind of like us to keep our eyes open for a good outdoor store," Jackie said. "If we can find another sleeping bag like mine, I think we can zip the two of them together. I know we can't with yours."

"That would be nice, too," Mark said, a smile crossing his face. "It's not cheap, but I think it's one of those things worth spending the money on. I don't know when we're going to come across a place like that, though."

"I was kind of thinking that Durango might be kind of an outdoorsy town, what with all the wilderness area around it, and there might be a good outfitter there."

"Fine with me," Mark said. "We'll check Taos out, and then head on to Durango."

It was hard to get up the next morning and strike the tent; hard to share a cup of coffee and their last bag of peanuts for breakfast, the last of their food; hard to finish packing the packs, and take one last look around the little mountain ponds where life had been so idyllic.

Coffee and peanuts didn't make for the best breakfast for hiking, but it was mostly downhill, and they made good time, especially after they got back to the road. There was a little food left at Rocinante that they hadn't taken backpacking with them, and they had sort of a brunch as they packed their gear in the plane, sorting out the mess that was still left after their hurried packing at Leadville.

It was but a short flight back over their camp to Taos. They circled their campsite for one last look, and Jackie took a picture out the window at the little ponds, sitting cold and lonely. She almost thought that she could see the rings of rising trout there, and wished that they had been able to stay longer.

Taos proved to be an interesting and colorful town, much more than a simple grocery stop, and the day slid on without them recognizing that it was evaporating on them as they explored some of the colorful merchandise in the stores, and the art galleries, and just drank in the atmosphere, a rather hippie atmosphere at that. "I swear," she told Mark at one point, "I'm going to barf if I hear the words 'far out' again today."

"Far out," Mark teased.

She grabbed Mark's shirt collar from behind, pulled it tight, and bent over behind him. "Blllaaachhh," she said, teasing back.

"All right, you've made your point," Mark told her. "I want to check out some of this turquoise jewelry."

The day got away from them; they wound up pitching their tent under Rocinante's wing at the little grass airport at the edge of town, long after dark. They'd had a good day, a good meal, a couple of drinks, and had met some interesting people, but somehow hadn't bothered to get the groceries they had come for.

They did the next day, though, and managed to get back to Rocinante before the day got too hot. They flew across the valley to the city airport and gassed up, then headed west, then north, through rolling, arid countryside toward Durango.

The airport at Durango indeed proved to be a long way away from town. They combined the gear they would need for a motel stay into one pack, along with their dirty laundry, and managed to get a ride into town with someone who'd been out to see the airport manager.

Their ride dropped them downtown. The town was located in a deep valley, with high mountains to either side, and was something of a ski and tourist town. The first thing they did was find the railroad station, where they got tickets for the morning train to Silverton. Nearby was a motel; they rented a room, but decided to put their showers off until later, when they would have clean clothes to get into. Finding a laundromat, they set their laundry to running, and found a place for lunch. After they finished their laundry, they shopped around for a sleeping bag that would zip up with Jackie's, and were a little surprised to find one that would work.

It was still early in the afternoon. "Knowing that we've got that shower waiting for us makes me feel even grubbier," Mark said. "What do you say we go back to the motel and clean up, and maybe come back down to the train station to watch the train come in before we have dinner?"

"Funny you should mention that," Jackie said. "I was thinking the same thing."

It was only a couple of blocks to walk back to their motel room. They no more than closed the door and the drapes before they were peeling their clothes off. "You want to go first?" Mark offered.

"I don't care," Jackie said, then smirked, "I wonder if the shower is big enough for both of us."

The next half hour was pure ecstasy. Warm water, wandering hands, soap-slippery bodies entwined and caressed in indescribable joy, and they even got clean in the process.

Even the mutual toweling off was sensual, and even though they had already given themselves a pretty good workout, they found themselves in bed without asking or thinking about it.

It was quite a while afterward, after a lot of cuddling and kissing, that they fell to talking. "Now, that's my idea of a shower," Mark said. "I'm glad you thought of it."

"I am, too," Jackie smiled. "It kind of makes me sorry that we decided to go shopping, first. We'll have to do that again before we leave here."

"Let's give the water heater time to recover. So now that you've made love in a bed, how does it compare to a beach or a mountaintop?"

"Don't forget a shower," Jackie smirked, then got thoughtful. "I guess it feels a little strange. I mean, every place else that we've done it is kind of out of the ordinary, so it's been fun. Somehow, though, I can't get over the idea of our doing it in a motel room is just a little bit sleazy."

That wasn't quite what Mark expected to hear. "How do you mean?" he asked.

"Oh, I don't know," Jackie said. "Don't get me wrong, it's fine, and I loved it, but somehow, it just doesn't seem right. Sneaking off to motel rooms to have sex is something that people do if they're not married, and just fooling around like they're not supposed to be doing."

"Does that bother you?"

She nodded. "Yeah, a little, I guess. I guess I just haven't gotten used to it, yet."

"Well, look, if it would make you feel any better," Mark said, "We can go over, get our money back on the tickets. We could get quite a ways west tonight, but even if we started in the morning, we could be in Las Vegas and be married by tomorrow afternoon."

"Thanks," she said, burying her head on his chest. "I appreciate the offer, and I know you mean it, but even if we do decide to get married, it really should be in Spearfish Lake, so we can have our families and friends there."

"Well, it would be a long day, even if we left at first light, so we'd better figure on two to get back to Spearfish Lake. Three days waiting, and you could still be a June bride."

She lifted her head to look him in the eye. "No, Mark. I don't want to go back to Spearfish Lake until we're done with this trip. It would be too hard to leave again. Besides, we can have fun together for as long as this trip lasts, but I still don't know about getting married, in the long term."

"Same thing?" Mark asked. It was the first time since that evening on the tiny sandy beach at Waverly that this question had come up, and Mark had rather hoped that it would have changed Jackie's viewpoint a little.

"Same thing," Jackie said. "I just don't know how fair it is to you. Traveling together and living together is fine, because it only lasts as long as it lasts. Marriage is something else, again."

"Well," Mark said, playing with her breast, "I'm not going to make an issue of it if you're not. You know how I feel. I'm ready when you're ready."

"Thanks," she said. "I knew you'd feel that way, but thanks, anyway."

"Well, all right. Now, we can stay here and play some more, or we can get up, get dressed, watch the train come in, and maybe have some dinner. Which would you rather do?"

"I'd like to play," she said. "But the train only comes in once a day. On the other hand, after supper maybe we can get cleaned up."

It was nice to get dressed in clean clothes. They walked down to the railroad station, to watch the little Rio Grande Southern narrow-gauge steam locomotive pull its trainload of passengers into town. It was an old-fashioned engine, almost a century old, and smaller than they would have thought.

Mark could remember seeing a steam engine on the tracks that ran through Spearfish Lake when he was a small boy, and then it had seemed just slightly smaller than an ocean liner. As he stood there and thought about it, he realized that the number of working steam locomotives that he had seen could be counted on the fingers of one hand, and Jackie, though a railroaders daughter, hadn't seen many more. She remembered her father saying that he hadn't been aboard a steam engine a half a dozen times in his railroad career; everything was diesel, now, and had been for years.

The half-sized engine showed signs of its use. They stood there and looked at it for a few minutes, then walked back up the street to find a place to eat.

They finally settled on a restaurant that was almost full with passengers from the train, but since they were in no hurry, it didn't matter. They settled into a booth, and a harried waitress brought them beer.

"We ought to call home, tonight or tomorrow night," Jackie said. "It's been almost a couple of weeks, now."

Mark nodded his head. "Getting on toward three weeks, I guess."

"We haven't had mail in that long, either. I suppose we ought to be picking out some place for the home folks to send our mail to us. Do you think we'd be a the Grand Canyon long enough to have our mail sent there?"

"I kind of hope that we can be in and out of there in a couple of days," Mark told her. "I'd kind of like to do the trail down to the river, but I'm not sure I'm very interested in hiking back up."

"Me either," Jackie agreed. That would be a long, steep sweaty hike. I've heard that you can rent horses or mules or something. Maybe we want to think about that."

Mark nodded. "That's expensive, and I've never done that much riding, anyway."

"I guess we mostly check the place out from the rim." Jackie agreed. "You're right, that won't take us that long."

"For that matter, I'm not even sure we want to stop,"Mark told her. "They've got a control tower there, and we don't have the frequency for it in Rocinante. I suppose we could call them up on Unicom and tell them we need light signals, but maybe the thing to do is to avoid the place all together. Gas up at some nearby uncontrolled field, and then just fly over the place. We'd probably see more from Rocinante than we would from the ground, anyway."

"Well, is there any place between here and there where we're likely to be for a few days?"

"No," Mark said. "In fact, the only thing I have on my list between here and there is Shiprock, and that's a fly-over thing, not a stop and go hiking thing. The only airstrip is a hell of a long ways away."

"So we're looking at the Grand Canyon, what? The day after tomorrow?"

"Day after at the latest," Mark nodded. "I kind of think that we ought to be getting a move on. Up to this point, we've flown for a couple of days, then stopped for up to a week, then flown on for a couple of days, then stopped. That's fine; that's what I had in mind. But I think we've seen enough of Colorado and New Mexico if we want to see something else, too."

"I could spend the summer here," she agreed. "But there are other things to see."

"Darn right. I want to see California and the northwest, and we've still got Yellowstone and the Tetons on our list, don't forget. The thing of it is, I kind of had Stellafane on the list, too. That's in Vermont, the last part of August, only about two months on. We've been two and a half months getting this far from Florida. I suppose if we don't get to Stellafane, we don't get to Stellafane, so that's not a real big loss, but we've got three months at the most before the good camping weather is over with in the north part of the country, and only a month or so longer before we'd have to be pretty far south."

"I see what you mean that we'd better be getting a move on," she said.

He shook his head. "That doesn't mean that we can't stop for a while if there's a good reason to stop. I just don't want to have to stop for a bad reason, or spend time in a place that we don't have to. We're going through money faster than I'd hoped, so if we're going to stay gone for a year, we're going to have to stop some place and get a job for a while. I'd rather put that off until next winter, when we're pretty well going to be restricted to the far south, anyway. That means we're going to have to watch our money, too."

"We could turn in our tickets for tomorrow and get a refund," she offered, "And get back on the move, tomorrow, rather than staying over the extra night. That would save us a bit."

"No, we've gone to this trouble, so let's do it. It'll give you a good letter to write to your dad, anyway. As far as the motel goes, we wanted a motel room, anyway, and we haven't spent that many nights in motels." He smiled and looked at her with a grin. "I was getting to the point where I needed a shower, whether it was with you or not."

"Well, where could we tell the folks that we're going to be able to get our mail?"

"Well, if we call them tonight, we need to figure on four or five days," Mark told her. "Let's see, we've got Durango tomorrow and travel to the canyon the day after. Then, I'd kind of like to see a couple of things in Arizona. Flagstaff, the meteor crater at Winslow, but there's not good places to land at either one. Flagstaff has a controlled field, and meteor crater doesn't have an airstrip close by. That's kind of a fly-over thing, like Shiprock, anyway."

"How about Kitt Peak?" she asked. "That's down by Tucson, isn't it?"

"Yeah," he nodded. "I've been thinking about that. It's probably going to be hotter than hell down there. 120 in the shade and no shade, that sort of thing. Besides, there's no need to stop at every major observatory we come to. We've already been to McDonald Observatory, and I want to see Palomar."

"Palomar?"

"Yeah, the 200-inch telescope, the largest in the world. It's near San Diego. That's probably a good place to get our mail. We can just make it five or six days away, and be there."

*   *   *

Durango, Colorado
June 20, 1971

Dad and Sarah:

I'm sitting here in a little restaurant in Durango writing you this. We just got back from the train ride we told you about last night, and that was really neat!

They call this train the "Silverton Train". It goes up through the mountains in a narrow valley, a canyon almost, for what must be fifty miles, up to this little town of Silverton. The track is hardly ever straight, and the views are always tremendous. There's some places where the roadbed is cut into the side of the mountain, and you look straight down to the river maybe four or five hundred feet.

The little engine that pulls this train is tiny; it's a lot smaller than the smallest switcher down at the yard in Camden. The tracks are narrow-gauge, three feet, and it's really strange to stand between the rails and see them close together. Of course, with the gauge small, everything else is on the small side, too; the passenger cars are half the size or less than they would be on a real train, and there's hardly room to stand up.

The engine is something like ninety years old, and it doesn't go real fast - - ten or fifteen miles an hour, I guess. It takes a long time to get up to Silverton, so a ride on this thing is an all-day affair. It's crowded, too; we were lucky to get tickets on such short notice, and I think every seat was filled, even the ones on the flatcar outside, where the old coal-burner got cinders in everyone's hair. We rode there for a while -- we traded seats with another couple -- and it's really neat to see the old coal-burner belch huge clouds of black smoke as it works its way up the canyon. And, I was told it's a 2.5 grade, so that old steamer really has to work, too, and the sound is something like you wouldn't believe.

It was after noon before we got up to Silverton. We had an hour for lunch, and to explore the town. It's an old mining town, and we were told that's rather quaint, although it just looked a little run-down to me. I'm sure that when the train pulled out the restaurant got out their other menus, the one with the regular prices. They must charge double or triple for the people off the train for lunch. We just had grilled cheese sandwiches and cokes, and decided to hold off getting a decent meal until we got back to Durango.

The trip back down the valley was a little quicker, since it was mostly downhill, but we got to see some of the views from a different angle, so it was all still pretty nice. They have an overnight photo developing place here, and we decided to get some film developed. If it comes out all right, I'll include some photos of the train and the place where we camped over by Taos, and hold off on dropping this letter off until we get the film.

I know you always wanted to come out here and ride this train, Dad. You ought to. It is really fun! I think Sarah would like it, too.

Anyway, tomorrow we're going to get moving again. We'll be heading on over to the Grand Canyon, and that's something I'm really looking forward to.

It was nice to talk to you last night, and yes, I'm having the time of my life on this trip. I'm so glad I decided to come on it with Mark. It may have been the best decision I ever made. We'll try to call a little quicker, next time, and not let so long go by, but it's easy to lose track of time.

The waitress just brought us our food, so I'm going to wrap this up. After we eat, Mark and I both want to go back to the motel and take a shower to wash the cinders out of our hair. I'll write again soon.

Love,
Jackie

3.

After checking out of the motel the next morning, they stopped at the photo store that offered the overnight photo service. There was quite a bit of film there, clear back to Twillingate, and they leafed through the photos one by one, remembering some of the experiences they shared. Jackie selected several to send to her father and Sarah, and wrote a quick note explaining several, and added at the bottom, "Show these to Mark's folks, will you?"

Mark shouldered their pack, heavy with clean laundry, as Jackie ran out to the curb to mail their letter. He followed her outside, just as she dropped the letter in the box. "You didn't include any of the nude photos, did you?" he smiled.

Jackie's hand shot to her mouth. "Oh, dear," she said, her eyes opened wide in shock. Then, she dropped the facade and went on, "Do you think I'm crazy or something?"

"Just checking," he smiled back.

They managed to hitch a ride out of town as far as the turnoff to the road that led past the airport, then walked miles before getting another ride that would take them to the airport. By the time they got to where Rocinante waited for them, the cleansing effect of all their shower time the previous couple of days had been pretty well overcome.

"We'd better do a little flight planning," Mark said. It's empty enough out here that we probably aren't going to be able to stop and get gas just anyplace." He spread maps out on the ground, and he and Jackie hunched down over them, measuring this way and that. "Let's face it, we need to gas up before we fly over the Grand Canyon. There aren't a lot of real good possibilities if we're not going into the Grand Canyon airport. It's a choice between Page and Winslow, and we go about as far out of our way to either place. It's a little farther to go by Winslow, but we'd fly over Canyon de Chelly and the Painted Desert, and we'd see Meteor Crater right after we gas up. There just isn't a heck of a lot along the way if we go by Page. Then, after we get done with the canyon, we can maybe gas up again at Kingman."

"That's going to eat up most of the day, considering what time it is now, and a couple of fuel stops, and lunch, and messing around over the canyon," Jackie said, running her finger over the cluster of maps that they had spread before them. "We're probably looking at a night stop at Kingman."

"Might be kind of a big place for a night stop," he commented. "We'll just have to see when we get there. Let's get a move on."

It was not to be the first day that they had basically done sightseeing from the air, but they agreed afterward that it was their best one.

They flew southwest out of the Durango airport. A little more than half an hour out, they came upon the ragged red crags of Shiprock, west of Farmington, New Mexico. Mark dropped down for a closer look, almost at the level of the peak. Below them, they could see a group of mountain climbers trying to work their way up the rugged, nearly vertical sides of the peak. "I can't help it," Mark told Jackie, "But that doesn't look like fun to me. I'm not real crazy about getting up on a stepladder."

"But you've flown all your life," Jackie protested.

"Yeah, but it's different when you've got an airplane strapped to your butt."

They circled Shiprock several times, and Jackie took some pictures of it through the window.

It was a dead reckoning run from Shiprock down to Winslow. With Mark watching her, Jackie had carefully laid out their compass course across the desert, where there were few good landmarks, and it turned out that she had worked it out on the nose. They flew low over Canyon de Chelly, with it's ancient Indian buildings, and a little higher over the florid colors of the Painted Desert.

Winslow, Arizona came up through the disk of the prop a little over two hours out of Durango, right where it was supposed to be. They stopped for fuel, dug some snacks out of the luggage compartment, and got some cold Pepsis from the airport machine -- no Cokes were in sight -- and got back in the little Cessna.

Fifteen miles west of Winslow, they circled Meteor Crater. About 30,000 years before, a meteor perhaps a hundred yards across had hit, gouging out a hole nearly a mile across. It looked massively impressive from the air.

"If there was a good place to land, it'd be fun to walk down to the bottom of that," Mark said. "But I think it'd be kind of a hot and dry walk, right now."

"We might have the best view of all from right here," Jackie agreed.

Their course to the Grand Canyon was almost north. They had worked out a compass course, but most of the way they could follow a dry-wash river bed, so they didn't bother with the compass. Miles before they got to the canyon, they could see it opening in front of them in the clear air.

What can you say about the Grand Canyon? Words cannot express it.

The Canyon is a chasm that slices through the plateau country of northern Arizona like a gigantic and impossible desert crevasse. It is more than two hundred river miles long. At its center it is more than a mile deep. If you built four Empire State Buildings in it, one on top of the other, they would not rise level with the rim. The canyon averages ten miles across, but some of its bays swing back for twenty, thirty, even forty miles. In all it covers more than a thousand square miles, but the vast bulk of this area is almost never visited. Even today, unexplored corners remain.

Mark and Jackie had seen their fair share of photographs of the place, of course, and they thought they knew what to expect, but even before they flew close, they saw the space of it, a huge, cleaving space that the photographs had done nothing to prepare them for: an impossible, breath-taking gap in the face of the earth.

As they flew closer, they saw the depth -- the depth and the distances. Cliffs and buttes and terraces, all sculpted on a scale beyond which they had never imagined, filled with colors neither red nor white nor pink nor purple, but somehow a combination of them all.

"Wow," Mark breathed. "I'll bet even Valles Marineris wouldn't hit you like this."

"Valles Marineris?" Jackie asked, not tearing her eyes from the window.

"It's on Mars," Mark said. "Discovered by Mariner 9 a couple years ago, so they named it Mariner Valley. It's bigger than this by far, but if you were standing at the bottom, you couldn't see the sides."

"It may be bigger," Jackie said, "But, My God."

They were out over the Canyon by now, looking down into the burning and apparently waterless waste of rock. They looked down at the huge, alternating bands of cliff and terrace, repeating but never repetitous. They looked away, as far as their eyes could strain, until the canyon dwindled away in the haze.

Flying over the Canyon was one thing, but to fly down in it was something else. Mark was flying now, his mind handling the plane on automatic while he and Jackie gaped from the window.

They turned westward to follow the course of the river. They flew this way and that over the rugged cliffs, with Rocinante's wings to carry them over ground so isolated and rugged that it seemed likely that no one had ever walked there.

Ultimately, it was Rocinante's fuel gauge that turned them away from this grandest of sights to see from the air. In their airborne exploration of this wonder, they had let the fuel get down lower than they liked, and while they weren't out of gas when they landed at the airport at Kingman, they pumped more into it than they had before.

"Any place around here we could camp out under the wing?" Mark asked the man at the fuel pump.

"I don't know if it would be OK if you did here, or not," the man said. "We had some avionics stolen out of a plane at night not too long ago, and the Sheriff has been keeping a pretty good eye on the place."

"Got any other ideas?" Jackie asked.

"Which way you headed?"

West, they told the man.

"OK, I've got an idea," he said. "You go west about fifty miles, and there's a little dirt strip at Taylor Springs, just over the Nevada line. It's a public field, so there wouldn't be any problem about you landing there, and it's pretty deserted, so I wouldn't think there would be any problem with you camping there."

Mark looked at Jackie. "It's another half an hour, but that's no problem."

They found the airstrip on the chart. "Looks good to me," Mark told the man. "Thanks."

It was hard to find the strip on the ground, since the land was pretty heavily desert. Finally, they saw an airstrip, with a building sitting at the end, next to a road. "There it is," Jackie said, and began to set up the landing.

She let Rocinante roll to a stop at the building at the end of the strip. There was a sign that they could read: "Bullhead Ranch," it said. There was an "Olympia" sign in the window. "Strange to have a fly-in bar," Mark commented. "I suppose we'd better ask if we can camp out here tonight."

"If we can, a beer is going to taste good," Jackie said.

They went inside. The lights were low and red, and it was hard to see in there. Dimly in the corner, they could make out three or four girls and a couple of cowboys, and there was some heavy necking going on, there.

They went up to a middle-aged woman who was behind the bar. "Would it be all right if we camped out in back overnight?" Mark asked.

"Didn't think you'd come here for business," the woman said. "Not the both of you, anyway. Probably shouldn't, though. It might disturb the customers."

"I thought the guy over in Kingman said the Taylor Springs airport was deserted," Jackie said.

"Oh, this isn't Taylor Springs," the woman said. "That's about three miles up the valley. We just put the airstrip in last fall, for the fly-in trade out of Vegas."

Mark started to say, "What fly-in trade?" but stopped short as the light dawned on him. Jackie didn't get it, yet, he saw. "Well, we can fly up there," he replied. "Any chance we can get a cold six-pack of Oly to go?"

"Sure thing, honey," the woman said as Mark reached for his wallet. In a moment, she set the cold beer on the counter, and rang up his change. "You want to come back without your young lady, some time, just remember that Bullhead Ranch is open 24 hours a day."

"You never know," he said. "Thanks a lot."

The sunshine of the fading day was still bright on their eyes as they walked back out to Rocinante, which they hadn't bothered to tie down. They had the beer in the cooler and were in the plane before Jackie asked, "What was that all about?"

"You don't know?" Mark teased as he started the engine. "I thought you brought me here because you were getting tired of all the attention I've been giving you."

"Huh?"

"It did occur to me that maybe I wasn't giving you enough attention," he said, turning Rocinante to face down the runway. "Who knows, maybe you were looking for a job."

Jackie shook her head. "I don't know what you're talking about," she said as Mark opened the throttle.

"I mean, why else would you bring me to a Nevada whorehouse?"

"You mean . . ."

"Yeah, they're legal in some counties in Nevada, but not in Vegas. There are air taxi companies in Vegas that do nothing that haul people out to whorehouses and back." They broke ground and turned north, looking for the other airport, never getting very far off the ground. It sprang up in front of them in only a couple of minutes, looking very deserted. "Bet they don't use this much since they built the strip down there at Bullhead Ranch," Mark commented as he set up for a landing.

"My God," Jackie said. "Don't you ever tell anybody we were in there. What would they think?"

"Oh, think of the stories it would make back home," Mark teased as Rocinante touched down.

"That's one kind of place I never thought I'd see the inside of," Jackie said, shaking her head.

They found tiedowns, set up camp, and cooked their dinner as the sun set behind the mountains. It was getting dark before they finished up their dinner and zipped the two sleeping bags together for the first time.

It felt strange to have their two naked bodies together in a sleeping bag. It was different from the motel bed the last couple of nights, but they cuddled each other closely as they lay there talking. "How can women do that, anyway?" Jackie asked.

"Oh, some of them are probably pretty good people," Mark said, thinking that Mei-Ling had been one of them. He'd never mentioned Mei-Ling to Jackie, and didn't plan to ever do so; that was one thing he intended to keep private.

"I just can't imagine it," she said. "If you'd been by yourself, would you have stayed?"

"Probably not," Mark said. "That's kind of expensive."

"Wouldn't it be a lot different that the two of us here, me and you."

"A lot different," he said. "We care about each other, and that counts for a lot. Being in love will do that to you. Of course, if you'd like me to slide back down there and make sure, I will if you want me to."

"That's not necessary," she said, pulling him to her. "I think I can give you all you can handle."

They wandered for the next couple of days, trying not to hurry, so there would be time for mail to reach them at Palomar. They rose early the next morning, and flew north to check out Boulder Dam. They turned west, and flew low to the south of Las Vegas and all the high-performance air traffic out of Nellis Air Force Base. Sliding up over the mountains, they flew down to Furnace Creek, sightseeing in the fantastic scenery of Death Valley. "There's no real reason to land there," Mark said. "But only a little over a week ago, we were at the highest airport in North America, and now we might as well land at the lowest."

It was hot when they landed at Furnace Creek, a good two miles lower than then had been at Leadville. They only stayed a few minutes, on account of the heat, then got back into Rocinante and let the plane carry them up to where the air was cooler. They stopped for fuel at Trona, but then had to backtrack nearly to Nevada to get around a maze of restricted areas before they could turn south.

They spent the night at Lake Havasu, Arizona, where they saw the beginning of the transplantation of the London Bridge to it's new location. "The developers kind of got rooked on that deal," Mark told Jackie. "They thought they were buying tower bridge, and that's that pretty, two-level Victorian one. London Bridge is just a plain-vanilla stone arch. I walked over it a couple of years ago, when I was on leave, out of Germany. It's going to be strange to see it here, if we ever get back here."

The heat was bad enough at Lake Havasu, but it was even worse at Calipatria, where they spent their next night near the Salton Sea. They wound up sleeping naked on top of their sleeping bags, and the night was so hot and heavy that they were almost ready to sleep naked under the stars.

Fortunately, it was cooler when they got to Pauma Valley, near Mount Palomar, the next morning. It was several miles to the telescope, but they were able to hitch a couple of rides to get there.

It got considerably cooler as they went up Palomar Mountain. Pines and spruces grew around them, and soon they could see the huge Hale Observatory dome, 170 feet in height, towering above the trees, glistening in the dry sunshine. They climbed the stairs and entered the glassed-in room where tourists could view the telescope. It was unbelievably huge; the 82-inch and the 107-inch at McDonald Observatory had seemed big enough, but this huge machine dwarfed them easily. It have been the largest telescope in the world for a nearly a quarter of a century now, and only then were people beginning to think of building one bigger.

Late in the day, they got back to the Pauma Valley post office; and there was mail for them -- a package each for Mark and Jackie.

They ate dinner in town before they went back out to the airport, and opened their mail.

There were a couple of short notes for Mark, a bunch of junk mail, and some magazines. He began to leaf through "Sky and Telescope," when Jackie let out a gasp. "Mark, how soon can we get back to Spearfish Lake?"

"Something the matter?"

"My mother died." She began to read the letter. "This is from Sarah," she said. "'Only an hour or so after you called yesterday, they called us from Camden to tell us that your mother died. They don't know why, yet; one minute she was the same as she had been for years, and the next minute, she wasn't breathing. We tried to call Durango to find you, but if you get this at Palomar, you'll know that we couldn't reach you.

"'I don't know what the plans are at this time. Your father is still the next of kin, I guess, since we don't know of any other relatives that your mother has, besides you. We should know more by the time you get this, but call home collect as soon as you get this.'"

Mark shook his head. "We're about as far away from Spearfish Lake as we're likely to get on this trip," he said. "If we cranked up right now, and flew all night, and got lucky on finding places open to refuel after midnight, then we might be able to make it back by this time tomorrow."

"Would an airliner be any quicker?"

"We don't have enough radio to get us into Los Angeles International, although we could get close and get a taxi, I suppose. You might be able to get a redeye as far as Chicago, but I don't think you could get to Camden from Chicago until sometime in the afternoon, and you'd still have to get a ride to Spearfish Lake. If we get lucky with refueling at night, we can just about get there as fast as an airliner with five times the speed."

"Mark, I don't know what I should do," she said, shaking her head. "Worse, I don't know how I should feel. I mean, I suppose I should be sorry, because it's my mother, but she's been the next thing to a vegetable for ten years now, and maybe I'm relieved, for her sake."

"Before we go racing off, we should call," Mark said. "I think there's a pay phone up at the administration building."

Both Walt and Sarah were at home when they called. "There's no need to race home," her father told her, as Mark leaned close to Jackie's ear to hear the conversation. "We called around in Durango, the railroad, the airport, the police, and like that, but when we didn't hear from you, we just decided to go ahead with the service, and we hoped you wouldn't mind."

"We can come back tomorrow or the next day if there's any need to," Jackie told her father.

"There's no need to," Walt replied. "We didn't have much of a service, but the preacher at the Baptist Church was nice enough to come over and handle it for us. We used to go there years ago, and he was nice about it. We had her buried in her family plot."

"I feel like I ought to have been there," Jackie told her father.

"Don't worry about it," Walt said. "I know you would have liked to be here, and we thought about holding off until we could get in touch with you, but we decided that she'd really died years ago, and all we were doing was finishing up the details. There's no reason to feel guilty about it."

Jackie asked if they had figured out why she had died.

"The autopsy didn't have any clue," Walt said. "It was like God had finally taken mercy on her and pulled the switch. Actually, I think I'm relieved, more than anything else. I've felt for years like I'm the one that should feel guilty, for giving up on her, but I realized that I needed to get on with my life."

"I know," Jackie agreed. "I always felt like there was something I ought to be able to do, but I could never figure out what it was."

"Try to remember the good times," Walt said. "There were some, even though you were pretty little, I think maybe you can remember some of them. Try to forget the harder times that came later, and just put them behind you."

"It's hard to forget," Jackie said.

"Maybe it's a little easier for me," her father said. "I remember your mother before you came along, and she was a good person, and we had some good times. The bad times didn't start until after you came along. It was kind of like she couldn't handle the responsibility of being a mother, but she tried hard. Maybe she tried too hard. We'll never know."

"I guess I never knew that," Jackie commented.

"It's over with, now," Walt said. "If you feel you need to do something, say a prayer for her, or something, and get on with what you're doing."

Jackie shook her head. "Dad, if you think there's any reason why I should be there, to be with you, or anything, we can be heading back tonight."

"There's no reason," Walt said. "Try to call home a little more often, maybe, and keep us up on what's happening on your trip. I don't know if you realize how much we enjoy your letters and calls. We're enjoying the trip right along with you. When you write to us that you've been to a place, we dig out old National Geographic articles or go to the library to get a book to read about it. We were just leafing through a book on the Grand Canyon when you called. You're seeing things and doing things that I'll never have a chance to do. Believe me, this isn't worth ruining your trip for."

They had been aware that Sarah was on the other phone, listening in, and now they heard her voice: "We both think a lot of you and Mark," she said. "All we want is for you to stay safe, and come home to us when you're ready."

"We've never had any plans about when we're coming home," Jackie told them. "About all we've planned is that we have to be back not later than next summer, sometime, when Mark has to be ready to go to work for the phone company, and we hadn't planned on coming home before then, unless we had to for something like this."

"You don't have to come home for this," Sarah reiterated. "Don't misunderstand me. We'd be just as happy if you came home to see us, but don't come on our account, because of this."

After they hung up the phone, Mark and Jackie walked slowly back to Rocinante. "It's up to you," Mark said. "If you want to go home, we'll go. We can get started now, and get maybe three hundred miles east before night sets in. I'd really rather not fly over that country in the dark, if I can help it, but we could spend the night some place, start at dawn, and be out over the plains by tomorrow night, and fly most of the night, there."

"I don't know," Jackie said. "I just feel guilty, like I ought to have been home when I was needed, and I wasn't there. But you heard Dad say that there was no need for us to rush home. I don't know what to think."

"It won't hurt us to spend the night right here and sleep on it," Mark told her. "At a minimum, we could be fresh when we start in the morning, and that'll count for something."

"I suppose you're right," she agreed, furrowing her brow. "But Mark, I just don't know how I should be feeling, right now. I mean, she was my mother, and I ought to be feeling sorry, but mostly I'm relieved, more for Dad's sake, than anything else. I mean, even after he married Sarah, I don't think he ever gave up hope. Even when he was on the Walsenberg turn, he was down in Camden every other day, and I think he was in to see her almost every trip he was on. I mean, he never told Sarah and me about it, but we knew about it. It was something we just didn't talk about."

"You said once that you hadn't seen her for years," he observed.

"Yeah, it's been six, seven, maybe eight years now," she said. "Just to see her got me so down that I never wanted to go back, and Dad never made an issue out of it." They walked along in silence for a bit longer before Jackie added, "Mark, I was just so scared that that could be me some day that I just never wanted to see her again."

"You've been thinking about it that long?" he asked, a suspicion dawning. "What made you think it might get passed on to you?"

"I don't know," she said finally. "I guess I always just knew that it could happen. Mark, it's just such a scary damn thing to have to live with that I don't know what to think any longer."

"Yeah," he conceded as they reached Rocinante. "I guess it would be, at that."

"You know the best part about being on this trip with you?" she said, thinking aloud, then answering her own question. "It's just being with you, making believe that I'm a normal person, that I can have a normal life. In Spearfish Lake, I was always being reminded that it could happen to me. I've been so happy just being with you, out in the country, that it makes me wish sometimes that we never go back. Maybe we ought to go back to Fort Collins and see if you can get a regular job at Waverly. Or, go back to Twillingate, and see if Mr. Thibodaux will hire you. Or something, I don't know, but sometimes I hope we never go back there."

Mark shrugged. "I suppose it isn't a got-to sort of thing, but that's a good job I have waiting. On the other hand, there are other good jobs out there, too. It's something we don't have to make a decision about until maybe this time next year, so why worry?"

She took him into his arms; he could see that there were tears running down her face. "That's what I like about you," she said. "'We don't have to make a decision' . . . 'We can go home'. God, you don't know what that means to me. I mean, so long back there at home, all the little minds and little mouths were going, and it was always, 'You don't want to have anything to do with her, you don't want to get involved with her, stay away from her,' always on account of my mother. Mark, you don't know how much I hated my mother for being what she was, how much I know that she screwed me up. I mean, I don't get that from you, and I never thought that would happen with a Spearfish Lake guy. I always figured that if I ever get married, I'd have to marry some guy from out of town that's never had to hear all that shit all his life. That's why, if we do ever get married, I want to get married in Spearfish Lake, just to show all those old gossips that Crazy Jackie can find a good guy to marry."

"They called you that?" Mark bristled.

"Not to my face," she sobbed. "Nobody had the guts to do that, but I knew about it."

"I never heard it," truthfully, "But then, I'm enough older that I might not have. We didn't exactly run with the same crowd. But if we do go back to Spearfish Lake and I do ever hear it, I'm going to get a reputation for punching people's lights out."

"Maybe they're right," she said. "I guess I sound a little paranoid right now. Maybe paranoia runs in the family, I don't know. I know it scares the hell out of me, and I'm scaring myself right now."

"Jackie," he said. "You're about the sanest, most level-headed person I know. If you're in the least little bit off your rocker, it's because you're too level-headed. It's all right to show anger, it's all right to show you're scared. I'm no psychiatrist, but I do know that you don't have to think you're crazy if you're just pissed off or frightened or confused."

She buried her face in his shoulder. "You believe in me more than I do," she said, "And that's not right."

"Somebody has to believe in you," he said, realizing that he had to lighten the atmosphere somehow. All of a sudden a thought came to him: "Look, what you have is a Catch-22 thing. You know what that is?"

"Never heard of it," she said.

"Famous book. There's these bomber crews in Italy, back during World War

II. They're flying mission after mission, and getting the shit shot out of them, and they're all afraid of dying. Well, the regulations say that anybody can take themselves off of aircrew status by declaring that the fear of dying has driven them crazy. But the regulations also say that only a sane person can fear dying, so they can't be taken off of flight status. If you think you're crazy, you're not."

"That doesn't make sense," she said.

"That's just the point," he replied. "It doesn't have to make sense, it's the Army. You're so afraid of going off the deep end that the fear could drive you there if you let it. What was it you told Bruce? Don't let your fears keep you from doing what you want to do? You gave him good advice."

She pulled away from him. "That was a totally different situation."

"Bullshit."

She was silent for a moment, thinking about it. All of a sudden, an incredible urge for a cigarette came over him. He knew that there were a couple of cigarettes left in the pack he'd bought in Fort Collins, weeks ago. They were in the side pocket of his pack, and he open Rocinante's door to dig for them.

"You know what I almost wish we could do?" she said from behind him. "I wish we could fly back to Twillingate and talk to Brother Erasmus."

He pulled a cigarette from the pack, and turned around to face her. "We could, I suppose. Or, we could call him. But I can just about tell you what he would say."

"What would he say?"

He sat down on the Cessna's tire and lit the cigarette. "He'd tell you that it's all God's will. That whatever happens, to you, or whatever, is God's will. Maybe he'd tell you that your mother's death is a sign from God, to get closer to him, to let the past be dead and buried. He'd quote you some Scripture from John or from Romans or something telling you to put your faith in God. And, he might be right."

She cocked her head sideways. "You don't believe in God, do you?"

He took a deep drag on the cigarette, and let the smoke relax him. He let it out in a long, slow cloud and said, "That's not right, and you know it. I'm not sure I believe in Brother Erasmus' God. I've always had trouble of conceiving of God in a church, but then I know that other people don't have that problem, and I respect their beliefs, and that's why we've been reading Brother Erasmus' Bible. But, I'll tell you that I can't stand out under a night sky, or look at M-31 without feeling the presence of God. You remember John, down in Texas? I don't know if Bhuddists believe in God, or what they do believe, but looking at Omega Centauri through John's telescope -- well, I don't know how a person can look at that and not feel the presence of a superior being, and I think John knows that."

She stood there thinking for a minute, then sat down on the ground next to him. "I think I agree," she said slowly. "I couldn't have put it in those words, but I've always felt a magic out under the stars, out with the telescope that I've never quite been able to describe."

"That's it, all right," he said. "I get the feeling sometimes when I'm flying, too. What I've been wanting to do is to find some way of making that feeling relate to Brother Erasmus' view, or something that kind of relates to how other people feel. Having a gut feeling and making sense out of it are two different things. I mean, I think I could explain the feeling to John, and he'd understand what I'm talking about, but I think he'd lose me when he tried to explain it. I just don't have it in me to turn my back on my Christian upbringing."

"I know one thing Brother Erasmus would tell you," Jackie said. "Faith isn't something that you can explain logically. Faith is something you have to feel in your heart."

"I'm sure that's what he'd say," Mark agreed. "I mean, I have faith enough to go out under the starlit sky tonight and pray for your mother, and pray for the load you're carrying to be lightened, and pray for guidance for both of us, and at least feel honest about it. I'm not sure I could walk into Brother Erasmus' church and do that honestly."

"I think you may be right," she said. "I think I feel the same way."

On the top of Mt. Palomar that June evening, the largest telescope in the world was turned toward the sky, seeing answers to some scientific puzzle about the making of the universe, or the makeup of it, or the future of it. Far down the mountain to the west, a much smaller telescope was also turned skyward, seeking answers of its own to questions that were in many ways the same. The larger of the two telescopes sought wisdom until dawn wiped the stars from the sky; the smaller one was put away much sooner, but in each case, the operators of the telescopes put them away with satisfaction, feeling that they were a little bit closer to solving their piece of the puzzle.

*　*　*

Pauma Valley, California
June 26, 1971

Dear Dad and Sarah:

Mark and I talked about it very late last night, and decided that we wouldn't come home just yet. A couple of different times we all but had the plane packed to leave, but we talked ourselves out of it.

We are still willing to come home if you feel in the slightest that it would do any good for us to be there, even if it would just do you good to know we are there. We will try to call home more often, but don't feel that if you want us to come home that it's going to put us out any, as we have no real plans, and there's no place that we have to be.

We've seen a lot in the few days since we left Durango. The Grand Canyon was magnificent, and we also saw Shiprock, Meteor Crater, Death Valley, and, would you believe it, the beginnings of the London Bridge, and the 200 inch telescope, of course. Somehow, though, I just don't feel like writing about those things right now, but I will try to in a day or two.

Mark and I are still trying to sort out how I feel about Mother's death. It's very difficult for me to describe, but mixed feelings gets off to a good start. Hopefully, in a day or two things will start to sort themselves out.

I don't know too much about where we're going from here, although south and west are out, for obvious reasons. Mark says he's not looking forward to flying through the Los Angeles metro area, but I kind of think that we'll at least head north, perhaps to Yosemite or up along the coast. Frankly, I'm torn between wanting to get on the move again and leave the heavy thoughts of this place behind me, and between sitting right here until we work them out. But, we've packed up the plane, so I guess we will be leaving.

Dad, I promise we'll call in a few days. If there's any reason we should head home, don't be afraid to let us know.

Love

Jackie

4.

"I make it a compass course of 270, right on the nose," Jackie agreed. "I don't know that I'm too crazy about it, though."

"Me either," Mark said as they studied the map spread out on Rocinante's horizontal stabilizer. "I don't know that the alternative is any better, though."

They had spent a sleepless night at the Pauma Valley airport. Jackie had more or less reached the decision to continue the trip, although she wasn't comfortable about it, and she lay awake turning the options over in her mind most of the night.

Mark had other concerns: North of them lay the Los Angeles metropolitan area, and getting through it wasn't going to be easy. If they'd had a good radio or two on board the Cessna, and a radar transponder, it would not have been much concern, but with the old 12-channel Narco, penetrating the maze of Terminal Control Areas, Airport Traffic Areas, Prohibited Areas, Restricted Areas, Warning Areas, Military Operating Areas and Air Defense Interception Zones was all but impossible.

There was one possible route, over Palmdale, where they could possibly sneak through without radio, but Mark imagined that the air traffic there would be heavy, both out of Edwards Air Force Base and from other people trying to sneak around the busy area without the hassles of having to deal with all the air traffic and the air traffic controllers. Any way you looked at it, it involved an awful lot of aluminum in a limited airspace.

Another alternative they had was to go clear back to Nevada, where there was a possible route near the state line that avoided all the closed areas, or areas where access was restricted by their limited radio.

There was a third route, and it was the shortest, but it took some deep breathing to even consider it: if they were to fly from over Oceanside airport out to Santa Catalina Island, then carefully head northwest from Catalina to the Ventura and Oxnard area, they could avoid all the restricted areas, if they kept fairly low.

The only problem was that it was over the water -- with only a single engine, virtually no radio or navigation equipment, and not even having life preservers.

Of course, Mark thought, the same thing could have been said of Charles Lindbergh, almost a half a century before, and he was going 3500 miles over water, not the mere 45 they would be facing.

If they got away with it, no one would question them; if they didn't -- well, it wouldn't matter, even though Mark decided he would file a flight plan, one of the rare times he had done so on this trip, in spite of all the mountains and deserts they had flown over.

They gave Rocinante the most careful preflight it had received on the entire trip so far, and topped the Cessna's tanks as full as they had been. They refigured their navigation several times, each time coming up with the same answers. It would be a dead reckoning run all the way to and from Catalina -- which, though it might not seem a lot for 45 miles, it was of more concern because of the fact that the visibility was only about four miles in the southern California smog. Just as bad, they would strike Catalina endways, making it a lot narrower target than if they were coming straight out from Los Angeles. They would only be over the water for twenty-five or thirty minutes or so, but for a fair portion of that they would be out of sight of land in the low visibility.

It seemed like a pretty risky thing to do, but going to Nevada again seemed ridiculous, too.

Mark tried to make light of it: "You remember the old song -- 'Twenty-six miles, across the sea, Santa Catalina is the place for me . . .' We just can't get that close without checking it out."

"I guess," Jackie agreed, aware of the risk they would be taking.

How must Lindbergh have felt to see the coast of Newfoundland fall behind him on that day in 1927? Mark thought he must have had a taste of that feeling as he saw the Oceanside airport pass below them. He kept the needle centered on the "27" on the magnetic and the gyro compasses, checked his watch, and resolved that if Catalina didn't turn up in 35 minutes, he was turning northeast toward land, Terminal Control Areas or no Terminal Control Areas.

In the seat next to him, Jackie watched the shoreline slide underneath them, much too close for comfort. Given a choice, she would have been up at ten thousand feet; even if the engine quit, they could glide to land, but they were going to be heading right across the climb corridor from El Toro Marine Air Station, and at ten thousand feet they stood too good a chance of tangling with some Marine jet with a pilot who had his eyes only on the gauges.

The unease that she felt at the overwater flight was only heightened by the unease that she felt at their heading. As much as she could rationalize the decision to head on, there was a strong desire to be heading back toward Spearfish Lake, not towards northern California, and perhaps the decision to press onwards had not been the right one.

Their long discussion of the night before had only brought back all the old fears she'd had because of her mother. How would her life have been different if only her mother had been normal! As it was, it had messed up her own life royally. Jackie had long since conceded that she had fallen in love with Mark, but was that fair to him? Look at the agony her own father had gone through, over the years and years that her mother had been down in Camden! Was it right to ask him to risk having to deal with that?

Lost in the problem, she stared out the window at the empty water sliding beneath them, then checked her watch; she was as aware of the time they would have to fly overwater as Mark was. Only five minutes since they had left the shoreline at Oceanside! It seemed like an hour, the way the hands were dragging on her watch. She checked the clock on the panel, to make sure that her watch hadn't stopped, but it read the same. Was Rocinante's engine sounding rough? It had always sounded rough when they were out over some trackless desert, but she knew it was only her own imagination talking to her. Her eyes went out the window again, staring at the ocean's waves passing below. There was nothing much to be seen out there -- no ships, no boats, only an occasional bird, down near the surface. She looked ahead; there was only a gray haze that merged seamlessly with the ocean.

After a long time, she checked her watch again. Only ten minutes! She shook her head; she had never felt the time drag so. Again, she turned her attention to watching the crawl by ocean below, but her mind was even farther away.

The minutes crawled by. Up ahead of them, she could make out a boat floating in the water below -- the first they had seen since leaving the mainland. It was almost directly ahead of them, and they were approaching it rapidly, giving her some idea of just how fast they were really moving. It was something to look at, even though something didn't look right . . . "God, Mark! It's upside down!"

"What?" Mark said, her cry breaking into his own thoughts.

"That boat down there! It's upside down, and there are a couple of people hanging onto the bottom!"

"I don't see it," Mark said, rocking Rocinante up onto one wing to try to get a better look out the far side of the airplane.

"I'll show you," Jackie said, reaching for the throttle. She pulled on the carb heat and slowed the Cessna to let it descend. In but a few moments, they were only about three hundred feet up, circling the overturned boat. Below them, they could see two people clinging to the the boat's keel. One of them was waving at them, and for a moment, they could see the other trying to wave at them, too.

"Mark, what do we do now?" Jackie said.

"We've at least got enough radio to call for help," Mark said, reaching up to turn on the old Narco that now seemed to occupy a more prominent part of the panel. In the next seconds, Mark did something he'd never done before: turned the channel to 121.5, the emergency channel, and keyed the microphone. "Any station on one twenty-one five, this is Cessna Zero One Zero Eight Romeo, over," he called.

The response was instantaneous. "Cessna Zero Eight Romeo, this is El Toro, go ahead."

"El Toro, we are about 20 miles east magnetic from Avalon," Mark called. "We are circling an overturned small boat, and we can see two people hanging on to it. Can you contact the Coast Guard?"

"Roger, can do, Zero Eight Romeo," El Toro replied. "We are contacting the Avalon Coast Guard Station now. We'd like a better position. Squawk seven seven zero zero and ident."

"Sorry, El Toro, Cessna Zero Eight Romeo is negative on the transponder," Mark replied, wishing for once that he'd had the money to install the radar beacon in the little plane.

"Roger that," the voice on the other end of the circuit said. "Santa Catalina VORTAC is one-eleven point four, repeat one one one dot four. Can you give us a bearing?"

"Uh, sorry," Mark replied, "We're also negative on the VOR."

The radio was silent for a moment as they continued to circle the boat. Mark could almost imagine the cussing going on in the El Toro tower at the moment. Finally, El Toro came onto the air again. "Cessna Zero Eight Romeo, can you pick up a little altitude? We think we have you on radar, but it's very fuzzy."

"Roger, El Toro," Mark replied, opening the throttle. "We'll pick up a little and see if that'll help."

"OK, Zero Eight Romeo," the Marine Air Station replied. "Can you give us a long count?"

Thank God someone down there has a direction finder, Mark thought. He keyed the mike, counted slowly to ten, then slowly back down to one.

"Radar contact!" El Toro said, with just a little note of victory creeping into the professionalism of his voice. "El Toro has radar contact on Cessna Zero Eight Romeo 28 miles from the Santa Catalina VORTAC, bearing zero nine zero! Be advised the Coast Guard has left Avalon with a thirty-one footer, and we'll pass the location to them."

"Thank you, sir," Mark replied. "If it'll be any use, we'll be glad to orbit this location to help them out."

"How long can you remain on station?"

"El Toro, if you can adjust our flight plan, Zero Eight Romeo can stay here at least two hours," Mark said. "Maybe a little more if we need to."

"Roger, Zero Eight Romeo," El Toro replied. "We'll contact the Coast Guard. Stand by."

Mark turned to Jackie. "I don't know about you," he said. "But if I was one of those people down there, and saw us fly off, I think it would just about kill me."

"Me, too," Jackie said. "If we throttle way back, I think we can stay at least three hours."

"Hopefully, the Coast Guard can be here by then," Mark said. "I just wish there was some way we could tell those people that help is on the way."

A new voice came over the radio. "Cessna Zero Eight Romeo, this is Coast Guard 244."

"Coast Guard 244, this is Zero Eight Romeo, go ahead," Mark replied.

"Zero Eight Romeo, we understand your intention is to orbit the survivors to aid in our locating them."

"Roger, Coast Guard 244," Mark said. "We can stay on station two and a half to three hours. What's your ETA?"

"Pretty close to an hour," the Coast Guard rescue boat replied. "We'll be there as fast as we can."

"We'll be here," Mark told them.

"Cessna Zero Eight Romeo, El Toro," the radio squawked. "Understand you are in contact with the Coast Guard. We can't read them directly. We will notify Hawthorne FSS of your change in flight plan. If you need someone to relieve you on station, give us a call and we'll launch someone out of here."

"El Toro," Mark said. "We'll be happy to stay as long as we can."

"Affirmative, Zero Eight Romeo. Keep us advised. El Toro out."

The next forty-five minutes drug by slowly. Mark and Jackie changed off on the duty of circling the capsized boat, a thousand feet or so above the water. It might have been dull for them, just flying in a lazy circle, but the knowledge of what was riding on their circling there made it anything but dull. After a while, Jackie dug around in the tightly packed luggage behind them with a great deal of difficulty, and managed to pull out her little binoculars. She could occasionally get a glimpse of the people in hanging on the boat. They had quit waving now -- they knew they had been found -- and Jackie could see with difficulty that one of the people was doing their best to hang on to the other one. "The Coast Guard better not be far off," Jackie said, explaining what she had seen. "I don't think they can hold out much longer."

"Well, maybe we can hurry them up," Mark said, reaching for the microphone again. "Coast Guard 244, this is Cessna Zero Eight Romeo," he called.

The Coast Guard boat answered right back, and Mark replied, "Be advised that we think one of the survivors is pretty weak. It's hard to tell, but it looks like they're having trouble staying conscious."

"We're running with four bells and a jingle," Coast Guard 244 replied. "I think we're getting close, but we're having trouble finding you. Say the color and type of your aircraft."

"Gray and white, single engine, high wing," Mark said.

"Negative contact," Coast Guard 244 replied. "Maybe when we get a little closer."

Jackie put the binoculars to her eyes, in the direction she thought west was. "I see them, I think!" she said. "I see a white boat, with some orange on it, headed toward us."

"Coast Guard 244," Mark called. "Are you white with an orange bow stripe like other Coast Guard boats?"

"That's affirmative," came the reply.

"We've got you in sight, we think," Mark said. "Looks like you're heading right for us."

"Ah, there you are," Coast Guard 244 replied. "You're just hard to see, that's all. We'll be there shortly."

In a few minutes, they didn't need binoculars to see Coast Guard 244; they could see the white boat, the blaze orange stripe on its bow, kicking up a big quarter wave as it raced toward the capsized boat. "Zero Eight Romeo, we have survivors in sight," the Coast Guard reported.

Mark and Jackie looked at the scene below them. "It looks like they have you in sight, too," Mark replied. "They're waving at you. They're both waving at you!"

It only seemed like a few minutes before the Coast Guard boat pulled alongside the capsized boat. Mark remembered El Toro saying that Coast Guard 244 was a thirty-one footer; the capsized boat was a lot smaller, perhaps the size of a fishing boat or a runabout. As they watched, they saw a Coast Guardsman go into the water to help assist the survivors aboard. A few minutes later, the radio crackled once again. "Zero Eight Romeo, we have two survivors aboard. You were right, one of them is in pretty bad shape, and I think they're both going to need to be in the hospital for a while. We've got a great big thank you for your assist, but not as big a thank you as they do."

"Roger, 244," Mark replied. "Glad to have been of assistance. El Toro, did you copy Coast Guard 244?"

"Cessna Zero Eight Romeo, that's a negative," the familiar voice of El Toro replied.

"All right," Mark said. "Coast Guard 244 has two survivors on board. Would you advise Hawthorne FSS that Zero Eight Romeo will be proceeding to Catalina and closing our flight plan there?"

"Roger, we'll be glad to," El Toro replied. "We show the Santa Catalina VORTAC 28 miles from you, course 270 magnetic. Well done, Zero Eight Romeo."

As Rocinante's nose turned west, Mark straightened out, and waved goodbye the little Cessna's wings goodbye to the Coast Guard boat below them.

Where once the distance over the water seemed the width of an ocean, and minutes dragged on like hours, it seemed as if they had barely straightened out on course when Catalina Island began to take shape through the haze. They flew down the coastline, past Avalon, and finally saw the cliff-top airport. Mark switched the Narco over to 122.8 for the Unicom frequency. There was a fair amount of traffic reported, and as they got closer Mark could see that the airport was fairly crowded.

It took them a few minutes to find the gas pumps. Mark and Jackie left Rocinante sitting in front of them, and were glad to get out of the Cessna's seat to stretch. They went into the office, found a direct line to Hawthorne Flight Service Station, and closed their flight plan -- and got a "Good job" from the man on the phone at Hawthorne; apparently they had been monitoring 121.5 all along.

"Hey," the girl behind the counter in the office said. "Are you two with that gray and white Cessna out there? Zero One Zero Eight Romeo?"

"Yeah," Mark said. "We'd like it topped off with eighty octane."

"We had a phone call for you," the girl said. "Chief Daugherty at the Coast Guard Station wants to talk to you. I'll call him for you, if you like."

"Fine with me," Mark said.

The girl dialed the Coast Guard Station and got Chief Daugherty on the line. "Those people from Cessna Zero Eight Romeo are here," she said. "I'll put them both on." The girl handed Mark a phone, and pointed Jackie to a phone on the table; she went over and picked it up.

The chief sounded a bit gruff. "Are you the guy who was flying Cessna Zero Eight Romeo?" he asked.

"Me and my fiancee," Mark said, beginning to wonder if he was in trouble.

"Well, we just wanted to say that we really appreciate your help," he said. "The thirty-one footer isn't back yet, but they tell us that the woman wouldn't have lasted much longer if you hadn't showed up and stayed with them. The guy was pretty far gone, too. Their boat flipped over on them yesterday afternoon, and maybe neither of them would have made it through the day if you hadn't happened along. Can I have your names, please?"

"Uh, Chief, are we in trouble or something?"

"No," the man said, "But I think the district will want to write a commendation for you."

"My fiancee, Jackie Archer, is the one that spotted them," he said. "Once we saw them, we couldn't leave." He gave Chief Daugherty their full names, and their Spearfish Lake addresses, and explained a little bit about their trip and why they were in that particular spot at that time.

After they hung up the phone, they went back outside to watch Rocinante get topped off, then rolled the Cessna away from the gas pumps. They went back inside to pay for their gas, bought Cokes, and sat down to unwind a little before continuing the second half of their trip. Mark thought that as long as they were there, it might be fun to explore the island a little, but the schedule of tiedown charges on a bulletin board inside the office gave him second thoughts -- an overnight tiedown at Catalina Airport was exactly the same figure as a month's hangerage at Spearfish Lake, and he got the impression that everything else was just as expensive. "You about ready to go?" he said to Jackie, who was lost in thought.

"Yeah, I guess so." she said.

"OK, I'll file our flight plan."

They were aloft on the second half of their interrupted flight to Camarillo Airport, outside of Oxnard, before they fell to talking. "We saved their lives," Jackie said.

"Yeah," Mark said. "I guess we did."

"I've been thinking about it an awful lot," Jackie said. "If we'd started back for Spearfish Lake, they'd be dying or dead by now."

"The woman might be, anyway," Mark agreed.

"We could have gone back to Nevada, too," she said. "After all, where are we heading? North? We could have done it just as well there, too."

"Yeah, I guess," Mark said. "Except that we'd be going over ground we'd already been over twice."

"I keep thinking about it," Jackie said. "I keep thinking what it must have been like, hanging onto the bottom of that boat, hoping and praying that some miracle will happen, hanging on for your life, and then all of a sudden, you look up, and there we are. It must have seemed like a miracle to them."

"Yeah, I guess so," Mark agreed.

"You want to know what really seems like a miracle?" Jackie said. "If I hadn't been feeling so rotten over my mother and all, I wouldn't have been staring out the window, and we'd have flown right over them and never seen them. And, my God, think how that would feel to see us fly right overhead and never slow down."

"We could have been half a mile to one side or the other and have never seen them, either," Mark said. "It was just dumb luck that we were where we were."

"But Mark," she said, a real question in her voice. "That's what I keep thinking about. What if it wasn't dumb luck?"

"But . . ." he fell silent. The Continental engine in Rocinante's nose drummed a humming into his ears for several minutes as they flew northward. "I'm sure Brother Erasmus would call it a miracle," he said finally. "But then, he sees God's hand in everything, every leaf that falls. I see a chain of circumstances, sheer dumb luck involved at every step."

"What's the difference between sheer dumb luck and a miracle?" Jackie asked.

"Only how you look at it, I guess," Mark said finally. "We haven't been in a church since Twillingate. Tomorrow's Sunday, I think. Maybe we're about ready to try again."

*   *   *

Arroyo Grande, Calif.
June 27, 1971

Dear Dad and Sarah:

Well, we're back on the move again, except that we decided that since this is a Sunday, we'd make it a day of rest. After all, we've been going every day since Durango, and all of a sudden it seemed like a good time to stop, get cleaned up, go to church, and have a decent restaurant meal, and maybe get a newspaper and find out what's happening in the rest of the world. We stopped a little early yesterday afternoon so we could find a discount store, and so I could find a skirt and Mark could find a decent shirt, so we could look a little bit more respectable for church. It was very strange to wear a skirt again; I haven't had one on since March.

Now that I've had a chance to think about it and talk it over with Mark, I feel more comfortable with my feelings about Mother's death. I don't want to say that everything makes sense, but at least I don't feel as troubled as I did yesterday. Mark suggested that we'd better sleep on any decision we made, and I guess I'm glad we did.

We went over to Catalina island yesterday, but decided not to stay, as everything is ritzy and kind of expensive, so we looked around and flew on back to the mainland.

We had kind of an interesting experience yesterday, except that I don't want to get into telling you about it right now. Mark and I aren't sure what it means, yet, and we're still trying to figure it out. Once we know what we think about it, I'll tell you the whole story.

We're heading on north from here, I guess. Mark says that he'd like to visit Yosemite Valley, but he's worried that it's wall to wall people in the summer, so maybe we won't go there. Or, maybe we'll just fly over it and call it good enough.

We tried to call this morning, but we didn't get an answer. We'll try again this evening, and then again in a couple of days.

I love you,
Jackie

5.

There was a spot right on the corner of the rain fly where the water dripping off Rocinante's drooped aileron drummed like an endless water torture. At least a hundred times, either Mark or Jackie threatened to go out, loosen the tiedown ropes on the wings and tighten the one up on the tail, to move that spot off of the rain fly and get rid of the endless thumpatathumpatathumpatathump. But, they'd never got quite irritated enough at the ongoing sound when they were laying down to do something about it, and it always seemed as if when they were up and about they never thought about it.

Three days now, they'd been weathered in by this rainstorm. The rain was never heavy, and at times, it almost quit, but there was nowhere enough ceiling or visibility to fly.

There were only two positions where it was possible to spend time in the tent: sitting up, or lying down. They both had done their fair share of either, and Jackie was getting stiff in either position. She laid in the sleeping bag with Mark, watching him sleep. She didn't feel sleepy in the slightest, and envied Mark his ability to take a nap at such times like these. She lay there for a long time, trying to drift off, but it just wasn't going to work.

After a while, she got up as quietly as she could, and pulled on panties, jeans, and a shirt, deciding to go sit in Rocinante for a while. She could turn on the radio there, and not bother Mark, and best of all, she would have the seat to rest her back against.

Since the tent was pitched under Rocinante's right wingtip, she didn't have to bother with one of the ponchos, which were thrown over the Cessna's wing strut so they might drip a little dryer.

With the plane's tail on the ground, the right seat reclined back a little uncomfortably, until Jackie realized that the general idea was to relax, and this was a relaxing position.

Only after she had been settled back in the seat for a few minutes did she realize that she had nothing more to do in the cockpit than she did in the tent. She though about digging out the aviation ground school books that Jack Daniels had given her back at Waverly, but she and Mark had been going through them very intensively over the past couple of days, more for anything to do than any real need to get them studied to take her written. But, she had realized that just then, even that left her cold. Thinking about some of those things would just build up the desire to get into the air again, and that, they couldn't do until the weather lifted.

She turned on her side a little, so she could look over into the luggage compartment, to see if there was anything there that could suggest something to do. There was; laying on the floor behind the left seat, half-hidden, was the blue notebook they used as a journal.

It really wasn't much of a journal; it didn't go into much detail. The eight days at Twillingate, for example, took all of three sentences, and the two weeks and more at Waverly took five. Still, she flipped through it anyway, using each entry to key her memory of some of the things that had happened. There were dates and places they'd stopped for fuel, or spent the night, and occasionally a line like "Flew over Grand Canyon." There were notes of when Rocinante had its oil changed and addresses of people whose addresses they wanted to save.

The last gave Jackie an idea. Early in the loose-leaf pages of the notebook was Roger and Kathy Griswold's address, back there in Arvada Center, and Jackie had thought on occasion of dropping them a note, to let them know how the trip was coming, but she'd never quite gotten around to it.

There was a ball-point pen in the pocket with the navigation stuff in it, down by her ankle. She pulled it out, flipped back to a blank page farther back in the notebook, and began to write:

Mendocino, California
July 8, 1971

As she wrote that down, she realized that it had been a few days since she'd written a real letter to Dad and Sarah, not just a few lines on a picture postcard. She thumbed back through the pages to the logbook part of the notebook, and checked the dates. It had been clear back at Arroyo Grande, almost two weeks before! It didn't seem like that long, Jackie thought, but she ran through her mind the dates that were on the pages. Five days of backpacking in the high Sierras, plus four days marooned in this godforsaken weather in this godforsaken hole, and then it snapped into place. Yes, it had been that long.

The letter to Roger and Kathy could come another time; it was time to get a letter written to Spearfish Lake. With this weather, it could be a nice, long letter, one she wouldn't have to feel guilty about. She flipped back to the page where she had started the letter, and began to write:

Dear Dad and Sarah:

I think I understand how Noah felt after it had been raining a week or so. It's only our fourth day of being stuck in this place by weather that's too bad to fly in, but it seems like it's been half of forever.

Actually, from what we saw of the place the first day we were here, it's really a fairly nice little town, but with the rain and the overcast skies, it's about as attractive as hell with the fires out. There's been very little to do in the rain, and we're all set to get out of here at the first break in the weather.

Jackie though of the route they might have to take to leave; she and Mark had studied the map over and over again. It would have been possible to fly down as far as some place like Santa Rosa or Petaluma without getting more than a few hundred feet up, by flying out along the shoreline of the Pacific. But it was clear that while the weather might be barely flyable in some spots, it might not be in others, and even if they went as far south as Santa Rosa, they would still have to get up to 2500 feet or so to clear the foothills north of San Francisco bay, and still stay out of the restricted areas. While they'd wanted to fly as much of the spectacular western coast as they could, and had managed a share, it was not going to be much fun if they had to put up with weather like this.

Reading the weather segments of Jackie's ground school materials gave them a possible solution to the problem of where to go. It was clear that much of the bad weather was "upslope", blowing in off the Pacific, and then generated by the Coast Range. If they could get over in the northern San Joquain valley, behind the coast range, then the weather ought to be better. Mark's twice-daily calls to the Flight Service Station in Oakland for weather information had confirmed it. Now, if they could only get a real break in the weather, both here and farther south, one that looked as if it might last for a few hours, then perhaps they could make their escape.

She picked up the pen and continued to write:

We've been wanting to stay close to the plane, in case the weather breaks, and it's all very tiring, after all the good weather we've seen. The weather has been perfect most days, clear back to Louisiana, and if it gets bad it only has for a few hours. We're not prepared to spend days weathered in, and it's getting to us. We've been spending a lot of time in the tent, or in a little place up the road a ways, but it's rather boring.

Jackie smiled. The "little place up the road" was a bar, and she could not imagine what a country-western bar was doing on the northern California coast. It had the advantage of being warm, and inside, out of the rain, but there wasn't much else that could be said for it. If someone could take an axe to that jukebox, it might not even have been a bad sort of place, but the jukebox was very loud and going all the time, all with country-western music that Jackie mostly had never heard of before. One time, she wandered over to the jukebox, willing to drop in a couple of quarters to hear something that was a little more top-40, but the only names she recognized were country-western, like Johnny Cash. There were a lot of names there that she'd never heard of before: Bob Wills, Roy Acuff, Tammy Wynette, Ernest Tubbs, Hank Williams, Lefty Frizell. Johnny Cash she could tolerate, even though she'd heard "Ring of Fire" so many times that she'd gotten thoroughly sick of it, along with others like "Harper Valley PTA." There were a couple that weren't so bad, and she'd laughed the first time she'd heard "If you give me 40 acres then I'll turn this rig around," but it wasn't so funny the fifth or sixth time.

The only song on the jukebox that wasn't country-western was "Horse With No Name," and it was obvious that it had been put on there as a mistake, because she instantly fell in love with it.

The loud jukebox had to be a ploy to sell more beer; get drunk enough and it might deaden the pain of the racket from that terrible music. Unfortunately, Mark and Jackie had agreed that only one of them could drink, since the other had to be sober enough to fly them out of there if the weather should break. It made it hard all the way around, and they only went to the bar when they absolutely couldn't stand the tent any longer, and a couple hours there made the tent look pretty good.

She continued to write:

I haven't been feeling real good the past few days. It's probably the weather that's gotten me down, plus being stiff and sore from sitting and laying in the tent so much . . .

That wasn't the real problem, and Jackie knew it, but there was no graceful way to say that she was having her period, and it was getting to her.

About once in every four or five times, it really made her crampy and miserable and irritable. This was the first time on the trip that she was having a bad one, but she had discovered something else that cut the edge. She remembered Kirsten saying one time that making love with Henry massaged away a lot of the crampiness, and Jackie had given it a try. Between aspirin and having sex four and five times a day taking the edge off the suffering, this bad one was going better than it had any right to, and it was starting to ease up, now.

But there was no way that she was going to tell her father and Sarah of the marvelous way she'd found to relieve menstural cramps. She chewed on the end of her pen and thought for a bit before putting it back to the paper.

. . . and Mark has been good about giving me massages to relieve some of the stiffness, but I think the real cure will be to get out of this place. We came here

because we were told that this town had a really nice July 4 fireworks display, and it was very good, but the weather closed in overnight, and here we are, still.

The fireworks were very nice. The Spearfish Lake Lions Club for years had sponsored a small display out over the lake at home, but it always seemed like it was over with as soon as it got started. This was supposed to be a big one, and it was, although not as big as some of those she had seen on television. They had lots of rockets, and some big mortars, and some of the biggest displays lit up the sign. She had "ooed" and "aaahed" a lot at the gaudy colors in the sky, and at the booms of the big cannon crackers.

It wasn't until the fireworks were over with that she had realized that Mark had been uneasy during the whole affair. She'd asked him about it, and had been told, "I've seen enough fireworks to last me for a while." There was something in the way he said it that made her realize that he was talking about Vietnam, and it gave her the feeling that he'd seen things there he wasn't prepared to talk about, so she didn't ask.

She realized that she should go back to Arroyo Grande and recap some of the things that had happened to them.

I guess it's been a couple of weeks since I wrote to you from Arroyo Grande, and I think I mentioned to you my buying a skirt in a Goodwill store and going to church. It's just a cheap skirt, and I'll keep it in case I need one again, or unless Mark needs a rag to clean the oil off his hands.

It was also a short skirt. She had known it was short when she bought it, but she was looking more for waist size than she was for length, and short skirts were in fashion. However, with her long legs, the skirt was even shorter than she had realized. It really wasn't a "going to church" skirt, more of a "going to party skirt", but she hadn't realized it until she put it on shortly before taking off for church, and there hadn't been a lot of choice.

Fortunately, this was California, and they had chosen a church that happened to not been too uptight. It also couldn't sing to hold a hill of beans; even a gituarist that gave a special presentation was dishwater. She'd been spoiled by the singing at Brother Erasmus' church, and she knew it.

But the embarrassment she felt over the skirt that morning was nothing against the embarrassment she felt that afternoon. They had agreed that since they'd been swimming in the Atlantic and the Gulf, they had to go swimming, so they'd put their swimsuits on under their shorts and t-shirts and hitched a ride to the beach.

It had turned out to be a "clothing-optional" beach, and Jackie had never seen so much bare skin in her life. Under the circumstances, she felt more embarrassed in her bikini than she would have thought, so, along with Mark, she had bitten the bullet and joined the majority.

She had often wondered what it would be like to do something like that; but then, most Spearfish Lake kids had wondered at one time or another how they would have felt if invited to the nudist camp out north of town, so that wasn't so strange. What was strange was that once she'd gotten over the initial embarrassment, she'd discovered that she didn't mind the group nudity. Not that it was something that she'd seek out for its own sake, but if the opportunity or the need arose again, it was good to know that she could handle it. But, that was something else that her father and Sarah didn't need to know.

We went swimming in the Pacific after church, and explored the town, which is kind of a neat little place, although kind of overrun by people out of Los Angeles, out for the weekend. We stayed at Arroyo Grande for a second night, and thought about getting on a bus and going into L.A. to do some sightseeing, but as it turned out, we didn't. After all, we've seen Disney World, Disney Land just seemed like more of the same thing. There were some other things in Los Angeles that we would liked to have seen, but somehow, it just didn't seem like it was worth the expense or the trouble.

It was more than the expense or trouble. Neither of them liked cities very much; Camden was too big a town for their taste. Disneyland was the one thing that could have drawn them, but after the countryside they had seen, the repeat of the cheap thrills of Disney World didn't seem worth the trouble.

They'd been in the plane, heading north from Arroyo Grande, before they really had gotten to talking about it. She had said to Mark that sooner or later they were going to have to go into a city on this trip.

"Why?" he'd asked.

"Because it's there," she had told him. "We want to sample the variety of this country, not just the wild and backcountry places."

"If I had to stop in a city, I would think that San Francisco would be the place to stop," Mark said. I've been there twice, but it was just to the airport, both times. I never even saw the Golden Gate, and figured that I ought to at least do that much. But I never did. Maybe we can stop there."

So, the next morning, we got up, and flew north a long ways to Mariposa-Yosemite airport, and managed to get a ride up to Yosemite National Park. Mark and I had talked about hiking the John Muir Trail from Sequoia to Yosemite National Park, but that's way up there in elevation, and it's longer than we had realized, too long to take all the food we would need. It would have meant three weeks on the trail! That's too much, much too much.

Both of them had been eager to do it, but it was just too much of a trip. It would have probably meant closer to four weeks than three, by the time they counted in side trips, bad weather, and goofing off, and there was no way they were going to be able to pack any four weeks worth of food. Given a little more time for planning, they might have been able to work out some sort of arrangement to pick up prepackaged food along the way, but they hadn't planned that far ahead. And, they hadn't wanted to.

Besides, it was as Mark had said, "There's so much to do in only a few months of summer, it would be kind of a shame to waste four weeks of it when we could be somewhere else, too."

"Maybe if we're still going next summer, we could come back and do it right," she had said. They had agreed that it was something to put on a list for someday. It was hard to think that they might still be traveling like this in another year. She hadn't even mentioned it to Mark, but somehow, this seemed unnatural to her, and there was a gut feeling that it would be coming to an end. Mark had that job that started in a little more than a year, and they might well be traveling until then, but there was obviously going to have to be an end to this trip, sometime.

She thought about that for a moment; the future seemed fuzzy after the trip ended. What would she do then? Not willing to think about it just then, she picked up her pen and continued to write:

There's so much in the way of neat back country in the Sierras that we had a tough time deciding to just limit it to Yosemite; you could spend a summer up there and it still wouldn't be enough. We settled for five days in Yosemite and the high country beyond. One night, at Yosemite, we camped in a camp full of some mountain climbers, that spend their summers climbing some of those sheer, tall cliffs there. Those people are crazy!

They were not only crazy to be climbing those steep cliffs, but they were crazy when they were in camp, too. They had kind of gotten absorbed into a party in the campground, and it was basically a blowout. The smell of marijuana filled the air, and there was a lot of beer around. The climbers were full of crazy antics, horseplay, and showing off, and the party went on much later than either she or Mark had been able to keep up with it.

When they saw some of those same climbers start for some sheer cliff the next morning, she'd been unable to believe it. How could they take on something as difficult and dangerous as that with hangovers like they must have, and virtually no sleep, to boot?

They stood and watched a while. It was clear that climbing the huge wall was not going to be a fast process. "Have you ever wanted to try that?" she'd asked Mark.

"I like flying," Mark said. "But any flight from there would have to be a pretty short one. Jumping out of a plane with a parachute in the army was bad enough, but those jokers don't even have chutes."

"I didn't know you'd done parachute jumping," she'd said.

"I've made eleven jumps," Mark said. "Except for the jump pay, that was eleven too many."

Jackie remembered the scene some more. It had been fun, although the floor of Yosemite had been crowded, and they packed their packs, and went to confer with a ranger, about where they could go in the back country. They told him where they had spent the night. "You stayed at Camp Four?" he said. "I don't know how those guys do that. Some of them are up here from April through October living like that. God knows what they do to make a living."

How to write about the back country in Yosemite? It was tough. Perhaps the best thing to do was just put the pen to the paper and try:

The back country of Yosemite is very pretty, but it's also very full of people, and we're just beginning to get into the height of the summer season. It was so difficult, after being used to being almost alone in the back country every other time we've gone backpacking. Virtually every campground we stayed at was full!

While the high country in Yosemite and beyond had been great, she couldn't believe the people! It was almost wall to wall people up there. Several times, she and Mark had reminded themselves of their little trip up into the Sangre de Christos from the airfield at Angel Fire, and how they hadn't seen another soul, and how peaceful and quiet it had been. Not that some of the people that they met weren't pretty interesting people, but in a crowd scene like that, it was difficult to get to know anybody. About all anyone wanted to talk about was the mechanics of backpacking, the gear, where they'd hiked, where there might be a free campsite, and after a while that got tiring.

"This isn't wild country," Mark had said. "This is a city without the flush toilets."

Still, we met some neat people at virtually every campsite, and a lot of people that we met envied us our trip, when we told them about it. We did get down the John Muir trail as far as Thousand Islands Lake and Devil's Postpile National Monument, but that involved a little getting rides to intermediate trailheads, and then managing to get more rides back to the plane.

She hadn't talked much to her father and Sarah about how dependent on hitchhiking they were on getting rides on the ground. Sometimes, they had to pass up going to some interesting place on the ground, just because it was too far to walk. That put a limit on their traveling, although on occasion they had been able to borrow a car for a little while, like to go to lunch at an airport, or something. They never went near an airport that was big enough to have rental cars, and they were expensive, but a car would have been nice to have.

When she was with Mark, she supposed that hitchiking was all right, but there was no way she was going to do it by herself.

Thinking back, it was amazing that she had taken a ride from Roger and Kathy, back there in Titusville, although that had worked out all right.

It had taken hours to get a ride from Devil's Postpile back to Toulumene Meadows, and then on up over the pass and down into Yosemite. It had eaten up most of a very frustrating day, and they were tired when they got back to the airport. It was as far as they had gotten from Rocinante on the trip, but there just weren't any alternatives when it came to airports. It made them realize that they were going to have to be more careful about picking their adventures when ground transportation was involved.

Still, it had been pretty countryside, and although she liked the hiking, somehow she couldn't see walking the length of that trail. She remembered how she had envied the people riding horses up the trail, and remembered how when she was a little younger, she would have loved to have had a horse. She'd only been on a horse a couple of times, and it had been fun and exciting. She imagined what a horse trip up that trail would have been like, and wrote:

It would be fun to do a horse-pack trip through this area; there seems to be a lot of horse-packing here.

Once we finally got back to the plane, we were glad to see it. We flew north up along the western slopes of the Sierras, partly just to sightsee, but partly to avoid all of the military airfields and commercial air traffic in the San Francisco-Sacremento area. Then, we turned west and flew around San Francisco bay to a little airport at Novato, which is just north of San Francisco. That was last Saturday afternoon when we got there. We managed to get a bus across the Golden Gate Bridge into San Francisco -- the first really big city we've been in on this trip. We spent some time sightseeing, then got a room at a Holiday Inn. Neither Mark or I had had a real bath or shower since Durango, just sponge baths and swimming, and I guess we must have smelled and looked like a couple of dirty hippies, so it was real good to clean up and feel human again.

There were a lot of hippies running around San Francisco, and Jackie had resented being mistaken for one. She didn't mind an occasional beer, but seeing life as "groovy" through a drugged-up haze and saying "far out" to everything didn't seem all that great.

Face it, she thought, you're a country girl, and you like it like that. Maybe with the life she and Mark were leading that summer, it would have been possible to mistake her for a hippie, but she knew Mark didn't intend to make a life of living like that, and she surely didn't either.

That had kind of taken the edge off of San Francisco, and that wasn't all that had happened:

We went and saw some of the sights, and had a dinner in Chinatown. I'm not too sure what it was, but I wouldn't want to be a stray dog running loose in that neighborhood!

The Chinese dinner had been incomprehensible and she hadn't cared for it. While they had been in the restaurant, Mark had talked with the waitress in Chinese, just a few phrases, before they broke out into English. She asked Mark where he had learned Chinese, and he told her that he only knew a few phrases, like "How are you," and "Where's the john?" She knew that he was fairly good with languages, and decided he must have picked it up in Vietnam, or someplace. She'd been living with Mark for so long, she thought she knew him pretty well, but it had proven that he was still capable of surprising her.

Afterwards, they had gone up to the North Beach district, which was supposed to have some pretty good night spots, and they were kind of hoping for a night on the town. One place they went into had proven to be a topless joint, and Jackie could not imagine when men saw in women running around topless. There was one girl in there that was fairly slender, but she had enormous breasts, obviously with the help of some plastic surgery. It looked like she was carrying a couple of droopy basketballs around on her chest, and Jackie could not imagine what it must have been like to have to herd around those enormous boobs. She shook her head remembering it; the things women go to for men! That was another thing she decided that she'd rather not tell her father and Sarah about, so she just kind of skimmed over it:

We checked out some other sights around San Francisco, and the next morning, we decided that we had played tourist too much, so we got another bus back across the Golden Gate Bridge -- that's quite a view, too -- and got back to the plane. One of the places we had wanted to visit was Point Reyes, which is supposed to be really pretty, but it was just too far without a car, and getting rides is always a pretty iffy proposition, We'd about blown our luck on getting rides up in Yosemite. It would be nice to explore this place for a summer with a car, though.

They had really wanted to explore Point Reyes, or at least, Mark had. It had the reputation of being extremely pretty, and not well visited, but even on the July 4 weekend, it seemed like it would have been as crowded as Yosemite had been, and that took some of the edge off.

They had talked about doing some more exploring with a car. They kicked around the idea of seeing if they could find some sort of a fifty-dollar clunker like

Mark had driven around Spearfish Lake, and just taking off with it for a week or two. But, on looking into it, they realized that with license and inspection and all the other stuff, it was a little steep for a car that they probably couldn't trust as far as they could throw a fit. Besides, there was an unspoken feeling that it was a little unfaithful to Rocinante.

The best they had come up with was a decision to do the trip with a car if they came back in another year, but that was a big if.

They were still kicking it around in the airport office in Novato when they heard someone talking about the fireworks in Mendocino, and decided that coming here had potential. Besides, it was someplace to go that they could fly to.

She thought for a minute, then added:

It was at the airport in Novato where we heard about the fireworks in Mendocino. Since we had wanted to fly up the coast -- it has the reputation of being really pretty -- we decided that Mendocino would make a really good place for a night stop. That was a mistake. We're still here.

Dad, Sarah, it would be real easy to spend a summer or even years in California. There's a lot to see, and we barely scratched the surface. I'm sitting here in the plane writing this -- Mark is taking a nap in the tent -- and it seems like a long time since Mark and I finished the wings and left on this trip, but it's only been just about three months. Those wings have carried us a long way so far, and we've seen things I never dreamed I would see. But there's a lot to see yet, so we're having to make a real effort to press on and not blow a lot more time in California.

Jackie leaned back and thought about it. Yes, there was a lot to see in California, but that was the case anywhere. Like she had written, she had seen things on this trip that she had never expected to see in her life. Some of the people they had met had been people she would have never met, if she'd chickened out and stayed in Spearfish Lake, like her fears had told her to do. She thought back over some of the experiences and the people.

Some of the places stood out, and the places that most easily came to mind often weren't the big tourist attractions, but just places that where people lived and worked, places like Waverly and Twillingate and Leadville. There were exceptions, of course, like Titusville and Yosemite, but all of a sudden she realized that the best memories came when they weren't acting like tourists.

It would be nice to have another Waverly or Twillingate experience, she realized. But, those weren't the things that they could plan; they just happened, and not just because they were automatically in a place for a few days.

She realized that she was running out of things to say, and there was still some business to attend to:

It's only been a couple of weeks or so since we got mail from you at Palomar. I guess what we'll have to do is press on for a few days, and then try to select some place where we'll be in a few days, then call you and let you know about it. It worked well last time, but I'll have to talk to Mark to see what he thinks. Getting mail works better when we're in a place for a while, but it's not often that we know we're going to be in a place for a few days, and the next time that we're fairly sure about is still a couple of months away. But, it would not be surprising if we stopped some place for a while. We've seen a lot of interesting sights while we've been moving every day, but we have better luck at meeting and getting to know interesting people when we're in the same place for a few days. That is, up until this place, anyway.

What else to add? She stared at what she had written, and decided that what she'd done added up to a pretty good letter. Her hand was a little tired from the writing, but maybe she could go ahead and do the letter to Roger and Kathy after all. It wouldn't have to be as big a letter; only a couple of pages would do.

She leaned back in the seat, to try and think if there was anything else she should add to the letter in closing. She looked out through the rain-spotted plexiglass of Rocinante's windshield, and all of a sudden realized that it wasn't raining, and the sky seemed a little lighter than before.

Maybe this was the break in the weather they had been praying for. She thought about it for a minute, then started to open the door to go and wake up Mark, so they could go and make a call to check the weather.

Only then did she remember her letter, and quickly scribbled:

The sky looks like it's breaking up a little, and maybe that will mean we can get out of here. I'm going to wrap this up, now.
Love,
Jackie

6.

It seemed strange to be back in the midwest again, after almost three months in the southwest and the west. The country below them was filled with fields and woods and lakes, rather than mountains and valleys and deserts. They'd made a big day of flying eastward, leaving the high plains in the early morning, crossing the corn belt, then watched the Mississippi spread beneath them, a lot smaller river than they had crossed near Baton Rouge what seemed like a lifetime before.

"You want to dig out the logbook?" Mark asked. "I seem to remember that Roger and Kathy's place was somewhere east of Arvada Center, but I don't remember for sure."

Jackie twisted around in her seat, and dug out the blue notebook. There was the note she'd written back in April at the Titusville airport: "5 mi E of Arvada Center. Barn with 'Griswold'." She read it to Mark, and commented, "Ought to be easy enough to find. Do you think there'll be a place where we can land?"

"It's a farm," Mark shrugged, "They ought to have a pasture or a hayfield or something."

"It'll be good to see them again," Jackie said, leafing through the pages of the logbook. They'd made a lot of stops since they'd left Geyser and the K-Bar Ranch. Yellowstone, Craters of the Moon, Bonneville, Wendover, Rock Springs, more than a week at Waverly again. At Waverly, they'd begun to realize that they would have to get a move on if they were going to go to Stellafane, so as soon as Jack had signed off Jackie's private pilot license and Fred had signed off her glider certificate, they'd gotten a move on, just this morning.

Before they'd said goodbye to Cumulus for the last time, Mark had asked, "You're sure you don't want to take a swing by Spearfish Lake? It's only about three hundred miles out of the way. We could drop in and see the folks, and not have to worry about a mail drop."

"We just got mail," Jackie said. "Besides, we agreed that we wouldn't go back to Spearfish Lake until the trip was over."

"Fine with me," Mark said. "I'd just as soon go way south of Chicago. If we went to Spearfish Lake, we'd be just as far ahead to go through Michigan to stay out of the Chicago area."

They were halfway across Nebraska before the idea of dropping in on the Griswolds had come to them. "It'll mean we'll have to go out of our way to the south to get around Chicago," Jackie said, "But, we've still got a few days to spare before Stellafane. I'd sure like to see how Kathy's doing, though."

They were back to the familiar navigation of the midwest, with the fence rows and roads marking out the directions of north and south and east and west. Mark was flying this leg from the left seat, and he got down low over the little town of Arvada Center, and picked out the road leading to the east, and started counting off the well-marked miles of the section roads as they passed under them. "There's four miles," he said. "Start looking for the barn."

Sure enough, about a minute late, they could see a large barn, with the word "GRISWOLD" worked into the shingles. In front of the barn was a large, old wooden farmhouse; next to the old farmhouse was a smaller, newer one, made of brick. Mark stood Rocinante on it's wing, and circled the house and barn a couple of times. Below them, they could see the door of the large farmhouse open, and someone short and wide and blonde came outside, with a small child following, and both of the people waved to them.

"That looks like Kathy," Jackie said. "I wonder whose kid that is with her."

"I don't know," Mark said, "but there's a nice field across the road," he said, setting the Cessna up for a landing. A minute later, Rocinante's wheels skimmed the wheat stubble as Mark set the plane down, and taxied up to the edge of the field across from the house.

Rocinante's propeller had hardly stopped turning before Kathy Griswold and a little girl were crossing the road to meet them. "I see you got our letter," Kathy called. "We figured we'd see you sometime."

"Where's Roger?" Jackie asked.

"Out with the baler," Kathy said. "I'd be out helping him, but I'm getting a little big for that," she added, patting her swollen belly. "Besides, I have to sit with Judith, here." She pointed at the little girl that was trying to hide herself behind her back. She continued, "He ought to be done for the day, pretty soon. Can you guys stay for dinner, or spend the night?"

"If you don't mind having us," Mark said.

"Not at all," the short blonde said. "We've been looking forward to seeing you again, and there's plenty of spare room, and plenty of hot water if you want showers."

"You don't know how good a shower would feel," Jackie said. "I'm ashamed to tell you how long it's been since we've had a shot at an honest-to-pete bath, not just washing up in a stream or a reservoir."

The blonde smiled, "Well, you're sure welcome to use ours."

"It sounds good," Mark admitted. "But, if we're going to stay the night, we might as well get the plane tied down, first."

They dug the tiedown stakes out from behind Rocinante's seat, the dirt from near-desert Colorado still fresh on them, and twisted them deep into the soft, fertile midwestern wheatfield. As the two swung into their well-practiced routine of tying the Cessna down, Kathy stood back and watched, which Judith warily peeked out from behind her.

Jackie noted how wary the child was. Maybe five or six, she had yet to say anything. Judy went over in front of Kathy, bent down and asked her, "Hi, my name's Jackie. What's your name?"

"Judith," the little girl replied.

"Judith, have you ever been flying?" Jackie asked.

Wordlessly, the little girl shook her head.

"Our plane's name is Rocinante," Jackie said. "Do you think you'd like to fly in it?"

Judith shook her head again, and tried to hide behind Kathy again.

"Would you like to sit in the plane?" Kathy asked, twisting around to look at the little girl, who just shook her head again.

Jackie shrugged, and Kathy looked back up and said, "Probably better not push her. Her mother keeps a pretty close thumb on her, and probably wouldn't appreciate you taking her flying, anyway."

"No problem," Jackie agreed. "Let us get some clean clothes out of the back, and we'll be ready."

An hour later, showered and feeling considerably fresher, Mark and Jackie and Kathy sat out in the shade of the back porch of the old farmhouse, watching Judith swing in the swing and run around the yard, carrying one of the barn kittens.

"Cute kid, but I wonder where she gets all that energy," Mark commented, watching her chase a kitten that had escaped from her grasp.

"It makes me wonder," Kathy said, "How I'm going to be able to keep up with one or more like that."

"I don't know how I could do it," Jackie said.

Just then, they could hear the roaring of a large tractor turning into the driveway. "That sounds like the Deere," Kathy said. "If they brought it, they must be done with baling for the day."

Sure enough, a large, green tractor pulled into the yard, pulling a baler and a load of hay bales, followed by a smaller, red tractor, pulling a hay wagon. With practiced ease, the green tractor stopped the hay wagon right next to an elevator leading up to the upper stories of the barn. The cab door opened, and Roger stepped out. "It is you guys," he shouted across the barnyard. "I saw the plane, and figured it must be you."

Mark and Jackie and Kathy got up and walked out to the tractor, as the red tractor stopped and two teenage boys got off of it and headed for the barn. "I'm looking forward to hearing all about what you've been up to," Roger said, "But we need to get these wagons unloaded first. Are you guys staying for supper?"

"I thought we'd have steaks, if you'd light off the grill," Kathy said.

"Sounds fine to me," Roger said. "You guys sure are looking good."

"Hey, Mr. Griswold," a young male voice sounded from the barn. "We gotta be gettin' home."

"O.K., Merle, just a minute," Roger called, then turned back to the waiting threesome. "Guess I'd better get on it."

"Anything I can do to help?" Mark offered.

"There's some leather gloves on the back of the tractor," Roger said. "Once I get a few bales off, you can hand them to me. Dad and Charlie had to take off and go milk and do chores."

"Come on, Jackie," Kathy said. "Let's collect Judith and go get started on supper."

By the time that Mark and Roger got the two hay wagons unloaded, any benefit that Mark's shower might have had was gone. He was hot and sweaty and tired, and wondered how bad it must have been for the boys, up in the hayloft. Oh, well, he thought, he could have another shower; it wasn't like it was going to be weeks before he had the chance again.

Finally, Roger shut off the elevator, and called to the boys, "All right, that's it."

In a minute, the two appeared, hot and sweaty, too. "Same time tomorrow?" the older of the two asked.

"Yeah, we've still got three days work here," Roger told them.

"Well, we'll see ya tomorrow," one of the boys said, as both clambered up onto the red tractor.

"Hey, Tom, I get to drive, this time," the younger one said.

"O.K., Merle, O.K.," the older one said as the younger one slipped into the seat and started the tractor.

Roger and Mark stood watching as the tractor drove out of the yard. "They're good kids," Roger commented. "Throwing hay bales around is a man's work, but they hung in there pretty good. Gets to be haying time, especially after school starts, and you got to take what help you can get. They were only able to work a couple hours after school, but I'm glad they could."

"Anything Jackie and I can do to help?" Mark asked. "We spent a couple weeks working on a cattle roundup, so I guess a little farm work wouldn't kill us."

"If you could stay around a couple of days and pitch in, it'd be welcome," Roger said. "We've got good weather right now, and I need to get this hay done while it holds."

"Looking at the weather forecasts we looked at earlier, you've got two, maybe three days," Mark said. "I guess we could help. We've got to be in Vermont the middle of next week, but we've got some time to spare."

"If you can stay a few days, I'd really appreciate it," Roger said. "Dad and Charlie are milking, and with school back in session, that's really leaving us shorthanded. Let's go get cleaned up, and then you can tell me all about what you've been up to."

The smell of steaks grilling on the back porch half an hour later filled the air. By then, Judith's mother had come and picked her up, and the four sat around in the lawn chairs, talking. "What was this you said about working on a cattle roundup?" Roger asked.

"That's quite a story," Mark said. "We were flying out across Montana, east of Great Falls. We'd stopped for the night, out on the grasslands in the middle of nowhere, and camped for the night. The next morning, we got up, and decided to find someplace to have a real breakfast. We were flying along this county highway, and there, out in the middle of nowhere, was this little restaurant with an airstrip along side of it, so naturally, we landed."

"Let me tell you, they really put on a breakfast," Jackie added.

"So anyway, we go inside," Mark explained, "And while we were sitting there, eating, we heard this guy over in the next booth bitching up a storm. Seems he had this Super Cub, with a pilot, and the pilot had nosed it over and screwed it up. 'Now I've got roundup starting tomorrow,'" the guy said, "'And I've got no plane and I canned that asshole, so no pilot, either.'"

Jackie smiled at the memory, as Mark continued, "Well, that got me curious, so I turned around and asked him what he needed a plane and a pilot for. It seems that the cattle tend to wander around maybe two or three hundred square miles, and they all have to be hunted down and driven to a central location, and it didn't take us long to make the connection."

Jackie shook her head. "It really wasn't what I'd imagined. It's not like what you see on TV. There really wasn't much I could do, except fly with Mark, now and then, but he hardly ever stayed on the ground."

"We put on three oil changes in two weeks," Mark said, "And I don't think I ever got more than five hundred feet above the ground, but I'll tell you that old guy knew every blade of grass out there. He could smell cattle hiding up some gully, and then we'd have to fly around and find someone to collect them. There weren't a lot of horses, mostly jeeps and pickup trucks."

"What did you do when Mark was out flying?" Kathy asked Jackie.

"Mostly I stayed around the camp. They gave me a clipboard and told me to keep records, and I just noted stuff down on a form, and never did get to understand most of it. I did get to ride a horse a little bit. That was something I'd never done before."

"Those guys put on a feed in camp," Mark said. "It was all good eating, but mostly I was too tired to enjoy it."

Mark and Jackie were at the roundup long enough to call for a mail drop at the nearest town, and one day they flew into town and got their mail. There were several letters and a box of cookies from Walt and Sarah, and an official letter in a large envelope from the U.S. Coast Guard. "You don't suppose this is what I think it is?" Mark had asked Jackie.

"Open it and see," she'd said.

Chief Daughterty, back on Catalina, had been right: it was a commendation for their role in the rescue of the people from their overturned boat. Included in the envelope was a letter from the couple, whose name turned out to be Pittenger.

They'd been heading from LaJolla up to Catalina in their open runabout two days before Mark and Jackie found them. It was a trip they had often made before, but this time, something went wrong with the engine. They'd tried for hours to get it running, without success, and sometime in the first night, a wave had turned the boat over. They tried repeated times to turn it back over, but never could, and spent the rest of the night hanging onto the boat as best as they could.

When the next day came, they tried again to get the boat upright. The weight of the outboard was like a keel, keeping the nose of the boat in the air, and they never could get it upright. While Paul, the husband, made dive after dive to try to get the motor free to jettison it, so perhaps they could get the boat upright, Wendy Pittinger hung on as best she could. He couldn't get the motor free -- he'd needed a screwdriver, and none was to be found in the overturned boat -- and they spent the rest of the day, and most of the night, hoping someone would come by, and no one did.

With the dawning of the third day, they were very cold and tired, and knew they couldn't last much longer. Once or twice, boats or planes went by in the distance, but they never could get their attention. When Mark and Jackie had appeared overhead, they thought at first it was a hallucination, but "The longer you stayed there, the more we knew it must be real."

Paul knew that the plane circling them was a land plane, and there was no way that it could pick them up, but it was some time before they realized that the people watching over them from above must have radioed for help. They were never aware of the Coast Guard 31-footer until it was almost on top of them, and neither had the strength to climb the boarding ladder.

"I don't know what put you right overhead, but I'm thankful you were there," Wendy Pittinger had written. "We couldn't have held out much longer. May God watch over you, the way you watched over us."

Between them, Mark and Jackie told Roger and Kathy the whole story. "It was such a chain of circumstances, that it's bothered us a lot," Mark said. "Was it really a miracle, or just a chain of circumstances?"

Jackie nodded. "I mean, if it was a miracle, it feels so strange to have been a part of it."

"It sounds like a miracle to me," Roger said.

"It does to me, too," Mark admitted. "I'm just not too sure how much I believe in miracles." He moved to cut off the discussion; somehow, it had gotten too personal: "Anyway, after we left the K-Bar and the roundup, we decided to head on to Yellowstone."

As they ate dinner, Mark and Jackie told the Griswolds of the hike they made through Yellowstone Park, where they'd been headed months before, when they'd gotten sidetracked at Waverly. From Yellowstone, they'd flown southward, to Provo, mostly because Mark wanted to fly over the Great Salt Lake. They'd gotten hold of a paper there, and discovered that the Bonneville National Speed Trials were on, out on the Bonneville Salt Flats. "I'd read so much about Bonneville in the hot rod magazines when I was a kid, I knew I wanted to see the place for real," he explained.

They'd flown out to the huge white expanse of the salt flats, and spent a couple of days watching the cars, talking with the drivers and mechanics. "It was kind of like being with astronomy people," Mark explained. "A bunch of people that are really enthusiasts about something, and it really turned out to be a great time.

When they'd left Bonneville, they'd flown a few miles down to the abandoned Wendover Air Force Base, mostly because Mark wanted to gas up and hose the salt off of Rocinante. "It was just a big old airport, and it didn't mean anything special to me," Jackie said, "But Mark said that it was as if the place was haunted. I asked him why, and he asked if I'd ever heard of the 509th Bomb Group. That didn't mean anything to me, of course."

"Me either," Kathy said.

Roger had been in the Air Force, so it meant something to him, but he just nodded his head and stayed quiet. "I could almost hear B-29s warming up there, taking off there, back in 1945," Mark said. "That's where the 509th trained, before they went out to the Pacific, and Hiroshima and Nagasaki."

"Yeah," Roger said slowly. "I think I can see what you mean."

From Wendover, two weeks earlier, they took a swing through southern Utah, down to Canyonlands, then back north to Provo, and from there, they followed the old route of the Overland Trail eastward, until they were in eastern Wyoming. "We were so close, that we decided to stop off and see our friends at the gliderport in Fort Collins," Jackie explained.

"The guy I'd filled in for before -- you remember, we wrote and told you about him," Mark said, "He wanted to take off to Iowa and see his dad for a few days, so I filled in for him again. While we were there, we got the guy who had soloed Jackie last spring to run her the rest of the way through her ticket."

It had involved several hours of solo cross-country flying, plus a trip down to Denver to get her written examination. Just the day before, Jack Daniels had her fly over to an examiner in Greeley, where she had her license signed off.

"I tell you," Jackie explained, "That's something that I never thought that I'd have happen to me, but then, there have been a lot of things on this trip that I never thought would have happened to me, even six months ago."

Six months ago, she thought with the statement, she hadn't even met Mark! A lot had happened in that time, things that she had never dreamed would happened to her.

The supper had long been finished, and the dishes washed before Mark and Jackie were about yarned out, telling about things that had happened to them. "You guys have been having quite a trip," Kathy said as they watched the deepening twilight from the porch. "When we left you, down there in Florida, we were wondering about the things you'd see and do, and I'm glad you've been having such a great time."

"It's hard to see summer come to an end," Mark admitted. "Pretty soon, it's going to be too cold for camping under the wing, unless we're way down south."

"I don't know about you," Roger said, "But Kathy and I have got to be turning in. We've got to do chores and milk in the morning."

"Anything we can do to help?" Jackie offered.

"There's not much you can do to help, not without knowing what's happening," Roger said, "But you can come and watch."

It was the first time Mark and Jackie had slept in a bed since a cold, windy, rainy night in Idaho before they'd stopped at the K-Bar, and the first time they'd ever slept together in a bed in a home, and it seemed strange. "I think we'd better just sleep," Jackie said, the strangeness getting to her, and Mark agreed readily. It had been a long day, with many hours in the air followed by a full evening, and both were asleep within minutes.

It was past the onset of astronomical twilight, but still well before dawn when Roger came to wake them. Mark and Jackie had gotten used to waking up early at the K-Bar, so it wasn't any trick to get around. There was hot coffee waiting in the kitchen; they each poured themselves a cup, and Kathy said, "We'll have breakfast when we get done."

"Do all your days start this early?" Jackie asked as they headed for the barn.

"Usually Kathy and I milk in the evening, and then the next morning, then Dad and Charlie milk in the evening and the next morning," Roger explained. "But we have to mess around with the schedule a little, so Charlie can have a day off. We have to pay him, so he gets a break, but that means that a couple of times a week we have to milk three times straight."

"That does get to be tiring," Kathy said, "But I grew up on a dairy farm, so I'm used to it."

"Kathy's not going to be able to help much longer, so we're messing around with the schedule a little. In another couple of weeks, Merle Watson -- that's the kid you met yesterday -- is going to help either Dad or me with milking each morning before he goes to school."

"It's going to seem strange, not milking," Kathy said, "But I suppose I'll make up for it with having to get up in the middle of the night."

The smell of raw, warm milk hung heavy in the milking parlor. While Mark and Jackie mostly sat back and watched, Roger and Kathy swung into a well-practiced routine. The cows didn't take much leading; they were used to the process, and about all Roger had to do to get the first group up to the milking stands was to open the parlor door. The process was highly automatic, and sterile, filled with the noise of pumps and machinery. "I kind of had this vision of pulling a stool up alongside a cow," Jackie said. "It's not like that at all."

"This isn't a small operation," Mark said. "I'll bet there's a hundred thousand dollars worth of equipment here in this room."

The milking was a slow process, taking a couple of hours to complete, and Roger and Kathy were in constant motion, keeping things moving. Very little talking went on; the noise level was high enough that it discouraged talking, anyway.

After a while, Jackie went back up to the house, and brought the coffeepot out to replenish everybody's supply. There came a minute when both Roger and Kathy didn't have anything to do, and came over to talk for a minute. "I see what you mean that there's not much we could do," Mark said. "You two have this down to a science."

"It takes a while to get the teamwork down," Roger said, "But we've had a few months to practice. It's going to get worse, just as soon as the hay gets in. We're buying out the Sorensen's dairy herd, up the road, and it's going to take another hour a day. Running a dairy herd like this is such a big job that it takes a lot of investment, and not everybody can do it. It just gets worse and worse, the stuff you have to have to put out a quality product."

"Are you going to be much longer?" Jackie asked.

"About an hour," Roger said.

"Why don't I go up to the kitchen and get started on breakfast in about half an hour?"

"Sounds good," Kathy said. "There's bacon and eggs in the refrigerator, and potatoes in the cabinet next to the sink. We're going to want a big breakfast."

"I figured that," Jackie replied. "Especially if you start the day like this."

Mark went with Jackie up to the kitchen. While Jackie started breakfast, Mark poured another cup of coffee, and commented, "That's a lot of hard work they do, and the day is just getting started."

Jackie nodded, "I don't think I'd care to be a farm wife. She's what? Six months pregnant? Something like that, and still going like that."

"Well, she's a farm girl, and brought up to it, I guess," Mark said. "I tell you what, though; it makes working on phones seem so darn much easier. I mean, I've had trouble coming to grips with the thought that a year from now, I'm going to be a phone man for the rest of my life, but how would you like to have to face a life like that?"

"I wish I knew what I was going to be doing a year from now," Jackie said. "For that matter, what we're going to be doing."

Mark could see that this was going to head off into another "Do we want to go back to Spearfish Lake?" discussion, and he didn't really want to get into that, right then. "I think we can knock running a dairy farm off of the list," he said.

Breakfast was just getting ready as Roger and Kathy arrived, followed not long after by George, Roger's father, and Charlie, the hired hand. The newcomers had a cup of coffee, while they worked out what they were going to do for the day.

It turned out to be a busy day. With a full crew, Roger and George spent the day running the baler, and stacking hay wagons full; and Kathy spent most of her day in a pickup truck, bringing loaded hay wagons up to the barn, and empties back out to the field. Jackie found herself unloading the hay wagons onto the elevator, and she discovered that it wasn't that bad a job to haul the heavy bales off the wagon and onto the elevator. Charlie and Mark had the worst job, stacking hay in the barn. It got very hot and sweaty very early, and it seemed as if the bales never stopped coming. Both Mark and Jackie's muscles ached by the time everybody broke for lunch.

It was even hotter in the afternoon, and Mark thought he was going to die, up in the hayloft. Fortunately, the two boys from the day before showed up to relieve Mark and Charlie, but it was hardly a respite for Mark; he went out to the field to stack hay on the wagons as it came off of the baler, while Roger drove the tractor and baler up and down the hayfields, so George and Charlie could set to the evening milking.

Finally, the time came when Roger drove the tractor and baler back up to the barn, with Mark riding on top of the pile of hay for the last wagon of the day. In short order, that load was stacked in the hayloft.

"Good God," Mark said to Roger and Kathy and Jackie as he saw the load going up the elevator, thirteen hours after the morning milking had started, "Is every day like this around here?"

Roger shook his head. "Not every day," Roger admitted. "It's probably worst when we're haying like this, and we get three cuttings a year. Each cutting takes us about a week to get done, and there isn't any other way to do it but go ahead and do it."

"I guess I'm just not cut out for this," Mark said. "I thought I was going to die."

"Well, we got a lot done today," Roger said. "More than I expected. We ought to be able to wrap this up tomorrow. I'm sure glad you guys volunteered to help us out. What do you say if we were to go jump in the lake and cool off, then have supper at the cafe?"

"Fine with me," Kathy said. "Somehow, I don't feel like cooking tonight."

Kathy turned out to be far past the bikini she had worn on the beach at Titusville the spring before, but within a few minutes, all of the rest of them were dressed much as they had been in Florida, and were splashing around in the lake a few miles away from the Griswold farm.

After a while, the splashing around in the lake cooled Roger and Mark off, and they sat down on the little scrub of beach, next to Kathy and Jackie. "Won't be much more swimming this year," Roger commented. "It seems kind of sad to see summer come to and end."

"Do things slow down much for you when winter comes?" Jackie asked.

"It slows down some, but there's still a lot to do every day," Roger replied. "It feels good to have busy days like this."

"I know," Mark reflected. "It seems to me that we've been happiest on this trip when we have things to do. When we don't have anything much going on, then things get dull."

"I've learned that, too," Jackie said. "The traveling is fun, and we've got to see a lot of things, but I guess I've learned that I'm not much for sitting around, not doing much of anything, either."

"You two have had a heck of a trip," Kathy commented. "I guess I'm just getting used to being a farm wife. Back last spring, I just envied you so much when we had to come back here and buckle down. All the things you've seen and done, the experiences you've had, though! That's been the trip of a lifetime! Are you guys planning on staying with us for another few days?"

"I guess so," Mark said. "I guess we're willing to stick around and pitch in as long as you need us to. Have you got something in mind?"

"Well," Kathy admitted, "I'd sort of like you to come to church with us Sunday."

"We haven't been to church since Arroyo Grande," Jackie said. "I supposed we ought to."

"We'd love to have you," Roger said. "I'd like you to testify about your experience with finding that couple in that boat off Catalina."

Mark shrugged. "I don't know that there was that much to testify about. We were just flying overhead, and there they were."

"You said that there was that long chain of circumstances that seemed like it was a miracle," Kathy said.

Mark shook his head. "I said it seemed like a miracle. I don't know that it was a miracle."

"It sounds like one to me," Roger said.

"Like I say," Mark protested. "I don't know. I don't know what to think."

Mark and Jackie agreed to go to church with the Griswolds, but decided they'd have to think about whether they wanted to talk about the Pittingers. The conversation wound off in other directions, and it was late that night before Mark and Jackie could share a discussion about it, while they lay quietly awake in bed.

"I don't suppose it can hurt," Jackie whispered.

"Well, I just hate to stand up and make a damn fool of myself, if I don't understand what happened, myself," Mark said. "I like Roger and Kathy a lot, and I don't mind going to church with them, but that just seems like reaching a little."

"I like Roger and Kathy, too," Jackie said, feeling comfortable with the touch of Mark's warm hand on her bare breast. "If something like that happened to them, they wouldn't be shy about talking about it in church."

"They were brought up with it," Mark replied, massaging the softness he held in his hand. "I have to admit, I have to envy the comfort they have with their beliefs."

"Yeah, even though they sort of had to get married in a hurry, it seems to be working out pretty well for them," she said. "I kind of envy them for just having settled down into a regular existance. They're happy with each other."

"I just hope we can stay as happy with each other as they are," Mark commented.

"Do you want to do what I think we want to do?" Jackie said.

"Go to church with them? I guess so," Mark said.

"I didn't mean that," Jackie said, rolling her nude body over so she could kiss him.

"We'd better try to be quiet," Mark whispered. "These springs squeak."

7.

There was no point in wearing themselves out after their busy week at the Griswold farm, so the first night out, they made a night stop at a small grass airport near Elmira, New York, and the next day flew on eastward to Springfield, Vermont.

After the summer that they had spent flying around in the Rockies and the Sierras and the Cascades, the mountains of New York and Pennsylvania and Vermont seemed hardly more than hills to look down on. But they were green hills, green with the late summer and the onset of an early fall, and they only made Mark and Jackie realize how much they had missed green in all of the browns of the high mountain west. How lush the countryside seemed, after the desolate and empty lands to the west -- and how full of people the countryside was, too. Where only ten days before, they might go fifty miles between towns, and a hundred miles between airports, now it seemed as if they were hardly ever out of gliding distance of an airport, and never out of sight of a town. It all meant a big change in perspective to them, after the wide-open spaces of the west that they had grown accustomed to in the past few months.

The clock was winding down on summer for them, by now; quite a memorable summer indeed. Ever since May, when they'd left the Texas Star Party, the only date they'd had in mind that they had possibly wanted to keep was the September 15 start of the Stellafane star party in Springfield, Vermont. Stellafane, far and away the oldest of the big events for amateur astronomers, was something that Mark had dreamed of attending for ten years and more, ever since he'd gotten interested in astronomy, and this was the best opportunity he'd ever had.

Properly called the "Springfield Amateur Telescope Maker's Convention," Stellafane was known by the name of the place where the meeting was held, at the observing site of the tiny Springfield Telescope Maker's association, where there was a really odd "turret" telescope, a real one of a kind thing, and a little gingerbread house once called "Stellar Fane" by Russell W. Porter, the man who had built it half a century before. Porter was revered among amateur telescope makers like Mark as being the man who started the whole idea of amateur telescope making. Before his death, not too many years before, Porter had moved on to greater things -- like designing the 200-inch telescope on Mt. Palomar that Mark and Jackie had visited back in June.

The flavor of the five-day event was much different than the Texas Star Party had been, partly due to the tradition of the affair, but partly due to the vastly different setting. Vermont seemed more like home to Mark and Jackie than Texas had been, what with the green of the trees and the lushness of the grass; unfortunately, it also had the same moisture-laden skies as they were familiar with back home, and not the bell-clear air and wide-open spaces of west Texas, that made the stars seem so close that you could almost reach out and touch them.

Perhaps more importantly, where the Texas Star Party had been an observer's convention, where the focus was on looking at the sky, Stellafane was more of a telescope maker's convention, where the latest creations of the telescope hobbiests were to be seen and admired.

Mark was a little surprised to not see their friend John from the Texas Star Party at Stellafane, for the size of his 24-inch telescope would have guaranteed long lines. But, Vermont was a long way from California, and perhaps it was too far to come; Mark had gotten the impression that John did not have a lot of money.

It was kind of a shame; Mark did not see any other big telescopes with low-pressure altazimuth mountings. The few really big telescopes that were there were on heavy equatorial mountings, that took a lot of work to set up.

Mark hadn't expected to win any awards for his little 6" f5 telescope that he had made years before; other than its short focal length, it was pretty run of the mill. His real interest was in sampling ideas; it was clear that a bigger telescope was in the works as one of his first priorities to be accomplished after the trip was over, and what it was going to be, and how he was going to do it was one of the ideas he was trying to settle.

Perhaps the biggest attraction for Mark was the line of swap tables to be found. Everything imaginable that might be of use to the amateur telescope builder was for sale there, both new things on the market, and the leavings of telescope maker's scrap boxes. There were books and charts, eyepieces and mirrors. One man had a table full of various kinds of electric motors, all salvaged from various machinery; a telescope thoroughly electrically controlled could be built out of his scrap.

But, it was a man with a table full of glass that drew most of Mark's attention. Laying on the table were a couple of 16 inch diameter pieces of porthole glass. "They're really too thin to make a good mirror," the man said, "Unless you put a really good support underneath them.

Mark wasn't so sure the man was right. John's mirror in the 24-inch telescope had been porthole glass, no thicker than the blanks on sale, for a mirror half again larger, and John's mirror had been plenty stable in its rather simple mount. After going back to the table several times, Mark finally asked what the man wanted for the porthole glass blanks.

"Three hundred," the man said, recognizing someone who had the bug to build a bigger telescope.

"Sorry," Mark said, "That's a little tight on the budget."

"How about two-fifty?"

"Well, let me think about it," Mark said.

He and Jackie walked about thirty or forty feet away. "You really want them, don't you?" she said.

"Yeah, that's just about perfect for what I want to build," Mark said. "He's still too damn high, and I don't want to blow our budget."

"Oh, go ahead and get them," Jackie said. "You'll be kicking yourself if you don't."

Mark walked back over to the table and offered the man a hundred and fifty dollars for the two pieces of glass. They settled on two hundred, and at that, the man helped pack the two pieces of glass in a cardboard box, with plenty of wadded up newspaper for packing.

The package was not light, and Mark's arms grew tired before he got back to their tent. "We're going to have to ship this home," he said. "There's no way we can fit this into Rocinante, along with everything else."

"I realize this is kind of a stupid time to ask this question," Jackie said, "But how do you make a mirror, anyway?"

"It's a big, slow job," Mark said, setting the package down for a minute. "This glass is a whole lot bigger than the little glass in the telescope we have now, and it'll take a lot more time, especially if we make the focal length short enough that we don't have to use a stepladder. You start out by getting a really solid work surface, like a 55-gallon drum filled with water. You take one of the blanks, and start rubbing it back and forth across the other, with grinding compound in between. Because you're working with the edge of the glass on the bottom, the one on the top gets hollowed out very slowly. We really don't have to take a heck of a lot of glass out of the center of the top glass. It'll be maybe a quarter of an inch, or so. I'll have to figure out how much. That's called hogging the mirror out. It's the first step, and maybe the easiest one."

"It gets worse?"

"Yeah," Mark said, remembering the hours he had put in while he'd been in Junior High, working on the six-inch mirror in the telescope that had traveled around the country with them. He found he was getting anxious to start pushing the glass and the grinding compound around on these two pieces of porthole glass. "After that, it really gets boring," he explained. Hogging the mirror out leaves scratches from the grinding compound, and the only way to get rid of those scratches is with finer grinding compound, which leaves smaller scratches, so you have to take even finer compound to get rid of them, and so on, and so on. When you finally get the scratches out, you have the really tricky part. At this point, the mirror is spherical, or at least a segment of a sphere, if you've done everything right. The next step is to take jeweler's rouge and pitch, and polish it out a bit more in the center, to make the mirror parabolic. Now, a parabola is a section of a cone, and it's harder to get. We're talking millionths of an inch here, and we'll have to test it on a special machine, work for a bit, test it again, maybe lots of times. It's a tedious job, at least to do it right."

"How do you get the mirror shiny?"

Mark smiled, and picked up the package again, to move on toward their tent. "That's really the easy part," he told her. "You put it in a box and you ship it to a guy in Chicago, along with a check, and a couple of weeks later, the mailman brings your mirror back, and it's the prettiest thing you ever saw."

"You're really looking forward to that time, aren't you?" she asked, following him along.

"Yes, I am," he admitted. "There's a special wonder that you can make something so fine, something that you can measure that finely. I'm not ready to give up the trip and go home to do it, but yes, I'm looking forward to getting started."

That afternoon, they managed to bum a ride to a nearby post office, where they got the glass blanks shipped off to Spearfish Lake, heavily wrapped and insured. Inside the package were several packages of grinding compound, pitch and rouge that Mark had bought elsewhere at the swap meet. There was a winter's work, at least, in that box, and he knew it would be an enjoyable winter.

The rest of the week at Stellafane went slowly for Jackie, but quickly for Mark. He spent a lot of time talking telescopes with other fanatics like himself, and described John's big telescope to several other people, mostly getting shaking heads in return. Several people said that a big telescope like that couldn't be any good; it was too cheap, and with the mount it had, it was useless for astrophotography. Mark conceded the second part, but he'd looked through the twenty-four inch, and knew the view was tremendous.

"I figured it out, finally," he told Jackie. "It's a western thing, this telescope of John's. You ever hear the phrase, 'East goes east, and west goes west, and never the twain shall meet'?"

"Of course," she replied.

"Well, it hasn't met yet. I guess I'm just a westerner in the east. Someday they'll learn."

The weather had been balmy for September, but late Saturday night, a cold front went through, bringing rain and a real damp, dismal bite to the air; it seemed as if it had become November overnight. They were lucky to grab a ride down to the Springfield airport with some people they had met at the gathering, but that was all the further they got; the clouds were too low, and the visibility was too thick to fly. They set up the tent under Rocinante's wing, and there they spent the night, wearing their insulated long underwear for the first time since June.

It was chilly that night as they huddled in the doubled sleeping bag, holding on tight to each other for warmth after they had made love, and pulled the long handles back on. "It's September," Jackie complained. "It's still summer. It's not supposed to be this cold yet."

"You know, back home, it always seemed like it was hotter than hell the first month of school, and it was hard to stay in the classrooms," Mark commented. "But it always seemed like there was a cold snap along in there that told us that winter was on its way."

The weather was somewhat better when they got up in the morning, and they quickly got dressed and found a little restaurant not far from the airport, where they could have some breakfast and warm up over coffee.

"I don't know about you," Jackie said, feeling warm for the first time in hours, "But right now, I'm all for cranking up Rocinante and making a big move south. If we go a few hundred miles to the south, we might be able to catch up with summer again."

"I suppose we could," Mark said, taking a sip of his coffee. "It's either that or go back to Spearfish Lake."

"It's a heck of a time to be going back to Spearfish Lake," Jackie whispered, more to herself than to Mark. "Think how cold it's going to get there."

Mark kept silent for a moment, with guilt hanging on him. He had not wanted to bring this up, but it had been eating at him ever since he paid for the mirror blanks. "We're going to have to do something," he said finally. "We just don't have the money to keep going much longer."

She was surprised to hear him speak of it; they had reached an understanding months before that they were going to have to be careful with their money, but they hadn't talked about it much. Most of the money they had spent along the way was Mark's money, after all; Jackie had known that he had about $5000 to spend on the trip when they left Spearfish Lake back in April. She had brought $500 with her from Spearfish Lake, mostly for emergency money, and had only dipped into it to the tune of about $200 or so, and not much of that had been for emergencies. "How's it holding out?" she asked.

"We've been spending it faster than I hoped we would," Mark told her. "We've spent a lot more on motels and restaurant food than I had expected, although I probably should have put off getting those mirror blanks. I wanted to keep some money in reserve in case we had major trouble with Rocinante. We can probably hold out another month or two without dipping into the reserve, although I kind of figured on living on that for a while when we get back to Spearfish Lake. I can't expect to go to work for the phone company for another eight or ten months yet, so I suppose that means that I'll have to get a job to tide us over."

"I'm not ready to go back to Spearfish Lake yet," Jackie said flatly, squirming in her chair a little. "Not if there's any way we can avoid it."

"I'd sort of planned on staying gone for a year, maybe a little more," Mark told her. "One of the deadlines that we're up against is Rocinante's annual inspection. If we have to get it done out on the road someplace, it's going to be expensive. If we're back in Spearfish Lake by the end of April, then I can do it with Ken Sawyer, like the last time, and it shouldn't cost nearly as much. We'd pretty well have to be getting back a couple months after that, anyway," he went on. Mr. Corman will probably want me to work for a couple months before Mr. Frybarger retires."

"That means we have to hold out another six to nine months," Jackie said, with all the old doubts about returning home upon her. Now there was a deadline imposed; she had never really come to grips with the thought that some day the trip would have an end. Now, here it was to confront. "I guess I'm just not all that crazy about the thought of us going back to Spearfish Lake at all, much less any sooner than we have to."

"Yeah, and we don't want to go back to Spearfish Lake flat broke, if we can help it," Mark agreed, pretty sure of what she was thinking about, but hoping to gloss it over. "It's going to cost some money just for us to set up housekeeping, and I figured we could dip into the emergency reserve for that."

He could see her tense up a little and frown a little. "What do you mean, for us to set up housekeeping?" she asked.

"Just that. Rent an apartment, get food and toilet paper, and like that. I can't see us living in a tent, and I can't see me going back to live with my folks and you going back to live with your folks."

She reached across the table and took his hand. "Now that you say it that way, I guess you're right," she said. "I've just never thought that far ahead. There's no way we can go back to Spearfish Lake and play at being good little kids again. We're going to have live together if we go back to Spearfish Lake."

"I don't think we can just go back to Spearfish Lake and shack up together," Mark said, nodding his head. "Spearfish Lake isn't California. We'd get just too much static from everybody involved. When we go back to Spearfish Lake, we're going to have to get married."

She shook her head. "Mark, let's not get into that again. We've been over that before."

"Yeah, I know," he told her. "But we're going to have to get into that, sooner or later."

"You're right, Mark," she said, groping for words. "I know you're right. We're going to have to get into it again, and you're right, we really can't just shack up together in Spearfish Lake without being married. If we were anywhere else, it wouldn't really matter, which is why I don't want to go back to Spearfish Lake any sooner than we have to. For that matter, I'm not too sure I want to go back to Spearfish Lake at all."

"You're still thinking that?" he asked, surrendering to the realization that they were going to have to talk about it.

Jackie sat quietly staring into her coffee for some time. "The thing is," she said finally, "It's been so wonderful being with you, away from all the little minds at home. I just don't want it to end. I keep wondering if we really have to go back at all."

They had been around this discussion before, too, Mark realized. "I think we're going to have to go back eventually, and at least not later than next summer," he said. "It's going to be tough to come up with some alternative that gives us the advantages that we get by going home. I mean, we know the territory, we have friends, there's a job there in a year or so that could provide a comfortable living for a lifetime. Our families are there, and that means a lot by itself. I grant you, there are some drawbacks, but I think the advantages outweigh them."

"I just hate to go back and put up with all the rumors and gossip," she said. "The fact that I ran off with you and have been living with you all this time will just add to it."

"Probably not as bad as you think," Mark said defensively. "If we go back to Spearfish Lake, and we go back married, or at least if we go back and get married right away, that ought to take away a lot of those kind of hassles. If we just try to be steady, respectable people, a lot of the gossip will die out in time."

"I'd like to think you're right," Jackie said in a small voice, then brightened. "Damn it, Mark, you know how I feel about getting married, but I don't think I can live without you, either. I keep thinking that if we're not married, and something does go wrong with me, then you can break it off fairly easily if you have to, and not be saddled with all the trouble and the pain that my father went through. But you're right, if we go back to Spearfish Lake, we'll have to be married if we want to live together. The question is, do we want to go back to Spearfish Lake?"

Mark sensed he would have to change the subject. The subject of marriage was out on the table again, and perhaps he could work back to it from a different direction, at another time. "Well, we don't have to go back to Spearfish Lake right away," he told her. "We've still got money to travel for a month or two, and I always figured that if I ran short of money I could stop and get a job pumping gas or busting suds for a couple of weeks, just to string things out."

"If we're going to do that, we ought to at least try to string things out over the winter," Jackie said. "I've got a few hundred left in the bank at home that I could contribute to the cause. But if we're going to stay gone over the winter, let's at least find a place where it's warm."

"Kinda figured that we were going to have to do that, anyway," Mark told her. "It's either that, or find an apartment or some place to live where it's warm. I can't see us spending the winter in the tent, freezing our butts."

"Me either," Jackie said. "I froze my butt sufficiently last night, thank you."

"Winter is coming," Mark agreed. "Whatever we do, I think we need to get south to think about it, if we're not going to make a decision to go back to Spearfish Lake today. I kind of hate to think about the weather pushing us around, but I guess that's what's happening. I kind of wanted to nose around New England some more, but this kind of weather is ridiculous. There's just one thing I want to do here, and then maybe we can see if we can find some warmer weather."

"What's that?" Jackie asked.

"There's a place I want to visit. A kind of a pilgrimage, I guess."

"Where?"

"Walden Pond."

Jackie nodded. "I'd kind of like to go there, too."

Rocinante's heater felt good as they got into the sky. While it was anything but a clear day, the clouds were up high enough that they had no trouble sneaking beneath them.

Getting to Walden Pond was a major hassle, however. All through their trip, they had avoided controlled airports, and metropolitan areas with their control zones, and the edge of Boston was no different. "Remember that bar in Mendocino?" Mark asked after a long study of the chart of the Boston Terminal Control Area. "How the jukebox was playing country western all the time?" Mark said as he tried to figure out a route for Jackie to fly.

"Can't forget it," she said.

"Remember, 'If you give me forty acres then I'll turn this rig around'? That's just what it feels like trying to work this thing out."

The best they could manage in finding an uncontrolled field was an airport at Marlborough, eighteen miles from Walden Pond. If Mark hadn't wanted to visit it so badly, he probably would have given it a pass, but he thought that it would be worth the effort.

It eventually took them five rides to cover the eighteen miles. "Thoreau thought this was almost wilderness," Mark said sadly. "It isn't any more. Today, he'd want to be out in the Sangre de Christos or the north Cascades."

Still, it was a thrill to walk through the woods of Walden Pond, with the smell of fall setting in, and to walk up to the small monument that marked the spot where Thoreau's cabin had stood.

"There's a tradition here, too," Mark said, reaching into his pocket and pulling out a small rock, weighing perhaps half a pound. "I read about it when I was planning this trip. When people come here, on a pilgrimage like this, they bring a rock from their homes, and throw it on that pile over there. This rock is from the shore of Spearfish Lake, and I've carried it with us since we left. Would you like to be the one to do the honors?"

Jackie was touched. "Of course, I will," she told him. "I've come to appreciate some of the things that he was trying to say, too." She took the rock in her hand and hefted it; it was a touch of home, that seemed to mean more to her now. She felt it's weight, and rubbed her hand over its glacier-smoothed surface. This rock was a part of home, and all of a sudden, she realized how much she missed Spearfish Lake. She stood there for a long time, looking at the rock and feeling it, before she threw it onto the pile in homage.

They sat down under a large tree, not too far from the marker and the pile of rocks, just to sit silently, and take in the feeling of reverence that this place gave them.

"You know, I do miss Spearfish Lake," Jackie said finally. "I mean, I know we're going to have to go back to visit, if not to live there. We could do that, and not have to be married."

Now it was Mark's turn to be silent for a while, turning his own thoughts over in his mind. Finally, he spoke: "We keep bringing up this question of whether we want to get married or not. I kind of wonder if the question isn't sort of pointless."

"What do you mean?"

"I keep thinking that we've already been married for a while, and just haven't signed the paperwork. Maybe we've been married since Waverly, almost certainly since somewhere after that. Palomar, or someplace"

"We've been living together longer than that."

"Living together, traveling together, yes, of course we have," he said. "Loving each other, about as long. But you and I thought about it an awful lot before we had that night under the stars out at Waverly, and I think that was a commitment that we both had plenty of time to think out ahead of time, and not put down lightly."

"I don't know but what you're right," Jackie said, reflectively.

"Maybe we are married, and just haven't signed the papers."

"I think we are," Mark said, his thoughts becoming clearer. "This morning, you talked about how it would be easy for me to let you go if something went wrong with you. You might think it would be easy for me, but it wouldn't. You said once that your dad visited your mother virtually every time he was down in Camden. It wouldn't be any easier for me to let you go. Yes, I think we're married, at least as far as I'm concerned."

"God, that's so sweet of you. I think you have more faith in me than I have in myself." She pulled him close and kissed him, a kiss that went on and on.

"It's possible that you're right," Mark said. "Sure, it's a risk, but what isn't? The point is, I'm the one that has to take the risk, not you. As far as going back to Spearfish Lake, well, that's a decision we don't have to make right now. There's no need for us to get back there before April, at the earliest, and that gives us plenty of time to think about what we want to do."

"We're probably going to want to go back," she said, a little reluctantly. "But if we're going to go back married, I'd kind of like to have the winter to think about it. Do you have any idea of where we could winter over?"

"It's going to have to be pretty far south," he replied, He'd thought about this before, but had never quite gotten around to organizing his thoughts about it. "Florida or the Gulf Coast, maybe south Texas, maybe southern Arizona or southern California. We've already been through that area once, but we skipped through some of it pretty quickly. Frankly, it wouldn't break my heart to find some place where we can stay in one place. That's really a pretty limited area for us to travel in."

"You said we had a couple of months before we run out of money and have to stop," she said. "That's gives some time to look for a place to stop."

"Yeah," he agreed, shaking his head. "But it's not quite that simple. I think we'd better stop before we run out of money. I just wish I hadn't bought those mirror blanks. That's a couple of weeks, right there."

"We both wanted you to have them," Jackie told him. "We both want the sixteen-incher. Maybe if we can find the right place to winter over for three or four months, you can have your dad ship the blanks to us, and we can work on at least hogging the curve out."

"I'll need a halfway decent shop to do the figuring," he replied. "Not to mention building the rest of the telescope. I kind of figured that was a project for when we get back home."

"We could get started on it, though."

"Yeah, but finishing it up is a project for Spearfish Lake, and there we are back at going back to Spearfish Lake again."

"If we have to finish it at Spearfish Lake, then we have to. That's a long way in the future," Jackie said, looking around her, and down the path to where Walden pond lay gray under the overcast skies. "I keep sitting here in this place, of all places, and thinking that while I'm pulled to going home, that's not what I want to do right now."

"What do you want to do?" he asked.

"What I'd really like to do is to find some quiet little place in the woods, near some water, where we can spend the winter, just the two of us, and maybe see if we can think a few things out," she said. "I keep thinking about Thoreau living here, how he wanted to have a little home in the woods some place, where he could just sort out what he wanted to do with his life."

"That's not quite right," Mark said. "Thoreau only stayed here a couple of years, and then he went back to town."

"Yes," Jackie agreed, "But think of everything that he thought out while he was here. There are still a few things that we need to get thought out, and all the questions aren't even clear to me."

"We've got all winter," Mark said. "There's no reason we can't find a Walden Pond of our own, some place. We've got a while to look yet, before we have to do something. Let's just find a place where it's warm."

8.

Gettysburg, Pennsylvania
September 25, 1971

Dear Dad and Sarah,

I'm sorry I haven't written to you for a few days, but we've been busy.

We had planned to stop at Spearfish Lake when we came through the midwest, but we got busy at a couple of places, and time sort of slipped by us, and all of a sudden we had to rush to get to Stellafane, which is a big star party up in Vermont. It's a lot like the Texas Star Party, only it's sort of different, too. Mark bought the glass to make the mirror for a bigger telescope, although that's a project that will have to wait until we get home, probably.

It was cold in Vermont! Winter is coming, and we've been heading south, trying to stay in front of it. It's been warmer here than it was up there.

We're back to playing tourist again. I had thought that Gettysburg was going to be boring with a capital B, but it turned out to be pretty interesting. I really didn't know too much about the place, other than a big battle was fought here, but Mark and I wandered all over the battlefield, and it's really interesting. Cemetery Ridge hardly qualifies as a hill, but when you go walking down it, it's just wall to wall monuments. Monuments wherever you stand, saying that this company or that regiment fought here. The monument companies a hundred years ago must have made out like bandits. The whole field must have been really crowded. Mark just walked around, shaking his head a lot. "What a field of fire! A modern-day company could have held this line, maybe," he said. "A modern battalion could have shot the hell out of Pickett's Division before they even got halfway across the field." I cannot imagine what it must have been like for those poor men back then. Hell on earth, I guess.

I don't know how we managed to spend three days here, but we did, and it was an interesting three days, at that. We're going to head on out of here in the morning, and fly south a ways, down into North Carolina, and spend a few days hiking the Appalachian Trail. Mark said that was one thing he had thought of doing instead of taking this trip, but I'm glad he decided to take this trip instead. He says this will probably be our last backpacking trip this year, and that makes me a little sorry, since we've had a lot of good times on our pack trips.

Anyway, since we didn't pick up our mail in Spearfish Lake after all, why don't you send it to us at General Delivery, Boone, North Carolina? I don't know the zip code; you'll have to look it up. We'll make a point of being there in a week or so.

Love,
Jackie

* * *

There was a little bite in the Pennsylvania air on the morning that they left Gettysburg. Fall was certainly coming, and bringing an end to the nice camping weather they had been experiencing since April. Now, with the oncoming winter pushing them southward, it was clearly going to be a race to stay ahead of cold weather, until they reached some place where they could spend the winter.

But, with Rocinante's speed, they could win any race with the climate, and there were plenty of things to see and do before they reached a place where they might expect to winter over, and, in that part of the country, there plenty of things to see and do.

In spite of their aversion of cities, and their inability to penetrate restricted areas due to Rocinante's limited radio, they spent a few days in Washington D.C., mostly at the Smithsonian. They'd not been much on visiting museums, but this one was special. When they tired of that, they had to take a very expensive taxi ride out to Suburban Airport, north of Washington and outside the Terminal Control Area.

After Washington, they killed a couple of days waiting for their mail to arrive by flying to Luray, visited the caverns there, and spent a couple of days doing brief hikes in Shenandoah National Park. They hiked on the Appalachian trail some there, but it only made them want to do a bigger trip, staying out for a week or more.

They flew on southwest to Boone, North Carolina. Their mail wasn't there yet, and North Carolina seemed like it was far enough south that they could expect to have a week or so of fairly decent weather, so they got back in Rocinante and flew a few miles west to Elizabethton, which was closer to the Appalachian Trail.

As this was October 1, they were pretty sure that this would be their last pack trip of the summer, and it was with a degree of sorrow that they sorted their gear out and packed their packs from Rocinante's luggage compartment one last time.

Still, it had become a practiced routine for them by now, and they had a good idea of what to pack and where to pack it.

The Appalachian Trail in this area generally follows the ridge tops of the Bald Mountains, and as the name indicates, it's pretty exposed. The views are often grand, and they spent days hiking along the trail. They rarely had to use the tent, as they could often find shelters available for their use in this off-season along this well-developed trail.

They were heading southwest along the trail, toward the Smokies, with the idea of going for a few days until they were ready to quit, then leaving the trail at a convenient road crossing and hitchhiking back to Rocinante. Their days were pretty much like any of their other hiking days when they wanted to hike. They got up early, and fought off the chill of the early morning air with a cup or two of coffee, then got on the trail. They would hike along steadily in the crisp fall air of an Appalachian morning, take a long lunch break, and shoot to arrive at one of the shelters well before dark, which was coming earlier and earlier with each passing day.

There really was not much notable happening from one day to the next, but five days out, as they approached Hot Springs, they hit a bad spot, and their hiking slowed. It looked like some sort of windstorm, perhaps a tornado, had come along and laid down trees over a wide-spread area, making the trail all but impassable. Their hiking rate slowed to half what it had been as they had to clamber over trees and fight to keep on the trail. "Somebody ought to clean this mess up," Jackie commented.

"Somebody is probably a group of volunteers," Mark told her. "Getting volunteers out to work on trail maintenance like this can be tough."

Their rate of progress had slowed enough that they came nowhere near making the shelter that night, and they camped at a waterless spot in the middle of the blowdown area.

The next morning dawned clear, with a distinct chill in the air. Winter was still chasing them. "We'll be out to 208 in the morning," Mark said as their morning coffee heated. "That's probably a good route to get back up to Greenville, and that would get us back up to 11 and give us a good shot back up to Elizabethton. Besides, we're running out of food. I think I've had enough of the Appalachian Trail."

"I'm just as glad," Jackie said. "I think I've had enough backpacking this summer to hold me for a while."

"You know, I think I'm just as glad that I didn't decide to end-to-end this thing," Mark told her. "We've had some good times on this trip, and there's been plenty of things that we'd have never done if we'd done nothing but hike."

Their packs were getting light when they shouldered them not too much later on. They figured it had to be four or five miles out to the road -- a couple hours hike at their normal rates, but probably much longer if the blowdown continued.

The going was even worse that morning than it had been the afternoon before. Mark estimated that it took them an hour to go the first mile.

They were just beginning to think about stopping some place to have lunch when they heard a chain saw roaring up ahead of them. "I'll bet someone is cleaning this mess up," Mark speculated. "If that's the case, the going ought to be easier once we get past them. What do you say we put off lunch, and have a real meal someplace like Greenville?"

It took them half an hour or more to reach the spot where the chainsaw was working, to find three people working at the blowdown: a thin, wiry, wizened man who had to be well into his seventies, and a couple about their age. Mark and Jackie's arrival made a good excuse for the little group to take a break. "You wouldn't happen to be Chris and Barb Monahan, would you?" the old man said.

"Afraid not," Jackie told them.

"I was kind of hoping that you would be," he said. "They said they might hike in from 212, to see what we're up against, and I thought they might be a couple of days early."

"You've got several miles of it," Mark told them. "I'm not real sure about the distance, but you've got five or six miles of it. We've been going through this stuff since this time yesterday."

"I know," the man said. "I went over it both ways last week to see for myself. "There's a lot of work here, and I don't know if we're going to get it done in two weeks. We're from the Huron Valley Chapter of the Sierra Club, and we're down here from Michigan to help out with this storm cleanup."

"You're a long way from home," Jackie commented.

"Well, the work needed to be done, and someone had to do it," the man said. "I had a call from a friend in the Appalachain Trail Conference right after this happened, and he told me if I'd like to lead another work trip, this work was waiting."

"We had a week of vacation time coming," the young man said, "And Vince talked us into coming with him."

"You do this kind of thing often?" Jackie asked.

"Well, since I retired, I've probably led a dozen work trips a year," Vince told them. "Not all on the Appalachian Trail, of course. In the winter, I go down and help out on the Florida trail. I go out west sometimes, too."

"That's dedication," Mark said.

"It beats sitting home and watching the TV, waiting to die," he said.

They stood and talked for a few minutes more, until Mark said, "I suppose we'd better be getting a move on."

"Yeah," the young man said, getting up and picking up the chain saw. "I suppose we'd better be getting back to work."

"You two have a good trip, now," Vince told Mark and Jackie as they shouldered their packs.

They started down the trail, which smelled of fresh-cut wood and fresh dirt. It had been nicely manicured, and they made good time. In less than an hour, they reached the road that crossed the trail.

"I suppose it's time to get our thumbs out," Jackie said. "They did a nice job on that trail."

"That they did," Mark agreed. "Are you feeling as guilty as I am?"

"I think so," Jackie said. "We've been hiking trails all summer, and the work is done by volunteers on a lot of them. I've been thinking that we've got the time, we ought to put something back."

"My feeling exactly," Mark said, stepping to the side of the road and sticking out his thumb as he heard a car approaching. "The only thing is, we need to go into Greenville and stock up on food, first."

It was mid-afternoon before they got back to the trail work party, their packs bulging with a week's worth of food. Mark had stopped at a hardware store, and bought an axe and a spade, as well, although he wasn't sure where he was going to stow them when they finally got back to Rocinante.

"The more, the merrier," Vince said, acting as if he wasn't surprised at their return. Mark and Jackie set down their packs, and set to work at clearing away the fallen timber alongside the others.

The young couple turned out to be Tom and Beverly Jeskey, also from Michigan. They'd planned a fall hike in the area, and Vince had known about it and roped them into helping. It was just as well, because Tom turned out to be a wizard with the chain saw. Mostly, he lead the way, clearing out the major obstacles, while Mark lopped branches to make the pieces easier to handle. The others drug the cut wood and limbs far away from the trail and scattered them, and worked at cleaning up the treadway and repairing minor erosion.

They pressed on for a couple of hours, and decided to call it a day as the sun was getting low. It turned out that the other three had made camp off the trail a ways, half a mile back, and it turned out to be a good spot to camp. Soon, several stoves were roaring with dinner.

Soon, the five of them were sitting around a roaring fire, working on their dinners. "I'm usually not too much on campfires," Vince admitted, "But we've cut enough downed wood, we might as well burn some of it."

"I'm glad you two showed up," Tom said. "There's no way that the two of us could keep up with Vince. With four of us, we might be able to wear him down."

"I don't know," Mark said. "You swing that chainsaw like you know what you're doing with it. Jackie and I come from timber country, and we know what it's like."

"I've picked it up here and there," Tom admitted. "Normally, I work in an electronics store."

"I'm a secretary, for U of M," Bev said. "Vince here won't admit it, but he's a retired math professor."

"How does a math professor become a lumberjack?" Mark asked.

"Oh, it's just something I got interested in," Vince told him. "It gives me an excuse to get out in the woods and get some exercise."

"He'll just about exercise you to death, if you half let him," Bev said. "We've been on trail crews with him before. Are you folks on vacation, too?"

"Well, sorta," Jackie admitted, and explained their trip around the country in Rocinante.

"It sounds like you've had a wonderful summer," Tom admitted. "I kind of wanted to do something like that, back before Bev and I got married, but then we got married, and got a mortgage, and bills, and jobs, and all that happy stuff, and now it's a miracle when we get out for more than a few days."

"You two were smart to grab the chance while you still can," Vince said. "I like to get around and see the country, too, but I'm getting too old to keep up with you young folks."

"Says the man that wears out everybody that's a third of his age," Bev smirked.

The evening soon became one of shared stories around the fire. Mark and Jackie, of course, had some good ones to tell from their experiences of the summer, and the others had some good ones, too. By the time the fire burned low, Mark and Jackie had discovered that they had found some new friends.

The next morning, Mark and Jackie were heating coffee while Vince was frying bacon and eggs in a large pan. "Is coffee all you two are going to have?" he asked.

"It's about all we ever have, unless we're near a restaurant," Mark told him.

"You can't work all day on just that," Vince said. "I'll just throw on some more bacon and a few eggs for you."

"You don't have to," Mark said, but was gald that Vince insisted, because by lunchtime, they were hungry. They rapidly destroyed the normal lunch they were used to eating, and Mark thought about hiking back down to the camp to bring more back, but he and Jackie decided that they could just suffer until quitting time.

By the time they knocked off for the day, they had cleared out another half-mile or so of the trail, and were sore and blistered from the unaccustomed work. At least, the Jeskeys looked as tired as they did, but there was no exhaustion visible on Vince, who appeared as chipper as he had in the morning. "That's really sickening," Bev commented.

"Let me tell you," Tom said. "There's this hiking club back home that organizes a hundred mile hike each summer. They have a sag wagon involved, so they don't have to carry all their gear. This hike is really popular with the retirees in the club. They've got these folks in their sixties and seventies that do these twenty-mile days, day after day, and they'll flat walk your hind end off if you half let them. The younger people in the club know enough to stay away from that little event."

"I don't know," Vince said. "I find they go kind of slow to suit me."

"That figures," Mark said, disgustedly, hoping that when he was Vince's age, he'd have half his energy.

They worked all through the next day, Friday, ending up a little less tired and blistered than they had been the day before, but another half a mile of trail had been fixed up and reblazed. That evening, Vince told them, "I'm halfway expecting the Monahans to show up this evening. They don't live that far from here. I've never met them, but I've heard that they're good trail workers."

Sure enough, as they sat around the fire along about dark, a couple carrying immense packs showed up, asking about the trail crew. "This is it," Vince told them. "What there are of us." He made introductions all around. Chris Monahan was a short, heavy-set man, with long hair and a beard halfway down his chest. Barb had long, straight hair, and both of them wore overalls. Mark and Jackie got a vague air of "hippie" about the two, although they were both a little too old to qualify.

"Sorry we couldn't make it earlier," Chris said. "Barb's brother was supposed to come and take care of the animals for a few days, but he kind of had a bout with a jail cell."

"Anything serious?" Vince asked.

"Got into a fight in a bar, and the cops sort of hauled his ass off for a while," Barb said. "He's kind of a jerk, anyway. We've got a neighbor that's going to look after them, but one or the other of us is going to have to go home every two or three days to make sure everything's all right."

Vince explained that they were working about a mile and a half from the camp. "Tom and Bev, here, are going to have to leave sometime during the day tomorrow," he said. "They've got to drive back to Michigan and clean up before they can go to work Monday, so I think tomorrow afternoon, we'll move the camp up ahead about two miles, and save ourselves some time getting to work."

"Working regular hours is a bummer," Chris said. "I've been around that block often enough, but it's what Barb and I had to do if we wanted our farm."

"Is it a very big farm?" Jackie asked, remembering the operation that Roger and Kathy Griswold had to deal with.

"No, just a little thing," Chris said. "Just enough for Barb and me to raise our food, and run some sheep for shearing, and have a milk cow. We don't eat meat, but we decided that it was all right to use animals, so long as we didn't use their bodies."

"I take it you two weren't always farmers, then," Vince observed.

"No," Barb said. "We've only had the place a couple of years, now. After Chris got back from Vietnam, we realized just how much we hated living in the city and working at regular jobs, so we went looking and found our little place up at Elk Hill, not too far from where I grew up."

"You were in Vietnam?" Vince asked. Mark kept quiet; he had learned to be careful about vounteering that he had been there, since there were a lot of people around that didn't appreciate it. Let someone else take point, for once.

"I was there with the bloody X," Chris said, and explained, "The Red Cross. Spent two years there, mostly saving money, but I left there in a real bad mood. When I got back, I just about didn't want to have anything to do with anybody, and then I met Barb, who I'd known in college. Her husband had left her with two kids, and I guess she sorta didn't want to have anything to do with anybody, either. So we wound up at Elk Hill."

"How big is your place?" Mark asked, confirming his decision to not say anything about Vietnam. Chris was the only person there that might understand him, and perhaps not even he would.

"We've got 51 acres," Chris said, "But a lot of it is wooded hillside that isn't even much good for grazing. Only about fifteen acres are worth a damn."

"We use a few acres of it to raise grain," Barb added, "And graze some of it. Mostly we have a big vegetable garden, so we don't have to spend a lot of money on food. We don't really have a cash crop, so we both have to work a little now and then to bring in some money. We've had to learn how to get along on less than we used to, but that's all right."

"Well, if you like what you're doing, I suppose that's the important part," Jackie commented.

After a while, Chris and Barb set up their tent. The fire burned low, and soon everyone was in their sleeping bags. As Mark and Jackie held each other tight in their doubled sleeping bag, they whispered back and forth.

"Those two sort of remind me of Thoreau," Jackie said. "You remember how he wanted to have a little place out in the woods, where he could be alone and in touch with nature?"

"Maybe a little," Mark said, "But somehow I get the feeling that these two are playing at it. I mean, it's not how they have to live.

"It seems pretty good to me," Jackie said.

"Seems dull as hell to me," Mark said. "It's not that I mind working. Hell, I like working, and I don't know how to sit around worth a damn. Want to bet they're waiting at the mailbox when their welfare check comes?"

"Yeah, maybe," Jackie responded. "But I do like the idea of a place out in the country, maybe with some animals around, and a big garden. Not from any high-minded principles or anything, but just because it would be a nice way to live."

"That thought has crossed my mind on occasion," he replied. "Maybe have a place big enough to have our own airstrip. I suppose that's something we'll want to think about when this trip is over, and we're looking for a place to live."

The next morning, the seven of them worked on the trail for a few hours in the morning, then went back to the camp. Tom and Bev tore down their camp, said their goodbyes, and began to pack out to the road. The rest of them packed their packs and moved to a new site, further up the trail, at a place beyond where they had been working.

After they'd set up camp in the new place, the afternoon was getting along. "We could go back to work, I suppose," Vince said. "But I've been thinking. We've been working all week. Let's take the rest of the day off."

"Got anything in mind that you want to do?" Mark asked.

"There's a place down off the ridge a ways that looks like it has the makings of a good swimming hole," Vince said, "Although it's getting a little cool for swimming, it probably wouldn't hurt to rinse off a little. Then, maybe we could hike out to the road and go into town for a beer and a dinner."

"We didn't bring swimsuits," Chris said.

Vince shook his head. "I don't mind if no one else does," he said.

They all walked down the mountain and stripped off their clothes, to go swimming in the ice-cold pool. No one was very crazy about staying in for long, but it was good to clean off some of the sweat and stink from the past few days.

They hiked on out from there to Vince's car, and went to town to find a good place for dinner. Trying to find something that would suit the vegetarian diet of the Monahans was not easy, but they finally settled for a dinner in a small restaurant they found along the road. It was barely dark enough to see by the time they got back to camp.

The next day, they worked. The Monahans proved to be good trail workers, a little to Mark's surprise. With Tom gone, Mark more or less inherited the running of the chain saw, and they made fair progress. By the end of the day, they had developed into a new team.

The next several days slid by rapidly. It was the end of the week before they finally had worked their way down to the end of the storm-damaged section of trail. In that time, they had moved their trail camp ahead again, and now it was going to be a half-day's walk out to the road and the cars, so they settled into camp for one last night around the campfire, before picking up in the morning.

"I'm sure glad you two showed up," Vince told Mark and Jackie. "I think I'd have been up here working by myself for at least another week to get this done, if you hadn't."

"Well, we were glad to help out," Jackie told him. "We've been doing a lot of hiking this summer, and it only seemed right to give something back."

After all the time they'd spent in the woods, it was good to get back out to the road and Vince's car and the Monahan's pickup truck. The Monahans offered to drop Mark and Jackie off at Elizabethton, which was not too far out of their way. Even though there wasn't enough room in the cab for the four of them, and Mark and Jackie offered to ride in the back, they were glad of the ride. They stopped in Greenville so Mark and Jackie could resupply their groceries, and rode through the crisp fall air up the road to Elizabethton. It was cold in the back of the truck, and they huddled together for warmth. "I suppose there's no need to hang around this part of the country much longer," Mark said, observing the turning leaves.

"It's going to be getting cold soon," Jackie agreed. "The weather has been nice to us, but I think that it's time to be moving south. Do you have anything else you want to do in North Carolina?"

"Just one thing," Mark told her. "I think we ought to visit Kitty Hawk. Call it a pilgrimage, I guess."

They were happy to see Rocinante again. They hadn't seen it for two and a half weeks, and at times Mark had worried about how the plane was making out. They unloaded their gear from the pickup truck, and said goodbye to Chris and Barb.

After they were ready to go, Jackie suggested, "What do you say we fly up over the ridge where we've been working? It'd be fun to see it from the air."

"Fine with me," Mark told her.

Rocinante started right away, and soon they were in the air over the ridge. The trail was down in the woods, and it wasn't easy to see.

What dismayed Jackie the most was how quickly the flew over it. It only took three or four minutes to fly over the trail that they had toiled on so hard for days. "It doesn't seem fair," she said.

"It does give you a different perspective," Mark agreed, shaking his head and turning east.

"Those were good people," Jackie said, "But somehow, did you get the feeling that we never got to know them?"

"I think you're right," Mark agreed. "I can't put my finger on it, but I think you're right. There's something unreal about them. But then, maybe there's something unreal about us, too."

"I don't follow you," Jackie said.

"I'm not sure I follow myself," Mark told her. "I'm starting to get the feeling that I've had enough of this trip. If we don't find a good place to hole up in the next few weeks, I think it's time to go home and get a job."

9.

October 21, 1971
Charleston, South Carolina

Dear Dad and Sarah:

We've been here at Charleston for a few days now, but I guess we're going to move on. Charleston is a pretty old town, with a lot of gingerbread architecture, and we've enjoyed wandering around and looking at it. Yesterday, we took a boat ride out to Fort Sumpter, which is kind of interesting for a quick trip.

The weather here hasn't been real nice. It's been chilly, and overcast a lot. I know that if we were at home, we'd probably have had snow on the ground by now, and all the leaves would be gone, but here, they haven't started to turn yet, and things are still pretty green. We're beginning to realize how much we missed the lush greenness of the north and the east by spending the summer mostly out west.

I don't know where we're going from here -- south into Florida, I guess. We've pretty well exhausted what we wanted to do here, and so I guess it's time to be moving on.

We did finally get back to Boone to get our mail, but not until we were halfway across North Carolina did we remember it. It got to us very late, as we told you when we talked on the phone, but we didn't plan to stop and work on the Appalachian Trail for as long as we did, and that sort of goofed up the schedule. If we'd known we were going to be here as long as we were, we would have had you send mail here, but since we're leaving, we'll have to set up another drop. For right now, don't worry about it. It's not impossible that we'll be home for Thanksgiving, anyway. We'll let you know, one way or another.

Love,
Jackie

* * *

Jackie put her pen down and turned to Mark, laying beside her in the tent. "Do you think we might be back in Spearfish Lake for the holidays?" she asked.

"If we don't find a place to light pretty soon, we're pretty well going to have to," Mark said. "I thought you weren't too crazy about going back to Spearfish Lake."

"Well, for a few days over the holidays, and staying there are two different things," Jackie replied. "I suppose a lot will depend on whether we find work or not."

"I don't know," Mark said. "I just can't get too crazy about spending the next six months busting suds in some restaurant, and that's the only sort of junk jobs there seem to be open around here."

"I suppose that waitress job might come through for me," she said, "But that's not enough for the two of us to live on, and I don't want to spend the next six months living in this tent around here."

"Me either," Mark said. "What's more, I don't want to spend the next six months in some big city. You got any ideas?"

"What about Titusville?" Jackie asked. "That's a fairly small town. It would be warmer there, and we might be able to catch another launch or two."

Mark shook his head. "I really doubt it," he said. "From what I hear, they've been laying off at Cape Kennedy a lot, and there may not even be much available in the way of junk jobs."

"Well, how about St. Augustine?" Jackie asked. "Maybe we don't stay there, but it would be a good place to go into the unemployment office and see what's happening. Maybe even some place over on the west coast would be even better. Some place like, oh, Naples. From what I remember from looking at the map, that's a fairly small town."

Mark rolled over onto his back and stared at the roof of the tent. "What it comes down to," he said finally, "Is that there's no point in staying around Charleston. Let's crank up Rocinante in the morning and fly down to someplace down south of Tampa somewhere, and check out the prospects. If we don't turn up anything in the next two or three weeks, let's just say the hell with it and go home. We'll still have a few bucks we can use to get through the winter with, and maybe I can get Mr. Corman to jump the gun on my going to work for him. Maybe we could move in with my folks, although I don't think either of us wants that. Push comes to shove, we can probably sell Rocinante for more than I've got in her."

Jackie was shocked. "Sell Rocinante? You don't want to do that, not after all the three of us have been through!"

"No," Mark said, shaking his head. "But it does give us something to fall back on, if all else fails. As far as that goes, though, I suppose I could get a bank loan on it to carry us through until I start in for the phone company."

A range of prospects fluttered past Jackie's eyes. "We've got a better chance of finding work somewhere away from Spearfish Lake in the winter than we do there," she said. "It's probably worth giving it an extra long try."

"A short term job is all right for the short term," Mark said, rolling over to face her. "The thing is, we've got to have made up our mind by next spring whether we're going back to Spearfish Lake or not. I think that means that we've got to find some job that's going to have long-term prospects that are at least partly as good as what I already know I have for the phone company."

Jackie nodded. That would mean going back to Spearfish Lake to stay, and all that doing so would mean. "That's going to be tough," she said. "It almost has to mean phone work."

"Yeah," Mark said. "And it means finding it in the south, somewhere. Now, that means that we would have nice winters, but the summers would be hotter than hell. I don't know about you, but you can dress up for cold, but there's a limit to how much we can dress down for the heat."

"There is that," Jackie said. She didn't want to concede it to Mark, just yet, but she was just about resigned to having to go back to Spearfish Lake and make the best of it.

But, perhaps they could put it off until spring. She put up the pad and pencil, then rolled over and took Mark in her arms. They lay there for a long time, just holding on to each other.

They had to detour far to the west to avoid the maze of military operating areas around Ft. Stewart, Georgia the next morning, before they could turn to the south. It was a beautiful day, crisp with the promise of fall, even for the deep south. They stopped at Tifton, Georgia, for fuel, and then continued south, still flying low across the piney woods, but even then they could see military traffic going overhead.

It was Jackie's turn to navigate, while Mark flew. Navigating in this country, at this point, wasn't a big deal; all they had to do was to hold a course of south, or perhaps a little to the west of south, until they ran into the Gulf of Mexico, at which point they would turn a little to the left to follow the coast southbound. It was the kind of navigation that both of them liked the best; the kind where they didn't have to pay a lot of attention, but just look out of the windows a lot.

Still, Jackie kept a sectional chart unfolded to at least keep a mental track of where they were going and where they had been. As they flew across the Florida border, she flipped the sectional over, to continue following the course on the back side.

Looking at the chart in that area brought back memories. She had held the same chart in her hand back in April, when they had run into the thunderstorms that had landed them at Twillingate. "You know," she told Mark over the noise of Rocinante's engine, "We're not that far from Twillingate. Maybe we ought to stop and return Brother Erasmus' Bible to him."

Mark nodded. "Sure wouldn't mind seeing him again," he said. "And this is as good a chance as any."

Twillingate proved surprisingly hard to find. Mark had never been quite sure of where it was; they had just happened on it when they arrived, and they had just happened on the highway southeast of Tallahasee when they left. On thinking about it, Mark thought he had a pretty good idea of where it was, but his idea proved to be wrong. In the end, they were reduced to picking up the shoreline of the Gulf well to the west of where they were sure that Twillingate would be, and then followed the coast eastward, a mile or so inland, until all of a sudden things began to look familiar.

The river and the little town sprang on them from out of nowhere. For a long time, all they had seen was pine woods and swamp, and then, all of a sudden, they were there. Mark banked Rocinante to circle the town.

Even from the air, they could see that there was a plane, a twin of some sort, sitting in the T-hanger. "Must be quail season's open," Mark commented, looking at the windsock. "I don't suppose Mr. Cowgill will mind if we land there again."

In the six months since they had left Twillingate, not much appeared to have changed from the air. It was still possible to see where the tornado had passed through, but with difficulty; a season's fresh growth had obliterated much of the damage. The runway was as neat as a pin. When they left, it had been cleaned off from all of the tornado debris, but now there wasn't even a sign of the debris where it had been stacked around the edge of the runway.

Mark braked to a stop in front of the T-hanger, and taxied Rocinante up to the tiedowns where it had been left for a week back in April. "It's strange," Mark said as he and Jackie tied the Cessna down. "Even more so than Waverly, I feel like we're coming home again."

They got Brother Erasmus' Bible out of the chart case where it had ridden for six months, and began to walk the familiar dirt road down to the church.

The church seemed familiar, friendly, standing in the middle of the small clearing in the woods in its neat white paint, with Jackie's silver and white sign on the front, with no trace of the roofless, damaged way they had first seen it. No one was around the church, though, and when they walked back behind the church to Brother Erasmus' cabin, no one seemed to be there, either.

"You've got to figure that Ethylene is out working some place, and that Brother Erasmus is out tending to his flock, and E.J. is in school somewhere," Jackie said. "They'll probably be back this evening."

Mark shrugged. "Well, if we've got to hang around, we might as well go into town and get something to drink, and maybe say hi to Mr. and Mrs. Thibodaux," Mark said. "After all, we've got nothing better to do while we're waiting."

The walk into town was familiar, although there were not a lot of people to be seen -- no surprise in the middle of a working day. The woman who ran the

General Store remembered them, though, and asked what brought them back to those parts. "Just visiting," Jackie told her.

They walked across the dirt street and up a ways to the Thibodaux house, which had the phone company in the front, and knocked on the door. "Come on in," they heard Paul Thibodaux's voice call.

They found Thibodaux sitting at the switch board. "Well, look what the cat drug in," he said. "I've thought about you kids a lot, and wondered what you've been up to."

"We've been around," Mark told him, and explained what had brought them back to Twillingate.

"Brother Erasmus will be out with the quail hunters," Thibodaux said. "I suspect you saw that plane in the hanger. That's the first one of the season. Ethylene will be putting on a big feed for them, so I wouldn't expect either of them back until late."

"Well, we'll just have to hang around till late," Mark said. "It wouldn't do to pass through and not see him. How's Bessie doing?"

Thibodaux shook his head. "She's not been doing well," he said. "She's been in and out of the hospital in Perry a couple of times, now. Gall bladder's giving her trouble, and they're going to have to operate. That's what I'm doing sitting here running the switchboard, instead of being out stringing wire for the new system."

"Are you having to do everything by yourself?" Mark asked.

"Pretty much," Thibodaux said. "I can get one of the guys from the phone company over in Perry to come over and help me out every now and then, and when I do, Miz Sprague will come over here and sit with the switchboard, but we ain't getting nothin' done to speak of. I know there's been many times I've sat here and wished you'd drop in out of the sky again."

Mark looked at Jackie, who nodded. "Well, Mr. Thibodaux," he said. "I've got to admit that Jackie and I have been kind of looking for work to hold us over the winter."

"Can't afford to pay you much," the tall Cajun said. "But I can afford to pay you about a buck an hour over minimum wage, and pay Jackie here minimum wage to sit at the switchboard and look after Bessie some while we're out working on the system. It's costing me to have all that new system sitting in boxes, and not paying for itself. The job won't last all winter, though. If we can get right to work on it, maybe it'll last till around Christmas."

"How long would it take to learn how to run the switchboard?" Jackie asked.

"I can show you how to run it in half an hour," Thibodaux said. "'Twould take you twenty years to learn how to run it the way Bessie does, to learn all the families and where everybody is all the time, but folks around here know that Bessie ain't well, so they'll understand."

"Give us a couple minutes to talk about it," Mark told him.

Outside, Mark said to Jackie in a low voice, "It's a job, and it beats the hell out of busting suds," he said. "But, if we spend two months here, it'll mean that's two months that we can't be looking for a permanent job."

She nodded. "That means the chances are that much greater that we won't have any choice but to go back to Spearfish Lake," she said, understanding Mark perfectly.

"On the other hand," Mark went on, "If we're careful with our money, that probably takes care of the worst of the money troubles until we have to be back in Spearfish Lake, so it puts the decision off until spring."

"Let's see if we can find a place to rent," Jackie said, the decision obvious to her. "If we're going to be here for two months, I don't know that I want to spend it living in the tent."

"That's going to cost," Mark warned.

"I don't know that it won't be worth it," Jackie told him. "I'm getting a little tired of living in the tent."

"Me, too," Mark admitted. "I can think of worse places to spend the next two months than Twillingate."

They went back inside and told Thibodaux that he'd hired himself a staff, but that they needed a place to stay. "It doesn't have to be much," Jackie told him. "Just some place where we can stand up while we're getting dressed."

Thibodaux leaned back in his chair and thought. "Ain't no place empty 'round here that I know of, not now that it's getting on to winter," he said. "S'pose there's a lot of people 'round here that would take you in for room and board, but I'd reckon that you to would want to be on your own."

"Hadn't thought of it that way," Jackie said. "But I guess you're right."

"Mr. Cowgill might have a place out to the plantation open for the winter," Thibodaux said, thinking aloud. "That'd be kind of a long walk, but I s'pose I could go out and pick you up and take you home, but it'd be better if you could stay closer in to town."

Mark shook his head. "I suppose we could live in the tent if we had to."

"Don't think there's no need to do that," Thibodaux said. "There ought to be something . . . well, of course." He reached for the switchboard, plugged a plug into a hole, and gave the handle a crank. "Well, good morning, Sue Ann," he said into the headset. "Is Homer out there?"

It took a couple of phone calls to track Cowgill down; he proved to be at the sawmill. Thibodaux explained that Mark and Jackie were going to help out with putting the new phone system in, and needed a place to live. "I was sorta wonderin' if you was going to be using the Billie Jean the next couple of months."

Mark and Jackie couldn't make out the other end of the phone conversation, but Thibodaux was silent for several seconds, listening into the headset. "That's right nice of you," he said into the mouthpiece finally. "Don't matter that it's up to the fish camp. They'll be a mullet fisherman hanging around somewhere."

Thibodaux thanked Cowgill again, unplugged the line, and turned to Mark and Jackie. "Just took thinking of it," he said. "Three-four years ago, a fella bought this shantyboat up around Mobile somewheres. He was gonna retire on it down on one of the canals down south. He was towing it from Apalachacola down towards Tampa or somewheres with this rowboat and this little bitty outboard, and he was out on the Guff and it kicked up some. He finally got it into the river here, and he was so damn seasick he said he never wanted to see it again. I think Mr. Cowgill give him a hundred bucks for it, and moored it up to his fish camp for when he had more Yankees than he had beds. He says he don't think he's gonna be using it this winter atall, and if you kids want to clean it up and fix it up, then he says you're welcome to live there."

"What's this shantyboat like, anyway?" Mark asked.

"Kind of like a houseboat," Thibodaux told them. "Not a real nice sort of thing made out of fiberglass and chrome like you see down south, but rough-built out of wood. Got a couple of beds, a wood stove, and like that. Be a little close in there, but probably it would seem like all the room in the world, after all the time you two have been living in that tent."

"Sounds like it would work," Jackie said, thinking to herself that it sounded sort of romantic. "What's Mr. Cowgill want for rent?"

"Just keep it up and clean it up, was all he asked," Thibodaux said. "He wants the new phone system in as bad as anyone, maybe more than most, and this'll get it in quicker. We'll have to pay some mullet fisherman to go up there and tow it down here, and that'll be ten bucks or so, and we'll have to find some place to moor it. Maybe down there by Brother Erasmus' church would be good, better than right down town, anyway."

Half an hour later, Mark and Jackie found themselves sitting in an old wooden rowboat, with an Evinrude outboard of uncertain age pushing it, being run up the river by an old black man named Samuel, who was of equally undetermined age.

Samuel wasn't much of a man to talk, but Mark almost thought he remembered him from the raisin' back in April.

The river was wide and deep and sluggish, barely differentiated from the swamp that surrounded it. There wasn't much of a channel, but it flowed now through huge areas of sawgrass and then through stands of cypress with Spanish Moss hanging from it. They had not gone more than a few hundred yards before Mark was totally turned around, but Samuel obviously knew it like the back of his hand; he barely gave the outboard and attention, but rolled a cigarette from a bag of Bull Durham and looked half-asleep.

It was an hour or more up the river before they finally came upon a little cluster of shacks perched on one of the higher pieces of ground they'd seen. A dock stuck out into the river, with three or four boats tied to it; just past the dock was what looked like a small shack, planted on a wooden barge. A porch roof stuck out over the deck on either end of the barge, and there were a couple of old wooden chairs on the deck. Samuel cut the outboard motor, and let the rowboat drift up alongside the floating shack, and lazily put a line on the barge.

"This the Billie," he said, the first words he'd spoken in half an hour or more. "We be wantin' the plank and poles."

Mark and Jackie clambered out of the rowboat onto the deck of the shantyboat. The cabin was unlocked; Mark took a brief look inside, and saw a double bed, a small wood stove, and a couple of boxes that looked like they might be used for dressers of a sort. "It's not much, but I guess it looks like home for a while," he told Jackie.

"It looks like it'll do," she said.

Mark turned to look at the mooring arrangement. The shantyboat was held away from the bank by a couple of poles, but four ropes held it there. There was a gangplank to walk across. "I guess what we'll have to do is to take in a couple of those lines, loosen the other two, pull in the poles, take in the other lines and get across the gangplank before this thing drifts off," he told Jackie. "That about right, Samuel?" he called to the old black man, who was lashing the rowboat tightly to the side of the shantyboat.

"It be," Samuel said. "I be keepin' you from driftin' off."

The next few minutes were sort of a shambles, as Samuel had forgotten more about boatmanship at the age of five than Mark and Jackie had ever known. It wouldn't have worked at all, except for Samuel keeping the shantyboat from drifting off, and the fact that the little breeze there was setting them toward shore, rather than away from it. Finally, Mark was able to get the last line cast loose, and he ran across the gangplank, pulled it in and stowed it on the roof with Jackie's help. Samuel started the old Evinrude, backed the unwieldy tow away from the bank, and swung it around to head back downriver.

Samuel and the old Evinrude couldn't push the shantyboat very fast, and there were places where they couldn't go very fast, anyway, along the twisting, winding waterway back to Twillingate. "Samuel, you tell us if you need us to do anything," Mark called. The old man nodded, and rolled himself another smoke, while Jackie and Mark found chairs on the front deck to watch the river slide by.

It was a lazy way to spend a couple of hours, just sitting there on the deck, looking at the swamp and the forest, looking at the birds that flocked around. There was a wider variety of birds along that stretch of swampy Florida river than either of them had ever seen before. It was the height of the migration season, and several of the waterbirds, ducks and geese especially, seemed familiar from their northern home.

Around them lay a vista without a trace of human occupation, except for the odd piece of junk floating in the water, where kingfishers were perching. Periodically the wind sent long ruffling waves through the grasses and the massed needles of sand pines on the shore. A boat tailed-grackle flapped by with a snail in his bill; a comorant was beating the water in his effort to get into the air while he was still wet. Seaside and Savannah sparrows sat on clumps of bear grass. Occasionally there were little patches of palm jungle, dense and shiny-leaved, the trunks of the younger trees covered lattice-like with the projecting frond bases of dead leaves. Huge, long-stemmed crowns of glinting green leaves sprang nearly trunkless from the youngest palms. The heard the flapping of the wings of great blue herons as they flew into the sky. It was mid-afternoon by now, and the air was quivering with the heat in this half-land, half-sea of unbroken subtropics, marsh beside jungle.

Jackie wished that she had her fishing gear from Rocinante; it would have been fun to troll a line out from the deck of the shantyboat, even though it seemed unlikely that she'd catch anything. She looked back at Samuel, in the rowboat alongside, and saw that he'd unlimbered a handline and was trolling it in the water, but for what she wasn't sure, but after a while, there was a fish flopping on the floor of the boat. Someone's dinner, she presumed.

Mostly, they just sat back and watched the forest and the swamp flow slowly by them. After a while, Jackie, then Mark, walked back into the cabin of the shantyboat, to get an idea of how much cleaning up would have to be done.

It was surprisingly clean. While it was dusty, it wasn't dirty, so to speak; it showed signs of having been kept up, although there were places that wanted paint. The cabin had some big windows on the side, and although they were dirty, it wouldn't be any big deal to clean them, and even as dirty as they were, it was interesting to watch the view of the riverbank floating past. "It's going to be a little cozy," Jackie said, "But I think we're going to like it here."

Eventually, they reached Twillingate. The waterfront of the little town was grubby and junk-cluttered, a real eyesore, which was probably why Thibodaux had said they wouldn't want to tie up there. The river here was wider, getting set for it's plunge into the Gulf of Mexico, and Samuel took them right past the down and around a little bend, then swung the tow around and pushed to toward shore.

"Right here's good," a familiar voice called. "Throw me that line, and let's get you tied up."

Mark and Jackie looked up, to see Brother Erasmus and E.J. waiting for them on the shore. "It's good to see you again," Jackie called. "How'd you know we were coming?"

"Mist' Thibodaux done called and said what you was a-gonna do," he said. "Figgered you'd need some help gettin' the mooring rigged."

"I saw how we took it apart," Mark said, as he picked up a line and started to swing it around, to toss it up onto the shore. "But I never figured out how we were going to get it back together."

"I drove you a couple of mooring posts," Brother Erasmus told them, picking up the line, as Samuel cut the motor. "Figgered we could moor you to trees for the others. It's sure going to be nice to have you folks back with us for a while."

With the help of Brother Erasmus, and Samuel, and E.J., all of whom appeared to know what they were doing, the shantyboat was moored to the bank in only a few minutes.

"Preacher," Samuel said as they finished up, "I done caught a little bass I thought you'd like to have for supper."

"Well, Samuel, I think Ethylene would like to have you and Mist' Mark and Miss Jackie to supper tonight," Brother Erasmus said.

"Don't guess I'd better," Samuel said. "Got to catch the turn."

"Tide don't wait for no man," the preacher commented. "You come on up for supper some other time, Samuel."

"Sure 'nuff," the fisherman said as he got back into his rowboat and cast it off from the shantyboat.

"Thank you, Samuel," Jackie called to him. "You've been a big help."

The black man nodded to her, smiled, and started his outboard once again. The four of him watched as he sped down the river toward the mouth. "Seemed like an interesting old guy," Mark said. "Not much to say much of anything, though."

"Old Samuel, he been fishin' this water seventy, eighty years," Brother Erasmus said. "He don't get much call to talk to people, but he do talk to them fish."

"Brother Erasmus, it's good to see you again," Jackie said. "We stopped off to give you back your Bible, but Mr. Thibodaux asked us to stay for a while. I'm afraid we left the Bible up to Mr. Thibodaux's house, but we'll get it to you."

"He say to come up and get his pickup truck, so's you can get your stuff from your plane," Brother Erasmus told them. "But Ethylene and me do want you to come to supper tonight, 'cause me 'n her 'n E.J. are gonna want to hear all about your trip."

"We'll be happy to," Mark told him.

"Supper'll be late," Brother Erasmus warned. "Ethylene is going to stop off and cook something for them. Miz Thibodaux ain't well, and it's done been hard for Mist' Thibodaux to run the phones and try to nurse her, too. Guess she gonna have to go to the hospital up to Tallahasee next time."

"We didn't even see her when we were up there," Mark commented. "She must have been asleep, or something."

"She been hurtin' bad, down in her chest," the preacher told them. "They gonna have to take out her gall bladder, or somethin'. Most everybody in town is sorry for her, 'cause everybody knows her like family."

Mark shook his head. "I suppose we'd better be getting back up there," he said. "I guess Mr. Thibodaux is going to want to show Jackie how to run the switchboard yet this afternoon, so we can get right to work tomorrow."

"Don't be forgettin', you're gonna be havin' supper with us tonight."

"We won't forget," Jackie told him. "We came back to Twillingate to see you, after all."

While Thibodaux took some time to show Jackie the ins and outs of running the switchboard, Mark took his pickup truck down to the airstrip, and unloaded Rocinante -- really unloaded it, even down to the charts and things like that. It was as empty as the airplane had been since they left Spearfish Lake the spring before.

He knew that Jackie would want to participate in the setting up of house-keeping on the shantyboat, but he decided that there was no reason he couldn't unload their things and put them aboard. It took several trips before he had everything transferred, but before he went back up to the Thibodauxs', he dug in his backpack and pulled out a pack of cigarettes. This pack dated back to Massachusetts, and was getting perhaps halfway gone by now, but this was a good time to lean back in the deck chair and have a smoke.

The decision to stay in Twillingate and work for Thibodaux for a couple of months set well with him, he realized; he was glad that Jackie had agreed to it so readily. One of the things that Mark had come to learn on this trip was that he was not much of one to sit around and do nothing. He could do it for a day or two, if they had to, but he was the sort of person that had to be busy at something, and the happiest times that they had spent on the trip were the days that they were busy with something. As it turned out, the trip had not been a bad idea, if only to learn that; besides, it had done wonders for getting the wanderlust out of his system. If this deal in Twillingate hadn't turned up, they probably would have turned Rocinante's nose toward Spearfish Lake before the month was out, or not much later than that.

It was a foregone conclusion that they had to be home by the end of April, but that was still six months away. Mark had been recognizing Jackie's reluctance to return to Spearfish Lake for months, now, and he was pretty sure that he understood why she had that reluctance, although perhaps she hadn't yet realized that to return there as a married couple would put a different spin on things. Well, she realized it in her head, if not her heart, he realized as he took a deep drag on the cigarette. Probably the reluctance to get married she had so often stated stemmed at least partly from the same reason: if they didn't go home, then they wouldn't have to get officially married, although they were married now in everything but name, and Jackie even admitted it.

Last night -- was it actually last night in Charleston? -- he had all but had Jackie admitting that she was ready to go back to Spearfish Lake to live, if not now, then when the time came. Mark suspected that she'd continue to come around to the realization that it was the only sound course for them to follow. The job with Mr. Corman was just too good to pass up; they could build a comfortable life from it.

Jackie's preoccupation with her mother was just as strong as ever, and Mark had become accustomed to it. There was no doubt that it was just as much a risk as it ever was, but there was no way of telling. The risk still seemed worth the benefits, much more so now than when they had last been here in Twillingate.

The cigarette was now getting down toward the end; Mark took a final drag on it, then tossed it into the river, where it made a little hissing noise as it went out. The afternoon was wearing on, Mark realized; it was time to get back in the pickup and get up to the Thibodauxs'. It would be good to sit and talk with Brother Erasmus and Ethylene tonight, he realized. Brother Erasmus was full of good common sense, and maybe some good would come out of it.

Back up at the Thibodaux house, Mark found Jackie sitting behind the switchboard, the headset on her head. Mr. Thibodaux was sitting at a table in the room, going over some paperwork. "I think I understand most of this manual for setting this system up," he told Mark, "But there's some things I don't understand, and I'd be pleased if you could go through this. I think you probably know more about it than I do."

"It's like any phone system," Mark said. "It's not that complicated, but it just seems complicated. I do need to read over the manual, because there are a lot of different ways to go about things."

"I s'pose you and Jackie ought to slide back down to the Billie Jean and get moved in," Thibodaux told him. "I don't know if there are any lights down there for you to read by after dark, so I'll send a hurricane lantern with you."

"Don't know how much I'll get read tonight," Mark told him. "We've got to unpack, and have supper with Brother Erasmus, and that's going to eat the time up a bit."

"We got mostly wire to string for the next few days, anyway," Thibodaux said. "And we'll be seeing our fair share of Brother Erasmus. He's been digging holes for poles for me."

Mark carried the hurricane lantern and a manual and a couple of technical books, while Jackie carried Brother Erasmus' Bible as they walked back to the shantyboat. "I still didn't see Bessie," Mark commented as they walked down the sandy road. "How is she?"

"Not good," Jackie said. "She seems like she's in a lot of pain, and the heat isn't helping. She'll be going to the hospital in another week or so for her operation, but she's going to be a while recovering."

"How'd you like working the switchboard?" he asked.

"It was all right, although there were only half a dozen calls all the time I was there," Jackie said. "It's a little difficult, since nobody gives a number. They just ask for Maizie or Elmore or somebody. Mr. Thibodaux says that'll end in time, as people learn that I don't know everybody."

"It's going to be a sad day in Twillingate when the dial system gets working," Mark reflected. "People will have to remember phone numbers, instead of just calling down to the exchange to ask Bessie if they know where someone is."

"I suppose you're right," Jackie agreed. "The whole community will have lost something that's been nice about being a small and warm and friendly town."

"It's happened all over," Mark said. "Twillingate won't be the first place to see that happen. In fact, it will be one of the last. It sort of makes me wonder if we're doing the right thing by helping Mr. Thibodaux out, but it's getting so that he really doesn't have much choice."

Back at the shantyboat, it took them a while to get their gear unpacked and to find places for it. It would seem strange to not be living out of their backpacks, to not be moving every day, to be able to get dressed while they were standing up.

The sun was sinking low by the time they finished up. "I suppose we'd better wander up to Brother Erasmus'," Mark said. "Let's try to not be real late. I need to spend some time going over this technical stuff."

"Don't let me forget," Jackie said, "I need to finish that letter to Dad and Sarah that I started yesterday, and tell them that they can send our mail here."

"Might as well," Mark told her. "It looks like we're going to be here for a while."

"So, you be goin' to stay with us for a while?" Ethylene asked.

"Couple of months, it looks like," Mark explained. "I haven't got much idea yet of how much work it's going to be to put in the new phone system, but that's what Mr. Thibodaux figures."

They sat and watched the twilight from Brother Erasmus' porch. It was late enough in the year that the mosquitos had pretty well backed off, and it was enjoyable to sit outside. Being from the north woods, Mark and Jackie knew what clouds of mosquitos were like, and had learned from childhood to put up with them. They figured that Brother Erasmus and Ethylene and E.J. probably had to have the same immunity.

Supper had been good; the fresh bass had been just about right to go around, when added to Ethylene's corn bread. It beat eating out of cans, anyway, which was what Mark and Jackie had grown used to over the past six months.

"You two sure have seen a lot since we saw you last," Brother Erasmus said. "We often prayed for you, that the Lord would keep his hands on you, and would keep you from danger."

"We got into trouble, now and then," Mark told him. Over dinner, he and Jackie had told the Greens about some of their adventures, like the thunderstorm at Waverly, the takeoff from Leadville, and the rescue of the Pittengers. They had also talked about many of the other things they had done and the places they had visited. "So, what's new around Twillingate?"

"Not a whole lot," Brother Erasmus said. "You already know about the new phones, and Miz Thibodaux. "Couple of people have died, but I don't think you met any of them. They been a few people married." He laughed, and said, "You remember, after the raisin', I said how it wasn't real Christian-like for them people to be sneakin' out into the bushes at a church raisin'?"

Mark smiled. "Yeah, I remember that. People will be people, I guess."

"It all worked out in the end," Brother Erasmus smiled. "We done had two weddin's out of that raisin'. Real weddin's, too, not just commissary weddin's."

"What's a commissary wedding?" Jackie asked. "I don't remember hearing that one before."

Brother Erasmus smiled. "Back in the teppentine camps, sometimes a couple would just move in with each other, without gettin' married in a church, and the commissary would just start puttin' what they bought on one bill, 'stead of two, and that was what we called a commissary weddin'. People still call it that, though we don't have the company teppentine camps no more."

Jackie shook her head; it sure sounded familiar. "That's what Mark and I have, I guess," she said.

"I often wondered about that," Brother Erasmus said. "What with the two of you not havin' the same last names, and all. I thought for a while you must have been related somehow, but never thought it was right to ask. You two plannin' to have a church weddin'?

Mark thought he had better explain; perhaps he could pin Jackie down a little more. "When we were here before, we didn't know if we wanted to get married. I don't think you could even say we had a commissary wedding then. We were just friends who were taking a trip together. We've made up our minds that we're going to get married, but it's going to wait until we get back home. We kind of thought that it wouldn't be right to get married somewhere away from our families."

"The good book says that a man and a woman should be married in the eyes of the Lord," Brother Erasmus said. "I guess you got good intentions, anyways."

"It took us a while to reason it out that far," Jackie said. "It was just kind of something we slipped into."

"Happen like that for a lot of people," Brother Erasmus agreed. "Course, often enough, they's a little one on the way to make it happen a little faster."

"Well, that's one thing we don't have to worry about," Jackie replied. "We've decided that we don't want any kids. Ever."

"Childr'n make a man and a woman come closer together," the preacher chided. "The book, it say, 'Be fruitful and multiply.'"

"I don't think the book says to multiply if the result isn't going to be fruitful," Jackie said, and found herself explaining about her mother, how she had been lost to the world for years, and how she had died last summer. "It bothered me real bad," she said. "It bothered the both of us. We came that close to getting in the plane and flying back here to talk to you about it. But I guess God was guiding us, because we didn't, and it was the next morning that we found the Pittingers.

Brother Erasmus, if that wasn't a miracle all the way around, then I don't know what a miracle is."

"The Lord was surely using you as his tools that day," the black man said, a little reverently. "But this heaviness about your mother is still on your heart, isn't it?"

"Yes, Brother Erasmus, it is."

The preacher leaned back in his chair and thought for a moment. "What you got to understand," he said finally, "Is that you ain't supposed to know what the Lord has got in mind for you, but that he's goin' to do to you what he's goin' to do, anyways. You just done told me how in dyin' your mama gave life to two people through the Lord's work. It ain't always our purpose to know what the Lord is up to, you just got to have faith that he knows what he's doin'."

"I think I know that," Jackie said. "But knowing it, and having the faith to truly believe it are two different things, especially with the example I've had."

Brother Erasmus shook his head. "Here you been tellin' me of an example that ought to be all anyone should need to show you how the Lord works. You are just goin' to have to reconcile yourself that you are the Lord's tools, and he's goin' to do what he wants. You be thinkin' about that some, and then we talk about it again."

It was after dark before they got back to the Billie Jean. Mark figured out how to light the kerosene lantern, and Jackie pulled out one of the pack stoves to heat water for a late cup of coffee. While the water was heating, Mark pulled out one of the technical manuals, and began to leaf through it, just to get some idea of what would be involved. "There's a lot of work here, but it doesn't look too strange," he concluded.

"I don't know," Jackie said. "I guess I'm still thinking about Brother Erasmus. I guess he didn't say anything I didn't expect him to say, but it was still good to hear him say it."

"About what I told you he'd say, back there in California," Mark agreed. In his own way, and for his own reasons, it seemed as if Brother Erasmus had come to pretty much the same conclusions that Mark had reached a long time before, but Jackie was still reaching for them. Perhaps it would help her deal with the uneasiness she still felt, he thought.

"I know," she said. "Have faith, and the Lord will provide, unless he decides there's a reason not to. You know, when you say it that way, it sounds sort of fatalistic."

"Well, it is," Mark said, glancing at another manual. "But, if it gives you some hope to cling to, then it counts, I guess."

"I guess I know we should be married, and not just a commissary marriage, like we've got now," Jackie said. "But Mark, I'm still scared."

"Jackie, I hate to say it, but I think you'll always be scared a little," he said.

"But remember what you told Bruce, back there at Waverly. Don't let your fears get the best of you."

"I guess you're right," she said. "The water's hot. You still want coffee?"

"Yeah," Mark said. "I'll even make it. Why don't you sit down and finish that letter to your dad and Sarah while we're thinking about it?"

*　　*　　*

PS: (Next evening) -- Guess what! We're back in Twillingate, and it looks like we're going to be here for a while. Mark is going to work for Mr. Thibodaux putting in their new dial phone system. I think I remember either writing to you about him, or talking about him on the phone. It looks like we'll be here for a couple of months, so I guess you can send our mail here. Mrs. Thibodaux, who runs the switchboard, has been sick, so I'll be filling in for her. Both of us ought to be pretty busy.

I'll write and tell you more later. I'm sitting here writing this by a kerosene lantern, and I'd rather do it in the daylight, but I want to get this out when the mail goes first thing tomorrow. -- J

10.

Autumn was even coming to northern Florida. The nights were chilly enough to make them cuddle together in the doubled sleeping bag for warmth, although they hadn't yet had to break out the long underwear or start a fire in the wood stove for warmth. Waking up each morning to the sight of the morning fog laying low on the river, and the softness of the light that filtered through the pine trees, made any discomfort that might have been involved worth the effort, however.

It was always chilly when they got up, and they both always hustled to get dressed. Though the afternoons were still sometimes warm enough to take a quick swim to clean up, it was never an appealing idea in the morning, although both of them could see how it might have been in warmer weather. Using the wood stove to warm their morning coffee seemed like too much work, but they still had their pack stoves that had served them faithfully all summer, and one was enough for the cup of coffee it took them to get their eyes open.

They had quickly fallen into a routine. Since it was still often uncomfortably hot in the afternoon, especially on the days that Mark and Mr. Thibodaux and Brother Erasmus had poles to set or lines to string, they had gotten used to getting up in the half-light of dawn, and not wasting any time as they got around.

After a few days, they had taken to getting up early enough to walk down to the Thibodauxs' early, and get some breakfast going there. While Jackie would never be the cook that either of the Thibodauxes were, she could handle pancakes and sausages and eggs, and Mr. Thibodaux initiated her into biscuits and pan gravy and grits. At least the Thibodauxs had a gas stove, although they still had a wood stove in the kitchen, and Jackie could handle that. The big breakfasts were welcome, and it soon became a family affair. On the days that Brother Erasmus worked with them -- and that wasn't every day -- he'd usually drop by in time for a cup of coffee before they got to work.

Bessie Thibodaux couldn't eat much; it seemed as if most food caused her gall bladder to act up. Most mornings, she stayed in bed, always trying to be cheerful, although usually in pain, and she limited her breakfasts usually to a cup of coffee, and maybe a piece of toast or two. She was looking forward to getting her surgery over with, so she could get back to a normal life.

After the men piled into the pickup truck and set off to work, at whatever it was they might have been doing, Jackie did the dishes, picked up the house, and answered the phone, of course. There always seemed to be a rush of calls between eight and ten in the morning, mostly from women, and Jackie guessed it was for the housewives to gossip after they'd gotten their men off to work.

As she worked, Jackie tried to be cheerful and helpful to Mrs. Thibodaux, who was recovering from one bout in the hospital and getting ready for the next. They quickly got away from "Mrs. Thibodaux" and "Miss Jackie", and became

"Bessie" and "Jackie" to each other, just as Mark and Mr. Thibodaux had fallen to using first names.

The men usually came back to the house for lunch, which Jackie made for them, but they tended to go back to work and knock off fairly early in the afternoon. Occasionally, Jackie and Mark would have dinner with the Thibodaux's, and once in a while with the Greens, or the Spragues, and they even went to dinner with the Cowgills once, but they would be more likely to go back to the Billie Jean to have their supper, which wouldn't be anything special, after breakfasts and lunches that were bigger than they had become used to.

The evenings were long and lazy. Often, Jackie would get out her fishing pole and make a few casts from the deck of the houseboat, more to have something to do than not. Once Mark got familiar with the technical manuals, he would often use the evening time for drawing.

After a few days, Bessie Thibodaux went off to the hospital in Tallahassee. Paul Thibodaux spent most of his days up there with her; Mark and Jackie would go down to the house to see him off, and Mark spent the day setting up the switching system. It was an old rotator relay system that had been salvaged from some place around Southern Bell, he discovered; not exactly an up-to-date piece of equipment, but one that would do the job that was asked of it, and Mark imagined that the price had to have been right. It took a little figuring out how to set up, and there were some areas of the equipment that didn't work quite right, and Mark spent much of his days with test equipment, the manual open in front of him, as he struggled to make the system make sense.

Jackie soon learned that Mark wasn't much company when he had a telephone technical problem in front of him awaiting resolution, and waiting for something to happen at the switchboard occasionally got boring. There wasn't much she could do to help him out, and just staring at the switchboard left something to be desired.

One day, she found some paint in a back room, and decided to repaint the "Twillingate Telephone" sign that stood in front of the building. It was a little tattered, and the lettering had been amateurish; besides, it would eat up some time. She took down the sign, and spread it out on a small table near the switchboard. By the time that Paul made it back from Tallahassee, the sign was completed and back in place. "Looks good," he said to compliment here. "It was you that did the sign down at Brother Erasmus' church, wasn't it?"

"Just something to pass the time," Jackie explained.

She didn't think much about it, until a couple of days later, when she got a phone call from Mrs. Sattler, who ran the general store. "Mr. Thibodaux said you did the sign for him, and that one for Brother Erasmus," she explained. "I was wonderin' if you'd be willin' to do one for me."

"Sure," Jackie said. "It gives me something to do."

From that point on, there was usually a sign taking shape on the porch of the Twillingate Telephone Company while Jackie was keeping an ear to the switchboard. It turned out that there were a lot of signs that wanted making in the area, and Jackie's work was better than what had been available. At first, she would have been willing to do the work for cost, just to have something to do, but Mr. Thibodaux told her that she deserved something for her time. Jackie found herself charging more than she thought the work was worth, but people were still happy to pay for it.

"Looks like you're getting a business going," Mark commented. "I wonder if how you'd do painting signs in Spearfish Lake."

"It's something to think about," Jackie said. "As far as I know, there's no one in town that does signs that does a good job of them. There used to be a guy down in Albany River that did a lot of the signs around town, but I think he died."

"You might be able to make a nice little business of it, then," Mark commented. "It seems like it'd beat being a part-time waitress."

"I can get away with brushwork and boards around here," Jackie told him. "But these plastic signs are something else again. I don't know anything about them."

"You can learn," Mark told her. "There's got to be someplace that you can pick up that sort of thing. Maybe in Camden, or something."

Jackie nodded. It was something that she'd never considered before. "I don't know that we could make a living at it," she said, "But I'm sure there would be some extra income there. If we go back to Spearfish Lake to live, it's something that I ought to think about."

Painting signs took some of the edge out of the boredom of the day, but after a while, sitting on the Billie Jean's deck and fishing and watching birds in the evening began to pall -- even quicker for for Mark than it did for Jackie. "I think I'll call home and have dad send me my acrylic box and some canvases," he said. "Maybe I could work on some of the drawings I've done, and turn them into paintings."

"You really should do that one of Roger and Kathy," Jackie said. "She's about due to have her baby any day now, so it might be kind of nice for her to have."

Mark smiled. "Maybe I ought to do that one of you and Kathy. You know, the nude one."

"I don't think so," Jackie said. "Maybe someday, but you might have trouble explaining it to Brother Erasmus if he should happen to look over your shoulder."

"You might be right at that," Mark agreed.

It still left Jackie with the prospect of boring evenings. She thought about it for a minute, then asked, "How about if we get the mirror blanks shipped to us, and you show me how to work at hogging out the mirror?"

"That's a lot of work, and it's going to be dull," Mark told her. "I mean, if you want to do it, it's got to be done, and there's no reason why you can't do it."

A few days later, Jackie got a call from the Twillingate Post Office that there were a couple of large boxes from Spearfish Lake. By then, Mark had scrounged up an empty 55-gallon drum from somewhere, and he set it up on the bank of the river next to the shantyboat. "This is going to be a big job," he told Jackie. "It's going to take maybe twenty hours, maybe thirty. All we have to do is to take something like an eighth of an inch of glass out of the center of the disk, but we have to do it slowly and carefully and precisely."

It proved that an hour or two at a time was about all that Jackie wanted to work on the mirror, and it was hard to tell if she was making progress. Still, for the hour or two that she ground away at the disk nightly, spreading grinding compound, working one disk over the other for a few minutes, then washing the used grit off with water from the river, and starting over again, it was pleasant work, until her hands got tired. Then, she'd put the glass blanks back into the storage box, put it under the bed, and sometimes grab her fishing pole and throw a lure out into the stream, while Mark sat at the easel he had set up on the deck.

It took Mark a couple of tries to get his hands back used to brushwork before the painting of Roger and Kathy on the beach at Titusville took shape. Mark took a little artist's liberty in the painting of the two; the Saturn launch gantry was closer in the background, close enough so that you could make out what it was. In deference to the knowledge of where this painting would be placed, Mark made Kathy's bikini a little less radical than it had been in real life.

The painting took shape over several evenings, layer on layer. Jackie was happy to just sit, fishing pole in hand, and look over Mark's shoulder as it progressed. "I think you're capturing them very well," she said at one point.

"It'll do, I guess," Mark said. "I'm not real happy with it, but it'll do for a practice job. I may just finish this one and start over on it again."

"Don't be so picky," Jackie told him. "I think it's a good job. Maybe when you get it done, you should put it aside and try something else."

"You could be right," Mark agreed.

A couple of days later, Mark couldn't think of anything else he wanted to add to the painting, so he hung it on one of the walls of the Billie Jean to cure, while he went on to something else -- a painting of the Billie Jean itself, with Jackie sitting on the deck, fish pole in hand. The swamp it was sitting in was quite clearly the river, but somehow it was a mystical, foggy bayou at the same time.

One day, Brother Erasmus happened by as Mark was painting. "I see you ain't the only one of you two that can handle a brush," he said as he stood and watched Mark work.

"I play at it," Mark said defensively. "It's just something I do for the fun of it."

They talked for a while, half an hour or so, before Brother Erasmus was on his way. By the time he was gone, Mark was tiring of the evening's work.

"You ought to do a painting for him," Jackie suggested. "Maybe of the church. I'm sure he'd like one, but I don't think he'd ask."

"Yeah, you're right," Mark said as he set to cleaning brushes. "We owe him a lot."

But the painting that Mark started next wasn't of the church, but of a sailplane in the air over Waverly -- not a sleek, high-performance piece of fiberglass, but a tattered fabric 2-33, sharing the sky with a bald eagle.

"Those were some good days we had out there," Jackie commented.

"Yeah," Mark said. "All in all, we haven't got much to complain about the way this trip has gone. We've had some bad times, but I think that the good has outweighed the bad."

The days passed swiftly. Mr. Thibodaux and Mark decided to work six days a week when they could, but in practice they usually didn't work too hard on Saturday, leaving the afternoons for painting and working on the mirror. It was what they could do on Sundays afternoons, too; every Sunday, they went to church, just to be part of the community. One week, they would go to Brother Erasmus' church in the morning, to enjoy the preaching and singing, and in the evenings, they would go to Reverend Sprague's church for the evening service. On the next week, they did it the other way around. As a result, they spent a lot of time in church, and got to know many more people around the community fairly well.

Mark was working on the sailplane picture one evening when Samuel, the hermit-like old boatman who had helped them move the Billie Jean dropped by, bringing them a catfish that he had caught. Quite to their surprise, hardly turned out to be the same fellow at all. "I likes to talk to folks," he told them. "I just don't take to workin' close with 'em as all." He sat in his old rowboat, piled high with nets, handlines, oyster poles, a tin-can anchor filled with cement, knives and rusty buckets, and it seemed appropriate for him. "I knows somethin' about this coast, 'cause it take more than one lifetime to know everythin' about it, the birds and the guff and the fish and the animals. I done got so some of 'em and I understand each other pretty good. You know seagulls talk if you give 'em a chance. You ought to hear 'em beggin' when I haul in my nets. Some days I got a trail or 'em followin' in the sky behind my boat."

It was more than they had ever heard him speak at one time before. "Is Twillingate your home?" Jackie asked.

"I got a little shack here where I stays in sometimes," Samuel admitted. "These old bones ain't as young as they once were, and when we gets a big freeze, I gots to have a stove to stay warm, an' I didn't usta have to have that. But that's where I stays, sometimes. Home is sort of out there, the salt marshes and Sand Creek and Lost Creek, Big Piney Island, Snake Hammock, this here Shakahatchee River, and like that. I can pretty well go where I wants to go, an' you got to keep goin' to places 'cause they changes so much in the seasons and freezes and droughts and storms. As long as the Lord keeps fish in the Guff, I can makes out fine."

They talked with Samuel some more, and he did most of the talking. He talked about he talked to God and to the birds while he was out by himself in his old skiff, and how he wanted to take the memory of all that was good on the earth along with his soul when he went to heaven. "I just be wantin' a chance to know the world before I got to leave it, is all," he told them

After a while, old Samuel had about talked himself out, so he said goodbye, started up his old Evinrude and headed toward the sea. Mark and Jackie just stood there watching as he puttered away. "We think we've traveled a lot," Mark said. "I'll bet he has never been more than forty miles from where we are, and I'll bet he's seen more than we'll ever hope to see."

"It's all a matter of how you look at it," Jackie told Mark. "You get right down to it, we haven't been a lot different the past few months."

"Old Hank Thoreau would have understood him," Mark said. "Remember, 'I have traveled extensively in Concord.'?"

Jackie nodded. "That's what I said," Jackie agreed. "It's all how you look at it. If you look at it his way, this is a pretty good place to live, and I'm not so sure he's not right."

"I wouldn't care to live like that," Mark thought aloud. "Much as I like this place, I don't think it would make much of a place for us to make a home."

"I don't know. I think I'd like it. I could see making a life out of living on this shantyboat."

"If we could afford to do it without working, then maybe that would be a possibility," Mark argued. "But, I don't think we'd like trying to live by fishing mullet or slashing teppentine."

"Well, no," Jackie said. "I didn't mean it like that."

"This is a fine place to live for a while," Mark told her. "I really like staying on this shantyboat. But I think I couldn't just sit back on my ass and do nothing. I've found that I have to be busy at something, or I go nuts."

"I know," Jackie agreed. "It was hard for me last winter, when all I had to do was to take care of Johnnie, it got pretty bad, there. It was a lot better when I got the job at Ricks, even though it only lasted for a while."

"I'll tell you what," Mark said, shaking his head. "We've got a month, maybe six weeks, before we'll have the system up and running. While this is a nice town, and it's got good friends and good people, I'm not even sure I want to sit on my butt here until spring, with nothing in particular to do."

"You had something else in mind?"

"Not really. It's just that while we have friends here, they're friends because we're workers, not just sitting on our butts. If we didn't do anything, then we'd be thought of as Yankees, and nobody would give us the time of day."

"You're right, I guess," she said. "It's just that when the time comes to leave this place, I'm going to hate to leave. We've made so many friends here."

"We have friends elsewhere. What's more, we even have friends at home, and I'll tell you, more and more, I get the feeling that when we're done here, it's time to go home."

"I even feel like that now and then," Jackie replied. "The only thing is, if I'm going to sit on my butt all winter, I'd rather do it here where it's at least a little warm, rather than up in Spearfish Lake where it'll freeze."

"There is that," Mark replied. "On the other hand, if we go back to Spearfish Lake, I don't think we'll lack for things to do for the four months or so before I go to work for Mr. Corman."

"Such as?"

"Such as, suppose we buy a house that needs some fixing up. It'd be a perfect time to do it."

"We haven't got the money to buy a house."

"Oh, we could get it," he replied, smiling. "I could take out a VA loan, knowing that I'm going to be going to work for Mr. Corman. There's other ways, too.

"It's something to think about," Jackie said, looking at the fish that Samuel had left for them. "How'd you like a late fish dinner? There's no way this is going to keep, with no icebox."

Mark said that they didn't have much choice in the matter. He volunteered to clean and fillet the fish, while Jackie set up both of the camp stoves to fry it, and sliced a few potatoes to go along with it.

There turned out to be quite a bit of fish there, and Mark and Jackie were wondering how they were going to be able to eat it all when Brother Erasmus showed up. "You like a little snack of some nice, fresh-fried catfish?" Jackie asked.

"I ain't going to turn it down," the preacher said. "I take it you must have caught something."

While she was cooking, Jackie explained what had happened. In a few minutes, the three of them sat down on the deck of the shantyboat for their late fish dinner. "I can't help but wonder about Samuel," Mark said. "I mean, he seems like a nice old man, and all that, but he sure seems a little strange."

"That's right," Brother Erasmus said. "Some days, he don't hardly say nothin', and other days, he's the friendliest man you could believe, and you don't never know what he's goin' to be like from one day to the next. I guess probably he's a little touched, but folks 'round here have kind of gotten used to it, and so nobody minds."

"He sure seems to know every tree and fish around here," Mark commented. "I suppose after a lifetime of learning about them, he's got a right to."

"The Lord's hand is upon that man," Brother Erasmus said. "Maybe more than most. I ain't sayin' that anyone else would be happy livin' like he does, but it's the way the Lord has him livin' so I guess it's all right for him. He can go out in that little boat of his and talk to the Lord, and sometimes the Lord talks back, and I think he can hear him a little better than the rest of us."

"I don't know," Jackie said. "I guess I just wish I could hear him a little better."

"The Lord is talkin' to you," the preacher said. "He's a-talkin' to you all the time, but you got to be listenin' for what he says. The Lord, he works in mysterious ways, and we can't always know what he's tellin' us, or why he's doin' it. He was a-talkin' to you through Samuel, tonight."

"But what was he saying?" Jackie asked.

"Don't rightly know," Brother Erasmus told her. "He would have been a-talkin' to you, not to me. I could have been standin' right next to you, and he'd have been talkin' to me, too, but he might not have been tellin' me the same thing he was tellin' you. Ask, and you shall receive, it says in the book. But, you gotta have faith, and know that the Lord does things his way."

Jackie shook her head and said, "It doesn't make a lot of sense to me, but to have Samuel drop by out of nowhere and give us a fish ought to tell me that there's something more there than meets the eye."

"See?" Brother Erasmus smiled. "You learnin' something, already."

The work on the phone system picked up once Bessie Thibodaux was back from the hospital. The surgery was fairly successful, and although she was very tender and couldn't do much, at least she wasn't in constant pain, which was a big improvement for everyone involved. Day by day, she was able to do a little more for herself, and Jackie's need to nurse her grew less and less. By the middle of November, she was able to sit at the switchboard for an hour or so at a time, perhaps a couple of times a day, and there was getting to progressively be less for Jackie to do at the Thibodauxs. If it hadn't been for the increasing amount of sign painting, it could have been boring, indeed.

In only a few more days, Thanksgiving was rolling around. "You kids are coming to the house to have Thanksgiving with us," Mr. Thibodaux told them. "'Course, that's 'cause you're gonna have to do a lot of the cookin'. If we half let Bessie, she'd kill herself in the kitchen, so all of us are gonna have to work at keepin' her takin' it easy."

"I've never really cooked a Thanksgiving dinner," Jackie told him.

"Well, it's something you really oughta learn, and there ain't no time like the present to learn it," he replied.

The thought of Thanksgiving, and the holidays to follow made Jackie feel a little uneasy. She had never spent a holiday season away from her home and family. She figured that it would have been a little easier for Mark, since he had spent three of them away, in Vietnam and Germany. The fact that they were going to be having a dinner with friends as good as the Thibodauxes were just didn't quite seem to compensate.

Still, it was good to celebrate Thanksgiving with friends. It was a lot of work for Jackie; mostly she and Paul Thibodaux made Thanksgiving dinner, with a little help from Bessie and Mark. It was quite a dinner; turkey, of course, but with a lot of side dishes. By the time the afternoon was over, they needed the walk back to the shantyboat, just to help walk off some of the overeating.

Mark got out the easel, and thought about working on a painting, but he just couldn't find the enthusiasm to work on it much. Perhaps he was a bit homesick, too, Jackie thought.

"What would you think if we flew home for the holidays?" Jackie asked. "It'd be a day or a day and a half, each way, assuming we caught the weather right, and we could stay there a couple of days. I don't think Mr. Thibodaux would mind."

"I don't think it's going to matter," Mark told her. "By the holidays, we ought to have the system pretty well wrapped up and running. There'll be some work taking the parts of the old system apart that he's not going to use, but there's no rush on that. Mostly, they could sit there and rot."

"You mean, we're going to be done here by Christmas?"

"Yeah, maybe a week or so earlier," Mark said. "I'd kind of figured that we could stay here until after Christmas, and then go somewhere else. Maybe home. There's no reason we couldn't be home for Christmas, but I thought you were the one that didn't want to go home until we were done traveling."

"Well, yeah," she said. "But now I'm not so sure about that."

"Actually, if we go to the trouble of flying up north, maybe we should just figure on staying there, at least for a while, and looking for a house, and maybe I can find a job to hold us until spring."

Jackie thought about it for a minute. There was the old question again, whether to go back to Spearfish Lake to stay, or not. It was no easier to come to grips with it now than it had been every time they had talked about it before. "I just thought we'd stay for a few days and then come back to Florida, or maybe even head out west, say southern California, or something," she said, trying to put off the decision a while longer.

"Well, we could do that," Mark said. "But there's other things we could do with that time. Like I said, if we were to buy a house that needs some fixing up, I could get a good start on it between now and April or May."

"You know," Jackie mused, "It's a little unreal for us to be talking about buying a house and fixing it up."

"Well, yeah," Mark said, "But it's probably the logical thing to do, and after I go to work for Mr. Corman, we won't have time like that available again."

"I know," Jackie said. "On the other hand, I keep thinking about a little house out in the woods, someplace where he could be away from people. Do you think we could have something like that?"

Mark nodded "It'd be the sort of place that I'd want to look for," he said. "Maybe not back in the woods, though. I'd want to be in some place that's open enough that I could build an observatory out there. Some place where we could get in out of the wind in the winter when we're using the telescope. It can get awful bitter out in the open with a telescope when the wind is blowing."

"We could do that," Jackie said. "That would be nice. I'd kind of like to have a big garage or shop area, so you'd have a place to work on things, like the new telescope, and maybe I could use it if I can get a sign painting business going."

"You've been thinking about that?"

"I have," she said. "You might have a good idea there. I don't think we could make a living out of it, but I could be wrong. Still, it would provide some extra income, and that would allow us to do some of the things we want to do, like go traveling when we get the chance."

"Maybe if we really found the right spot, some abandoned farm, say," Mark said, still dreaming, "We could have room enough for our own airstrip. It'd sure be nice to just be able to go out in back, roll Rocinante out of the hanger, and go flying."

"Could we have a sailplane?" Jackie asked.

"I suppose we could if we wanted to," Mark said. "Spearfish Lake really isn't glider country, but there are openings here and there if you got low and had to land, so we'd really have to learn to be careful about that. The one real hangup is that Rocinante doesn't have enough guts to tow one, even a real light one, even at that low an altitude."

"That could be a problem," Jackie said, reluctant to give up that particular dream. "I don't really want to have to give up Rocinante."

"I don't either," Mark said. "But, there are a couple of options. If we found the right field, and it would have to be a long one, we could probably work out a way to do auto tows, or maybe a winch tow from the ground. Plus, there are conversions available. Maybe when the time comes to give Rocinante's engine a major, and it'll need one sometime in the next few years, maybe we could hang a bigger engine in the nose. As far as that goes, the Stinson probably has got enough guts to do the job. It's not a problem that can't be solved, but we've got a few years to solve it. We just aren't going to be able to afford a sailplane on top of Rocinante, right away, anyway."

Jackie shrugged. "Well, it's something to think about, I guess," she said. "Do you have anything else you want in a house?"

"A fireplace would be nice," Mark said. "It'd be nice to sit down in front of a fire on a cold winter's night, just to make the time pass in the evening, just to cuddle up and get a little romantic."

"That would be nice," she said.

"The thing is," he said. "I don't want to have to screw around with wood heat. As much wood as we would have to cut, that could really get to be a pain in the ass."

"You know Mr. Tovio, out in Amboy Township? Kirsten and I used to pal around with his daughter," Jackie said. "They've got wood heat, and I seem to remember that you roast on one side and freeze your butt on the other. I'm with you. I like central heating. Do you think we can find a place like that?"

"I wouldn't be surprised," Mark said. "I've kind of got an abandoned farm in mind, maybe four or five miles out of town. The house is fieldstone, so it ought to be in pretty good shape, but I've got no idea what the interior of the place must be like. I don't know if it could be bought, or how much it would cost, but it would be the first place that I'd want to take a look at."

"If we had a farm, could we have a horse or two?" Jackie asked. "When I was a little girl, I always wanted a horse, but it was always out of the question, since we didn't have a place to keep it."

"Don't see why not," Mark said. "I don't know what we'd use a horse for, except maybe to ride, now and then, but I wouldn't mind having one."

The dream was taking more shape in Jackie's mind. She could see a brightly lighted kitchen, a comfortable living room, a warm bedroom with a large bed. "It is kind of a dream, isn't it?" she reflected to Mark.

"It's not the sort of thing that we could put together right away," he said. "But there's no reason we can't have all of that, and more, over the course of a few years, if we go back to Spearfish Lake. That's not one of those things we can automatically plan on doing anywhere else."

"I agree," she said. "We'd have to go back to Spearfish Lake if we want to do all that. It's just that I'm still not too crazy about the idea of going back to Spearfish Lake."

"That's one of the reasons for wanting a place out in the country," Mark said. "It wouldn't be like living in town, with all that means. We wouldn't have to spend any more time in town than we wanted to."

"Yeah, but still," Jackie protested. "We'd still have to spend time there, and put up with all the gossip."

Mark shook his head. "I don't think that matters. We agreed long ago that if we went back to Spearfish Lake, we'd have to be married, and that'll end a lot of the gossip. A lot of the stuff about your mother will die out in time, and the rest of it, we can afford to ignore. Like I told you once, to hell with the little minds. I think you worry about that too much."

Jackie looked out at the dark, still waters of the river for a moment. "There is the other thing to worry about, too," she said finally.

"Your mother?"

"Yeah."

"We've been over that before until it's almost boring," Mark said. "As I have said before, it's a risk, sure. But it's more a risk that I have to take, than you have to take, because I get a choice in the matter. I don't think it's that big a risk."

"I still don't think it's fair," Jackie said.

"Let me tell you something I've never told you before," Mark told her. "You remember the day I walked across the causeway for water, back in Titusville?"

"Yeah," Jackie said. "That seems so long ago. We've come a long way since then."

"We have," Mark said. "I thought about this whole thing of you and your mother and us lot on that hike. You know what struck me the hardest?"

Jackie shook her head, and Mark continued. "It struck me that while I have no idea what went wrong with your mother, it had to have something to do with the fact that there must have been some kind of stress that she wasn't able to handle. I mean, I don't know what that stress must have been, but it seems to me that there ought to have been something. You think I'm on the right track?"

"You might have something there," Jackie said.

"I think I do," Mark told her. "Well, anyway, what I figured out was that the two of us, traveling together on the trip like this, ought to put a fair amount of stress on you. I just kind of figured that I could just sit back and see how you handled it, and then make a decision from there."

"I never realized that you thought of it like that," Jackie said, a little coldly. "What did you decide?"

"Isn't it obvious?" Mark said. "We wouldn't be sitting here talking about getting married if I had decided any other way."

"Is that what we're talking about?" Jackie said.

"Of course it is," Mark told her. "What else did you think we were talking about?"

Jackie was silent for a long time. A blue heron came gliding in over the trees, and splashed down onto the river. Finally, Jackie got up, went over, sat down next to Mark, and put her arms around him and kissed him -- a long, deep French kiss that went on and on. "Well, all right," she said. "I think you believe in me more than I believe in myself, but I can't ask for much more than that. Let's go ahead and get married."

"How about going back to Spearfish Lake?" he asked.

"I think so," she told him. "But, let's go home for the holidays before we make up our minds for sure."

"Let's get married while we're there," he suggested. "It'll drag the stay out for a few days, but at least we can do it with our families around."

"We can do that," Jackie said. "I don't want a big wedding. Just a few friends. Maybe not even in a church."

"I figured you'd want a church wedding, anyway," Mark observed.

"Well, yeah," Jackie said. "But, there's no church in Spearfish Lake that I'd really like to get married in."

"Me either," Mark said. "I mean, it's kind of beside the point, since we want to get married in Spearfish Lake, but the only church I'd really want to get married in is right up there on the top of the hill."

"You mean, by Brother Erasmus?" she asked.

"That's just what I mean," he said. "Can you think of anyone better?"

* * *

November 27, 1971
Twillingate, Florida

Dear Dad and Sarah,
It's a little early to tell yet, but it looks as if Mark and I will be home for the holidays. The work on the phone system is going pretty good, and it looks like we're going to be able to be free for a few days.

The weather here has been getting colder. We actually had frost a few days ago! You don't think of that happening here, but it does. Mr. Thibodaux said that two or three years ago, they actually had a couple of inches of snow! It was gone the next day, but that was really pretty strange for around here, he said. A lot of the leaves have turned color now, and some of the trees have lost their leaves, but it doesn't seem like fall.

I told you about this houseboat that we're living on. It's kind of nice. We've been swimming on the warm afternoons, right off the deck, and it's been fun, although the water is getting a little too cold to stay in very long. I guess winter even comes to Twillingate.

I'm really looking forward to being home for the holidays. If we're not home then, we should be shortly after, since it will depend a lot on how the work on the phone system goes. I'm really looking forward to Mark and I sitting down and talking to you and telling you about everything that's happened since last spring. It's kind of strange to look back and think about everything, since so much has happened, and I know there have been things that we've never talked about on the phone, or told you about in my letters. It'll be good to be home again.

Love,
Jackie

11.

It was a good week after Thanksgiving when the news came.

Mark called into the central office, to check a circuit. This would about complete the party line out at the plantation, and there wasn't a lot of work to do yet. A couple more circuits had to be finished, and there was several days worth of phone installation waiting, but the work at Twillingate was visibly coming to an end.

Bessie answered the phone. It was good to hear her on the circuit again, even though her time as "Central" was coming to an end; she was getting better, so much better that Jackie had come with Mark and Paul a couple of times, this being one of them. "Brother Erasmus is a-lookin' for you," she said.

"Did he say why?" Mark asked.

"He said that some mullet fisherman found old Samuel's boat a-driftin off'n the river mouth, and there weren't no sign of Samuel. He wants you to go get in your plane and look for him, or his body, anyways."

"Don't see why not," Mark said. He hung up the phone and asked Paul if he would drive them to town.

They stopped by the phone company office, where Brother Erasmus was waiting, but he couldn't add much to what Bessie had told them. "They found the skiff about a mile offshore," he said. "I done asked around, and no one has seen old Samuel for two-three days, but that ain't strange. Don't guess nobody saw him."

"We saw him head out on the tide about three days ago," Jackie said. "We didn't think anything of it."

"You was about the last people to see him, then," Brother Erasmus said. "I can't believe the boat would have drifted too far from where it was found, and if'n he'd fallen over a couple days ago, it'd either be ashore or a long ways away."

"I can't make any promises," Mark told him. "That's still a big area to look over, and really, a body is a pretty small thing to try and find."

It was strange to get in Rocinante again. They had not been in the cockpit of the little Cessna in almost a month and a half. There had just never been the need to go flying, although a couple of times they had talked of flying into Perry or Tallahasee for a movie or something, just to go somewhere besides Twillingate. But, there had always been some reason why they didn't have any need to.

As Mark taxied Rocinante down the runway and ran the engine up, a lot came back to him. He and Jackie had put a lot of miles onto Rocinante's wings in the past few months, and it seemed almost like normal.

"This is probably going to be pretty hopeless," Mark observed. "We'll give it a shot, but I don't think we're going to find anything."

They picked out an area perhaps a couple of miles square off of the river mouth, and flew low over it, back and forth, searching out the windows. Below them, they could see several of the local fishing boats, out on the same mission, and they didn't seem to be having much luck, either. They kept it up until

Rocinante's gas gauge began to reach an alarming level. "Guess we'd better break off and go to Perry and get some gas," Jackie observed.

"Yeah," Mark said, a little disappointed. "We can come back and look some more." He picked up some altitude and turned to the east, in the direction where he now believed that Perry was. They flew there, landed and gassed up quickly, and flew back to Twillingate, and searched for an hour more, until the light began to get bad. They made one last pass right up the shoreline, right down low, in hopes that old Samuel's body might have drifted ashore. They had done that before, and found nothing, but with the light in a different direction, there was the possibility that they might find something now.

It was not to be. Reluctantly, they picked up a little altitude and flew back to the Twillingate airstrip, where Mr. Thibodaux, Brother Erasmus, and a handful of others were waiting for them.

"No sign of him," Mark reported. "Of course, if he fell overboard and drowned, you'd expect his body to sink. If he had a heart attack and fell overboard not breathing, it might not, I think. But, we didn't see anything."

"'Twas bound to happen sooner or later," Brother Erasmus said. "Old man like that, he ain't gonna go on forever. I 'spect, if'n he had to die, he'd want to die in his boat."

"That skiff was his life," Thibodaux observed. "I don't think he would want it any other way."

"Don't think he would have wanted us to find him," Brother Erasmus observed. "I think he'd wanted to have been buried in the sea."

"You might be right," Mark said.

"He was a nice old man," Jackie said. "It would have been nice to know him better, but I'm glad to have known him at all."

By then, the day was shot for doing any more work on the phone system. Thibodaux gave them a ride back to the shantyboat. "What do you want for supper?" Jackie asked.

"Don't know," Mark said. "Open a can or two, I guess. I guess I'm not real interested in eating, anyway."

Mark set up the easel. He had been working on a painting of the church for Brother Erasmus, and he'd been trying to work on it at times when the preacher might not drop by, in hopes that it might be a surprise. Somehow, this didn't seem like the time to work on it, and it seemed likely that this would be a good time for him to drop by, anyway.

"How about working on the mirror?" Jackie suggested.

"I just can't get interested in that right now, either," Mark said. Jackie busied herself with making a light supper, while Mark dug out his pack of cigarettes and pulled one out. He sat back in a chair, with his feet on the rail of the houseboat, and just stared out across the river.

After a while, Jackie brought a plate of stew out to him. He flipped the cigarette over the rail, and it died in the water with a hiss. "It's got you down, huh?" Jackie observed.

"Yeah, I guess it has, a little," Mark said, putting his feet down and digging into his stew. "He was a good old guy. This river, this ocean, was his life. I guess this is where he was supposed to be, and I guess that was how he was supposed to end up. This was his home."

"Kind of a different way to live," Jackie said, digging into her own plate.

"Yeah, but it was right for him. It wouldn't be right for you or me, but it was right for him."

"Well, I agree, I guess," Jackie said. "Still, it was nice to see his way of life."

"Yeah," Mark said. "We've been doing a lot of seeing how other people lived. I guess that's what we set out to do on this trip -- see things, get to know other people. We've done pretty good. But, while it was fun to do, I don't think it's how we're supposed to live."

"You're talking about going back to Spearfish Lake, aren't you?" Jackie asked.

"I guess I am," Mark said. "Now that you mention it, I guess that's it. Jackie, I think that's where we belong."

"You really want to go back there, don't you?"

"I don't think I ever wanted to do anything different. Like Samuel belonged here, I've always felt we belonged there. Think how out of place he would be in Spearfish Lake. That's how far out of place we would be if we were to stay here. I know you've never been real enthusiastic about going back, but I've been willing to consider what you want. I still am willing to, for that matter. But there's so much in favor of going back that it's hard to consider not doing it."

"I'm not against going back," she said, sitting down beside him. "I've just enjoyed being away from Spearfish Lake, where no one knows us, where we're judged on what we are, not what we were or what our parents were. That's been kind of nice to not have to carry that baggage around with us."

"I agree, it's been nice," he said. "But the longer we stay in a place, the more of that sort of baggage that we'll pick up. That'd happen in any small town, and

I don't think that either you or I are the kinds of people that could live in a city, and stand it or each other for very long."

Jackie looked out over the water for a while. "Well, you're probably right," she said. "The only big city we've been in on this trip was San Francisco, and I was just as happy to get out of there. I suppose that if we have to live in a small place, it might as well be Spearfish Lake, where at least we know where everything is."

"We can always change our minds if it gets to be too much, or too hard," Mark told her. "But if that happens, we can do it on our own time, and make sure we have a good place to be jumping to."

"I suppose," Jackie said. She looked up, and added, "Here comes Brother Erasmus. Did you want to talk to him about him marrying us?"

"I don't know that this would be too good a time, considering Samuel and all," Mark said. "We'll have to see."

The preacher came up the gangplank and said, "Just wanted to thank you two for the time you took to look for Samuel."

"Just wish we could have found him," Mark said. "I take it that none of the mullet fishermen found anything?"

"Not a thing," Brother Erasmus said sadly.

"Are you going to be planning a memorial service, or something?" Jackie asked.

Brother Erasmus leaned back in the chair, "No," he said. "Not now, anyways. It still might be a little early. After all, he could have been up the coast somewheres, and his skiff could have drifted off on a rising tide. I think we's best wait a while."

Mark nodded. "Yeah, that makes sense. He could be walking home from somewhere, and then think how you'd look if he did."

"Yeah, don't want to be in no rush to bury someone who maybe ain't dead."

They sat and talked for a while, about one thing and another. It was nice to sit on the deck of the shantyboat, to talk with a friend, and they knew that there wouldn't be a lot longer that they'd be doing that. Mark and Jackie had made a lot of friends in Twillingate, and they were going to be sorry to leave, although it wouldn't be much longer.

Finally, Jackie realized that now was as good a time as any to drop a question on Brother Erasmus. "You know that Mark and I are going to get married," she said. "We've got a little problem, and I thought maybe we'd like to hear your opinion on what to do."

The preacher asked what the problem was.

"We decided long ago that if we were going to get married, we ought to get married at home," she said. "The problem is, there's not a church at home that we feel like getting married in, and somehow I feel like we ought to get married in a church. And, we'd like for you to marry us in yours. I just don't know how we handle it."

"Well, I's glad to hear you gettin' married," Brother Erasmus said. "But you done set yourself a problem."

"Yeah," Mark told him. "Anything we do seems like the wrong thing."

The preacher smiled. "I'd be glad to marry you," he said, "But you're right. You should be gettin' married at home, 'fore family and friends. Course' I'd like to see you get married in a church, too."

"I had one idea," Jackie said. "I thought that maybe we could get married twice. Once, here, in the church, and maybe not even bother with a wedding license. Then at home we could have the official thing. Maybe just a civil ceremony, at home, to deal with the paperwork."

"Might work," Brother Erasmus said after thinking about it for a bit. "The only thing is, I'd be happier if you had a church wedding, or at least one by a preacher, back home, too, since that would be the real official one."

"I suppose we could do that," Mark said. "The thing is, the churches back home seem so cold and impersonal, after going to yours and Reverend Sprague's."

"You get out of it what you put into it," Brother Erasmus said. "If'n you expectin' it to be cold, then it will be. You two ain't been goin' to church at home, I take it?"

"Not for years," Jackie said. "My dad had kind of a problem with the church, what with the problems he had with my mother, and we just sort of quit going. But, they were pretty good about the funeral service for my mother, Dad said. I suppose we could ask the preacher there."

"Now, you makin' me wonder," the preacher said. "You two always acted like you was saved, but I guess I never done asked you about it. Have the two of you taken Jesus into your heart as your savior?"

"I guess," Mark said. "I've never really thought about it in those exact words, but yeah, I guess it comes down to that."

Brother Erasmus turned to Jackie, who was sitting there, thinking. "Me, too," she said finally. "I couldn't have said that when we were here last spring, but somewhere between then and now, I guess that I've come around to thinking like that."

"Then it's real important that you get into a church when you get back home," the preacher said. "Might be the Baptist Church up home, but might not be, too. We's independent here, but I can get along with the Baptists. Ain't no reason you cain't shop around a little. You should be baptized into your church, but I take it you ain't never been baptized, either?"

"I was as a baby, I guess," Mark told him.

"Now, that's what we call sanctifin'," Brother Erasmus told him. "That's for when you was a kid, and you hadn't been able to make a grown-up decision to follow in the path of the Lord. You really ought to be baptized, and the sooner the better."

"What's the big rush?" Mark asked.

"Well, first, it's important," the preacher said. "'Specially if'n somethin' should happen to you. It signifies to the Lord that you're one of Jesus' children. An' it helps you to set in your own mind that you've chosen Jesus' path. We can get you two baptized Sunday."

"Brother Erasmus," Jackie smiled. "Do you remember the eunuch in Acts? How he and Phillip are riding across the desert in his chariot, talking about this sort of thing?"

"You mean, where he says, 'See, here is water. What is to prevent me from being baptized?'"

"That's it," Jackie said, waving her hand around the shantyboat. "There's water all around us."

Wet and dripping, Mark and Jackie went into the shantyboat to change. Dried off, they came back out on deck, where Brother Erasmus waited. "Now that we've got that out of the way," he said, "We can talk about a weddin'. A Twillingate weddin', that is. When do want to do it?"

"I'd rather we didn't let it go too long between here and home," Jackie said. "I don't want to do anything too big or elaborate. Maybe just some Sunday, after church. Mark, are we going to be ready to leave by Christmas?"

"Easily," Mark told her. "It'll be tough to drag out until then."

"Then how about the Sunday before Christmas?" Jackie suggested. "Then, we can work out something for right after Christmas, whether we travel until spring, or stay in Spearfish Lake."

"Sounds all right," Brother Erasmus said. "Now, if you don't be mindin', I'd like to go get on some dry pants."

"Remember," Mark said, "We don't want to do anything special. Just a short service. No gifts or anything like that."

"I'll take care of everythin'" Brother Erasmus said as he departed. "Don't worry, we'll do it right."

"That scares me a little," Mark said to Jackie after Brother Erasmus had left.

"What?" Jackie said.

"What his idea of doing it right might be, and what mine is."

"Yeah," Jackie reflected. "We might get more than we bargained for."

The next few days slipped by quickly. As the days dwindled down, Mark carefully repacked the glass blanks for the mirror in their shipping crate. With a little help from him, Jackie had been able to get most of the glass hogged out from the mirror, but it would take bench testing at home to tell if it was enough. Then, the mirror would have to be polished and figured, so there was still a lot of glass work yet to come.

With the blanks in the mail, heavily insured, Mark wrapped up the paints and brushes and the paintings that he had done in the last six weeks, and shipped them off to Spearfish Lake -- all but two.

One of them was the painting of Roger and Kathy, on the beach at Titusville. Mark still wasn't perfectly happy about it, and thought he could do better if he started over, but finally decided it was best left well enough along. They thought about shipping it to the Griswolds, but Jackie suggested that there was room enough in Rocinante to take it with them, and they could have the fun of dropping it off in Arvada Center.

The other painting not shipped to Spearfish Lake was the one of Brother Erasmus' church, that Mark had been trying to work on without Brother Erasmus finding out. It wasn't just a picture of the church sitting quietly in the woodland, but a much more ambitious project -- Mark had painted the church as he remembered it during the roof raising, back in the spring, with most of the community gathered around, rafters being handed up, shingles being carried up ladders, and the building swarming with men with paint brushes, hammers and saws. In the courtyard of the building, the women of Twillingate, both black and white, were gathered around tables, setting up a great community feast. Mark thought that it said more about the community and the church than any quiet painting would have.

It was the one painting that he really would have liked to take with him as a souvenir of the little town, but somehow, he thought it meant more there. Jackie did take a couple of pictures of it, and Mark thought that some day, he might like to do the painting again, just to remind them of this place.

The work on the phone system progressed, and slowly it came to life. It still only worked locally, but every few days another line or two went into service, and Bessie and Jackie found themselves answering the switchboard less and less often. Finally, there came a day that Mark and Mr. Thibodaux, armed with wirecutters, cut loose the old Rhinelander switchboard from it's wires and carried it out to the garage. "Too bad you don't have a museum here," Mark said. "That's a real museum piece. Why don't you call the state historical museum and see if they'd like to have it? It might be better than just hauling it out to the dump."

"I don't know but what it should be in the parlor," Paul said. "Bessie and I have spent a lot of years being slaves to that board. The kids, when they were home, used to answer the phone if she or I was busy, sometimes when they was just four and five. This is sure a big day in my life, and I hear you got a big day coming in yours this Sunday."

"Is it this Sunday, already?" Mark said. "I thought we had another week."

"That's a single man talking," Thibodaux said. "Trying to drag it out as long as he can."

"Not hardly," Mark told him. "Jackie and I have been a long way getting this far, and once we're past it, then we can worry about other things."

There was still work to do on the system, as well as taking out some of the old phones, and Mark and Thibodaux concentrated on that. Back at the Thibodaux house, Bessie and Jackie kept waiting for the bell that would never ring again to go off on the switchboard, and time lay especially heavy on Bessie's hands. "What you gonna wear Sunday?" she asked one day. "I don't suppose you're gonna get married in blue jeans?"

"Why not?" Jackie said. "I don't want an all-out wedding dress. I thought about getting a knee-length white skirt, and a white blouse, but that looks too much like a waitress' uniform, and this is one day that I'd rather not be reminded that I'm really nothing but an unemployed waitress."

"Well, we ought to be able to come up with somethin'" Bessie said. "Let's go over to the general store and see what kind of fabric they've got."

"I suppose it won't hurt to think about it," Jackie told her. "But really, blue jeans are all right with me."

The two of them got up and headed for the door. They were no more on than on the porch when Bessie stopped. "Who's going to stay with the phone?" she asked.

"Bessie," Jackie reminded her, "That doesn't matter any more."

"Lord sakes, child," Bessie said. "I wonder how long it's going to take me to get over that. I been answering that board for over 40 years, and it doesn't seem right that I won't have to answer it no more."

It felt strange for Jackie to pull on the blue and white dress on Sunday; it was the first time she had worn a skirt since Arroyo Grande, back in July, and in that time Jackie had come to the conclusion that she preferred to wear pants, preferably jeans. It had taken Bessie and her a couple of days to design and sew, but it fitted nicely and it looked as if it would serve the occasion.

Before the church service, Brother Erasmus got them off into one corner, and said, "We might's well do the paperwork now. You did get a weddin' license, didn't you?"

"No," Mark said. "Like we said, this is just for the church wedding. We'll do the official one up in Spearfish Lake, but this way, both of them will be important to us."

"I don't like it," Brother Erasmus told them. "It ain't right, but I guess we's kind of stuck with goin' through with it, anyway. You got to promise me that you'll get a weddin' license for when you get home."

"We will," Jackie promised, although remembering that she had suggested to Mark that they skip the wedding license there, too, just to leave his options open, but Mark had drawn the line at that. "I thought you understood that this what what we'd agreed on."

"I remember you sayin' it, now," Brother Erasmus said. "I guess, so long as you do it right, with a preacher, when you get home, it'll be all right. Guess I should have cleared that up before this, but now we got a weddin' set, and people be expectin' it, so's I guess you get a commissary weddin' in church. Lord won't mind, and the state of Florida better not, either."

The church service that morning was pretty normal, although the church was a little more crowded than usual, and there were more white faces there than usual. The singing was hearty, and Brother Erasmus preached a good sermon. The only mention of Mark and Jackie's wedding came during the announcements: "Now, most of you know Mister Mark and Miss Jackie, who came to us last spring right ahead of the Devil's Wind that took the roof off of this church. They stayed to help put it back on. They came back to us, to help with the new phones, and they're going to be getting married here, about half an hour after the service is over. You're all invited to stay around and help us celebrate their decidin' to spend their lives together."

The church was packed during the regular service, but afterwards, it grew more crowded, rather than less. A lot of people that wouldn't normally be at the regular service came into the building: the Thibodaux's, the Cowgills -- Mrs. Cowgill out for the first time in a long time -- Reverend and Mrs. Sprague, the lady who ran the general store and her husband, and a lot of other people -- some of whom they only knew by faces, and some of whom Jackie only knew by their voices.

"We're gathered here together to celebrate the marriage of this man and this woman," Brother Erasmus said. "Now, we all know that a lot of people get married out of the passion of the moment, and they're the people that we say marry in haste and repent in leisure. That can't be said of these two people. They've made no haste in gettin' married, but they've taken their time to be sure of what they're doing.

"Now, marriage is a sacred thing, and it shouldn't be rushed into. It's a commitment in the eyes of God, and it's a commitment that's for a long time. The Lord wants us to do the right thing, but sometimes we have to make sure what we know is the right thing to do. Sometimes, there's good reasons to decide not to get married, if a man and a woman aren't right for each other, so it's well sometimes to wait and think about what you want to do and be sure of what you're doin'.

"Mark," Brother Erasmus said, turning to the groom, "Do you take this woman to be your wedded wife, to love her and honor her, for richer or for poorer, in sickness and in health, from this day forth, till death do you part?"

Mark turned to Jackie, and said, "In sickness and in health . . . I do."

Both Mark and Brother Erasmus could see tears come to Jackie's eyes; they could just hear her whisper, "You didn't have to do that."

"I wanted to," Mark whispered back. "I meant it."

"Jackie," Brother Erasmus said in a voice loud enough so the congregation would hear, "Do you take this man to be your wedded husband, to love him and honor him and obey him, for richer or poorer, in sickness and in health, from this day forth, till death do you part?"

As quickly as the tears came to Jackie's eyes, they were gone. "I do," she said quietly.

"Then by the power vested in me, I hereby declare you man and wife."

Once the service was over, Mr. Thibodaux took a few snapshots with Mark's camera -- of the two of them, with Brother Erasmus and without. Then, they went outside.

Mark and Jackie shouldn't have been surprised to see over a hundred people waiting outside the church for them to come out. Beyond, they could see tables set up, covered with food, like at the church raising in April. "You didn't have to do this," Mark quietly said to Brother Erasmus.

"We don't get a lot of weddin's in Twillingate," he said. "But when we do get one, we likes to do it right."

Mark raised his hands over his head to call for silence. "While I've got you together," he said. "There's something special I'd like to say."

The crowd grew silent, and Mark continued, "Jackie and I have been traveling all over this country since last spring. We've had some great experiences, and met a lot of great people. But, we've never made better friends, or enjoyed ourselves more than we have here. Now, Brother Erasmus has become an especially good friend, and we felt like we had to do something for him. Paul, did you bring it?"

Thibodaux brought Mark a large, flat package, wrapped in brown wrapping paper. "Seems to be appropriate to me to be giving gifts at a wedding, but in this case, it's better for the bride and groom to give, rather than to receive. Just by you people being yourselves, you've given us the greatest gift of all. Now, this is a little gift to repay some of that. We're giving this to Brother Erasmus, but it's really for all of you."

He handed the package to the preacher. "You shouldn't have done this," he said.

"Not the first time today," Mark said.

Brother Erasmus opened the package, with the painting of the "church raisin'" inside. He held it out to look at it. "I kinda wanted to ask you to do somethin' like this for me," he said, "But I didn't want to ask."

"You didn't have to ask," Mark told him, as the preacher held the picture up to the crowd to see. "We knew you wanted it."

There were half a dozen people around the airstrip the next day as they loaded Rocinante. They hadn't packed their luggage in the plane in almost two months, but they hadn't forgotten how. There was a place for everything, and everything went into its place. There was enough room on top of the pile for the painting of Roger and Kathy. Once they were ready to go, they went down the line of people, shaking hands and thanking each one.

Mark and Jackie took a little extra time with Mr. Cowgill. "We want to thank you for letting us use the Billie Jean," Mark said. "It's been our first real home. I'm just sorry we couldn't take it back to the fish camp for you, but we'd never find the way by ourselves."

"That's all right," Cowgill said. "Might have it rented for down here sometime, anyway."

There were special thanks for Paul and Bessie Thibodaux, and for Brother Erasmus and Ethylene, and then it was time to go. Mark and Jackie got into the plane -- Jackie on the left, this time -- and she started the plane. It took a minute or two to taxi out to the end of the runway and do the runup, and then she started it rolling. They waved to the little knot of people standing by the T-hanger, and then Twillingate was gone.

Jackie set Rocinante on course to the north, climbed to cruising altitude, and throttled back to a cruise. "I wonder if we'll ever go back there?" she mused.

"Don't know," Mark said. "I'd kind of like to. Maybe someday. Maybe not. Who knows?"

"That sure was a nice party yesterday," Jackie said. "What with all the food and the dancing, it wore me out. I never thought that on my wedding night, I'd be happy to just go to bed and go to sleep."

"Well, our wedding has been kind of an ongoing thing," Mark told her. "You can consider our wedding night to be that night back at Waverly."

"I don't think then," Jackie said. "We may have gotten married then, I think, but I don't think I realized it until Walden Pond. What do we celebrate for an anniversary?"

"Doesn't matter," Mark said. "Waverly, Walden, Twillingate yesterday, Spearfish Lake next weekend. Let's celebrate all of them," he laughed, and she laughed with him.

"You know what's funny?" she said. "I can just see us going to the preacher in Spearfish Lake, and him giving us a big, solemn pitch about all the counseling sessions we have to have before we get married, and us telling him that they don't matter, we're already married, and we just want to do it one more time."

After a while, they stopped for gas, but it was getting dark as they approached Kentucky, so they made a night stop before they continued on the next day. It was getting along in the afternoon before they approached Arvada Center. "I'd better do the landing," Mark said. "It'll be the last one on the trip that's away from home, and you can land us at home."

"Home," Jackie said. "I'm actually going to be happy to get there. Twillingate started to feel like home, but I guess Spearfish Lake really is home."

Mark took a low pass over the field they had landed in the summer before. There didn't seem to be any wind, and the field was still short stubble, but from the patches of light snow and the general appearance, he guessed that it was frozen solid. Winter had come to the north country, only a few days before Christmas. He took a low pass over the house, and while circling, they could see Roger and Kathy come outside to wave at them. With that, Mark swung the Cessna around and landed, as Roger and Kathy drove up.

"It's good to see you two again," Roger said. "We've been wondering when you might drop in."

"It's good to see you, too," Jackie said. "Kathy, you look different from when we last saw you."

"It was a little boy," she said. "He's just the sweetest baby. Can we get you a cup of coffee, or anything?"

"We really should stay with the plane," Mark said. "There's no way we can tie it down in this hard ground. We can only stay for a few minutes, anyway. I want to make it home before dark tonight, and nobody at home knows we're coming, but we can have a chance to talk next weekend, if you like."

"What's next weekend?" Roger asked.

"We're not sure exactly when, yet," Jackie said, "But we thought you two would like to stand up for us at our latest wedding."

"Your latest wedding?" Kathy asked. "Do you want to explain that?"

"It's a long story," Mark said. "Let's just say it's our official wedding. We kind of got married unofficially the day before yesterday, but it takes a little telling."

"Of course we'll be there," Roger said. "You can call and give us the details."

"Since we're probably not going to see you until after Christmas," Mark said, "We thought we'd like to stop and give you this, too." He reached into Rocinante's luggage compartment and pulled out the package.

"Can we open it now?" Kathy asked.

"If you like," Jackie said.

The Griswolds pulled the wrapping paper off of the package. "That doesn't look like me," Kathy said when she saw the picture.

"That's what they all say," Mark smiled. "I've heard you say that before."

Roger looked at it. "Looks pretty good to me," he said. "That'll make a great reminder of our honeymoon. Is last spring as long ago to you as it is to me?"

"Afraid so," Mark said. "It was as long for us as it was for you."

"So you're getting married, finally?" Kathy asked. "I know this is a silly question, but where are you two going on your honeymoon?"

It was a question that had never occurred to Jackie, but she had an answer: "What would we want to go on a honeymoon after we get married for? We're just finishing the best honeymoon you could possibly ask for."

-- 30 --